Jon Stoc.. ...ie
Cardamom Clu............... *Spy Running* a..u ......s *Traitors Play*. He
works at the *Daily Telegraph* and lives in Wiltshire with his wife
and three children.

Praise for the Daniel Marchant trilogy:

'As elegant as le Carré and as cynical as the twenty-first century . . .
exactly what we need from a spy novel now'   Lee Child

'A Jason Bourne sweat-fest with George Smiley's brain'
                                                       Daily Telegraph

'Picks up more or less where le Carré left off'   *Guardian*

'[Stock] has emerged in the past few years as a stunning espionage
novelist'   *The Australian*

'*Dead Spy Running* is a rip-roaring race of a read that never lets
up until the finishing tape – and a bit beyond' Robert Goddard

'As strong as Bourne, as clever as Bond, but with a voice set for
Generation Next, Jon Stock has done the impossible in Daniel
Marchant and created THE new spy'
                                   Stephen Gaghan, director of *Syriana*

By the same author

The Riot Act
The Cardamom Club
Dead Spy Running
Games Traitors Play

JON STOCK

Dirty Little Secret

blue door

Blue Door
An imprint of HarperCollins*Publishers*
77–85 Fulham Palace Road,
Hammersmith, London W6 8JB

This paperback edition 2013
2

First published in Great Britain by Blue Door 2012

ISBN: 978-0-00-730077-8

Typeset by Palimpsest Book Production Ltd, Falkirk, Stirlingshire
Printed and bound in Great Britain by
Clays Ltd, St Ives plc

For Stewart and Dinah

1

Salim Dhar looked over the limestone cliff and tried to imagine where he would fall. For a moment, he saw himself laid out on the flat rocks eighty feet below, the incoming sea lapping at his broken body. He stepped back, recoiling, as if he had caught the stench of his own death on the breeze blowing up from the foreshore.

He glanced around him and then out to sea. The moon was full, illuminating the fluorescence in the crests of the waves. Far to the west, the lights of reconnaissance planes winked as they criss-crossed the night sky, searching in vain for him. Somewhere out there a solitary trawler was drifting on the tide, crewed by men who would never see the dawn.

Dhar limped along the cliff edge to the point where he had climbed up. His flying suit was waterlogged, his left leg searing with pain. He knew he shouldn't be here, standing on Britain's Jurassic coastline, but the pull had proved too much. And he knew it was his only chance. After what had happened, the West would be hunting him down with renewed intensity. The American *kuffar* would increase their reward for him. $30 million? How about $155 million – the price of the US jet he had shot down a few hours earlier?

But would anyone think to search for him so close to home?

In another life, Britain could have been his home. He pressed a foot against the rocky ground. Tonight was the first time he had stepped on British soil, and he was surprised by how good it felt: ancient, reassuring. The air was pure, too, caressing his tired limbs with its gentle sea gusts.

He looked down at the foreshore again, rocks latticed like paving stones, and imagined his body somersaulting towards it. Would he survive? His descent might be broken by one of the ledges – if he was lucky. In the training camps of Kashmir and Kandahar, luck had been a forbidden fruit, on a par with alcohol. *You who believe, intoxicants and games of chance are repugnant acts – Satan's doing.* Instead, Dhar had been instilled with the discipline of planning. 'Trust in Allah, but tie your camel to a tree,' as his explosives instructor had joked (he was mixing hair bleach with chapatti flour at the time).

Now Dhar was rolling the dice. His plan was uncharacteristically reckless, possibly suicidal, but there was no choice. At least, that's how it felt. He needed to see where his late father, Stephen Marchant, had lived, where his half-brother, Daniel, had grown up. Tarlton, the family home, was not so far from here. He had seen it on the aeronautical charts. If he was to follow in his father's footsteps, he had to be sure, root himself deep within the English turf.

Dhar stumbled as he picked his way down the steep path, pain shooting through his leg. His knee had been cut when he had ejected. Instinctively he checked for the mobile phone in his pocket. It was still there, sealed in a watertight bag with the handgun. He had taken both from the trawler that had rescued him earlier in the Bristol Channel. If everything had gone to plan, he would now be being debriefed by jubilant Russians back in the Archangel Oblansk. But everything hadn't gone to plan. Dhar had blinked, and listened to the other man in his cockpit: Daniel Marchant.

He thought again about the trawler. First the captain's phone had rung, then he had drawn his gun, but Dhar had been ready. Thinking quickly, he had disarmed him before turning on the remaining crew members. It was after nightfall when he had finally abandoned the trawler, making his way ashore in its tender with the captain. He was below him now, propped up against a rock beside the tender, hands tied, drunk on vodka.

After reaching the bottom of the path, Dhar checked on the Russian. It was important that he was sober enough to speak. He dragged the tender further up into the shadows of the cliff and tore at some long grass to use as crude camouflage. The blades cut into his soft hands and a thin line of blood blossomed across his finger joints. He cursed, sucking at a hand, and went back to the Russian. He couldn't afford to be careless.

'Walk,' Dhar said. After the captain had risen unsteadily to his feet, Dhar pushed him in the direction of the cliffs. He meandered across the flat, stratified rocks, head bowed like a man approaching the gallows. There was no need for Dhar to threaten him with the gun. He had seen what had happened to his crew.

Dhar looked up at the cliffs ahead: layer upon layer of limestone and shale, crushed over millions of years. The compressed stripes reminded him of the creamy *millefeuille* his Indian mother used to smuggle out of the French Embassy in Delhi when she was working there as an *ayah*. She was here somewhere, too, he hoped. In Britain, the land of the man she had once loved. Daniel Marchant had promised he would look after her.

When they reached the foot of the cliff, Dhar signalled for the Russian to sit. He circled like an exhausted dog before slumping onto the rocks, trying in vain to break his fall with his tied hands. Dhar stood over him and pulled out a bottle of Stolichnaya, his actions tracked by the man's aqueous, frightened eyes. Squatting down beside him, he unscrewed the lid and poured vodka into

3

the Russian's mouth, watching it trickle in rivulets through the stubble of his unshaven chin. His swollen lips were dry and cracked. Small flecks of white, sea salt perhaps, had collected in the corners of his mouth.

Dhar had thought about what lay ahead many times in the last few hours, trying to banish the notion that he had nothing to lose. He could have stayed on the trawler, made his way south to France and on past Portugal to Africa, Morocco and the Atlas Mountains, where he had hidden once before. But he knew he was deluding himself. Without Russia's protection he would have been caught by now, picked up by one of the search planes. So here he was, in Britain, a country he had never quite been able to wage *jihad* against.

'You've been to the pub, a nice English pub,' Dhar said, his face close to the Russian's. He could smell the vodka on his breath, mixed with what might have been stale fish. 'And you fell down the cliffs on your walk home. Too much to drink.'

He waved the Stolichnaya in front of the man's eyes like a censorious parent.

'Are you going to kill me?' the man asked. Dhar had chosen him because his English was good, better than his crew's. He had heard him talk to the coastguard on the ship-to-shore radio.

'Not if you do as I say,' Dhar lied. He was certain that the man was an officer with the SVR, Russia's foreign intelligence service. It would make his killing more straightforward, despite the company he had provided during the long row ashore, the talk of his young family, twin sons.

Dhar tucked the bottle in his flying suit and pulled out the sealed bag containing the mobile phone and the gun. Don't rush, he told himself. There was no hurry. According to a map he had found on the trawler, the stretch of shoreline they were on was near a place called East Quantoxhead. The signpost at the top of the cliff, on the West Somerset Coastal Path, had said they were one mile from Kilve, where there was a public house. They would find him easily enough. The Quantocks were not exactly the Waziristan hills.

Taking the phone out of the bag, Dhar dialled 999 and held the receiver up to the Russian's mouth. With his other hand, he pressed the barrel of the gun hard against the man's temple. Afterwards, he would drag his body back to the boat and hide it in the shadows.

'Talk,' he ordered, cocking the gun. Dhar's head was clear, purged of twins. 'You've had a fall, hurt your left leg.' He pointed the gun at the man's thigh and fired. 'And now you need help.'

2

Daniel Marchant sat on the rock, throwing stones into Southampton Water. It was past midnight, and he still didn't have a strategy. Lakshmi Meena was asleep in the room behind him. To his left and right, a high green steel fence, topped with barbed wire, marked the perimeter of Fort Monckton, MI6's training centre at the tip of the Gosport peninsula.

Marchant was on a small private beach in front of the Fort's accommodation block. Two old cannon and a row of dark inlets in the sea-facing wall were a reminder of the Fort's role in the Napoleonic Wars, while an MoD sign saying NO LANDING ON THE FORESHORE hinted at its current purpose. The accommodation was usually occupied by MI6's most recent recruits, fresh-faced graduates on the Intelligence Officers' New Entry Course, but the latest batch had left for a two-week stint in Helmand station, and the rooms were empty.

He glanced up at the row of white sash windows, checking that there wasn't a light on in his room. It was a warm night, and he had tried to sleep with the window open, but sleep had never come. How could it, after what he'd just been through? A few hours earlier he had nearly died in a plane with Salim Dhar, and he knew he wouldn't be thanked for it. Never mind that he had thwarted one of the most audacious terrorist attacks ever mounted against mainland Britain.

And now this. He had already woken Lakshmi once to talk to her about the letter in his hands, but he hadn't been able to share its contents. Perhaps it was training. A genuine trust had built up between them over the past few weeks, a rapport that was edging towards something stronger, but she was still a CIA officer, although he suspected not for much longer. She was too honest, too nuanced for Langley. And she had become too closely associated with him.

But he knew it was more than training. As long as the contents of the letter remained known only to him, he could discount them, imagine they weren't real. He read them again, holding the paper up in the moonlight.

> . . . *Moscow Centre has an MI6 asset who helped the SVR expose and eliminate a network of agents in Poland. His codename was Argo, a nostalgic name in the SVR, as it was once used for Ernest Hemingway.*
>
> *The Polish thought that Argo was Hugo Prentice, a very good friend of your father, and I believe a close confidant of yours. He was shot dead on the orders of the AW, or at least of one of its agents. Hugo Prentice was not Argo.*
>
> *That mistake was a tragedy, destroying his reputation and damaging your father's. The real Argo is Ian Denton, deputy Chief of MI6.*

An hour earlier, while Lakshmi was sleeping, he had tried to call his Chief, Marcus Fielding, but the line was busy. He never liked leaving messages. He would call again when he had gathered his thoughts. Not for the first time, Marchant was struck by the solitude of his trade. He threw another stone towards the sea, harder this time. It missed the water and ricocheted between rocks like a maverick pinball.

Ian Denton had been good to him over the years, shared his distrust of America. And he was different from the smooth set at MI6, an outsider: a quiet northerner from Hull. But his awkward stabs at camaraderie at the terrace bar, the whispered words of encouragement in the corridor – they had all been a pack of lies.

'Are you OK down there?' It was Lakshmi, who had appeared at the bottom of the stone steps down to the beach, wearing an oversized dressing gown. Her left wrist was in plaster. Marchant knew as soon as he saw her that this time he would reveal what was in the letter. He understood that look in her eyes, the weariness of isolation. The CIA was about to throw the book at her for failing to bring him in. She had crossed the divide, reached out to a fellow traveller. Fielding had promised Marchant that his own job was safe, but the Americans were after Lakshmi's head, too. And they would get what they wanted, sooner or later. They always did.

He held Lakshmi's gaze and then looked at the stone in his hands, rubbing it between finger and thumb. If only he could break free, leave the distrust behind.

'I couldn't sleep,' he said.

'You were going to share something earlier,' Lakshmi said, walking over to him. Her feet were bare except for ankle chains, which tinkled like tiny bells as she crossed the stony beach. The sound brought back childhood memories of India, Marchant's *ayah* approaching across the marble floor with sweet *jalebi* from Chandni Chowk.

'Maybe if you told me, you might get some rest,' she continued, standing beside him now, tightening the cord on her dressing gown as she shivered in a gust of wind. She rested her hand on Marchant's neck and began to work the tight muscles.

Marchant breathed in deeply. There was no point being enigmatic. If he was going to tell her, he would be blunt about it.

'The Russians have got an asset high up in MI6,' he began, raising a hand up to hers. 'Very high.' He needed to feel her warmth. Or was it to stop her slipping him thirty pieces of silver? It was the first time he had told tales out of school.

'I thought he'd been killed.' Lakshmi's tone sounded casual, which annoyed Marchant, even though he knew it was unintentional. She was referring to Hugo Prentice, his close friend, fellow field officer and mentor in MI6. Prentice had been accused by the Poles of working for Moscow, and was gunned down in front of Marchant on the streets of London. The Americans had been only too ready to believe that he was a traitor. For Fielding and Marchant, it had been harder to dismiss him so quickly.

'It wasn't Hugo. None of us wanted to believe it was him, but we did. We forced ourselves, recalibrated our pasts. Now it turns out it wasn't him after all.'

'And that makes you mad.'

'It makes me feel cheap, sordid. Hugo was a family friend. Close to my father. He looked out for me.'

'Perhaps now you can remember him as he was, without the guilt.'

Marchant let his hand drop, and picked up another stone. 'Aren't you going to ask me who the traitor is?'

'I can't do that, Dan,' she said, ignoring his flippant tone. 'You've got a career to return to. You're a hero, remember? The man who talked Salim Dhar out of killing thousands.'

Marchant laughed. Sometimes Americans saw things in such black and white: heroes and villains, good and evil. His world wasn't like that. 'Try telling that to Langley. To James Spiro. I was in the plane that shot down a US jet.'

'Spiro won't listen to me.'

'Are you definitely leaving the Agency?'

'I've got no choice.'

'Then there's no harm telling you who the traitor is.'

9

This time Lakshmi returned his smile and sat down on the rocks next to him, close, her injured wrist slung playfully over his knees. 'Let me guess, now. Marcus Fielding?'

They laughed together, the tension gone for a moment, a sudden brightness in her tired eyes that gave him hope: for them, the lives they had chosen. The thought of Fielding, Chief of MI6, being anything other than loyal was risible, they both knew that. Known as the Vicar, Fielding was the one constant in Marchant's life. Lakshmi liked him, too. She had met him a couple of times, once at the Chelsea Physic Garden, and had warmed to his professorial ways. He had even visited her in hospital, brought her honey mangoes from Pakistan and Ecuadorian roses.

'It's true,' Marchant said. 'He's defected to the Royal Horticultural Society – to head up their fight against moles.'

Lakshmi smiled again and fell silent, running her front teeth over her lower lip. They both knew better than to fall under Fielding's avuncular spell. A few weeks earlier in Madurai he had turned Lakshmi and Marchant against each other for his own cold purposes, and he would gladly do so again if circumstances required it.

'Spiro once told me that he thought you were a traitor,' she said, her good hand sliding up Marchant's leg, working the thigh muscles.

'Sounds like Spiro – the guy thinks he's James Jesus Angleton. Spiro also suspected my father for years, particularly when he was tipped for the top. I don't think the CIA ever really got over Kim Philby.'

'Don't tell me who it is, Dan.' Lakshmi was serious now, almost whispering, her sweet breath warm on his neck, her hand squeezing the top of his thigh. 'You've got to go on, continue the fight. No one can stop Salim Dhar except you.'

But Marchant was no longer listening. His phone was vibrating, and there was only one person who rang him at this time of night: Fielding. He stood up to take the call, instinctively turning away from Lakshmi as if to shake off their intimacy, worried he had been caught.

'It's Paul here,' the voice said. 'Paul Myers.'

'Paul? How are you doing?' Marchant asked, relieved, walking down the beach. He turned and waved a hand of reassurance at Lakshmi, but he could already feel the shutters coming down, protocol kicking in. Myers had been injured when Dhar had bombed GCHQ's headquarters in Cheltenham after downing the US jet. The bomb was meant to have been dirty, but Marchant had talked Dhar out of it.

'Bit of a headache. Ears still ringing. But I'm back at my desk. Well, working from home. Spent the afternoon at A&E. The doc told me to stay away from GCHQ for a while.'

'It could have been worse, trust me.' Marchant felt bad that he hadn't been to visit Myers, but Fielding had insisted on him staying at the Fort in the aftermath of the attack.

'So I gather. I suppose I should be thanking you.'

'Any time. What's up?'

'I couldn't help listening in on the crash zone. I should have been resting, but you know how it is.'

Marchant knew exactly how it was. Myers lived and breathed for chatter, drawing it down from the ether with the dedication of a drug addict. Intercepts, voice-recognition, black-bag cryptanalysis, wiretaps, asymmetric key algorithms: he was a privacy kleptomaniac. The more measures people took to ensure their communications were private, the more Myers wanted to listen in. If Myers hadn't been working for GCHQ, he would still have found a way to eavesdrop.

'I picked up something just now that I thought you should know about,' he continued.

'About the crash?' Marchant asked, glancing back at Lakshmi, who was heading up the steps to their room. Once again she had

11

got under his skin, come too close when he should have been focusing elsewhere.

'Maybe.'

According to Fielding, a trawler had been found with its auto-pilot on, drifting west in the Bristol Channel with three dead Russians on board. There had been no sign of Dhar, which troubled Marchant. He also remembered counting four crew when he had been in the sea with Dhar.

'A Search and Rescue Sea King from RAF Chivenor was called out a few minutes ago. A man rang in from the coast, near Quantoxhead. Said he'd fallen down a cliff on the way home from the pub at Kilve. I was listening in on the call. He sounded in a lot of pain. And drunk.'

'It's the weekend, isn't it?' Marchant knew Myers was one of the best analysts at GCHQ, but this time he wondered if he had been on the beer too. Marchant didn't blame him. He had been lucky to survive the bomb blast.

'He also sounded Russian.'

3

Marcus Fielding was surprised to see the lean figure of Ian Denton already in position at the long coffin-shaped table, talking quietly with the Foreign Secretary. Less surprising was the sight of Harriet Armstrong, his opposite number at MI5, chatting with the Prime Minister at the far end of the airless conference room. She had always been good at the politics. As he watched them, silhouetted against a flickering mosaic of flat TV screens, the thought crossed Fielding's mind that this might be his last COBRA meeting.

A part of him flinched at the idea. He wasn't ready to step back from the fray. There was still so much to do, battles to be won, not just in the war on terror but in Whitehall. He knew he should be more like Armstrong and Denton, sweet-talking the politicians, but he had always preferred dealing with field agents rather than Foreign Secretaries. He was a Chief who liked to stay south of the river.

If this was to be his final COBRA, he wouldn't miss the dimly lit Cabinet Office room with its low ceiling and brown curtains along one wall. It was past 1 a.m., but time was meaningless here. Night didn't follow day. Instead, the room was trapped in a penumbral stasis. The air conditioning was too warm, the coffee cold. As for the meetings, they had become increasingly ineffective, a forum for political posturing rather than swift operational responses. That was why he liked to meet privately beforehand with the heads of MI5, the Joint Terrorism Analysis Centre and the Defence Intelligence Staff, away from ambitious ministers with their own agendas. Only this time, they had quietly demurred.

Fielding took his seat, nodding at the Director of GCHQ. It wasn't reciprocated. Dhar's bomb might not have been dirty, but it had still knocked some sugar off 'the doughnut', as GCHQ's Cheltenham premises were known. Fielding felt a knot begin to tighten in his lower lumbar. Tonight wasn't the moment for lying supine on the floor, as he was prone to do when his back played up. He was prepared for the meeting to be tense. For many of those gathered around the table, MI6 was in the dock. He also knew that he could never reveal the one piece of intelligence that might save his career.

'Welcome, everyone,' the Prime Minister began, looking down the room. His jacket was off, his tone businesslike. No small talk. 'Marcus, I think it's best if we start with you?' In other words, Fielding thought, you got us into this Christawful mess, you can get us out of it.

'The UK threat level remains at critical,' Fielding began, glancing at Armstrong, who cast her eyes down at the printed agenda. 'And in our opinion it should remain so. As we know, yesterday's attacks on the Royal International Air Tattoo at Fairford, where an F-22 Raptor was destroyed, and on GCHQ at Cheltenham, were carried out by Salim Dhar in a Russian SU-25 fighter jet. Although we think it was partly an act of proxy terrorism on behalf of the Russians, Dhar was essentially operating on his own.'

A dissenting shuffle of papers. 'And with more than a little help from one of your officers,' the director of GCHQ said. 'Daniel Marchant *was* in the cockpit with Dhar?'

The gloves were coming off quicker than Fielding had expected.

14

'As I outlined to the Americans in our earlier JIC meeting,' he replied, trying to ignore the knots tightening like serpents, 'Daniel Marchant succeeded in talking Dhar out of a far worse attack. Two points I'd like noted, please.' A glance at the COBRA secretary. God help him, he thought: he was starting to sound like a politician, covering his arse at every opportunity. 'First, the Russians wanted Dhar to wipe out a delegation of Georgian generals who were at the air show to sign a deal with the US. Dhar pulled out of the attack at the last moment – thanks to Marchant. It should also be noted that the attack would have killed the US Defense Secretary, a point that seems to have been overlooked in Washington.

'Secondly, Dhar's plane was armed with a thousand-pound radioactive dirty bomb. Caesium-137 – nasty stuff, particularly in a conurbation the size of Cheltenham. It was always his intention to fly on to GCHQ, twenty miles to the north-west, and drop this bomb on the building. In the event, he pulled out of that plan too, again thanks to the bravery of my officer, Daniel Marchant. Instead, Dhar opted for a conventional explosive that I gather caused only minor structural damage.'

'And killed one of my colleagues,' the Director of GCHQ added.

A pause. Fielding thought about offering his condolences, but it seemed trite in the circumstances.

'Thank you, Marcus,' the Prime Minister said, after waiting in vain for Fielding to commiserate. 'I think it would be fair to say that while those gathered here understand the role of MI6 in all this' – a dry cough from the sidelines. Was it really Denton, Fielding wondered – 'the Americans don't. I've just come off the phone to the President, who is demanding to know why an MI6 agent was in a plane that destroyed $155 million-worth of USAF aircraft.'

'It's no exaggeration to say that our relationship with Washington is in tatters,' the Foreign Secretary said. 'Trade meetings cancelled, diplomatic initiatives dropped.'

'I've just been informed that the proposed new Joint National Security Board has been put on ice,' added the government's National Security Adviser, glancing up at Fielding.

'And the NSA's Echelon cooperation thresholds on SIGINT have significantly risen across the grid in the past few hours,' the director of GCHQ said. 'It's as if the UKUSA Agreement didn't exist.'

'I also understand France has now been asked to head up NATO's joint sea exercise off Cape Wrath next week,' said the Joint Chief of Staff. 'It's normally our shout.'

Things must be serious if the Americans were cosying up to the French. For the first time, Fielding wondered if he would be forced to reveal his ace in the hole, but he knew he couldn't. It was a secret that only he and Marchant were privy to.

'It's with all this in mind,' the Prime Minister continued, 'that I've asked the Foreign Secretary to head up a Cabinet working group that will focus solely on rebuilding all aspects of our relationship with America. Ian Denton will oversee intelligence sharing, which of course lies at the heart of the partnership.'

Credit where credit was due, thought Fielding. Denton had played a blinder, distancing himself from a discredited Chief of MI6, and climbing into bed with the Foreign Secretary. Another knot tightened.

'At the heart of our strategy is doing all we can to help the US find Salim Dhar,' the Foreign Secretary said. 'It's the only thing that will pacify Washington, and it's the least we can do, given Dhar's unfortunate connection with Britain.' He glanced at his watch. 'As of thirty minutes ago, when Fox News broke the story against our wishes, I'm afraid it's now common knowledge that Salim Dhar's father was Stephen Marchant, the late Chief of MI6,

16

and his half-brother is Daniel Marchant, a serving MI6 officer. Ian here will be working closely with JTAC, GCHQ, Five and of course Six over the coming weeks.'

'And we still don't know any more about Dhar's last movements in UK waters?' the PM asked.

'We've got Sentinel and Sentry cover, they're combing the entire area,' said the Joint Chief of Staff. 'So far, just the one abandoned trawler and three dead crew. A few minutes ago we picked up the acoustic profile of a Russian Akula-class submarine off the coast of Ireland, south-east of Cork, heading out to sea. It might have been part of Dhar's original exit strategy, but I'm not sure how keen the Russians would be to help him, given he failed to attack the Georgian generals. I'm afraid Salim Dhar seems to have vanished into thin air.'

4

Dhar sat against the rocks, watching through narrowed eyes as the man descended towards him. The noise of the yellow Sea King helicopter was deafening, the downcurrent from its blades instilling a sudden panic in him. It took all of his self-control to stay where he was, pinned to the ground like quarry beneath a hovering hawk. His instinct was to run, along the foreshore, into the sea, anywhere. The helicopter brought back too many memories: his hasty departure from the Atlas Mountains, the unnecessary killing of the Berber messenger.

The winch man was almost with him now, spinning on the rope like a dangling spider. He had a luminous orange stretcher under one arm and his feet were out to the side, to protect himself from the cliff face. Dhar checked for the handgun in his pocket. Earlier, he had dragged the Russian back to the boat and ordered him to remove his outer clothing. Then he had shot him, a double tap to the forehead and a prayer for the thousands of Muslim brothers slain by the SVR in the Caucasus. Struggling with his injured leg, he had climbed out of his flying suit and put on the Russian's jacket and bloodied trousers, watched by his hollow stare.

If the dead Russian had seemed to disapprove of Dhar's new outfit, his distorted features had formed a smirk when he had

18

reached for the vodka bottle and, for the first time in his life, tasted alcohol. He had closed his eyes as the liquid burnt against the back of his throat. *You who believe, intoxicants and games of chance are repugnant acts – Satan's doing.* Allah would forgive him, would understand how important it was that his rescuers thought he was drunk. It was only drinking from the grape that was *haraam*, wasn't it? And hadn't the caliph Haroun Al-Rashid occasionally indulged?

Dhar sat perfectly still now as the winch man touched down beside him, unhooked the stretcher and leant in close to his face. The alcohol's alien effects made Dhar's head spin when he closed his eyes. He hoped that his breath carried its sinful traces. Why hadn't he thrown the half-empty bottle away, instead of slipping it into his inside pocket?

'Can you hear me?' the winch man asked, checking for vital signs. Dhar had decided that unconsciousness was the most credible state after a drunken cliff fall. The winch man had seen the bloodstains on his leg, the ripped trousers and the dark bruising below, and was now checking the wound. Tentatively he pulled back the material and spoke into his helmet mike.

Dhar couldn't catch the exact words, but he heard something about an incoming tide. Five minutes later his head was whirling like a dervish as the stretcher lifted into the sky. It was a relief when he was finally eased in through the side door of the Sea King. Then, after slipping his arms free of the stretcher straps, he was on his feet and pointing the gun at the winch man and his colleague.

'Remove your helmets,' Dhar said, glancing up towards the cockpit. He had intended to shoot them both, but something made him change his mind. He hoped it wasn't the vodka. The two men exchanged nervous glances and looked back at Dhar. Did they doubt him? Dhar felt another wave of panic, and raised the gun to their heads.

'Remove your helmets!' he barked.

It would be so much easier if they were dead, he thought. Without hesitating, the men unfastened their helmets and dropped them to the deck. Dhar motioned at the open door and they edged towards it. Had they realised who he was?

He watched as the winch man stood with his legs bent, head down, like a nervous child on a high diving board. The helicopter had arced out across the sea after picking up Dhar, and was heading towards the shore again. They would be over land in a few minutes. The winch man held onto the side, bent his legs further, and this time he was gone, dropping away in the darkness with a fading scream. The second man glanced at Dhar, at his gun, then he jumped too.

5

Lakshmi stood in the window, looking out across the Solent. It was well past midnight, and Marchant was still on his phone, pacing about at the far end of the beach, close to where a line of perimeter fenceposts waded into the water like determined bathers. A solitary yacht was heading into Portsmouth under engine, sails down, navigation lights on. Her body was beginning to ache, a cramplike pain tightening her limbs. She told herself it was her wrist, but she knew it wasn't.

Her imminent departure from the CIA was timely. She and Marchant would have more chance of making a go of things if one of them was in the real world, where people were straight-forward and honest, and used the regular mail rather than brush passes to communicate. A year earlier, they had circled each other like wild animals in Rabat, where she had been sent to keep an eye on him. Everyone had thought Marchant was crazy to believe that Dhar would show up in Morocco, but the renegade MI6 officer had been proved right.

She still didn't fully understand why he had ended up in a Russian fighter jet with Dhar, but she believed him when he said a far worse disaster had been averted. And she had assisted him, in her own small way. She was glad she had done that, even if it had triggered something she hoped was behind her.

She went over to the bed and wrapped herself in a blanket, trying to stop the shiver that had set in. She thought again about the Soho restaurant where she had helped the Russians lift Marchant in a firefight. One of them, dead eyes beneath a black balaclava, had raised a machine gun to her head. She would have been killed if it hadn't been for Marchant, who had screamed at him not to shoot. A stray bullet had already shattered her wrist.

She closed her eyes, trying to put out of her mind the paramedic who had turned up within minutes of the shooting. He had just been doing his job, a routine medical injection for trauma as she had slumped on the floor of the restaurant in agony.

The pain had dissipated within seconds, replaced by a surge of liquid pleasure that had spread out from her body like nectar. Time had begun to slip, too, taking her back three years to when she had been a medical student at Georgetown University. Her life had moved on since then.

She stared at the old wall of the Fort, tracing the lumps and cracks in its whitewashed surface. It would be only a matter of hours before she would be taken from here and flown back to Langley to be dismissed. Spiro would know that she could have done more to stop the Russians, that she had disobeyed orders. Her father would be disappointed, her mother relieved. They had always wanted her to be a doctor, but her father had recently begun to take pride in her work – not that he could boast about it to his Indian friends in Reston. 'Government business' was all he was allowed to say.

Wiping her nose, she noticed a voicemail message on her phone. It was Spiro, and he wasn't ringing to fire her. After the message had finished, she got up from the bed, walked over to the deep-set window and called Spiro back. The blanket was still around her shoulders.

'Do I have a choice?' she asked, watching Marchant on the beach below, trying to ignore a rising nausea.

'You're an American, of course you have a choice. This isn't India, for Christ's sake.'

'In that case, it's a no.'

'Listen, if it's not you, we'll get someone else. It's as simple as that. I wasn't sure how you'd feel about another woman getting up close and personal with Marchant.'

'What makes you think he'll drop his guard so easily?'

'He's done it before. You never knew Leila, did you?'

Not personally, she thought, but she felt as if she did know her. Marchant had talked often about Leila, the MI6 officer who had betrayed him.

'And by all accounts, it's not just his guard that he's dropped with you.'

Lakshmi ignored the innuendo. 'He's told me nothing. He's a professional.'

'All the more reason we need someone like you. Can you believe it? The Brits are defending him. Fielding thinks Marchant's a frickin' hero. Try telling that to the head of the USAF. It's a total clusterfuck. If Marchant's helped Dhar once, he'll help him again. It's in the blood. Only this time we need to stop him. I'm just sorry you got hurt.'

Lakshmi wasn't falling for Spiro's sudden concern, not for one minute. She had taken up Fielding's offer to stay in the sanctuary of the Fort in order to keep away from him.

'I'm not interested.'

There was a pause, as if Spiro was idly looking around for something, a cigarette perhaps. Her reaction didn't seem to surprise him.

23

'Have you spoken to your folks recently?'

She didn't like his change of tone: small talk concealing something more sinister. Her arm began to shake. 'Give them a call some time. They'd appreciate it.'

Before Lakshmi could say anything, Spiro had hung up.

6

'Primakov wrote me a letter,' Marchant began, sitting on the rocks. He would return to Lakshmi in a minute. The wind coming in off the Solent was cold, and he was exhausted.

'Go on.' Marcus Fielding sounded tired too, more tired than Marchant could ever remember him sounding. Marchant felt guilty about his news.

'He says that there's a Russian asset high up in MI6. The letter was written after Hugo died. Primakov thinks the mole framed Hugo to protect himself.'

'And does he give a name?' Fielding asked.

Marchant paused. 'Your deputy.'

There was a long silence. Marchant wondered if the news surprised Fielding, or if it confirmed a previous suspicion. Fielding was inscrutable face to face, even more so at the end of a phone line.

'You know Primakov never liked Denton,' Fielding said eventually. 'There was history between them.'

'I didn't know.'

'I'll look into it.'

'You think it might be Primakov's revenge? From beyond the grave?'

'We owe it to Hugo to find out. I know someone in Warsaw who might be able to help.'

7

Dhar stumbled as he approached the two pilots in the cockpit of the Sea King. He wasn't sure if it was his leg or the vodka. The noise was deafening, disorientating. The co-pilot clocked him first, his eyes widening in panic. As Dhar raised the gun, a finger to his lips, the pilot turned and saw him too. He seemed calmer, glancing at Dhar and then past him, down the helicopter, to see what had happened to his crew.

Dhar was familiar with the cockpit of an SU-25, but the Sea King's controls were alien to him. He knew, though, that he would have to move fast to disable its communication systems and prevent the pilots from raising the alarm. It would be equipped with U/VHF and HF radios, as well as intercom, but Dhar didn't have time to familiarise himself with the panel of dials. Instead he grabbed the flex coming out of the back of the pilot's helmet and ripped it from its socket. Then he did the same with the co-pilot, jerking his head back as if he had pulled his hair.

'Take them off!' Dhar shouted above the noise, waving his gun. After they had removed their helmets, he tossed them into the back of the helicopter, where one clattered and rolled out of the open door. The sight of it plunging into the night like a severed head seemed to shock the co-pilot. One of his knees began to bounce uncontrollably.

The helicopter was approaching land. 'If you want your frightened friend to live, fly back out to sea,' Dhar said, leaning in towards the pilot. The pilot hesitated for a moment, as if thinking through his options, and then moved the stick. The Sea King altered course. 'And if you try anything – calling for help, attempting to land – I will kill you. I know how to fly.'

Dhar couldn't be sure, but both men seemed to believe him.

'What do you want from us?' the co-pilot asked, unable to hide the fear in his voice. 'We're just SAR pilots.'

'I don't want anything from you,' Dhar said, pressing the gun against the man's temple. A few seconds later, the co-pilot was standing at the open door, looking back down the helicopter at Dhar in disbelief, and then he was gone.

'Now we head for Kemble,' Dhar said, slumping into the co-pilot's empty seat and picking up a chart. It was good to be airborne again.

8

Lakshmi lay in the darkness, thinking about Spiro's offer. Marchant was still outside on the rocks. She had considered joining him again, but the call from her father a few minutes earlier had changed everything.

'He explained he was from the IRS,' her father had said, sounding like a broken man. 'Said the company's books were not in order, and accused us of all manner of damn things: tax evasion, money laundering.'

'Slow down, Dad,' Lakshmi had replied, already detecting Spiro's hand at work. 'Did he give you a name, a number?'

The caller had left enough details for Lakshmi to be certain it was a sting. Somewhere on the Langley campus a junior officer would be sitting by a phone in an empty office, ready to field any calls to the Internal Revenue Service.

'You know it's all lies,' her father had continued. 'I trained as an accountant in Madurai, best results in my year. How dare he accuse me of these things?'

'I'm sure it's just a mistake,' Lakshmi had said. The last time she had heard him this agitated was on the day after 9/11, when he had been stopped by police officers in a shopping mall and detained for eight hours. 'Leave it with me. I'll make some enquiries.'

'I'm sorry to have bothered you with this, Lakshmi,' he had said, almost in tears. 'Twenty-five years it's taken me to build the business, isn't it. I came to this country with nothing, just –'

'Dad, leave it with me. Everything will be fine.'

She walked back over to the window. Below her was the man she thought she loved. If she quit the Agency, Spiro would still follow through on his threat. He was that kind of man. The only way she could protect her father was if she agreed to his terms. She had no choice. For a moment, she understood how Leila must have felt when the Iranians threatened to kill her mother if she didn't spy for them. Whenever Marchant had spoken of Leila, she had hoped she was different, not the sort to betray those closest to her. Now she was about to join the club.

She looked again at Marchant, his tall rower's frame silhouetted in the moonlight, then dialled Spiro's number.

'I've made my decision,' she said.

'And?'

'I'll do it.'

'You're smarter than I thought.'

'I need to know my cover story. Marchant thinks I'm about to quit the Agency.'

'Actually, we were going to fire you, then put you on trial. Let's stick with that, shall we? You're on the run, you got too close to Marchant. Disobeyed orders. Grossly violated your duties. A warrant's been issued for your arrest – it will give you some cred- ibility. We just won't bring you in.'

'What's Marchant's current status?'

'Fielding's defending him, but he won't be around for much longer. I'm seeing to it personally. As soon as Fielding's out of the way, we'll pick Marchant up from the Fort. Until then, I want you to stay close to him. Find out what the hell he was doing in that plane with Dhar, why he didn't take the guy down. I won't expect you to make contact. It's essential you don't arouse Marchant's suspicion – unless you've got important intel. Even then, be careful. It pains me to say it, but Marchant's good.'

'There's one thing you should know.'

'Go on.'

'Marchant says there's a Soviet mole, high up in MI6.'

The information was a down payment, something to reassure Spiro that more would follow. He seemed unimpressed.

'Tell me something I don't know.'

Five minutes later, Marchant crept back into the room. Lakshmi was in bed, eyes closed, dreading his return.

'Are you OK?' she whispered in the darkness. She had hoped her voice would sound stronger.

'I've just come off the phone to Fielding.'

'How was he?'

'Tired, defeated. He's been in a difficult COBRA meeting.'

'And?'

'I'd say his days are numbered.'

Marchant slid off his jeans and climbed into bed. His body was cold. She couldn't bring herself to hug him.

'I know how he feels,' she said.

'Have you heard from Langley?'

'Not officially. One of my colleagues rang. A friend.' She closed her eyes again, bit her lip.

Your legs are sweating. Are you OK?' he asked.

'I caught a chill on the beach.' But she knew she hadn't.

'And what did this friend say?'

'The Agency want to throw the book at me.'

'For not stopping the Russians?'

Lakshmi hesitated, doubting whether she could go through with this. She wanted to cradle Marchant in her arms, feel his warmth. Then she thought again of her father.

'Disobeying orders, gross violation of duties,' she said, repeating Spiro's words. 'A warrant's been issued for my arrest.'

'They won't be able to touch you here. That's why Fielding sent you. He saw this coming.'

They lay in silence, listening to the water lapping at the rocks beneath the window. Already she could feel them drifting apart on the tide of professionalism swelling back into their lives. And she hated herself for it, for the games they were forced to play.

'I helped you in the restaurant because I believe we won't win by force alone,' she eventually said, for her own benefit as much as his. She turned towards him, resting her broken wrist on his chest. The cast trembled against his skin. 'There are other ways of winning the war on terror. I despise Spiro, his brutal approach to intelligence-gathering.' She paused. 'And I did it because I wanted to be with you. You do know that?'

Marchant turned towards her. 'I'm very grateful.'

'What's going to happen to us? To you?'

'It doesn't look good. An MI6 officer apparently defects to Moscow only to show up in a hostile Russian plane with Salim Dhar. Without Fielding to protect me, I'm buggered.'

She thought again of Spiro, his instructions to find out more, and swallowed hard.

'Why didn't you kill him?' she asked, as if it was the most natural question in the world. But she knew it sounded forced. She was no good at this any more, not with someone she loved.

'Dhar? You haven't asked me that before.'

'I know you can't tell me everything, Dan, but you never talk about him, the whole half-brother thing. Is that why you wanted the Russians to take you? And why you didn't kill him?'

But Marchant didn't answer.

9

Dhar knew it was a risk taking the pilot with him, but he might be useful in the hours ahead. For a few brief seconds, watching the blades spin down in a remote corner of Cotswold Airport in Kemble, he had considered shooting him, but again a calm voice in his head had urged restraint. Instead he had bound his wrists with a bandage, taped his mouth with a roll of plaster and told him he was dead if he tried anything.

They were now walking in the darkness towards the perimeter fence in the north-east corner of the airfield, the pilot leading, Dhar limping behind. In his left hand he held a set of bolt cutters he had found on the helicopter, stored with other safety equipment. He had ordered the pilot to head for Kemble because it was less than two miles from Tarlton. When he was being trained to fly in Russia, he had often studied this area on a map, wondering if, one day, he would ever get to see the home where his father had lived. That moment was now approaching.

Dhar glanced at his watch as they reached the fence. Time was not on his side. Air Traffic Control had twice tried in vain to contact their helicopter during their approach to Kemble. A wider alarm might not have been raised by their failure to respond, but it was a risk. A more worrying call had come in from Search and Rescue's regional headquarters at RAF Valley in Anglesey, which they had also ignored. The only good news was that the control tower at Kemble was deserted, just as Dhar had hoped. Kemble had no licence for night use.

Dhar told the pilot to stand with his face to the fence. Again, he wondered if it would be easier to shoot him. He pulled out his gun and pressed it against the back of the man's head, suddenly impatient. What was he doing, dragging this *kafir* with him? For a few long seconds he thought about squeezing the trigger. The pilot looked down, preparing himself for death. He was composed, Dhar had to hand it to him. He hadn't panicked when Dhar had first appeared behind him in the cockpit, hadn't flinched with a gun to his head, unlike his craven co-pilot. Dhar loosened the bandage around his wrists and handed him the bolt cutters.

The pilot knelt in the wet grass and cut away at the bottom of the wire mesh, watched by Dhar. Once he had finished, Dhar tossed the cutters into the undergrowth and pushed the pilot through the gap with his gun, following after him. For a while the vodka had numbed the pain, but it was excruciating as he crouched down. When the pilot was a few feet ahead of him, Dhar took a swig from the Stolichnaya and slid the bottle back into his jacket. It was medicinal, he told himself, but he knew it was more than that. His life, so ordered up until now, was slipping out of control.

Two minutes later they were standing beside a main road, hidden in the shadows of a dirty lay-by. The road was empty, but Dhar could hear the distant sound of a car. If the pilot was going to try anything, now was the time. Dhar pressed the gun into his back and waited as the vehicle's headlights swept round the corner. It was a solitary police car, driving fast, blue light flashing, but no siren. Instinctively he grabbed the pilot's arm and pressed the gun harder into his back as it drove past them. He told himself to relax.

Once the road had cleared and the night was quiet again, Dhar pushed the pilot forward. Somewhere in the dark woods up ahead, an owl hooted. It was only one mile to Tarlton.

10

'I need to know why Marchant was in the cockpit with Dhar,' Ian Denton said, sitting back in Marcus Fielding's official Range Rover. 'At least, I need to know what I can tell the Americans.'

Although Fielding lived in Dolphin Square, he had offered to give his deputy a lift to his home in Battersea after the COBRA meeting. It was out of his way, but he owed him an explanation, and this was their first proper opportunity to talk. There was no anger in Denton's voice – quiet, with a drop of Hull – no indication of any resentment at having been excluded. As far as Fielding knew, Denton had never objected to MI6's tradition of need-to-know, its culture of compartmentalised knowledge. Even as deputy, he wouldn't expect to be informed of every operational detail. But there was a new-found confidence in his manner, a lack of deference that made Fielding wonder if the Foreign Secretary had already offered him his job.

'We knew the Russians were shielding Dhar,' Fielding said as his Special Branch driver, separated from them by a soundproof glass divide, turned right onto the Embankment. 'The only way to get to him – and to stop whatever atrocity he was planning – was to persuade the Russians that Marchant wanted to defect. You'll understand why I could tell no one at the time. Nikolai Primakov, Moscow's cultural attaché in London, had agreed to

35

work for us again. He had access to Dhar, and acted as our middle man.'

'Just like old times, then.'

'Quite. Primakov likes working with Marchants.'

For the first time, Fielding detected a trace of bitterness in his deputy, the Hull accent less suppressed. Marchant's father, Stephen, had recruited Primakov in Delhi in the 1980s. It had been a game-changing signing in the Cold War, as good as Oleg Gordievsky, and had fast-tracked Stephen to the top of MI6. Denton, then a young officer in the SovBloc Controllerate, was the contact man, clearing the dead-letter drops and trying – in vain – to keep Primakov sweet. The two men had not warmed to each other.

'As far as I can recall, we never got round to telling the Americans about Primakov,' Denton said.

'No, and I would ask you, in your new role, that it should stay that way.'

The last thing Fielding needed was some CIA goon going over the Primakov files.

'That could be a problem. As part of our efforts to rebuild trust with Washington, we've agreed to an independent investigation into the events at Fairford and Cheltenham. It's no secret that the Americans want to throw the book at Marchant and Lakshmi Meena.'

'Then it's up to us to protect them, isn't it?'

Fielding had expected a witch hunt. Top-down, no stone left unturned, the usual Whitehall hysteria: craven civil servants running around doing the Americans' bidding. It was why he had sent Marchant and Lakshmi to Fort Monckton. They would be safe there, at least for the time being.

'What the Americans are struggling to understand – and I see their point – is why Marchant didn't eliminate Dhar.' Fielding thought Denton looked increasingly at home in the Range Rover, sitting back, at ease, elbows out, his sinewy body expanding with new authority. In the past, he had never relaxed when Fielding had given him a lift, perching on the buttermilk leather like a watchful lizard. 'Once he'd won his trust by defecting,' Denton continued, 'there must have been opportunities to kill him. In Russia. On board the plane.'

Fielding could never tell him the real reason why Marchant hadn't killed Dhar. He could never tell anyone. He tried to change the focus.

'I think we're forgetting who we're dealing with here,' he said. 'When Marchant reached Russia, Dhar forced him to shoot Primakov, a family friend, for being a Western spy. The bigger question is why Dhar didn't kill Marchant. He could have done so at any time. Marchant was exceptionally brave.'

'So why didn't Dhar kill him?'

Fielding turned away, looking down the Thames as they drove over Battersea Bridge. It was almost 3 a.m. He always felt depressed when he saw Albert Bridge at night, lit up like a gaudy old whore in pearls. 'Perhaps he was curious. They're half-brothers, after all. And Dhar only met his father once, when he was in jail in India. Maybe Marchant reminded him of his father, I don't know.'

'The Americans want answers, Marcus, not cod bloody psychology.'

'I don't remember you always being so ready to oblige them.'

Fielding was struggling to remain civil as the Range Rover drew up outside a nondescript terrace house on Battersea Bridge Road. Denton's anti-US views had been well known in the Service, causing Fielding enough problems in the past. It appeared that he had put them to one side with the promise of promotion.

'They also want to find Dhar. Marchant was the last person to see him alive. I assume we can circulate his Fort debriefing?'

'It will be on desks in the morning,' Fielding said.

Denton got out of the car and leant in through the open door.

'Thanks.' He tapped the roof, as if he'd just chosen the vehicle in a showroom. 'For the lift.'

'There's one thing I can tell you,' Fielding said. 'Daniel Marchant's one of the good guys. Trust me. Let's not throw him to the lions. Not yet.'

11

Marchant lay staring at the vibrating phone. It was still dark outside, and for a moment he didn't know where he was. He didn't even know if he was awake. His dreams had been about dead sailors and Dhar. The phone display said that 'Dad – Home' was calling. He hadn't been called from that number since his father had died seventeen months before.

The call was from the family home at Tarlton, outside Cirencester in the Cotswolds. Nobody lived there any more. The house was closed up, and would remain that way until Marchant decided what to do with the place. As the only surviving member of the family, he had inherited his father's flat in Pimlico, where he now lived, and the large family house in Tarlton. He could never envisage living there, but he hadn't been able to bring himself to sell it.

Marchant slid out of bed, checking that Lakshmi was asleep. Her eyes were closed, her breathing uneven. He would call a doctor in the morning, get her wrist checked out. Careful not to wake her, he stepped into the bathroom, closing the door behind him. He was glad the phone was on vibrate, as he could tell himself it was the phone and not his hand that was shaking. Who would call from his home? And at 4 a.m.? Once a month, his father's cleaning lady dropped by to check on the place, but she would only ring if there was a problem. Perhaps there had been a fire?

'Who is this?' Marchant said quietly.

'Your pilot.'

12

Omar Rashid wasn't comfortable with promotion. For a start, he had too many people in his SIGINT unit who were twice his age. It was just plain awkward asking a fortysomething analyst at the National Security Agency to work a bit harder. It was like a freshman telling a senior how to hit on girls. But the new job had its perks. Instead of trawling through the real-time night traffic in AfPak, hoping to nail some careless *jihadi* in an internet café in Karachi, he could sit back in his small office and catch a bit of girl-on-girl action on RedTube while others did the hard work.

He blamed Salim Dhar, whose voice he had picked up in North Waziristan a few weeks earlier. Only it hadn't been his voice. Dhar had duped them, strapped a tape recorder to his cell phone and planted it with six kidnapped US Marines. None of them had stood a chance when the Reaper deployed its Hellfire missiles twenty minutes later. His boss had taken the drop, leaving the unit without a leader.

In all the confusion and recriminations that followed, someone seemed to overlook the fact that it was Rashid who had made the original intercept, and he was given the job. Promotion by incompetence, that's what he called it. What fiasco would it take for him to reach the top of the NSA?

'Sir, we have a priority level five,' his PA said, putting her head around the door. He switched browser windows, confident she had seen nothing, and checked out her rear as he followed her into the main room. One day he would be brave enough to ask her out for a drink, maybe the Havana Club in Baltimore.

'What've we got?' Rashid said, an awful sense of déjà vu washing over him. His unit normally sat at separate terminals. Now, though, most of them were gathered around one analyst's screen. Like everyone else in his department, he had been told to temporarily redirect his unit's efforts to the UK, where GCHQ was in need of cover after Salim Dhar had run amok. His last known act had been to eject from a Russian jet over the Bristol Channel, from where he was thought to have been picked up by a Russian sub, but nobody was sure. Who said the Cold War was over?

'One hundred per cent voiceprint recognition,' the analyst said.

'Salim Dhar?' Rashid's tentative words hung in the air. For a few brief minutes, the name had brought him fame and the promise of fortune, but now he had come to dread it. They all had.

'On a watchlist number. Calling a cell phone in Portsmouth, UK.' And then he added, for Rashid's benefit: 'Real time two-way.' This time, in other words, a tape-recorded Dhar was almost impossible.

'Cell IDs?'

'Receiver handset's encrypted. We're working on it.' The analyst looked across at a colleague who was crunching numbers on his screen.

'What about Dhar's?'

'Sir, signature and profile of a secure hard line. So far no number.'

'A hard line? What the hell's he playing at? And no number ID? I thought you said it was on our watchlist.'

'It's got some heavy-duty masking encryption at the local level.

Looks like it's been rerouted at source. The Brits may have a better idea. Somebody call down to GCHQ?'

Rashid had seen the images of 'the doughnut', and the bomb damage to its central courtyard. It had been showing on the news channels all afternoon. The iconic building had stood up well to the attack, and there had only been one casualty, but its operational capabilities had been affected. GCHQ had a large contingent working on the floor below, where morale had taken a nosedive. He had been down there earlier for a chat, and had returned with one eye on the window, scanning the skies for rogue Russian jets, wondering if the NSA might be next.

'Sir, the cell ID's location.'

Rashid walked over to the analyst who was sitting on his own.

'Fort Monckton, MI6 training centre,' Rashid said, reading from the screen, which was now showing a crystal-clear satellite image of Portsmouth harbour, a pulsating blue icon radiating out from the southern end of the Gosport peninsula.

'And we've got the hard-line number for Dhar. It's presenting as the main switchboard for MI6 headquarters, Vauxhall Cross, central London. Seems like the entire MI6 phone network is on our watchlist.'

Rashid didn't want to think about the ethics of eavesdropping on their closest ally. There were other things on his mind. He ran a hand through his hair and wondered what he'd done to deserve Dhar. It was beginning to feel personal between them.

'Is it just me, or does anyone else sense the Brits aren't being entirely straight with us? Hold that call to GCHQ, and get me the DCIA's office.'

13

Marchant closed the door of his room, confident that Lakshmi was still sleeping, and walked down the corridor to the kitchen at the far end. Nothing had changed. It was here, five years earlier, that he'd first cooked Leila a meal – grilled mackerel, steamed samphire – when they were IONEC recruits, starting out on their careers. They'd eaten it cross-legged on the floor of her room like students. He pulled open a drawer, removed a kitchen knife and slid it inside his jacket before heading down the stairs and out into the courtyard.

The place was silent, except for the cry of a distant seagull. There was an archway on the opposite side of the courtyard. It was the only entrance into the Fort complex, and beyond it was a grass-roofed gatehouse with a light on inside. He knew most of the guards from his time at the Fort as an IONEC recruit. Hewn from the same granite as Oxbridge porters, they were long-suffering and had seen it all before, their manner a mix of respect and contempt.

He walked up to the gatehouse and knocked on the glass to get the sleeping guard's attention. Marchant didn't blame him. There were no recruits in residence, and it should have been an easy shift.

'I need a car from the pool,' Marchant said, glancing at the bank of flickering CCTV screens. The guard wasn't familiar, but Marchant's face in the window triggered something in him, recognition followed by a crude attempt to disguise it.

'I've got orders to let no one in or out.'

Marchant raised his eyebrows. 'No one? I thought everyone was in Helmand.'

'You're not to leave the site, sir.'

'Says who?'

'It's for your own safety. Chief's orders.'

So Fielding had sent him to the Fort for his personal protection. It was less obvious than Legoland, the staff nickname for MI6's headquarters in Vauxhall. The Americans wouldn't come looking for him down here. Things must be worse than he thought between Washington and London. Marchant glanced at the steel gates that rolled open and shut like a modern-day portcullis. Instead of feeling secure, he felt like a prisoner. The Fort was surrounded by twelve-foot-high MoD fencing on all sides, topped with barbed wire and security cameras.

'OK, I'll ring him in the morning.'

'Anything else I can do for you, sir?' the guard asked, glancing at the clock to remind Marchant of the unreasonable hour.

'No, it's fine.'

'Good night, sir,' the guard said, watching Marchant as he turned to walk back through the archway. There was only one way to escape.

14

Fielding had been sleeping fitfully when the phone rang. It wasn't his mobile, but the secure landline that linked his flat in Dolphin Square with COBRA, the home numbers of key colleagues of the Joint Intelligence Committee, and 10 Downing Street. The ring tone had an urgency that made him get out of bed and walk quickly across the living room to answer the phone.

'Marcus, I need to know what's going on with Salim Dhar.'

It was the Prime Minister.

'I'm not quite sure what you mean by "going on".'

'This is not the time for bloody semantics. The Americans have intercepted a call from Dhar to Fort Monckton in Gosport.'

Fielding's brain began to process the PM's words, assessing the possibilities and implications. It wasn't in his nature to panic – that was one of the reasons he had risen to become Chief – but the multiple scenarios that were spooling through his mind made him pass the receiver from one hand to the other.

'Daniel Marchant is currently recovering at the Fort,' he said calmly, starting with what he knew. But he couldn't help wondering why he was hearing about the intercept from the PM, and not from GCHQ or another intelligence colleague. It had clearly been discussed already, and he had been excluded. This wasn't an operational call, it was political. 'Where was Dhar ringing from?'

'According to the Americans, Vauxhall Cross. Your headquarters.'

Fielding let out a thin, dry laugh. He knew it was impossible for Dhar to be in Legoland. In the course of a life spent in espionage, he had witnessed far more cock-ups than conspiracies. But if that was what the Americans believed, he had a problem.

'And how do they know this?'

'The NSA's traced the number, and it's presenting as MI6's main switchboard.'

'With respect, if I were to ring you from this line and the NSA managed to intercept and trace it, which is unlikely, the number would show as MI6's switchboard. And Dhar's definitely not here.'

Fielding couldn't resist a quick glance around his flat: Oleg, his Lucas terrier, asleep in his basket in the corner; a flute resting against a sheet of Handel on a music stand in front of the fireplace; a proof copy of the new biography of Lawrence of Arabia open on the Indian coffee table.

'Marcus, the Americans are convinced we're holding Dhar. The President is calling me in five minutes. I need to give him my word that we're not.'

'We're not. Of course we're bloody not.'

'So why the hell's he ringing Daniel Marchant from a secure MI6 landline?'

'I have no idea. He might not have been. The last time the NSA supposedly intercepted a call from Dhar, it was a set-up and six US Marines died.'

'They want access to Vauxhall Cross, to search the building floor by floor, room by room. And they want us to arrest Daniel Marchant.'

'I would advise against that. Dhar may call him again, which would be more useful to us.'

Fielding might be too late to save Marchant, but the Americans would be allowed into Legoland over his dead body. Unfortunately, he suspected he was already dead. Denton would have his job by morning.

'What are Fort Monckton's orders?'

'To keep Marchant on site. Don't worry, he's being closely guarded.'

'I hope he is – for all our sakes.'

Fielding didn't have time to feel threatened. 'What did Dhar say to him?'

'Marchant asked who was speaking, and Dhar said, "Your pilot." That's it. As if we needed to remind the Americans of MI6's role in the Fairford attack. Marchant should have dealt with Dhar when he had a chance.'

In other words, Fielding thought, ignoring the PM, Dhar's message wasn't as important as the fact of the call itself. He was telling Marchant where he was. And it looked as if he was still in Britain, which meant that something must have gone catastrophically wrong with his escape plan.

There were numerous MI6 facilities across the country, all of which had secure landlines that were routed through the main switchboard. Fielding hadn't been entirely straight with the PM: although the numbers would show up as MI6, each one had its own unique signature that could be identified by a private-key-encrypted handset. He could only assume that Marchant had seen at once where Dhar was calling from, and had hung up.

'Tell the President that Marchant's going nowhere, and we haven't got Dhar.'

'So where the hell is he?'

'I don't know.' Only one person knew, and that was Daniel Marchant. Fielding would call him now, try to warn him, but he feared it was already too late. 'It's important we don't jump to hasty conclusions, given Dhar's history of phone calls,' he continued. 'You know it won't look good, the Americans going into Legoland?'

'The truth is, Marcus, I'm not sure I can stop them.'

15

Marchant didn't look back at the gatehouse as he walked away. He knew already that calls would be made, measures taken. What he wasn't prepared for was the speed with which security would be ramped up on the base. As he passed under the archway and back into the courtyard, he heard voices to his left. Two guards were approaching from the direction of the indoor firing range, stopping to chat outside the main door to the accommodation block. They wore plain blue uniforms, and weren't the usual 'MoDplods' who guarded military bases.

He had run up against them once on a training exercise when he was an IONEC graduate. After being dropped in the centre of Portsmouth, he and the rest of his class had been told that they had one hour to get back to their rooms without using the base's main entrance. Marchant had swum round from Gosport, only to be met on the beach by a guard who had given him a very physical welcome.

Tensing at the memory, Marchant retreated into the shadows of the archway, out of sight of the two men and the gatehouse. Above him were the rooms where visiting top brass stayed. (Fielding had a room reserved solely for his use.) Marchant couldn't hear what the guards were saying, but after several minutes one of them walked on, leaving the other outside the main door, which was at the northern end of the accommodation block. Behind him was an alleyway that led through to a flight of stone steps down to the beach. Which was where Marchant wanted to go.

He felt for the kitchen knife under his jacket and then cut left, keeping one eye on the guard as he kept close to a wall that ran across to a hangar. It was in there that he had been trained in anti-kidnap techniques. British diplomats and royalty were occasionally sent down for training too, which had always been a laugh, as the IONEC students got to play the bad guys.

After working his way around the hangar, Marchant came to the lab where he had learned how to forge passports and take covert film footage. From here it would be possible to approach the guard at the main door without being seen, providing he kept behind a parked van. He inched forward until the guard was barely five yards away.

It was clear that he had been told to stay where he was, but every few minutes he went for a short walk, wandering away from Marchant down to an external staircase that led up to the first floor of the accommodation block. There was a chance that Marchant could run the five yards and slip down the steps to the beach during one of these walkabouts, but the risk was too great.

He waited for the guard to set off again, but it was as if he had suddenly become more diligent. For ten minutes he remained rooted to his post outside the door. Marchant could hear his breathing, the sound of his shoes as he rocked gently back and forth, the slow rhythm of bored guards everywhere. He wondered if it was the same man who had met him on the beach. It had been an unnecessary show of force. Marchant had been exhausted, having failed to anticipate the strong tide, and he had got closer to his room than any other student. But as their instructor, a former sergeant in the SBS, had pointed out, they weren't being trained to become nursery-school teachers.

The guard was finally on the move, a slow meander down the side of the building towards the staircase. Marchant ran across the narrow gap between them, checking again for the knife in his jacket. In one movement, he pulled back the guard's head by his hair and punched him hard in the throat. As the man doubled up, clutching at his neck, Marchant kneed him in the face and brought a hand down hard across the back of his head. Before his body collapsed to the ground, Marchant was already dragging him over to the doorway. He pulled him inside and propped him against the wall.

'He doesn't look well,' a familiar voice said.

Marchant glanced up to see Lakshmi standing at the top of the stairs. She looked terrible, sallow around the eyes. Had her wrist become infected?

'He'll live,' Marchant said. Lakshmi had surprised him, and she knew it. 'I've got to get out of here. Are you OK?'

'You should have woken me. I could have helped,' she said, nodding at the guard. Marchant didn't doubt her, even with one wrist in plaster. He had only seen her engage in physical combat once, and it had been enough to convince him that the Farm, the CIA's equivalent of the Fort, trained their people well.

'I was going to. Fielding's in trouble. He's taking too much heat from the attack at Fairford. I need to see him, tell him about the traitor. It might be enough to save his job.'

'Can't you call him?'

'Too risky.'

'So what do you want me to do? Kiss you goodbye at the picket fence and go back to bed?'

'Of course not.'

Marchant wanted to confide in her, explain why he really needed to get away from Fort Monckton. He could tell her about the phone call from Dhar, and take her with him. But he knew he had to go alone. She had already become too close to him for her career to survive. If she was found with Dhar, she would spend the rest of her life behind bars.

'I want you to go the gatehouse, chat up the guard on duty, distract him from the security-camera screens.'

'Flash my tits at him, you mean?' She was angry, the sudden outburst out of character.

'I've got to go.' He glanced at the guard. 'I'll be back by morning. Just talk to him. All you have to do is talk. Please? And get that wrist looked at again.'

Her wrist was not the problem, it was the rest of her body that was in pain. Lakshmi didn't know why Marchant was in such a hurry to leave, but it clearly had nothing to do with Fielding. All she knew was that she wanted him to go, to leave her alone for what she needed to do. She tried to think about what she had seen earlier: Marchant with his back to her, holding the phone that had woken her from her troubled sleep with its insistent vibrating. And the words she had glimpsed on the screen: 'Dad – Home'. Then she thought about her own father, the anxiety in his voice.

'OK,' she said quietly. 'I'll go to the gatehouse.'

'Thank you.'

'And if anyone discovers that you've left?'

'Tell them I've gone to see Fielding.'

16

Fielding worked fast after the PM had hung up. First he rang Marchant, but his phone went straight to voicemail. He didn't leave a message. Then he called the duty officer at Legoland, giving a password that authorised an emergency lockdown. The main green gates of the pedestrian and vehicle entrances on Albert Embankment were always shut at night, but within moments a second set of barriers rolled into place behind them. At the same time, steel blinds closed on all the windows and the order went out that nobody was to leave – or enter – the building until further notice.

The last time Legoland had shut down in anger was in 2000, when the IRA had damaged an eighth-floor window with a Russian-built RPG-22, launched from Spring Gardens across the railway track. Fielding tried not to dwell on the fact that this time the threat was from Britain's closest ally.

These latest developments were beginning to remind him of the 1960s, when relations between Britain and America had been at an all-time low. Fielding had been rereading the files, hoping to learn lessons from the past. Washington, still reeling from Kim Philby's defection, had been appalled at the election in 1964 of Harold Wilson, whose Labour government was against the US's Polaris nuclear-missile programme. President Johnson was equally suspicious of Britain's intelligence establishment, believing that it was still riddled with Soviet spies. The President duly dispatched two spooks to London to review the effectiveness of MI5. Accompanied by the CIA's London head of station, they were granted widespread access, including to MI6's headquarters, without anyone on the British side knowing their real purpose.

Their damning report concluded that the UK had insufficient counter-espionage resources, and that MI5 was leaderless under its Director General, Roger Hollis. If James Angleton, then head of counter-intelligence at the CIA, had got his way, MI5 would have been run by Americans and become an outpost of the CIA's London station. *Plus ça change . . .*

The most recent analysis to cross Fielding's desk suggested that 40 per cent of the CIA's efforts to prevent another atrocity in homeland America were now being directed at the UK. What was the ghastly phrase someone at the Agency had used to describe Britain? 'An Islamic swamp,' Fielding recalled, as he tried to ring Marchant again.

17

The captain of the thirty-two-foot yacht was relieved they had finally reached Portsmouth. He didn't much care for Spinnaker Tower, but it was good to be drawing close to it at last, having seen its sail-like profile on the horizon for what seemed like an eternity. In a few minutes they would moor for the rest of the night in Gosport Marina. It had been a tiring crossing, taking longer than it should have done, and both he and his future son-in-law, brewing tea below, were exhausted. They should have arrived before sunset, but the wind had been against them, making them miss the tide coming around the Needles.

But at least the trip had been a success. *Jacana*, an old Seadog ketch he had owned since the 1970s, was lower in the water than normal, thanks to the haul of wine that was stacked up in boxes below decks. His daughter's wedding was in a few weeks, and she thought it would be fun to buy the wine in France. He had spent far too much in the cellars of Saint-Vaast, where the prices were inflated for British visitors, but they had enjoyed tasting the wines, and the trip had been 'a chance to bond', as his daughter had put it.

It was as he adjusted his woolly bobble hat, the butt of many family jokes, that he heard the call. How far away the person was, he wasn't sure, but he knew at once that someone was in the water, on the port side.

'Hello?' he called out, cupping his hands. 'Who's there?'

'Over here!' the voice shouted. Then he saw a waving hand and a figure clutching to a yellow racing buoy, fifty yards away.

'We see you!' he called back, turning the wheel hard to port. 'Coming across now!' He leant in to the cabin. 'Forget the bloody tea, and get yourself up here! There's a man overboard!'

Daniel Marchant watched the yacht as it adjusted course and headed towards him. He had spotted it from the shore fifteen minutes earlier, and timed the hundred-yard swim out to the buoy. He didn't think he had been seen by the two security cameras mounted high up on steel poles either side of the beach. As he had slid off the rocks and into the sea, the cameras had stayed pointing to the left and right, scanning the public footpath that ran along the shoreline. He reassured himself that they were set to detect people trying to breach the Fort's defences, not to escape from them. Lakshmi, too, must have kept her word. He was worried about her.

Now, though, he had to concentrate on his escape. There had been no opportunity to create a cover story. Instead, he would have to improvise, judge the mood. The boat was bigger than he had thought, and he hoped there wouldn't be too many people on board, too many questions.

'What the hell happened to you?' the captain asked, manoeuvring the yacht alongside the buoy. A younger man had already lowered a rope ladder over the gunwale and was holding out a boathook for Marchant to grasp.

'Long story. Bet someone I could swim across to Portsmouth.'

'Are you drunk?'

'Not any more,' he said, hauling himself up onto the rope ladder.

'We can take you into Gosport Marina, but then you're on your own.'

'Suits me.'

Five minutes later, Marchant was in the cockpit with a blanket wrapped around him, cradling a mug of steaming tea. He wasn't as cold as he looked. There seemed to be only two people on board, a father and son perhaps. Their bags were packed, but the older man, who spoke with a faint Glaswegian accent, had explained that they were going to spend the night on board, as they were too tired to drive home. Marchant needed to establish only one thing: the whereabouts of their car keys.

After finishing his tea, he climbed down into the cabin and placed the mug on the draining rack beside a tiny sink. He paused a moment, looking around at the cupboards, the foldaway table and a bank of electrical equipment on the other side of the cabin doorway. An old leather Morris Minor key fob was hanging next to the depth finder. His father used to sail a Westerly 22 out of Dittisham when Marchant was young. He too had kept the car key hanging up in the cabin, beside an ancient VHF radio. Marchant slipped the key off its hook, slid it into his jeans pocket and returned to the cockpit. Just his luck that they drove a car even older than their boat.

'Thanks for the tea,' he said. They were decent people, and he regretted having to steal their Morris Minor, but he needed to reach Dhar before dawn.

18

Ian Denton had taken the decision to represent MI6 on his own at the COBRA meeting. The committee was sitting through the night, but key players had dispersed for a few hours' sleep, replaced by deputies. Now, though, heads and chiefs had all been recalled, with the exception of Marcus Fielding. Nobody objected to his absence.

'Marcus has assured me that Dhar is not being held at Vauxhall Cross,' the PM began, glancing at Denton. 'I passed that information on to the President. Daniel Marchant is being held at Fort Monckton. I passed that on too, but I can't say the President was reassured.'

The mood was worse than Denton could ever remember at a COBRA meeting. 'I've checked with security at the Fort,' he said, hoping to inject some optimism. 'They've got strict orders to keep Marchant on site. Extra security has been put on his door.'

'Did you sense any shift in Washington?' the Foreign Secretary asked.

'None,' the PM said. 'We remain an irrelevance. And we must be prepared for the Americans to act unilaterally. The President's words, not mine.'

'Any progress on where Dhar was calling from?' Harriet Armstrong, Director General of MI5, didn't look up, but her question was intended for the Director of GCHQ.

'An MI6 facility, that's all we know,' he said, shifting awkwardly in his seat. 'Although we were obviously involved with setting up Six's comms network, it's a private-key encryption. Nobody else can access it. That's how these things work. And I'd be lying if I said we were enjoying the full support of the NSA on this one.'

'I may have something,' Armstrong continued. 'An incident in Gloucestershire was red-flagging on the grid as I arrived. A SAR helicopter made an emergency landing earlier tonight at Kemble in Gloucestershire. All three crew are missing. Local police are liaising with RAF Valley in Anglesey.'

Denton looked up. He had taken a train to Kemble once, a few years ago. What had been the occasion? A private lunch, to mark Stephen Marchant's appointment as Chief of MI6. Tables covered with white linen in the apple orchard, a jazz band, competitive croquet. He had never felt so out of place. The journey from Kemble station to the Chief's house had taken less than five minutes.

19

Salim Dhar moved around the bedroom, looking for something that would link the place to his mother. The air was stale, the mood one of finality rather than grief. There were no sheets on the double bed, just a pile of folded blankets at one end and some pillows without their covers. The bookcases were empty, the cupboards bare.

He limped over to the bedside table, where there was a small bronze statue of Nataraja: Shiva as lord of the dance. The figure was familiar to him, a distant memory from the days when he had been a Hindu, like his parents, who had called him Jaishanka Menon. He had converted to Islam partly to spite the man he thought was his father. The statue's weight surprised him, and he wondered at its significance. It was the only trace of India in the room.

He picked up a leaflet from the dressing table. It was the order of service for the funeral of Stephen Marchant, the man who had turned out to be his real father. There were Christian readings, but Hindu ones too, and a passage by Kahlil Gibran, an Arab described in a footnote as a Maronite Christian influenced by Islam and Sufism.

Only when you drink from the river of silence
shall you indeed sing.
And when you have reached the mountain top,
then you shall begin to climb.
And when the earth shall claim your limbs,
then shall you truly dance.

As he put the service sheet down, something caught his eye. A photo had slipped to one side in a silver frame on the dusty windowsill. It showed a middle-aged Western woman, standing in front of Qtab Minar. She didn't strike Dhar as a picture of happiness: a wry, confused face squinting into the Delhi sun. But it wasn't this photo that interested him. There was another one behind it, a corner of which was visible.

Dhar turned the frame over and removed the back. An image of his mother fell onto the table. She was wearing a turquoise sari and standing in front of the British High Commission, where she had once worked. Her smile was radiant, beaming out at him across the years and the continents. He smiled back at her and slid the photo into his pocket. She was here now, somewhere in Britain. *Inshallah,* one day they would be together again.

20

Lakshmi sat on the edge of the bed at the Fort, holding a sterilised syringe in one hand, her phone in the other. Marchant had only been gone ten minutes, but she couldn't wait any longer. As requested, she had flirted with the guard in the gatehouse, distracting him without having to flash her breasts. By the time she had returned to the room, the guard at the bottom of the stairs had gone too, dragged into one of the empty rooms by Marchant. The alarm would be raised shortly, either when the guard regained consciousness or his absence was noticed, but by then she would be immune to the storm raging around her.

She looked at the needle's point, turning it in the light of the bedside lamp. Her damaged left wrist was sore in its cast, the most painful it had been since she had left hospital. But it wasn't hurting enough for what she was about to do.

Everything had been going so well before she was sent to Morocco to spy on Daniel Marchant. For two clean, healthy years she had worked for the Agency, signing up amid the optimism of a new presidency. Life as a field officer hadn't always been what she had hoped. At times it had been hell. In her first year at Langley, Spiro had constantly reminded her that she was a woman in a man's world. He had also tried to sleep with her, but she had dealt with that. The career change was working: her bad habits had been left behind at medical school.

Her father would have been happier if she had continued with her studies at Georgetown University, but he hadn't known her secret – which was ironic, given that it was an act of rebellion against him. She would ring him now, explain the real reason why she had dropped out, prepare him for the shame it would bring on the family. He would be at home, checking emails at the kitchen table, worrying about the call from the IRS.

She brought his number up on the phone's screen and looked at the image of him: never smiling, always formal, as if he was holding his breath. Then she held the phone to her ear, listening to the distant ring.

'Dad? It's me. I need to tell you something.'

'*Ennamma Kannu?* I'm so glad you called.' She could hear him place a muffled hand over the phone, letting her mother know it was their only daughter. 'I've just had another call from the IRS. The whole thing was a hotchpotch, a terrible mix-up. They're not investigating me any more.'

'That's good,' Lakshmi said. Spiro must have moved quickly. 'That's so good.'

'I'm just glad we didn't waste time worrying unnecessarily. I always knew the charges were false.'

Lakshmi had to smile. Who was he kidding? He had nearly worried himself to death. Just as he had constantly worried about her over the years. And she had always done his bidding, forgoing alcohol, unsuitable men, meat, even caffeine. Her rebellion, when it finally came, had been extreme.

'I wanted to say,' she began, 'that I know you were mad at me for dropping out of Georgetown –'

'Baba, you know that's not the case. And we're so proud of you now, the important government work you're doing.'

'I know, but –' she paused, holding the syringe. 'It was a difficult time. I wasn't well. I needed a change of direction.'

She thought back to the first and only meeting she had attended, when her habit was becoming hard to hide. Twenty strangers – hobos, storekeepers, journalists, a librarian – sat on plastic chairs in a circle, united by narcotics. Up until that anonymous gathering, her addiction had been private. Nobody knew about the stolen hospital supplies of diamorphine hydrochloride, better known as heroin. Shame had made her cunning, and she had concealed her secret life with the ingenuity of a spy. Certainly the vetters at Langley never found out when they later questioned her fellow students and tutors.

As she had sat there, listening to other people's stories, the futility of her own rebellion had become all too apparent. No one she cared about had noticed anything. To her friends and family she was still the same clean-living, hard-working Indian girl from Reston, Virginia. Only a group of strangers knew that one of the brightest medics on campus was mainlining. For two weeks she sweated and vomited, vowing never to take drugs again.

'You studied hard,' her father said.

'I've got to go,' she replied, pursing her lips, fighting back the tears.

She had studied hard all her life, that was the problem. At her father's behest she had spent every waking hour at her books, shunning nights out in Georgetown, politely declining dates, turning her back on life, all so she could study. It wasn't his fault, she realised that now. Hard work was the curse of the immigrant, a response to the constant need to justify oneself. What was the point of telling him that she hadn't always been studying in Georgetown? That she had nearly thrown her life away, the opportunities he had given her, and was in danger of doing so again?

'I just wanted to check you were OK, about the IRS and every-thing,' she said.

'It's all good. Everything's fine.'

She said her goodbyes and put the phone down on the bed, looking again at the needle. The paramedic was to blame. After diagnosing that a single gunshot wound had shattered the lower radius and ulna of her left forearm, he had injected her with a 30mg ampoule of diamorphine hydrochloride. It had dulled the pain, like the good analgesic it was, but it had also mimicked the body's endorphins, triggering a cascade of euphoria that had swept up her student past and laid it out in front of her in all its spar-kling glory.

She sat back, trying to relax. Her dressing gown was drenched in sweat. Rolling up one sleeve, she tied a pair of knickers around her upper arm, tightened the elastic as hard as she could and flexed her hand again. Then she broke open two glass ampoules, one full of sterilised water, the other containing powdered diamor-phine hydrochloride BP.

Although she knew the door was locked, she still looked up to check as she drew the sterilised water into the needle and squirted it into the powder. She shook the solution gently and then searched for the vein at the top of her forearm, sank back against a pillow and sobbed with joy.

21

Marchant soon got used to the loose gears of the Morris Minor Traveller as he drove up the A34 towards Newbury. Downhill, the car sat comfortably at 75mph, but it began to shake violently at 80mph. The slightest incline reduced its speed to 50mph. The one time he lost his nerve was when he accidentally pulled out the tiny brass ignition key, only for the engine to continue working.

The radio worked only intermittently, but the noisy heater produced warmth of a sort. His clothes were sodden and he was shivering, but at least his wallet and phone were dry, sealed in a food bag he had taken from the kitchen.

The Traveller had been easy to find in the marina car park, as it was the only one of its kind. After Marchant had thanked his rescuers and jogged off down the jetty, telling them he was staying at a friend's house in Gosport, he had quickly spotted the car's distinctive ash frame in the distance. The boat had taken a mooring on one of the furthest jetties, at least five hundred yards from the car park, and he was confident that they hadn't seen him drive away.

His mobile phone lay on the passenger seat beside him. He had removed the battery as soon as Dhar had rung him. The call would have been picked up by GCHQ, and probably by the NSA too, who would have been monitoring his number. (Rumour had it that the NSA was now listening in on all MI6 comms traffic.) Dhar's voiceprint would have been recognised and matched within seconds. He must have known that. What was he playing at? More importantly, what the hell was he doing at their father's house in the Cotswolds?

Marchant realised that his fears about the missing Russian from the trawler were well-founded. And Myers had been right to be suspicious about the Search and Rescue Helicopter. Dhar must have come ashore with one of the Russians and somehow got himself to Tarlton, using the sailor's voice to avoid his own being detected.

It would only be a matter of hours before Dhar was caught. Was he hoping for some kind of protection from Britain? If the Americans reached him first, would he talk, reveal their secret? Or perhaps he realised the game was up, and wanted to see his father's home before he was killed.

Marchant thought again about the call. The only thing that had bought Dhar time was that he had chosen to ring from the home of a former intelligence Chief. MI6 had yet to downgrade the security on the line. A few weeks after his father's funeral, Marchant had been down to comms on the second floor of Legoland and singled out an attractive female technician he had spotted a few weeks earlier.

'I'm going to be living there at weekends,' he had said. 'It would make sense if the line stayed.'

'You know it's against protocol,' she had replied. 'Chief and deputy, heads of controllerates – they get secure landlines because they're important. Last I heard, you were just a cocky field agent.'

'What will it cost me?'

'A drink after work.'

He had struck worse deals in his time. It turned out she had admired his father, thought he was a great Chief, and felt sympathy for a bereaved son. She would have to put in the order for a downgrade, but cuts in the department budget meant it would be a while before it was processed. She would oversee its delay personally.

After too many drinks at the Morpeth Arms, he had walked her home to Vauxhall, but turned down coffee. Back then, there had been Leila to think about. Eighteen months on, the line was a forgotten memo and still secure, routed through MI6. But his own mobile phone, despite the encryption, would have been tracked to Fort Monckton, which was why he had removed its battery. He thought of Lakshmi, hoping she was safe. They would come looking for him at the Fort, and she would tell them he had gone to see Fielding.

It was 4 a.m. when he eventually reached Cirencester, two hours after he had left Gosport. He took the road to Tetbury, turning left to Kemble after a few miles. He didn't want to drive up to Tarlton in the Traveller. There was a chance that the sailors had noticed it had been stolen and had already raised the alarm. He needed to leave it somewhere it wouldn't draw attention.

At Kemble, he turned right into the railway station and a big car park that he remembered. He used to cycle here from Tarlton in the university holidays when he went up to London, leaving his bike against the railings in a well-tended garden beside the platform. There had been no need to lock it, as it was a sit-up-and-beg Hero his father had brought back from India. Modern bikes were stolen regularly from Kemble, but nobody had wanted this one.

He found a quiet corner, away from the station, and parked the Traveller between two other cars. One was an Aston Martin, the other a BMW. The Traveller might stand out more than he thought. Then he went over to the garden beside the platform, just in case there were any unlocked bikes there. But it was empty, the flowerbeds still well tended. Shivering in the dawn light, he set off back down the road and began the two-mile walk up to Tarlton.

22

James Spiro looked out onto a deserted Grosvenor Square and glanced impatiently at his watch. The Marines were running behind time. In his day, if you weren't five minutes early, you were late. For a moment, he felt the same churn in his stomach that he used to get in Iraq before a contact. Back in the first Gulf War, the Brits had been allies, decent fighters in Operation Desert Storm. How times had changed.

He didn't believe Salim Dhar was really holed up in Legoland, but he couldn't afford to take any chances. After all, who would have guessed that an MI6 officer would be sitting with Dhar in a Russian jet when it took down an F-22 Raptor? He had spent all evening in the crisis centre at the American Embassy, listening to Turner Munroe, the US Ambassador to London, fight a losing battle with Washington. As far as the President and the Pentagon were concerned, there was a good case for withdrawing Munroe in light of the air-show fiasco. The special relationship, if it ever existed, was over, and as Spiro pointed out, it could be argued that Britain had been complicit in an act of war against the US.

But Munroe had displayed a dogged loyalty to Daniel Marchant.

'Let's not get too trigger-happy here,' the Ambassador had said in a lengthy video conference with the White House. 'We could have been discussing the death of the US Defense Secretary. Marchant has form when it comes to persuading *jihadis* not to blow people up. I should know.'

Fifteen months earlier, Marchant had helped to talk a suicide bomber out of killing Munroe and countless other competitors in the London Marathon. At least, that was Marchant's story. Spiro had begged to differ. In tonight's discussions with Washington, Munroe had consistently fought Marchant's corner, calling for restraint until all the facts were known. But the President's anger had prevailed. The CIA's London station was given *carte blanche* to do all they could to find Salim Dhar, last known location somewhere in UK waters.

Spiro, as head of the Agency's National Clandestine Service, Europe, was put in charge of the mission. His first call was to surround MI6's headquarters with a deployment of US Marines who were based permanently at the embassy. He had also given orders for Daniel Marchant to be picked up from Fort Monckton. Fielding couldn't protect him any longer. Denton had given assurances that Marchant was being held securely, but Spiro knew better than to underestimate Marchant.

'Go in the back door,' he had told the captain of USS *Bulkeley*, a destroyer moored in Portsmouth on a meet-and-greet hosted by the Royal Navy. The captain explained that he would need authority from the Pentagon before giving the order to deploy a unit of Seals against an ally he had just been on exercise with. Spiro had anticipated friction. The US Navy wasn't in the habit of taking orders from the CIA, or storming British military bases. He gave the captain the name of someone to speak to, and told him to get on with it. 'And leave the woman out of it,' he added. 'She's one of ours.'

He had expected to hear back from Lakshmi Meena by now, but she hadn't rung, which made him wary. He had hoped to hear from his wife, too, but that was another story. It had been three days since they had spoken, and he had no idea where she was.

He pushed her to the back of his mind and thought again about Marchant. As a former Marine, he wished he could be with the Seals when they beached at Fort Monckton. It would be the final humiliation of Marchant and MI6. Instead, Spiro had to settle for the lead jeep as it rolled out of Grosvenor Square five minutes later and headed down Regent Street towards Vauxhall. There were six US Army trucks behind him, carrying a hundred Marines in total. The sight of American forces on the streets of London would send a clear message to the Brits, causing acute political embarrassment. Better still, Spiro hoped, it would scare the crap out of Fielding.

'Ain't London a beautiful city when it's empty?' he said to his driver as they rumbled around a deserted Piccadilly Circus at 3 a.m. Above him, the advert for Coca-Cola flashed in the night.

23

'I think I know where Dhar might be,' Denton said, turning to the Prime Minister.

'Go on.'

The room fell silent as everyone looked down the table at Denton. He paused, calculating the implications one more time. On balance, it was better to share his hunch with COBRA rather than with the Americans, but there wasn't much in it. He studied the tired, expectant faces and thought that the British establishment had never appeared so weak. If he was going to become a Chief with any power, he would need US support. To win that, he had to give them Dhar on a plate. But he didn't trust them to capture him. The British were still better at some things.

Just as he was about to speak, an aide to the Chief of Defence Staff came into the room and whispered something to his boss.

'A contingent of US Marines is currently making its way down Regent Street,' the Chief of Defence Staff announced, trumping Denton's announcement. 'It's an unauthorised movement. Any US troop activity on UK soil must be cleared first with –'

'Of course it's bloody unauthorised,' the PM said. Denton had often noted how, in times of crisis, the military defaulted to mindless protocol.

Everyone in the room turned to look at the staccato images now streaming live from traffic cameras on Piccadilly Circus. For a moment, Dhar's location was no longer important. Denton had known it was coming, but the sight of the US military on the streets of London was still chilling. Fielding must have anticipated it too. A few seconds earlier, Denton had received a staff alert informing him that Legoland was in lockdown.

'They're heading for Vauxhall Cross,' the PM continued. 'Unilateral action, just as the President warned.' He turned to the Chairman of the Defence Advisory Committee, who had been summoned from his club to join COBRA. 'It's too late for the papers, but I don't want to see these pictures tomorrow morning on *The Andrew Marr Show*.'

'That might be difficult,' the Chairman replied. 'The best we can do is put out an MoD release explaining that it's an exercise.'

'If only it was,' the PM said. 'I hope to God Dhar's not there.'

'He's not,' Denton said. 'And even if he was, the Americans wouldn't find him. Fielding's locked down the building.'

'That could be interpreted as the actions of a Chief with something to hide.'

'Just pride.' Denton paused, looking around the room at his pale, flabby colleagues. Most of them had been up for twenty-four hours. 'Dhar's not in London. He's gone to his father's house. Stephen Marchant had a big place in the country, in a hamlet called Tarlton, just outside Cirencester.'

A murmur swept around the room, followed by shuffled papers and disbelieving asides.

'I know it's been a long night, but are you seriously telling me that Salim Dhar is hiding in the Cotswolds?' the PM asked. 'Wouldn't he want to be as far away from here as possible?'

'It would explain the MI6 number. As Chief, Stephen

Marchant's home was installed with a secure landline. My guess is that it was never downgraded after he died.' Denton turned to the Chief of Defence staff. 'How long would it take for the Increment to reach Tarlton?'

24

Dhar stood by the grave in the half-light, reading the words that had been carved into the stone. 'Stephen Marchant 1949–2009. *Semper occultus.*' He didn't know what the words meant. If Marchant showed up, he would ask him. Time, though, was running out – for both of them. He had left the pilot in the house, tied up and gagged. He still wasn't sure why he had chosen to keep the man alive. Perhaps it was for his own self-preservation. One kidnapped *kafir* wouldn't be enough to barter with when they came for him, as he knew they would, but it might stop him being killed.

He glanced around and knelt awkwardly, trying to ignore the pain in his leg. His father was buried at the back of a small and ancient church, separated from the main house by a gravel drive. It was the first time he had been to a Christian burial site, and he began to recite the last verses of the Surat al-Baqarah, the second chapter of the Holy Qur'an.

'. . . *Our Lord! Lay not on us what we have no strength to bear. Pardon us, forgive us and have mercy on us. You are our Protector; give us victory over the disbelievers . . .*'

Tears pricked his eyes as he prayed in the early-morning still-ness. A gossamer mist hung over the surrounding fields, and his knees were wet with dew. He was here to honour his real father, whom he had only met once, at a black site in South India, but images of another man kept rearing out of the shadows.

Life had been hard when he was growing up on the fringes of Chanakyapuri in New Delhi, where his parents had worked at various foreign embassies. The man who claimed to be his father used to beat him regularly with a wooden baseball bat: back of the legs, arms, soles of his feet when he slept late. His mother had suffered terribly too, hiding when her husband returned from yet another party at the American Embassy, drunk on bourbon and Coke. Dhar couldn't blame her for turning to another man.

He leant forward and kissed the top of the gravestone, the sound as his lips touched it exaggerated in the quietness. Silence at dawn felt alien to him. Where was the *muezzin*, calling the faithful to prayer? Where were the mosques in this sterile land they called the Cotswolds? That was the hardest thing for Dhar to accept: that his father had been an unbeliever. It was painful enough that he had worked for an infidel intelligence agency, but he had come to terms with that. Now, though, he had to deal with the *kuffar*, whom he could feel closing in all around him.

25

Fielding walked briskly along the south side of Grosvenor Road. Oleg was at heel, surprised but happy to be on a night-time walk. They had slipped out of the Dolphin Square flat unnoticed by the Special Branch guard down on the street, which gave Fielding a kick. He might not be Chief for much longer, but he hadn't lost any of his old field skills.

He wanted to see for himself if Spiro had really parked his tanks on MI6's lawn. The threat, relayed by the PM, had sounded real enough, and as he turned south onto Vauxhall Bridge, dawn beginning to break over London, he knew his career with the Service would soon be over. They weren't tanks, but two large US military lorries were positioned across the road, stopping what little traffic there was at that time of the morning. He could see more US military vehicles down by the bus station, closing off all approaches to the usually busy junction. It was a scene not unlike the ones that had recently caused Fielding to wake in the middle of the night, dripping in sweat: tangible proof of Britain's submission to America.

Up in front of him a solitary car was turning around, followed by a motorbike, both being instructed by a helmeted US Marine waving a gun. A gust of wind blew up from the river. Fielding tugged at his coat collar and considered turning around too, but he wanted to see if Spiro was there, tell him to his face that he was making a fool of the United States, and not just MI6. He was certain now that Dhar had made his way to Tarlton, the Marchant family home, from where he had rung Daniel on an old secure line. It was a desperate decision for a man on the run, but perhaps he had nowhere else to go.

There was nothing Fielding could do about it. What power he still had was slipping through his fingers like desert sand. It was up to Marchant now. He would find a way out of the Fort, and make his way to Tarlton. That was what he was best at: kicking out against his own system. Like Fielding, Marchant would want to know what the hell Dhar was playing at. He just hoped that others wouldn't get to Tarlton first.

He kept walking, tugging at Oleg, who seemed less eager to confront the scene up ahead.

'No access, sir,' the Marine said as Fielding approached the roadblock.

'Is Jim Spiro around?' Fielding asked. 'Tell him it's Marcus Fielding, Chief of MI6.'

The Marine looked him up and down, then got on his radio mike. Two minutes later, Spiro was sauntering over as if he had just conquered London. Fielding was surprised he wasn't smoking a stogie.

'Nobody seems to be at home,' Spiro began, looking over his shoulder at Legoland. The lights were all out and the windows shuttered. 'We knocked on the front door, like the polite people we are, but there was no answer. Don't suppose you've got a key?'

'If I had more time, I'd gladly show you around.'

'Where is he, Marcus?'

'He's not in Legoland, for Christ's sake.'

'I kinda figured that. Not even the Brits would be that dumb.'

'So why are you here?'

'Wanted a drive through London without the traffic. And our trucks are cheaper than those open-topped buses. Or them crazy Yellow Duck tours. We're bringing Marchant in too, by the way. He took the call. He'll know where Dhar is.'

'And when you find him, what then? Will our problems be over?'

'I reckon the world will be a safer place with a dead Salim Dhar, don't you?'

Fielding didn't answer. Without realising it, Spiro had gone to the core of what had been troubling him ever since he and Marchant had signed off on their deal. Would their plan lead to a safer world? It didn't matter now. The operation was in pieces, shattered before it had begun.

Fielding turned and walked slowly back across the bridge. If this was what the intelligence community had become, there was no place in it for him. He glimpsed an oystercatcher in the mud down on the Thames. At least he would have more time for birdwatching. He wasn't interested in going back into the City, or working in oil, despite various approaches that had already been made. The money was eye-watering, but he had never wanted for much. And he hadn't talked Gaddafi out of his nuclear ambitions in order to feather his own nest.

He would call up old friends he hadn't seen for years, cook them pomegranate chicken with *fattoush* salad, *baba ganoush* and sesame couscous cakes. There would be time to spoil his godchildren with trips to Russian circuses. Improve his flute-playing. And travel. Ever since reading *From the Holy Mountain* he had longed to journey through the lands of the ancient Byzantine Empire, visiting monasteries, churches and Stylite hermitages.

There might even be time for love. He knew what the office gossip was: the Vicar was gay – either that, or celibate. It wasn't surprising. He had made a conscious, cold-hearted decision to put that side of life on hold when he joined the Service fifteen years earlier. There had been a woman in his life once, when he was working in emerging Middle Eastern markets before he had joined the Service. Later, during his initial vetting process, questions were asked about her. Kadia's parents were Libyan, and she and her family had spent a life in exile, mostly in London. Despite her opposition to Gaddafi, Mossad had passed a file to MI6 suggesting she had links with Palestinian terrorists. It turned out to be untrue, but he had learnt his lesson. Love had nearly ruined his career before it had started.

As he was nearing Dolphin Square, a 4x4 Subaru with blackened windows slowed down beside him. Fielding tensed, suddenly regretting his decision to go out without protection.

'Get in,' the voice said. It was Turner Munroe, the US Ambassador to London.

26

The platoon of sixteen men from Seal Team 5 sped across Portsmouth harbour in two Zodiac Combat Rubber Raiding Craft, leaving HMS *Victory* and HMS *Warrior* to port. The inflatable rubber was bulletproof, but no one was anticipating incoming fire, not until they reached the shore in front of Fort Monckton.

Despite their professionalism, there was unease in the team. Forty-eight hours earlier they had been simulating a terrorist asymmetric swarm attack with the Royal Navy in the Irish Sea. Afterwards, they had spent a drunken evening in the bars of Portsmouth with their colleagues from the SBS. Now they were being told to lift a member of MI6 – allies in the war on terror, last time they checked – from a British military training base, and to expect resistance on the ground. The head of the platoon had queried the order with the captain of USS *Bulkeley*, who shared his discomfort. But the mission had been confirmed by the head of US Special Operations Command.

The two Zodiacs skidded up the sandy beach at the same time. Seven Seals, armed with M4 carbines, jumped out of each one and ran up either side of the accommodation block, leaving two men to keep guard on the beach. They didn't know which room Marchant was staying in, so they started from the outermost rooms on the ground and first floors and worked inwards, kicking open the doors and clearing each one.

Lakshmi heard them coming, but she wasn't frightened. She felt safe in her bed, protected from the outside world by the blankets and the diamorphine hydrochloride that was coursing through her veins. It had already reached her brain, transforming into morphine and triggering her opiate receptors. In turn they had released a sweet surge of dopamine that was orgasmic in its intensity. She knew it all, had studied the medical effects at Georgetown until the words had blurred on the page.

Despite her overwhelming sense of contentment, she still had the presence of mind to hide the syringe in the bedside table moments before the Seals burst in through her door.

'Hands where we can see them!' one of them shouted while another made for the bathroom.

'It's OK, everything's OK,' she said. 'I'm CIA. Lakshmi Meena. ID's over there.' She nodded at the bedside table.

'Where is he? Daniel Marchant? The Brit,' a more senior Seal asked, coming into the room behind the others.

'Dan?' She paused, smiling wanly.

'Don't fuck us about, lady. Where is he?'

'He's gone home.'

27

There were no lights on in the house as Marchant crept up the driveway, keeping off the gravel and in the shadows. It was strange to be back. He had spent some time here after his father's funeral, but it had been a harsh February, and the place had never really warmed up, despite the roaring fires he had made in the sitting room. It had been his intention to visit at weekends, but he had never made the journey, and the longer he stayed away, the harder it was to return.

He wished he had come before. The sight of the house at dawn triggered happy memories, stronger and more lasting, it seemed, than those of the funeral, when the place had been full of dark suits and white lilies and forced conversation. An air of guilt had hung over proceedings that day. Friends and colleagues knew they could have done more to stop the CIA from driving his father out of office and into an early grave.

But those dark memories were fleeting. It was here in the orchard, on the other side of the drive, that Marchant had spent some of his most blissful days with Sebbie, his twin brother. For a few years they had come here every summer, escaping the heat of Delhi to play in the shade of the Cotswolds, climbing trees, throwing water balloons, chasing the cat. He had returned in the aftermath of Sebbie's death too, hoping the wounds would heal.

Now, in the family home, he was about to meet another brother. He knew he didn't have long. He might even be too late. Despite the heavy encryption, the call would already have been traced. It felt as if he was here to say goodbye. Dhar would be dead within hours; there was no escape from here.

He walked around to the back of the house, where a rusting greenhouse leant against the rear wall. His father used to call it the conservatory. A door to the kitchen was inside. Marchant was about to slide the greenhouse open when he saw that the window in the kitchen door had been smashed. Dhar must have come in this way. There used to be a complex alarm system installed in the house, including floodlights, but it kept going off for no reason. Marchant had deactivated it after the funeral.

Moving quietly, he stepped into the greenhouse, lifting the glass panel as he slid it to avoid noise, and then stopped. He could hear a muffled sound inside, and what he thought was a chair being scraped across the tiled kitchen floor. He walked up to the kitchen door and looked in through the broken glass. A man in a flying suit was sitting on a stool, arms and legs tied and mouth taped. He was trying to shuffle his way across the room. When he saw Marchant, his eyes widened with fear or relief, it was hard to tell which.

Marchant put a finger to his lips and opened the door. The man must have been from the Search and Rescue helicopter that picked Dhar up.

'Where is he?' Marchant asked. The man nodded at his bound feet in desperation. He was clearly expecting to be released, but Marchant wasn't going to be rushed. First, he needed to find Dhar.

28

'I'm not happy with where things are going,' Turner Munroe said. He was in the back of his official car, with Fielding beside him. Oleg was in the footwell. 'Not at all happy. What I just saw in Vauxhall is an embarrassment – to Washington. It shouldn't be happening. I knew Spiro was going ahead, but I needed to see it with my own eyes.'

'Me too.'

'You know I've worked hard over the last few years on the relationship. We're meant to have a presidential visit next year, when it's set to be upgraded from "special" to "essential". That might not sound like a big deal, but it is in my world – the culmination of a lot of hard work by my staff in London. I'm not prepared to see it all going to waste over one lousy jet.'

'Quite an expensive one, I gather.'

'Production's already halted on it. The F-35 will be the game-changer. And hey, we spent twenty billion last year on aircon alone in Afghanistan.'

On paper, Fielding should have despised Munroe. The Ambassador was widely regarded in Whitehall as a hawk, and he had been a surprise appointment by the incoming President in 2008. Like Spiro, he had fought in the first Gulf War and believed that military intervention was the only way forward in Iran.

He was also a fitness fanatic, running 3.30 marathons around the world, whereas Fielding limited himself to a daily swim in the basement pool in Legoland. If all that wasn't enough, he preferred Bruce Springsteen to J.S. Bach.

But despite their differences, Fielding was more than happy to step into his car. It was Munroe's behaviour in the chaotic aftermath of the London Marathon that had changed his opinion of him. He had gone away, studied the evidence, and concluded that it was Leila, not Marchant, who had tried to kill him. Marchant had saved his life. And it seemed he was prepared to be equally open-minded about Marchant's role in the air show. Unfortunately, his was a lone American voice.

'There are people in Langley who want you out of office, Marcus, you know that.'

'They've almost got their wish.'

'You're not going down without a fight, though?'

Fielding paused, looking out of the window at a slowly waking London. The street cleaners were out already, sweeping up the excesses of the night. He was too tired to fight.

'The latest CX to cross my desk points to a Russian mole high up in MI6.'

'When wasn't there?' Fielding knew what was coming. The Americans had long suspected him of treachery. He had been too close to Stephen Marchant, his predecessor.

'My source says it wasn't Hugo Prentice.' Fielding flinched at the name of his old friend. No one had wanted to believe Prentice had been a traitor, least of all Fielding. 'Apparently someone framed him to protect themself.'

'And Langley thinks it was me?' Fielding asked, wondering for the first time if there might be more to Primakov's allegations about Denton than he had thought. Nothing would make him happier than clearing Hugo Prentice's name, even if it were posthumously.

'They want to believe it was you, but there's no evidence.'

'There's a surprise.'

'Find the mole and your position will be safe. Nothing scares us Yanks more than British intelligence run by Moscow.'

'And does your source know who this mole might be?' Fielding thought again about Denton. Why was he reluctant to point the finger at his deputy? Because it was he who had appointed him? Fielding had brought Denton on over the years, encouraged him to apply for jobs, happy to see the cosy old mould of MI6 being broken by an intelligent grammar-school boy from Hull.

'I'm working on him. First, I wanted to check that you had the stomach for a fight. And that you're close to finding Salim Dhar. That would kinda help the relationship.'

'We're close.'

29

Marchant walked into the high-ceilinged hall, stood still and listened. Somewhere far above him, he could hear the sound of a muffled voice. It wasn't Dhar's. He had heard it before, a long time ago, but he couldn't place it at first. Then he remembered. What was Dhar doing?

He looked around and saw the old phone on a corner table. Above it, numbers had been written in ink by his father on a piece of paper stuck to the wall. He went over and saw his own mobile number next to the word 'Daniel'. His father had never called him 'Dan', despite all his friends using the name. There were no work colleagues on the list, unless his father had given them codenames, which wouldn't surprise him. He noticed, though, that the ink was green – a private joke.

Slowly, he moved up the stairs, thinking back to those times when, after a night out as a teenager, he had tried to reach his room without waking his father. He had always heard him. Marchant liked to think the reason was his father's training, but he knew now that it was his own unsteady legs. Sebbie had died when he was eight, in a car crash in Delhi. They'd never got to share the teenage years, the parties, the dope, the girls. Sometimes Marchant wondered if that was why he had consumed so much alcohol in his life: he was always drinking for two.

He reached the landing, and listened again. To his right: the guest room, the bathroom, his father's bedroom. He preferred to call it that, even though he had shared it for a while with his mother. She had played only a small part in his childhood, retreating into herself with depression, and was dead by the time he was seventeen. His father's brief affair in Delhi with Dhar's mother can't have helped. Or perhaps it was a reaction to his wife's illness. He had never found out.

His and Sebbie's bedrooms were on the top floor, where the voice was coming from. He knew what it was now, even though it was still muffled. It was the first record his father had ever bought him: *Sinbad the Sailor and Other Stories*. Dhar must be playing it on the old wooden-cased HMV player in his room. The door was shut, but he could see that Sebbie's was open. It hadn't been a conscious intention to turn it into a shrine, but he and his father had decided to leave it as it was when he had died.

Marchant crept up the last flight of stairs, stopping to look at a photo of his father, Sebbie and himself. They were standing in front of the Taj Mahal. As he passed the leaded window, he thought he saw a flash of light over by the chapel, on the far side of the garden. It was a tiny Norman chapel of rest, where the hamlet gathered for services on special occasions. His father's funeral had been at the bigger church in Rodmarton, down the road, but he was buried here.

He waited to see if the light appeared again, but there was nothing. Dawn had broken but it was still difficult to see clearly. He carried on up the stairs, thinking of Sebbie and how they used to race down them, bouncing on their bottoms. At the door he paused, listening to the story of Sinbad, and glanced behind him. He could see Sebbie's bed, a toy tiger propped up on the pillow. Taking a deep breath, he turned and opened his own bedroom door.

Dhar was sitting on a pile of brightly coloured Indian cushions, his back to the wall. He had an unusually shaped bottle in one hand, a gun in the other. An empty bottle of vodka was lying on the carpet beside him.

'You took your time,' he said, pointing the gun at him.

30

Denton was touching 100mph in the outside lane of a deserted M4 when he took the call from Spiro on the hands-free. He had been weighing up when to ring the Americans, but Spiro had made the decision for him.

'I've just had word from Lakshmi Meena at the Fort,' Spiro said. 'Don't suppose you know where Daniel Marchant likes to call home? And don't say Tora Bora.'

Denton breathed in and slowed to 90mph. He was already looking forward to a time when he would be driven by someone else. He needed time to think.

'We're on it,' he said. It was important to keep Spiro sweet, but he didn't want his heavy-handed men messing things up.

'Meaning?'

'We've worked out where Dhar was calling from. We'll have him for you by daybreak.'

'Good of you to share that, Ian. In case you hadn't noticed, the whole of the goddamn Western world's looking for Dhar. I thought you and I had an understanding.'

'He's yours, just let us bring him in. He's half-British, remember, caused us a lot of problems. We've got a reputation to restore.'

'Too damn right you have. Just make sure it's you and not Fielding who gets the knighthood. And don't go claiming that reward either. We haven't got $25 million to spare. I guess you know Marchant's with Dhar, too?'

Denton didn't know, and slowed up some more, his hands tensing on the steering wheel as he glanced in the rear-view mirror. He had assured the PM that Marchant was under lock and key at the Fort. It wouldn't look good if he had escaped. He couldn't afford to put a foot wrong if he was to become Chief.

'I thought he was at Fort Monckton.'

'So did we. My men just took a look. Seems he left a while ago.'

'We'll hand him over with Dhar.'

'I'd appreciate it. And where might this handover be?'

'How does RAF Fairford sound?'

'I like the symmetry.'

Denton knew it would appeal. Fairford was not only where Dhar had wounded American pride by shooting down one of the USAF's most prized jets; it was from there that Marchant had been renditioned after the London Marathon fifteen months earlier.

'Put a plane on standby,' he said. 'I'll call within the hour. And when you've got Dhar –'

'We'll pull out of Vauxhall. We're two peas in a pod, Ian.'

Denton could think of nothing worse, but he knew many such compromises lay ahead. Finding a way to get on with Spiro would be the least of them. His relationship with the military had never been straightforward. 'There's a need in this family to make amends,' Denton's father, a sergeant major with the Green Howards, used to bark at him when he was growing up in Hull. No one ever talked openly about it, but his grandfather had been a conscientious objector. Denton chose grammar school and Oxford instead of the military, before signing up to MI6. His father had not hidden his disappointment, but it was the closest Denton could get to making amends. He had liked his grandfather, whose objections had been more to the officer class than to war itself.

He glanced at his watch and accelerated again, choosing Miles Davis on the CD player. It suited night-time driving. Before leaving London he had called the SAS headquarters at Hereford and spoken to the MI6 liaison officer. Denton had worked with him once in Basra, and had been present when he had taken the previous year's IONEC recruits through their special forces training at the Fort. His mantra had been borrowed from the US Seals, whom he revered: 'The more you sweat in peacetime, the less you'll bleed in war.' They hadn't got on. The officer, public-school educated, now had overall responsibility for the Increment, a covert unit of special forces that MI6 could call upon at any time.

The unit was already heavily deployed in Afghanistan and Yemen, providing MI6 field officers with protection. Its members were drawn mainly from the SAS, but it also recruited from other special forces, including the SBS and the SRR, who provided reconnaissance, and 8 Flight Army Air Corps. After Denton's phone call, two of its Eurocopter Dauphin helicopters had scrambled and were now making their way to Kemble, each one ferrying ten men.

The plan was for one team to proceed on foot from Kemble to Tarlton, where they would isolate the hamlet, surround Stephen Marchant's house and carry out as much surveillance as they could. Once they had confirmed Dhar's presence, they would call in the second team, who would come in low by helicopter. As they fast-roped onto the roof of the house, the first team would enter by the ground floor. Denton would be waiting a mile down the road, ready to accompany Dhar to Fairford once the operation was complete.

He dialled through to the liaison officer at Hereford again.

'It's Ian,' he said. 'Daniel Marchant might be with the target.'

'One of yours, isn't he?'

Denton heard the contempt in his voice, and told himself it was mutual. Neither side appreciated the other's skills. Just as MI5 didn't enjoy working with the police, so MI6 resented being increasingly asked to share operations with the military.

'He was.'

'Expendable?'

Denton paused. It would be easier if Marchant was out of the way, but Spiro was expecting him. 'No.'

He hung up, and thought about what lay ahead. After a discussion with the Chief of Defence Staff, the Director of Special Forces and other military top brass who had been summoned from their beds to attend COBRA, the PM had authorised the mission to capture Dhar. It was short notice, but it wasn't as if the target was hiding in hostile territory. He was in the Cotswolds. If anything went wrong, the operation could be dismissed as an exercise.

The PM's main concern was to pre-empt the Americans. A raid by the US on British soil would be politically humiliating, possibly fatal, for the coalition, which still had to deal with the problem of Vauxhall Cross. However, the PM had agreed for Dhar to be handed over to the Americans at the earliest opportunity. The government would win global credit for capturing the world's most wanted terrorist, the special relationship would be back on track, and Denton's right to take over as Chief of MI6 would become unarguable.

31

'Turn it off,' Dhar said, waving the gun at the wood-encased record player in the corner. 'Then sit down.'

Marchant went over to the old HMV, given to him by his father, and lifted the needle off *Sinbad the Sailor*. After clicking a switch, which released a dusty hiss, he sat down on the carpet, cross-legged like Dhar, and tried to gauge the extent of his drinking, the state of his mind. His words were clear, but his eyes, usually as bright as onyx, were unfocused. It was the one scenario he hadn't expected. Injury had always been a possibility, the reason Dhar had sought sanctuary here. There was a patch of blood on the carpet, and his trousers were ripped. But alcohol? That was meant to be Marchant's curse, not Dhar's.

'I wasn't expecting us to meet again so soon.' Marchant nodded at Dhar's leg. 'What happened?'

'It's nothing.' Dhar winced, taking another sip of vodka from the bottle.

'Looks painful.'

'I said it's nothing,' Dhar repeated, raising his voice. He was still holding the gun loosely in one hand. Marchant felt like someone who had released an animal back into the wild, only to find it on his doorstep the next morning, tired and hungry. Dhar's life couldn't be in graver danger. Didn't he know they would be coming for him? After a pause, Dhar spoke again, quieter this time. 'I'm sorry,' he said. 'I'm glad you came.'

'They'll have tracked your call, you know that.'

'And you will protect me.'

'That wasn't the deal.'

Christ, Marchant thought. He really does expect the UK to offer him sanctuary.

Dhar smirked. 'The Russians weren't so pleased to see me.'

'I can't do anything, Salim. It's too late.'

'It's OK, I know. I don't expect you to. Not now. Maybe later. Share a drink with me.'

Dhar passed the unusually shaped bottle to Marchant, who glanced at the label, trying to get his head around the situation. Binekhi was a brand of Georgian *chacha*, or grape vodka, that Nikolai Primakov used to give his father. Dhar must have found it in the drinks cupboard downstairs. For the past year, Marchant had stayed off the booze, except on his final night in Marrakech. It had been easy to stay sober in Morocco, a Muslim country. Now he was being offered a drink by Salim Dhar, of all people. To refuse would cause tension. He closed his eyes and let the vodka slip down smoothly.

'There was nowhere else for me to go,' Dhar said, taking the bottle back. 'Besides, I have always wanted to see this place for myself.'

Marchant watched Dhar take in the bedroom as if it was his own, a rare smile on his drawn face. He had missed the drink, despite the trouble that inevitably followed.

'Have you had a look around?' he asked. For a moment, Dhar reminded him of his father. He had never noticed it before, but when Dhar smiled, one of his cheeks dimpled in the same way, creasing the skin around his hollow eyes. His father had been a drinker too. Bruichladdich whisky. Maybe they would move on to that when the vodka was finished. Already he was feeling less concerned, adjusting to their dangerous predicament.

'I've seen your brother's bedroom,' Dhar said. 'It must have been a painful loss. I'm sorry.'

Marchant didn't want to go down that route, not now, but he suddenly felt Sebbie's presence, here in the house they once shared. He gestured for the bottle again, and drank long and deeply, wiping his mouth with the back of his hand.

'We were close. Mates, brothers. The twin thing. He died in Delhi. 1988. A government bus hit us at a crossroads, shunted our jeep thirty yards. Sebbie was in the front seat, didn't stand a chance. My mother survived, but never really recovered. I'm over it now.'

Dhar seemed happy to buy into the lie. 'I found a photograph of my mother,' he said, changing the subject.

'Shushma?' Marchant asked.

'It was in our father's bedroom, hidden behind a photo of your mother.'

Marchant didn't like the idea of Dhar snooping around his father's possessions, but then he checked himself. He was Dhar's father too. In similar circumstances, he would have done the same.

'I also visited our father's grave.'

Marchant glanced across at the window that overlooked the tiny church. *Always secret, always loyal.* He knew the grave was not as well tended as it should have been. When all this was over, he would come back and cut the grass, maybe plant some flowers.

'Tell me something about him,' Dhar said. 'What he was like when you were growing up.'

'Our father?' Marchant paused. He took another swig and passed the bottle back to Dhar. 'Well, because of his job, we didn't see him so much, but when we did, he made up for it. Spoilt us rotten. Drove us too fast through the countryside in his old

Lagonda, took us wild swimming in the Thames, up near Lechlade. He'd grown up in Africa, you see, always liked big open spaces. The great outdoors.'

'We all do.'

'And he used to take us camping in Knoydart.'

'Where?'

'The remotest place he could find on mainland Britain. No creature comforts. Just moss to wipe our bums, fish he'd caught in the loch, and a mouldy old canvas bell tent. He always bought us kippers at Mallaig after the ferry back. Sebbie hated them.' Marchant paused, remembering how his father used to pinch Sebbie's nose with one hand and spoon in kipper with the other. 'We were very young when we lived here, before we moved to Delhi. After we came back, things were different.'

'No Sebbie.'

There was a long silence before Dhar continued. 'When they take me, I want you to promise something. You must help with my escape.'

Was it the vodka talking, Marchant wondered. What was he thinking? That the Americans would send him on community service? 'That might not be so easy.'

'The *kuffar* will take me to Bagram. Maybe later they will transfer me to Guantánamo.'

'Two of the most secure prisons in the world.'

'You will find a way to help. The Iranians want me to work for them again. We share a dislike of America. If it's Bagram, the Islamic Revolutionary Guard Corps will secure my freedom – they have many friends in Afghanistan. And it's been done before – four brothers escaped in 2005. But they might need assistance. And if it's Guantánamo, I'm sure your female American friend will help you.'

Marchant tried not to react, but Dhar's comment took him by surprise. How did he know about Lakshmi?

'And when I'm free –' Dhar said. He paused, looked around the room and then lowered his head, speaking more quietly. 'I will keep my promise, and do all I can to protect Britain.'

Marchant closed his eyes, his head beginning to spin. It was the first time he had heard Dhar confirm their arrangement: he was prepared to work for MI6. That was what he couldn't tell Lakshmi when she had asked why he hadn't killed Dhar. And it was what Fielding hadn't been able to tell anyone either. Between the two of them, they had agreed that Dhar would be more valuable as an MI6 asset than dead. 'A back channel into the global *jihad*,' as Fielding had put it.

So Marchant hadn't killed Dhar when they had met in Russia. He had tried to turn him as they had approached Britain, flying at five hundred feet. It had been an incalculable gamble, but now it was worth it. Seeking refuge in Tarlton had seemed suicidal for Dhar, but his confident talk of freedom had given the operation new life. Marchant just had to figure out a way to honour his side of the deal.

'Bagram isn't exactly an open prison,' Marchant said. 'I can't see a way to help if they take you there.'

'The West's senses have been sharpened by technology. Maybe all I'm asking for is a blind eye, a deaf ear.'

Marchant watched Dhar as he became lost in thought, studying the Binekhi label on the vodka bottle. Did he mean GCHQ?

'When you first told me our father was not working for Moscow, I was shocked, angry,' Dhar continued. 'I had wanted to believe he was a Russian agent.'

Marchant thought back to the terrifying moment when he had broken the news to Dhar in the Russian SU-25 jet. Up until that point, Dhar had believed – hoped – that both Daniel and their father were Russian moles, all three of them united in their fight against America. But it hadn't been as simple as that.

'Our father didn't like America,' Marchant said. 'But he never betrayed Britain.'

Dhar nodded, a distant smile in his eyes. 'And I don't expect you to betray your country either. My war is not with Britain, despite its weak attitude to America. This is the land of my father, and you have promised that my mother is safe here. But if you will not help with my escape, I cannot guarantee Britain's safety. There are many brothers who wish to destroy this country. I can only do so much to stop them. They will be angry when I am taken – the talk is of a nuclear hellstorm – and only my freedom will bring you peace. Now you must go. The clumsy *kuffar* are waiting outside for the moment to strike. I saw them just now from the window, moving about like elephants in the orchard. But first we have a toast – to our joint *jihad* against America.'

32

The Increment had been briefed that Dhar had landed at Kemble earlier in the evening and it didn't take long for the first team to find a bolt-cuttered hole in the airport perimeter fence. They made a bigger incision of their own and moved through in single file, the whites of their eyes bright against their blackened faces. There were several fields nearer the target where they could have landed, but the stakes were too high. Dhar was a professional, and Kemble airport gave them cover. No one would question a helicopter coming in to land there, even out of hours.

It was almost light by the time they reached Tarlton. They had kept to the edges of fields, moving quickly and silently in the morning mist. After splitting into two, one group approached the house across a field at the back, spreading out behind a dry-stone wall that marked the perimeter of the garden. The other moved down the single-lane track that led to the house and beyond to the chapel. When they reached the drive, they dispersed into the orchard and checked in with their forward reconnaissance colleagues, who confirmed Dhar's presence in the house. They waited for the sound of a helicopter.

33

Fielding managed to slip back into Dolphin Square without his Special Branch protection officer spotting either him or Oleg. Two–nil to MI6. He carried the dog in his arms as he stepped through the tradesmen's entrance of Nelson House, putting him down again once they were safely inside. Turner Munroe had taken them along the Embankment, up to Sloane Square and then back to Pimlico, promising to find out more about Russia's penetration of MI6.

As Fielding let himself into his flat, he tried to think of a time when the Americans hadn't accused Britain of harbouring a Moscow mole. For as long as he could remember, the CIA had been suspicious of Stephen Marchant. Their wariness had become part of the culture of MI6. And who could blame them, after the débâcle of Philby, who had been destined to become Chief after a stint in Washington? Spies had long memories.

He still couldn't dismiss the possibility that the latest American intel was referring posthumously to Hugo Prentice. The Polish case against him had been strong. It was a tragedy that Prentice had been killed before he could be questioned. Fielding still struggled to accept that one of his oldest friends in the Service could have betrayed a network of Western agents in Poland.

If the Americans were convinced that he himself was the mole, as Munroe had suggested, he would have to deal with those allegations as and when they arose. His closeness to Stephen Marchant had never endeared him to Washington, but that would not be sufficiently damaging, given that the case against Marchant had never been proven. Unless the real mole had managed to frame him.

Fielding poured himself a small glass of malt, slid a Telemann cantata into the CD player and went over to his desktop Mac in the corner of the room. It was no longer possible to dismiss Ian Denton, who was now the obvious candidate to replace him as Chief. Fielding had been wrongfooted by his deputy's ambition in recent days. Up until now Denton had seemed a born number two, happy to troubleshoot for his Chief, to complement his skills rather than challenge them. That was partly why Fielding had chosen him as his deputy.

Denton was the Moscow man to his camel trader. Between them, they made a good pair, had the world covered with their respective areas of expertise: Denton the SovBloc, Fielding the Arab world. But something in Denton had changed. An innate wariness of Washington had been replaced by a desire to please the Americans. And any personal loyalty had vanished too, giving way to a naked determination to succeed Fielding as Chief.

Fielding couldn't blame Denton if he felt marginalised. He hadn't been privy to Daniel Marchant's fake defection or their plan to turn Salim Dhar. But it was still a long walk from disaffected deputy to traitor.

'What do you reckon, Oleg?' Fielding asked, logging into the Legoland network. 'Is this the "unkindest cut of all"?' Oleg raised his head from his cushion, then went back to sleep.

Fielding called up a secure personnel file on Denton, wanting to know more about his troubled relationship with Primakov, the man who had accused him of being a traitor. According to his

Developed Vetting profile, a complaint had been made against Denton shortly after he had started working for the SovBloc Controllerate, while he was helping Stephen Marchant to run Nikolai Primakov. Both men had recently returned from Delhi, Marchant settling into a short London stint, Primakov rising up the KGB's ranks in Moscow.

Primakov was constantly asking Denton when he could defect, something that was not in the young field officer's gift. There was little love lost between them, and Primakov eventually requested for Denton to be replaced. His next batch of CX included information that suggested Denton was working for Moscow. The matter was discreetly investigated by MI6's Director of Counter-Intelligence and Security, who dismissed the allegations out of hand. On this occasion, Primakov was judged to have been an unreliable source. As a precaution, though, Denton was transferred to another job. Had Primakov remained unreliable? Had Denton been falsely accused for a second time?

Fielding's thoughts were interrupted by his landline ringing. It was the secure link to COBRA.

'I thought you should know that we've found Salim Dhar,' Denton said.

'Congratulations. How did he find the Cotswolds?'

There was a pause on the line before Denton spoke quietly. 'It would have been helpful if you'd told us.'

'I think you mean it would have saved arses. It was pretty obvious, wasn't it?'

'Nothing's changed, Marcus. They just want me to oversee the search for Dhar.'

'"They"?'

'The Prime Minister's office.'

At the request of the President, Fielding thought. 'Will Spiro let everyone get back to work now? You've seen the scenes at Vauxhall, I presume.'

'He's promised to pull his men out once we've handed Dhar over. He thinks Marchant's with him.'

'So you haven't actually got Dhar yet.'

'Within the hour. Marchant too. Spiro wants a chat with them both.'

'You remember what happened the last time they took Daniel?' Marchant had been waterboarded at a black site in Poland, and might well have died if it hadn't been for the intervention of Hugo Prentice.

'That was before he helped to shoot down a US jet. I'm not sure we've got a choice. Besides, what the hell's Marchant doing with Dhar anyway?'

Fielding understood his deputy's frustration. It went to the heart of their differences: the continual denial of information about Daniel Marchant and Salim Dhar. Fielding was unable to answer him; more so now than ever.

34

After too many toasts to their shared *jihad* against America, Marchant changed into some of his old clothes. They were too small, but at least they were dry. He left Dhar sitting cross-legged on the floor of his bedroom and crept back down the stairs, keeping away from the windows. He knew he had to move fast. If Dhar was right, the 'elephants' would be storming the house within minutes. He didn't want to be around when they arrived, although he would like to know if it was American or British special forces that Dhar had spotted in the garden.

He stopped in front of the fireplace in the hall and listened, holding the handgun that Dhar had insisted on giving him. Silence, only memories. It was more than twenty years since he and Sebbie had played together in the house. They used to spend hours honing a variation of hide and seek with the local farmers' children. After being given two minutes to hide, the twins' challenge was to get out of the house and into the garden without being seen. Every time they would emerge at the far end of the lawn, running back across the grass shrieking and laughing.

It was their first shared secret: the priest hole beside the fireplace, and the passage that led out to the garden. Their father had shown it to them on their sixth birthday, when they were brave enough to crawl down the tunnel with torches, but not old enough to understand why Catholic priests had once needed to hide.

Marchant didn't have a torch now, and there was no time to look for one. After checking on the pilot, who was still tied to the stool, head bowed, he closed the kitchen door and went back to the fireplace. The pilot wouldn't have much longer to wait before he was released. The fireplace was surrounded by oak panels, one of which, on the right-hand side, could be opened. He felt along the bevelling. At first he couldn't find the latch, but then his fingers lifted a small wooden peg and the panel gave way, swinging back into the dark.

His father had always encouraged their games, and was particularly proud of this one. He had even joked once that the priest hole might come in handy when the men in white coats came to take him away. Now it was saving his son's life. Marchant climbed into the cramped space and pulled the panel closed behind him. It didn't feel right to be leaving Dhar on his own, but there was no other way. If he came with him, they would survive on the run for a few days at the most. The only chance for him to be free again was to be taken alive.

Marchant stayed still for a few moments, crouching in the confined space as his eyes adjusted to the darkness. His sense of balance had gone. One sip of vodka would have been enough to placate Dhar. He should have taken a single slug and passed the bottle back. Instead he had gone down to the cellar for the Bruichladdich.

The oldest parts of the house dated back to the sixteenth century, when it had been built by a wealthy Catholic family that was fearful of being caught at prayer. There used to be a concealed chapel in the loft, linked to the priest hole in the hall by hidden stairs that ran up the outside of the chimney block, but a fire in the early 1900s had destroyed the roof, which had subsequently been rebuilt.

He felt his way forward, crawling over the damp, mud-like floor. He had always gone first, Sebbie following behind, both trying not to be frightened. Their fear was usually outweighed by the thought of running down the lawn towards their startled friends, except for one time, when their torch had died. Sebbie had panicked and started to sob in the darkness. Marchant had kept going, his own fear rising. He should have stopped to comfort his brother, and he felt guilty again now as he moved slowly down the sloping tunnel, wondering what was happening above.

35

Dhar knew it was a gamble, but he had run out of options. It felt strange being unarmed, but by giving Marchant his gun he hoped he might prolong both their lives. The first few seconds would be crucial. He had to look as passive as possible, hands clear of his body. The cowardly *kuffar* were terrified of suicide belts, so he stood up from the cushions, and almost fell over as his leg collapsed beneath him. He told himself it was the wound, but he knew it was the alcohol. It had tricked the winch man on the cliffs and kept the pain at bay for a time, but opening the whisky had been a mistake. Never would he let such vile liquid cross his lips again.

Leaning against the bed, he unzipped the flying suit and turned it down at the waist, revealing his bare, skinny torso, thin wisps of black hair on his chest. He caught sight of himself in a mirror by the door, and saw that his shoulders were red and bruised. Then he moved closer to the mirror and looked at his eyes, which were tired and bloodshot. Had there really been no other choice but to come here? He cursed himself again for the drink and tried to clear his head, thinking through the choices that had been open to him.

But he knew, as he heard the first sounds of an approaching helicopter, that there had never been any choice. The decision to come here hadn't been about his future but his past, over which he had no control. His need to see his father's house, to feel the security of a family home that had been denied to him, had been overwhelming.

He turned and sat down in the middle of the floor, putting a hand out to stop himself from falling. Then, ignoring the pain, he crossed his legs, closed his eyes and rested his hands on his knees, pressing his thumbs and index fingers together, just as his mother had taught him. *Samyama* meditation had helped them both get through the darkest days in Delhi, until he had finally had enough and fled for Kashmir.

This time there would be no running away.

36

Marchant saw the helicopter before he heard it. He had been scanning the horizon to the west, more out of habit than anything else. It was where he and Sebbie used to look for the Hawker Hunters taking off from Kemble. His instinct was to get as far away from the house as possible, but he knew that ground troops were already in position in the garden and would see him. He was lucky they hadn't spotted him already.

The passage from the priest hole had brought him up into a group of tall conifers at the back of the garden, forty yards from the house. He had managed to open the hatch without noise or difficulty, even though a thick layer of rotting grass cuttings had been dumped on it by the old gardener who still came once a month. It might have been safer to stay in the tunnel, but Marchant had decided to take the risk. He needed to see the moment when the troops stormed the house. The noise and confusion of those few seconds would provide him with his only opportunity to escape.

As the helicopter swept in low over the fields and hovered above the roof of the house, the tops of the trees swaying in its down-draught, Marchant saw that it was an unmarked Eurocopter Dauphin. At least that was something. The Eurocopter was the SAS's chopper of choice, which meant the British were running the show. Dhar would have a marginally better chance of not being shot dead on sight. But he began to wonder as a series of loud explosions cut through the noise of the helicopter. Ground troops had emerged from the orchard and hedges and were storming the house from the front and back, throwing stun grenades in through broken windows. At the same time, men were fast-roping down from the helicopter, landing on a flat-roofed extension at the rear of the house and smashing their way in through the top- and first-floor windows. It was time to break cover.

He darted to the stone wall that ran along the back of the conifers, jumped over it and ducked, turning to see if anyone had noticed him. The house was now shrouded in smoke, the early-morning air thick with adrenaline-charged shouting and barked orders. British orders. The helicopter had moved away from the house and was banking around to the south. Marchant assumed it would be used to take Dhar away when he had been captured. In which case it would soon be touching down in the field he was in, the only clear space in the area.

He ran north, keeping his head down and using the wall as cover. After a hundred yards he jumped back over the wall and cut across a paddock where two ponies stood anxiously, frightened by the noise. His sudden appearance scared them even more, and they bolted away from him as he headed for the lane that ran down from Tarlton to Rodmarton.

Crossing the road would be risky – Marchant guessed that the village would have been sealed off before the raid – but there was a covered footpath on the other side that would get him out of the area quickly. He also hoped, as he climbed through a hole in the hedge, that he was far enough out of Tarlton to be beyond any roadblocks. He was wrong.

37

Dhar felt very close to his mother as the first window shattered and smoke swirled all around him. He remained calm, sitting in the position she had taught him, knowing that any sudden movement would cost him his life. And he felt close to his real father too, here in his house.

The British – he was sure the soldiers now swinging in through the windows were British – were attacking the home of one of their own, a former Chief of MI6. However well trained they were, that would make them tread more carefully, pause a fraction of a second longer before squeezing the trigger. At least, that's what Dhar told himself as the two men kneeling a few feet in front of him trained their weapons on him.

'Hands above your head!' one of them shouted. His voice was muted by the gasmask he was wearing, but Dhar could still hear the anger in his voice, fear mixed with aggression. He was wearing full body armour, his face blacked out, darting eyes unnaturally white.

'Neptune located,' the other one said into a radio mike. 'Top floor, room two.'

'Higher!' the first one shouted, almost screaming now.

Dhar raised his bare arms, wondering what weapon the *kuffar* thought he might be about to reach for. The vodka bottle?

Moments later, the second soldier took a flash photo of Dhar with a small digital camera. Dhar could hear more soldiers running up the stairs. He began to choke on the fumes, and realised that it was a gas of some sort. The last words he heard were spoken by the second soldier: 'ID confirmed. It's Dhar.'

38

Marchant paused in the hedgerow, cursing his luck. There was a roadblock – two army vehicles, a police car and an Audi – thirty yards to his right. A group of soldiers standing in the middle of the road had a clear view of where he had hoped to cross the lane. He would have to keep going to the end of the paddock, parallel with the lane, and cut across the next field once he had passed the roadblock. There was less cover there, but he could pick up another footpath at the far end of the field that would eventually take him down to the Tetbury road. It was further, but he had no choice.

Keeping his head low, he ran along the edge of the paddock, hidden from the lane by the hedgerow and trees. As he drew close to the roadblock, out of sight on the other side of the hedge, he slowed down, trying to minimise any noise. His breathing was heavy, more from fear than exercise. The flashing blue light of the police car was visible through the trees, but the foliage provided enough cover for him not to be seen. The soldiers were talking on a radio. Marchant stopped to listen.

'Neptune's located, sir.'

'Any sign of Marchant?'

'No, sir.'

'Keep looking.'

Marchant froze. It was Ian Denton's voice. If the deputy Chief of MI6 was heading up the hunt for Dhar, it meant that Fielding was already finished. And so was he. There were already too many unanswered questions about what an MI6 officer was doing in a Russian plane that had shot down a US jet. He could see where it was all heading: Denton would take the credit for Dhar's capture; the Americans would anoint him as Fielding's successor; and the world would never know that he was working for Moscow.

No one could help him now. He crept past the roadblock and climbed over the paddock fence. Checking behind him, he set off across the field, accelerating into a sprint. There was only one thing he could do that might save him and Fielding: prove that Ian Denton was a Russian mole. For as long as Marchant had been with MI6, the Americans had suspected the Service of being penetrated at the highest level by Moscow. At one point they had thought it was his father. He had nailed that lie. Now Denton would make sure that the suspicion fell on Fielding, and by implication himself.

By the time he reached the cover of the footpath, the helicopter had touched down in the field. Marchant turned to watch, hidden behind trees. A group of soldiers was escorting a bare-chested Dhar towards the helicopter. Dhar was stumbling, barely able to walk, and had a black hood over his head. Marchant wondered what the deal was. Would he be handed over secretly to the Americans, or would the British make some political capital out of his arrest? There would be a price to pay if they went public: *'There are many brothers who wish to destroy this country. I can only do so much to stop them. They will be angry when I am taken – the talk is of a nuclear hellstorm – and only my freedom will bring you peace.'*

As Marchant watched the helicopter rise into the sky, drop its nose and head south, he considered his options. The search for him would already be widening. Airports, stations and ports would be on full alert. He was small fry compared to Dhar, but Denton – no doubt supported by Spiro – would be on a roll after Dhar's capture, and wouldn't stop until both of the men who had been in the cockpit of the Russian jet were captured.

He needed to get out of the country, but he didn't have access to his own passport or the half-dozen cover-identity passports he kept with it. They were in his flat in Pimlico, which would be under surveillance. He had no money either – just a phone he couldn't use. Perhaps Lakshmi could help him. He was reluctant to involve her any further, but he had nothing to lose, now that her career was effectively over. He also wanted to be with her – too much.

Whatever he did, speed was of the essence. It was still only 6 a.m. If he could get back to Kemble, he might be able to reach Gosport in the Morris Minor and return it to the car park before its owners noticed it had been stolen. But it wouldn't be out of honesty. He wanted to borrow something else from them.

Before that, though, there was another person he needed to visit. And Marchant wasn't sure how pleased he would be to see him.

39

'I gather he wasn't even armed,' Spiro said, turning to Denton. The two men were in a group of US and British officials, some in uniform, who had assembled in the officers' mess of RAF Fairford. On a big TV screen in front of them, the Prime Minister was giving a hastily arranged news conference about the capture of Salim Dhar.

'No resistance at all,' Spiro continued. 'Stripped to the waist and sitting cross-legged on a carpet. Just sitting there, drunk as a fiddler's bitch. Maybe it was a magic carpet, and he was worried about flying under the influence.'

Denton ignored Spiro's laughter. He was trying to listen to his PM, who had been woken early in anticipation of Dhar's capture.

'Today we should all salute the bravery of our British special forces and the intelligence services, who have worked tirelessly to capture Salim Dhar. As is often the case in such matters, those who deserve the greatest praise must remain anonymous. But they know who they are, and it is thanks to them that our world is a safer place this morning.'

'I guess that made it harder to shoot him,' Spiro said.

'And let this be a warning to anyone else who seeks to destroy our values and democracy with violence and terror. We will hunt you down, however long it takes, wherever it takes us . . .'

'Our instructions were to capture him alive,' Denton said.

'This morning, I ordered Dhar to be handed over to our American allies at RAF Fairford, a historic airfield that symbolises our close relationship.'

If you ignored all the 'Air CIA' rendition flights that had passed through Fairford, Denton thought. Politicians had conveniently short memories.

'Come on, Ian. You know how these things are,' Spiro said. 'Trials are wasted on these guys. And they're too high-maintenance in jail. Nothing but trouble.'

'Dhar left British soil thirty minutes ago on a United States Air Force plane – an official flight, registered with UK air-traffic control – and will be brought to trial in accordance with international law. I spoke with the President of the United States a few minutes ago, and he assured me that justice will not only be done, but will be seen to be done.'

'Seems like your President has other ideas,' Denton said. Spiro wasn't about to go away, and he had to work out how to deal with the idiot. At least he had kept his word and pulled his troops out of Vauxhall. The bridge had reopened for business by dawn.

'Dhar's my prisoner now. It's anyone's guess what might happen when he squeals. Where's Marchant, by the way?'

'We're still looking for him. According to Forensics, he was at the house with Dhar shortly before the raid. Left through a priest hole.'

'A what?'

'A secret hiding place once used by Catholic priests to flee persecution.'

'Tell me you're making this stuff up.'

Denton didn't have the energy for a history lesson. It was already a matter of acute embarrassment that Marchant had slipped the net.

'We'll find him.'

Denton still felt bitter that Fielding hadn't told him the full facts about Marchant and Dhar.

'By the way, are we bothering to keep Marcus in the loop, or has Elvis already left the building?'

'He's still Chief, and will remain so until the Foreign Secretary decides otherwise. That's the way these things tend to work in Britain.'

'We'll see about that,' Spiro said, putting an arm around Denton's shoulders before walking away.

40

Marchant had only been to Paul Myers's cramped digs in Montpelier in Cheltenham once, but he could still remember the squalor: empty pizza boxes on the floor, a bike with two flat tyres, remote-control planes and computers covering every surface. If anything, things were worse this time as he picked his way across the floor, cleared a BLT sandwich wrapper off the sofa and sat down. In addition to the bank of computer screens, some of which were on, there was a pile of circuit boards, bits of phones and other electrical equipment scattered across the unmade bed.

'You need to get a cleaner,' Marchant said, noticing that the bike was now on its side in the corner.

'Do you think so?' Myers asked, coming into the room with two mugs of tea. He was always drinking tea. 'I thought it was what the magazines call scruffy chic.'

'You look better than I feared.'

'Really?'

'Actually, you look shit. But you're alive, which is something. And you're not about to die slowly of radiation.'

'It's true about the dirty bomb, then?'

'It's true.'

Myers whistled, which always struck Marchant as odd. He didn't

123

know anybody else who whistled. Then again, he didn't know anybody like Myers.

'You've seen the latest news?'

'About Dhar?' He had heard a scratchy bulletin on the car radio.

'They caught him in the Cotswolds. That won't have done much for his *jihadi* credentials. I guess the tourist-information people recognised him when he asked for the nearest tea shop.'

Myers laughed awkwardly, then gulped at his tea when he saw that Marchant wasn't smiling.

'You were right about the SAR helicopter,' Marchant said. 'He must have got the Russian to make the emergency call, knowing we would have recognised his voiceprint.'

'And taken the chopper to wherever he wanted to go on his sightseeing trip. What was he playing at?'

'He went to my father's house. I was there too.'

Myers nearly choked on his tea.

'I need your help, Paul,' Marchant continued. 'The Americans are on my back.'

'When weren't they?'

'I need a phone that won't give away my location, some money and regular updates from the GCHQ grid.'

'Is this about Dhar?'

'The Americans didn't take too kindly to one of their jets being shot down.'

'I won't ask what you were doing in the cockpit.'

'Damage limitation. Let's leave it at that.'

'Do you know how many calls are made on UK mobile networks each day? Two hundred million. Not even Echelon can listen to them all. The only way people like me are going to be alerted to a keyword or recognise a voiceprint is if we're already monitoring the number you're dialling from or the number you're calling. Having said that, your best bet is talking over the internet using VOIP. Put your call through an anonymous routing network and a proxy server, throw in a botnet for luck, and you're safe.'

'What happens if I don't have internet access?'

'Buy a bunch of unlocked pay-as-you-go phones. They're ten quid at Tesco. Use each one once, then chuck it away. And vary the network operators. One call on Orange, the next on Vodafone. That's what the drug dealers do. Keep a phone just for incoming calls and give me the number. If you need to call me, I've got a pay-as-you-go that I haven't used.'

'And if I want to contact someone whose line is monitored?'

Myers didn't answer. In keeping with his dysfunctional manner, he stood up without explanation and started to rummage through the pile of electronic detritus on his bed.

'Try this,' he said, holding up what looked like a regular pair of bud headphones and a mike. 'It's a hands-free unit – with a difference. When you talk into the mike, it modulates your voice.'

'And makes me sound like Darth Vader?'

'Same principle, but no. It just plays around with your vocal cavities and articulator patterns. Enough to confuse the NSA's voiceprint-recognition software. What sort of updates are you after from the grid?'

'Anything to do with Dhar.'

'That's a big ask.' Myers bent over one of the computers and scrolled down a list of websites. 'The traffic's gone haywire since news of his capture broke earlier. Literally hundreds of *jihadi* chatrooms. The guy's got a following bigger than bin Laden.'

'What about Iran?'

Myers cast his eyes downwards. 'I've only just been put back on the desk. I asked for a transfer after, you know, all that business with Leila. It was too painful.'

'Of course. I'm sorry.' Leila had been half-Iranian, and Marchant

125

wasn't the only one to fall for the MI6 officer's exotic charms. Myers had been obsessed with her.

'My line manager kept me away from the region for a while, then said she couldn't do without me.'

'I'm not surprised.'

Myers was GCHQ's leading Iranian intel analyst, fluent in Farsi and, crucially, the complex ways of the Islamic Revolutionary Guard Corps.

'Could you listen out for any mention of Dhar? Particularly along the Iranian border with Afghanistan?'

'I thought he'd been dumped by Tehran?'

'Seems they're interested in him again.'

'There's been a lot of IRGC activity along Iran's eastern borders recently. They're trying to counter what they think are proxy terrorist attacks by the CIA. Jundola, Mojahedin-e Khalq, the usual suspects.'

Marchant was glad Myers was working for the West. His knowledge was forensic. 'If Dhar's sent to Bagram, which seems likely, the Iranians will definitely try to spring him.'

'And?' Myers asked.

'I just need to know, that's all.'

'Don't you think the whole world might know if Salim Dhar escapes from Bagram?'

'I want to know before it happens.'

41

Fielding looked around his office, knowing it was for the last time. Most of the pictures were from the government's private collection, except for the two Turners, which he had borrowed from Tate Britain. They would be returned across the water by his successor, who was more into Lowry, but he was damned if the Matt cartoon would stay. It showed a man in a trenchcoat and dark glasses on top of a Christmas tree, where the fairy should be. He had commissioned it for the Service's centenary year Christmas card, and knew exactly where it would hang in Dolphin Square.

Anne Norman, his principal PA, had provided him with a clear plastic box for his personal possessions. He felt like a prisoner checking into jail. It hadn't taken long to fill the box: desk photos of his twelve godchildren, his Montblanc pen and a bottle of green ink (a present from Hugo Prentice when he became Chief), the ten-volume *Book of the Thousand Nights and a Night* (Sir Richard Francis Burton's 1885 limited edition) and a photograph, kept in his top drawer, of Kadia, the woman he might have married if his career hadn't intervened.

As he put the framed Matt cartoon in the box, face down in a half-hearted attempt to conceal it, he heard Ian Denton outside, talking to Anne. He might have had the decency to wait, Fielding thought. Only a few minutes earlier he had been in a meeting in St James's with the Foreign Secretary, at which he had offered his resignation. Instead, it had been agreed that he would go on sick leave for the foreseeable future. Denton would step up as acting Chief.

'We don't want to make a fuss,' the Foreign Secretary had said. 'Not now. The coalition's in a fragile state. I'm sure you understand. It's the Cold War all over again, only this time with our closest ally.'

Fielding listened to Denton's voice outside. Anne was being polite, but she was clearly stalling him, knowing that it would be awkward for him to enter the office before Fielding had left. If she had to, she would physically block Denton's way. She had done it before, shielding him, in her formidable crimson tights and red shoes, from pushy politicians. Fielding would miss her.

He walked back over to his desk. There was still the safe to check. Unlike others in the building, only the incumbent Chief and the Foreign Secretary knew its combination, which changed twice daily. Traditionally, it contained documents that were for C's eyes only – 'God's access'. Some of them – deniable operations, details of crown jewel assets – were enough to bring down governments if they were ever made public. Fielding had always played by the rules of the Service, but there was one document he didn't want his successor to see, regardless of whether he was or wasn't Moscow's man.

It was a single watermarked sheet of A4 paper, handwritten by Stephen Marchant, and read many times by Fielding over the past few years. Beginning with the thoroughness of a witness statement, the former Chief had outlined his recruitment of Nikolai Primakov in Delhi in the 1980s and how the Russian had, on his return to Moscow, risen to become head of K Branch (counter-intelligence) in the KGB's First Chief Directorate.

The document went on to describe – in increasingly charged language – how Moscow Centre had, over time, become suspicious of Primakov. In order to protect his source, Marchant had taken the controversial decision to let himself be recruited by Primakov. Operating with the sole knowledge of his then Chief, Giles Cordingley, Marchant had proceeded to hand over high-grade American product to Primakov, none of which compromised Britain, in return for the continued flow of priceless Soviet intelligence.

Denton had been heavily involved with the running of Primakov, but he had not known that Marchant was effectively a Moscow asset. No one had, particularly not the Americans. To this day, Washington had no knowledge of Primakov, let alone the pact that Stephen Marchant had signed with him. Now, with Denton due to become Chief, or at least acting Chief, it would only be a matter of time before the Americans became convinced of what they had long suspected: that Britain could not be trusted as an ally. Denton would be sure to tell them about Primakov and the US intel, given that he owed his promotion to Spiro.

Fielding knew, as he started to spin the numbers on the heavily oiled wheel, that he had to move fast. The Americans wouldn't just point the finger – once again – at Stephen Marchant. They would accuse him of guilt by association: he should have informed them of what amounted to treachery by proxy when he had first become Chief. Daniel Marchant wouldn't come out of it well either.

'I'm afraid the combination's already been changed.'

Fielding paused for a moment and then stood up. Denton was inside the office, standing by the door. Anne had uncharacteristically failed to keep him at bay. Then another figure appeared beside Denton, and Fielding understood. It was a member of security, thick-necked, no smile. Had it really come to this?

'No problem,' Fielding said, clicking shut the plastic lid on the box. 'The contents of the safe are your responsibility now. To be honest, it's a relief to be free of the burden that comes with them.'

'If there's anything personal in there, I can have it sent round to Dolphin Square, with your other possessions,' Denton said, nodding at the box on the desk. 'I'm sure Anne will arrange it. Once it's been checked.'

For the first time, Fielding tried to look at Denton as a Moscow asset. If he was, he guessed it was a recent development – five years, at most – which made it marginally less unpalatable. If Denton had been working for Moscow during the 1980s and 1990s, Primakov would have been blown, given that Denton had helped to run him. But Primakov wasn't blown, nor was he used by Moscow to feed false information to London. The intelligence had always checked out.

'One word of advice, Ian,' Fielding said, walking to the door. 'Never ignore a gut feeling. If you find you don't like working with Spiro, there's probably a good reason.'

As Fielding passed through the door, Denton called out behind him.

'That Matt cartoon. I was looking forward to seeing more of it. I'll tell security it was yours, shall I?'

Fielding didn't answer. Anne had her eyes cast down as he passed. He wasn't sure if there weren't tears welling, too.

'Perhaps you could bring the box yourself,' he said quietly, pausing by her desk. 'Then we could say goodbye properly. Maybe share a pot of fresh mint tea, extra sweet, just how you like it.'

Before she could reply, he was gone, watched by cameras into the lift, and again as he crossed the foyer towards the row of security pods by the main entrance. He walked through one of them, conscious that the guards were keeping a closer eye on him than usual, and collected his company mobile phone on the other side. He was surprised that it hadn't been withheld. They would send for it shortly, like an ex asking for her CDs. But there was no official car to take him home. Instead, he turned right and headed over Vauxhall Bridge, knowing that he would have to move fast if he was to leave the country.

42

It was 10 a.m. by the time Marchant arrived back at Gosport Marina. He had hoped to be there earlier, but it had taken longer to buy the five pay-as-you-go phones, each one from a different shop so as to avoid suspicion. He had borrowed £500 from his old friend and received an assurance that Myers would keep him updated about any intel relating to Dhar and Iran's Revolutionary Guard. There was no one at GCHQ who knew the region better.

After leaving the Traveller parked on the road outside the marina, Marchant walked towards the grid of floating jetties, keeping an eye out for police. The older man had talked about having a lie-in after their long Channel crossing, but Marchant assumed that they would have raised the alarm about their missing car by now. As he approached the boat he spotted him in the cockpit, drinking from a Scottish mug. There was no sign of the younger man. Their bags were stacked up on the stern. It was clear that they hadn't been to their car or spotted Marchant.

Five minutes later, Marchant was back on the jetty, having returned the car to its original slot in the car park. The small brass ignition key was in his hand as he approached the boat for the second time.

'Just thought I'd come and say thanks for picking me up last night,' he said. 'And apologise for delaying you after such a long journey.'

'Not at all,' the older man said. 'Nice of you to come back. I would have been too embarrassed.'

'Can I help with your bags?' Marchant asked.

'You could if we knew where our car key was. We've looked everywhere for the damn thing, but it seems to have vanished. My son-in-law's walked into town to find a garage.'

'Let me have a look. I'm good at finding things.'

Marchant climbed aboard and went below decks. He soon found the key he was looking for, hanging from a hook by the ship-to-shore radio. But it wasn't for the Traveller, it was for the boat's diesel engine. He had remembered seeing it hanging from the fob when it was in the ignition the night before. Checking that the man wasn't looking, he slid it off and put it in his pocket, then pushed the car key down a slot beside the steps, where it could have fallen from the hook above.

'I think I've got it!' Marchant called up to the man.

'Have you really?'

'It's just a matter of retrieving it.'

The old man proved adept with a carving knife, and soon managed to slide the key out from the slot.

'I think we're quits now, don't you?' he said, a hand on Marchant's shoulder as they climbed back up into the cockpit.

'Are you off, then?' Marchant asked, trying not to sound as if he was hurrying him along.

'We've just got to take down the ensign, lock up and we're done. I'll call my son-in-law now. Tell him the good news.'

Marchant left him to it and retreated to the shower block, where he washed. He was confident that no one had followed him from Kemble to Cheltenham, or from Cheltenham to Portsmouth. As he splashed water on his unshaven face, he thought how tired he looked. It was twenty-four hours since he had slept. He would try to get some rest once he was on their boat and heading across the English Channel on autopilot.

First, though, he needed to find Lakshmi.

43

The two brothers didn't speak as they drove through the Pembrokeshire countryside. There was nothing more to say. They had sat together to watch the BBC news about Salim Dhar's capture, and before the bulletin had ended they were halfway to the lock-up where they kept the truck. It was also where they kept two hundred kilos of carefully dried ammonium nitrate, made from fertiliser bought at separate locations; one forty-litre barrel of liquid nitromethane, sourced from a drag-racing track; and ten kilos of Tovex Blastrite gel sausages used for avalanche clearing. To ensure a stronger blast, they had also stolen ten kilos of zinc dust.

It had taken five sweaty hours to mix the ingredients, which were divided between three barrels strapped to the floor of the van, and it was a relief when they were finally on the road out of Easton in Bristol and heading across the Severn Bridge to Wales. Like many others in Britain, the brothers had become followers of Dhar after he had come so close to assassinating the American President in India. His widespread appeal wasn't hard to explain, particularly now, after his spectacular attack on the Fairford Air Show.

They told themselves that Dhar wasn't like other *jihadis*. His targets were strategic, focused on halting American imperialism.

Politicians and the armed forces were fair game, instruments of Empire. Civilians were off limits. 7/7 had left both brothers uncomfortable. Britain had been craven in its support for the war in Iraq, but why kill commuters?

Up until Haverfordwest, they had stayed on the M4 and A roads. Now they were heading down a narrow lane, tensing every time the van drove over a bump in the uneven surface. An indigo sky spanned above them, a high summer sun beating down on the surrounding fields, but the world around them was no longer important.

'We should have got out of Bristol more,' the older brother said, looking ahead. 'It's beautiful here.'

'Beautiful,' his younger brother replied, his head turned away.

After passing through a hamlet called Tiers Cross, they knew they were only minutes from their target: an American-owned oil refinery in Milford Haven. They had staked it out in recent weeks, posing as trainspotters. Railway tracks ran along the eastern boundary, and some unusual shunting engines had proved a useful draw for enthusiasts. Their plan, though, had not required much reconnaissance. It relied more on God's will and the element of surprise.

They would approach the northern entrance to the refinery at speed, passing the staff car park on their right, and break through the temporary security barrier. An adjacent, more sophisticated carlock was currently under construction. If it had been finished, they had a problem. A row of eighteen oil storage tanks would be immediately ahead of them once they were through. It was just a matter of how far up the road they could get before being stopped. Ideally, they would be able to park up in a gap beyond the first twelve tanks, as there was a group of four bigger tanks on the opposite side of the road. Then, *Inshallah*, they would detonate their incendiary cargo.

As they passed through Robertson Cross, glancing nervously at the refinery now visible up ahead, they both said quiet prayers. The younger of the two, barely eighteen, noticed his brother's hands tighten on the steering wheel and felt sick. Without warning, he wound down the window and retched. Salim Dhar would approve of the target, he reminded himself, wiping the vomit from his mouth with the back of his hand. His upper body had begun to shake.

Oil went to the heart of the US's relations with its allies. And few innocent people would be killed. There was a small chance that the subsequent toxic aerosol cloud of hydrofluoric acid might inflict burns on the surrounding population, but that couldn't be helped. *Inshallah*, the attack, the first of many, would be a reminder to Britain that there was a price to pay if it continued to cooperate with America.

'It's OK,' the older brother said, pulling the van up beside a gate. They sat in silence for a few minutes, engine off. Cows grazed in the field next to them. 'Bro, take a look at the video again. It will remind you why we're doing this.'

After loading a video file, he passed his phone to his younger brother. They watched the footage for a few moments, occasionally checking the mirrors for traffic. The lane was deserted, the countryside hushed. The images were from a video that had been released by WikiLeaks three months earlier and widely circulated among jihadis. It showed two US Apache helicopters gunning down a group of people, including two Reuters journalists, in the Iraqi suburb of New Baghdad in July 2007. The footage included dialogue from the crews of both helicopters, each of which was armed with 30mm cannon.

The brothers watched, shaking their heads in disbelief as the helicopters circled the men in the street below, then started firing on them.

'Light 'em all up.'
'Come on, fire!'
'Keep shootn'.'

The helicopters continued to circle the scene. After eight men had been gunned down, the American crews made idle chatter.

'Hotel two six, Crazy Horse one eight.'
'Oh yeah, look at those dead bastards.'
'Nice.'
'Two six: Crazy Horse one eight.'
'Nice.'
'Good shootn'.'
'Thank you.'

'Now you understand why we are doing this,' the older brother said, putting the phone back in his pocket and turning the key in the ignition. 'Come, we must go.'

44

After filling up with diesel at the marina, Marchant steered the Seadog out past the MoD fuel jetty and into Portsmouth harbour's small boat channel. A yacht was approaching from the opposite direction. He was worried that someone might recognise him, but he made himself wave at the passing crew, who appeared to be in training. They waved back.

It was important to appear normal, just another boat out for a sail on a July afternoon in the Solent. In an attempt to disguise himself, he had put on a woolly bobble hat that was lying behind the wheel, pulling it down to just above his eyes. Although the sun was out, it was still cold on the water and a hat didn't look out of place.

On the far side of the harbour, warships old and new were moored up in the Royal Navy dockyard. The aircraft carrier HMS *Illustrious* was the biggest, overshadowing HMS *Cattistock*, a mine counter-measures vessel that was moored nearby. Marchant had been on board *Cattistock* once, when he was based at Fort Monckton. Its hull was made out of glassfibre-reinforced plastic to avoid setting off mines. Behind *Illustrious*, the sleek, angled lines of HMS *Daring*, a Type-45 destroyer, brought back less happy memories of the Indian coast, off Maharashtra, where he had been picked up by an American Littoral Combat Ship.

He told himself the Royal Navy wouldn't be searching for him, but the sight of an MoD Marine Police launch made his stomach tighten. It seemed to be patrolling the waters in front of *Illustrious*, a policeman standing in the stern with a Heckler & Koch MP7 submachine gun slung across his body.

Marchant tried to ignore the launch and focus on what lay ahead. He never liked attempting the same trick twice, but there was no other way of getting Lakshmi out of the Fort. She would have to swim, as he had. According to his watch, she should already have entered the water. By the time he was off the Fort's foreshore she would be at the yellow buoy, where he would lift her aboard.

The decision to take her with him had not been an easy one. His guard dropped in her presence, just as it had with Leila. But he wanted to trust her. Besides, he would need her help if Dhar was ever to escape. He would finally have to reveal that Dhar had agreed to work for MI6, but he could live with that. Her loyalty no longer lay with the CIA or Spiro, who wanted her behind bars. And her mind was open enough to understand the logic of turning Dhar rather than killing him. *We can't win by force alone. There are other ways of waging war on terror.*

He also missed her.

He went to the stern of the boat, leant over and checked that cooling water was coming out of the engine. Crossing the Channel in a 1970s yacht wasn't the quickest exit he would ever make, but it was the best option in the circumstances. He just hoped that his old friend Jean-Baptiste was enjoying his usual summer break from Paris on the Cotentin peninsula in Normandy. He would ring him once he was clear of the Isle of Wight.

Earlier he had called Lakshmi at the Fort. She had sounded pleased to hear from him. Almost too pleased. He guessed she was demob happy. No one had come looking for them, she had said, which was encouraging. Perhaps Fielding was still in play, and able to protect them. Either way, they couldn't afford to hang around. Spiro would be keen to tie off the whole operation, now Dhar had been caught. He wouldn't rest until they were both in the custody of the CIA.

As the boat motored up towards the rendezvous, Marchant's mood dipped. He glanced astern and saw a cross-Channel ferry bearing down on him, rising out of the water like a leviathan. It had been years since he had sailed on his own. He checked his watch again, pulled out one of the £10 phones and plugged in the hands-free that Myers had given him. After the phone had booted up he rang the guardhouse at the Fort, adopting what he hoped was a golf-club secretary's reedy tones.

'It's Stokes Bay Golf Club here. Thought you should know you've got some possible intruders trying to climb your perimeter fence down by the 9th hole. Unwashed peace protestors by the look of it.'

The public golf course was adjacent to the Fort's far perimeter fence, which had always struck Marchant as odd. A few yards from the fairway, young IONEC officers were being instructed in a very different kind of driving: how to negotiate roadblocks at speed. Slipping the phone overboard, he hoped his call might create enough of a diversion for Lakshmi's afternoon swim to go unnoticed.

45

'I think you should come over and read it for yourself,' Denton said, sitting at the desk that had been so recently vacated by Fielding. He had rung Spiro at the American Embassy, hoping to catch him before he left for Bagram.

'I'm kinda busy, Ian. Flying out in a couple of hours. Can't it wait till I get back?'

'I'm not sure if it can.'

There was a pause while Denton heard Spiro talking to someone in his office at the US Embassy. Denton sat forward and looked again at the sheet of A4 paper, which he had found in the safe as soon as Fielding had gone. He knew he must share it at once with the Americans. It would shore up his own position and weaken Fielding's.

'OK, I'll come around now. But I don't want to find myself locked out of Legoland again. Fielding's gone, I presume?'

'He's left. But you might want to talk to him when you've read this.'

Denton hung up, walked over to the door and asked Anne Norman if she could ring down for some tea.

'A mug, if possible. Tetley. Two bags, dash of milk.' Insipid Moroccan teas weren't for him. And if she was asking, he preferred the canteen's sausage sandwiches to halloumi. He knew Anne was upset about Fielding's departure, but the sooner she got over it, the better. He had work to do.

Back at his desk, Denton tried to clear some papers from his in-tray. Top of the pile was a memo from the station head in South Africa. According to reliable sources in Durban, Iran's Revolutionary Guard was attempting to ship a high-performance powerboat back to Bandar-Abbas under a Hong Kong-flagged merchant vessel called the *Amplify*. The DTI in London and the US Commerce Department's Bureau of Industry and Security were trying to block the export, suspecting the boat might be intended for military use.

Denton tried to focus on the memo, but Stephen Marchant's copperplate kept drawing his attention. What Marchant had written was shocking, rewriting a part of his life he had thought was immutable history. As a junior field officer in the SovBloc Controllerate, Denton had worked closely with Marchant on Primakov. He had never liked the Russian, who had made it clear he preferred dealing with the more cultured Marchant. When they did talk, he was always asking for a new life in the West, 'somewhere civilised like Oxford'. Denton was tempted to exfiltrate him to Marfleet, the deprived ward in Hull where he had been born, but his brief was to fob him off with MI6's grubby money. Eventually he was moved to another job.

It had never once occurred to him that Stephen Marchant was handing over American product in return for Primakov's. Why would it? Marchant had been more dedicated to the Service than anyone he'd ever met, a Chief-in-waiting from the moment he had joined.

He sat back and looked around Fielding's office, now his own, taking in the view of the Thames. A solitary maroon canal boat was heading down towards Westminster. It reminded him that he hadn't been on his own boat, moored near Oxford, since Easter. He would get down there even less now, but it was a small price to pay for a job he had never thought would be his. Those who said modern Britain was classless had never worked for MI6. Despite endless protests to the contrary, the Service had always been the preserve of the privileged, a public-school club without the tie.

He was beginning to flick through some images of alleged torture in Bagram, the subject of an internal investigation he was overseeing, when an MI5 alert flashed up on his main computer terminal. A terrorist attack had just taken place at Milford Haven oil refinery. Moments later, his comms console lit up and Anne put her head around the door.

'Harriet Armstrong on priority line one,' she said.

'Put her through.' Denton had little time for the Director General of MI5. She had been too close to Fielding, head girl to his head boy.

'I'll keep this quick, as I'm about to brief the PM,' Armstrong began. Denton could hear the tension in her educated voice.

'Are we sure it's hostile?' he asked, already thinking through the implications for his own Service. He hoped the perpetrators were homegrown, her problem. 'Wasn't there a fire at Milford Haven last year?'

'This was a five-hundred-pound truck bomb, Ian. Look, I've got to go, but clearly I'm going to need all the help you can give me on this one. I hope things won't change just because Marcus has gone.'

'I know he was very supportive, as I will be,' Denton said, looking at the images of Bagram again. He turned one photograph on its side and peered closer at the shackled victim. His arms had been tied behind his back to his ankles, and he was hanging from a beam like a trussed-up fly.

'Thank you,' Armstrong said. 'By the way, it's an American-owned refinery. You might want to keep out of Spiro's way.'

46

Marchant stared out into the thick fog, wondering if his boat was about to be mown down by a supertanker. The brutal sound of a ship's horn had woken him from a restless sleep in the corner of the cockpit. Lakshmi was below. She was in a bad way, still recovering from her cold swim out to the buoy.

He couldn't see anything on either bow, but he thought he could hear the sound of distant propellers above his boat's diesel engine. Perhaps he was imagining it. But just as he began to relax, a deafening foghorn sounded again, closer this time. Christ, where was it? He must be crossing the shipping lanes. All he needed was a supertanker on autopilot, steaming through the Channel at 15 knots, crew asleep, bridge deserted.

He went down to the cabin, glancing at Lakshmi, who was shivering feverishly, barely conscious. She would need medical attention when they reached France, which would complicate matters. He had rung Jean-Baptiste, who was expecting him, but hadn't had time to explain about Lakshmi. He turned on the VHF radio, tuning in to Channel 16 in case the tanker was trying to communicate. Silence. Beside him, Lakshmi moaned, her eyes still shut. They hadn't looked right, the pupils dilated, when he had pulled her into the boat. He knew she was on medication for her arm. Had she accidentally overdosed? Had someone drugged her?

The foghorn sounded again. He considered letting off a distress flare, but the last thing he wanted was to attract the attention of the Coastguard. A Search and Rescue helicopter would be sent out to investigate, and he would be back in England before he had even left it.

Back in the cockpit, Marchant peered over the side and listened again, hoping the fog would clear. Then he heard the horn sounding for a third time, more distant now. Wherever it was, it had passed him. He checked the autopilot bearing and sat down, pulling the bobble hat over his eyes.

His tired mind turned to Salim Dhar, and how he had managed to get himself to Tarlton on a Search and Rescue helicopter. He would already be in Bagram. There was something about Dhar's resigned manner that hadn't added up, even taking into account the unfamiliar consumption of vodka and whisky. It was as if he knew he had to be captured if he were ever to be free again.

Marchant had heard about the jailbreak in 2005 that Dhar had mentioned. It was the only time anyone had ever managed to escape from Bagram. Various conspiracy theorists had pointed the finger at the CIA. Had a deal been done – four prisoners allowed to escape in return for four captured US soldiers? Had one of the prisoners, whose name was initially covered up, been a long-term CIA agent? Or were they 'released' so they could be killed, given that one of them was due to testify in America against a prison guard accused of torture?

Just as he was beginning to fall asleep, Marchant heard something else – this time it was the sound of a loudhailer. He thought he was hallucinating. Perhaps there had been no foghorn, and there was no one hailing him now. But there was, and the voice was getting louder.

47

A few minutes after the fireball had risen more than three hundred feet into the Welsh sky, a man walked briskly down the high-hedged lane in the far west of Cornwall. He was carrying a large, steel-lined briefcase. There weren't many visitors to Skewjack, two miles from Land's End, just the small team who worked at the cable station, which he was now approaching.

It was here that 'FA-1' and other crucial submarine fibre-optic cables linking America with Britain terminated after reaching land at nearby Porthcurno and Sennen. There were similar sites at Bude and Southport, but the man liked to think he had been assigned the most important. For it was at Porthcurno that one of the world's first submarine telegraph cables had made landfall in 1870, linking Britain to Portugal and later to India.

He should have arrived an hour ago, but he had been held up by traffic on the drive down from Truro. For a moment he feared he might be too late. The award-winning building, with its low curved-steel roof that barely troubled the countryside, would be surrounded by armed guards. But as he turned into the entrance, heart racing, he was relieved to see that security appeared to be as low-key as ever: CCTV cameras and a secure main entrance.

It had taken a few months to be recruited by the firm that carried out maintenance at the site, but he had more than enough

IT qualifications, and the call eventually came through. He was also from Bangalore, which he liked to think had helped his application: the company that owned the cable was Indian. The positive-vetting process was thorough, but nobody discovered his 'missing month' after he had left Bangalore University with a degree in computer science engineering. It was then that he had met Salim Dhar in a Kashmir training camp, offered up his considerable IT skills to the cause and been instructed to lie low as a sleeper in Britain until he was needed.

He had been on two maintenance visits to Skewjack before, once with his predecessor, and once on his own. The staff were always friendly to him, and today was no exception.

'Oh, hi, Pradeep. Thought you'd forgotten us,' Vicky said, getting up unnecessarily from her desk. She was the youngest – and prettiest – member of staff. Last time she had flirted shamelessly with him, and she seemed happy to pick up where she had left off. Perhaps they didn't get many visitors this far west.

'How could I forget you, Vicky?' Pradeep said, managing a shy smile. He was content to play along with the charade, as it allowed him to confirm her mobile phone number. He would need it later.

'Text me, promise?' she said, after they had exchanged details. 'Sometimes I make it up country, even as far as the bright lights of Truro.'

'Sure,' he said. In the interests of cover, he had texted her following his last visit: one message, rich in sexual innuendo. The next would be blunter.

After turning down an offer of tea, explaining that he was running late, he left the staff in the open-plan office to carry out what they assumed was routine maintenance in the main termination hall. It was here that the three-inch-thick FA-1 submarine cables – part of a £1 billion 'figure of eight' fibre-optic loop with Long Island in America and Brittany in France – connected with

Britain's landline infrastructure. There was also a connection to 'FEA', a fibre-optic cable that linked in thirteen countries from Britain across Europe to Japan. As the site's manager liked to remind him, the capacity of its cables made Skewjack one of the largest-bandwidth communications stations in the world.

Twenty minutes later he had placed eight packs of PE4 plastic explosive as close to the cable housings as possible, linked to a phone-operated detonator. The blast would be enough to penetrate the steel wires, aluminium, copper and polycarbonate that protected the fibre-optics. He then said his goodbyes, unable to muster the smile he had arrived with, and walked back to his car. He had left it down the road to avoid the CCTV cameras.

Sitting in the driving seat, engine running, he pulled out an unused pay-as-you-go phone from the glovebox and texted Vicky, his fingers shaking. 'This is a bomb warning. Your building is rigged with explosives. Not an exercise.'

Then he drove off towards Sennen as fast as he could. He would give them two minutes.

48

Images of the burning oil refinery were showing on the main screen in Denton's office as he tried to tell James Spiro about the document he had found in his safe. Denton was at his desk, the photographs of torture in Guantánamo stacked neatly to one side. Spiro was pacing around.

'This better be good, Ian. I've got Washington screaming down my neck telling us to pull out of this goddamn country altogether. Do we have to provide the security for your oil refineries too?'

'I wish I could say it's an isolated incident, but I fear it won't be. The Salim Dhar backlash has begun.'

Denton also had people giving him grief. MI5, GCHQ and the Prime Minister all wanted answers about the terrorist attack, but his priority was to get the contents of Fielding's safe into the open as soon as possible.

'So what have you got?' Spiro said as he sat down on the sofa, glancing at the TV screen. A few seconds later he was up on his feet again, pacing the room.

'I found a document – more of a confession – written by Stephen Marchant.'

Spiro looked across at him, his interest piqued.

'Fielding ran a Russian agent in the 1980s and 1990s,' Denton continued. 'Someone very high up in the KGB and later in the SVR.'

'Does he have a name?'

'Nikolai Primakov.'

'He was one of yours? What the hell was he doing trying to recruit Daniel Marchant?'

'I wish I knew. My predecessor kept the details of Daniel Marchant's activities very much to himself. Need-to-know.'

'You were his deputy, for Chrissake.'

Spiro had an uncanny habit of hitting raw nerves, Denton thought. Perhaps that's why he had excelled at enhanced interrogation techniques.

'What I do know is that the Russians were shielding Dhar,' Denton said. 'The only way we could get to him was by convincing Moscow that Daniel Marchant wanted to defect.'

'They can have him.'

'Primakov was the middle man. Unfortunately, it still doesn't explain why Marchant didn't eliminate Dhar when he was brought to him.'

'Too damn right. And it doesn't explain why he then got on a plane with him and starting bombing the crap out of GCHQ either. And that was after he'd shot down one of our Raptors.'

'I think this document might help.'

Denton got up from his chair, walked around his desk and handed the sheet of paper to Spiro.

'I'll need it back. For safekeeping.'

Spiro sat back down on the sofa, falling unusually quiet as he began to read.

'So, we were right all along,' he eventually said. 'Stephen Marchant, Chief of MI6, was handing over US-frickin' intel to Moscow. And we officially pardoned the guy, wrote our suspicions out of the history books. They'll need rewriting now.'

'It would seem so,' Denton said, taking back the sheet.

'It kinda makes sense, though, when you think about it. I mean, look at his two sons: Daniel Marchant, the most treacherous officer ever to be employed by MI6 – and that's saying something – and Salim Dhar. You couldn't make it up.' He paused, glancing again at the screen. 'I wish someone'd put that fire out.'

As they sat in silence, Denton almost felt pity for Spiro. Some difficult conversations with Washington lay ahead of him. There was also the issue of Spiro's wife, Linda, who had gone missing. Denton had never met her, but by all accounts she was a bit of a livewire who was currently having a mid-life crisis. Spiro had confided in him earlier. It had been a surprise to learn that they were still married. Denton had always thought Spiro was divorced, like him and practically every other intelligence officer he knew.

'What gets me,' Spiro said after a while, in a tone close to sober reflection, 'is that Fielding defended Stephen Marchant last year, when we were throwing the book at the whole family, accusing the father, the son, of treachery. And there he was, knowing full well that Stephen Marchant had been a goddamn traitor all along. It's institutional treason, that's what this is, Ian. Where does this leave Fielding?'

'In Moscow, as it happens. I just took a call from our station chief. Fielding arrived at Domodedovo airport on the 5 o'clock flight from Heathrow.'

49

'You are entering a restricted military area. Please alter course now.'

The fog was thick and swirling. Marchant still couldn't tell where the loudhailer was coming from, even though it had repeated its message several times.

'I hear you, but I cannot see you!' he called out, cupping his hands.

Then he saw it, a black rigid inflatable, approaching fast from the port bow. Two men in naval uniforms were on board, one of them waving at him to turn to starboard as he repeated his message over the loudhailer.

Marchant flicked off the autopilot and spun the wheel sharply to the right. There was no reason for them to suspect he was in a stolen boat, or on the run. He just had to do what they said and they would leave him alone.

'Sorry, I couldn't see you in all this fog,' he said as the inflatable came alongside.

'Forty-five degrees to starboard and you'll be fine,' the man replied. Marchant knew immediately that everything was going to be OK. There was no menace in the man's voice, he was just doing his job.

'Nothing about restricted areas on my chart,' Marchant said, making a bit of a fuss. He was a proud sailor, he told himself.

'It's a routine naval exercise,' the man said. 'Keep on this bearing for ten minutes and then you can revert to your original course.'

Marchant was desperate to know more, but he resisted probing further. As the inflatable bore away to port and disappeared back into the fog, he wondered what sort of exercise it was. In his first month at Fort Monckton, he and the other new recruits had been taken out into the Channel to watch the SBS seizing control of a suicide container ship, packed full of explosives and 'Hazard A' cargo. Such exercises were becoming more common as the Olympics loomed on the horizon.

He turned on the ship's radio to see if anyone was transmitting, but there was silence. Next, he scanned the airwaves on the ordinary radio until he caught the faint sound of a news bulletin. His hand froze on the dial as he listened to the newsreader:

'The Home Secretary has confirmed that the police and security services are treating the explosion at a Milford Haven oil refinery as an act of terrorism. She joined the American owners of the plant in condemning the attack. There is no information yet on the number of casualties, but police fear a cloud of toxic gas could spread over the surrounding area. The town of Milford Haven has been evacuated as a precaution while firefighters continue to tackle the blaze.'

So Dhar had been as good as his word. Marchant didn't like the thought of Britain under attack. It was a personal affront. He had felt the same after 7/7, an acute mix of anger and failure. Fielding had once told him that success in the intelligence services was like anti-matter. It could only be measured by what hadn't happened. Failure was solid, tangible, there for all to see.

As soon as he was close enough to France to get a signal, he would ring Myers, find out if he had heard anything coming out of Iran. *If you will not help with my escape, I cannot guarantee Britain's safety.* He was still at a loss to think how he or anyone else in the UK might help to get Dhar out of Bagram, but there might be a way to take some of the credit if the Iranians were successful. Somehow, he had to stop Britain from burning.

50

'I want this to go out to all station chiefs,' Denton said, standing beside Anne Norman's desk. 'Immediately.'

Anne still took dictation in shorthand, proudly, even though it added to the amount of paperwork that needed shredding each day. She picked up her pen and pad, crossed her red tights, and started to write as Denton talked.

'Marcus Fielding stood down from his duties as Chief of MI6 earlier today. The decision was taken by the Foreign Secretary in the light of the attacks on the Fairford Air Show and GCHQ and the role played in them by a serving MI6 officer, Daniel Marchant. For reasons not yet known, Fielding left Britain for Moscow earlier today and was seen arriving at Domodedovo airport at 1700 hrs GMT.'

Anne paused, her hand hovering above the paper. There had been many difficult moments during her twenty-five-year career, which had spanned five Chiefs if she included Denton, which she didn't. Booking her old boss onto a military flight on 12 September 2001 from Brize Norton to Andrews Air Force base had not been easy. It wasn't the logistics, although ATC Brize Norton initially refused to clear the flight. It was the fear that she might never see Marcus Fielding again. Taking Denton's letter was proving harder. Fielding had been good to her, better than any of them. But now he had fled to Moscow, which could mean only one thing. She bit her lip and continued to write:

'Interpol has been informed, and an international warrant for Fielding's arrest has been issued. If any officer identifies him, he should report his location at once to London station and await further instructions. Interpol has also issued a warrant for the arrest of Daniel Marchant, whose location is unknown. His high-threat status remains unchanged, both here and in the US.'

51

Jean-Baptiste was waiting on the quay at the French fishing village of Portbail, standing beside an orange Citroën Mehari, the car he kept at his mother's nearby château for ferrying guests around. It was a plastic jeeplike vehicle used by the French army, who valued its agility, and was powered by the same 600cc engine found in 2CVs. Marchant had been taken for many bumpy rides through the sand dunes in it over the years. He was amazed the car was still in one piece. Jean-Baptiste wouldn't hear a word said against it.

'Ah, *la voiture en plastique,*' Marchant said as he stepped ashore. It was nighttime, but the moon was full, which had made the Channel crossing easier.

'*Bien sûr,*' Jean-Baptiste replied, hugging his old friend. 'You've put on weight.'

'And you're still ugly.' Marchant knew that nothing could be further from the truth. Jean-Baptiste always seemed unaware of how attractive he was to women, and he looked even more stylish than usual in his polo shirt and three-quarter-length shorts as he took a rope from the yacht's bow.

He was tall, big-framed, and at first glance appeared clumsy, but he had better hand–eye coordination than anyone Marchant knew. He lived a sophisticated life in Paris, but he had been brought up rooted in the *terroir* of the Ardèche, and had an earthy assurance about him, one reason why he was such an effective field agent. He could blend into any environment, adopt any cover with ease. And like every self-respecting Frenchman Marchant knew, he preferred his steak *saignant*, drank wine from Madiran and read Carl Sagan.

'Do you have any bags?' Jean-Baptiste asked after the boat had been made secure. Marchant had picked up from the owner that it was a twin-keel, which made things easier. The small, sheltered port of Portbail became a muddy sandpit at low tide, and the boat would have tipped over if it had been single-keel.

'No bags, but I have a passenger.'

'Are you serious?'

'There was no time to tell you. Sorry. My credit ran out.' Marchant could have called back on another of his pay-as-you-go phones when he had rung earlier, but he hadn't.

'You sounded different on the phone. Your voice. Like –'

'Darth Vader?'

'Him, yes.'

'Must have been bad reception.' Marchant would talk to Myers later about his voice modulator.

'Where is he?' Jean-Baptiste asked. 'Your stowaway.'

'It's a she.'

Jean-Baptiste gave him a mischievous smile. Marchant wished it was that simple.

'And she's not well. I couldn't leave her behind.'

'Does she have a name?'

'Lakshmi,' Marchant said, speaking quietly, keeping an eye on the boat. Last time he checked, she was in a deep sleep, but he didn't want her to appear while they were talking.

'The Hindu goddess of wealth. What's wrong with her?'

'I'm not sure. She works for the Agency. At least she did. She's in trouble with Langley for helping me. She took a Russian bullet in the arm on my behalf. I owe her one.'

'She'd better come with us then. Let Clémence take a look at her.'

Marchant could feel Jean-Baptiste's bonhomie slipping away. He should have warned him about Lakshmi. He was already asking a lot of his old friend. Now he was involving his wife, Clémence, too. She was a doctor with Médecins sans Frontières.

Two minutes later, Marchant stood in the cockpit of the boat with Lakshmi draped in his arms. She was still asleep, wearing an ill-fitting woollen jumper and yellow oilskin trousers. He was aware that it wasn't a good look, but it had been all he could find after pulling her out of the water.

'Can you take her?' Marchant said, checking that nobody was about as he stepped up onto the deck. The quay was deserted, except for two locals fishing off the end of the harbour wall. They had their backs to them and seemed preoccupied.

Jean-Baptiste lifted Lakshmi into his arms and carried her to the Mehari, where he laid her in the back, making a pillow for her out of an old jacket.

'She doesn't look well, Dan,' he said. 'Is that where she was shot?' he continued, gesturing at her wrist. Marchant nodded. He didn't enjoy seeing Lakshmi lying in the back of a plastic car, looking like death and wearing ridiculous clothing. And standing over her felt like an invasion. Perhaps he should have left her at the Fort, where she might have been safer.

'She doesn't normally dress like that. Her clothes got wet.' Marchant had put her jeans and top in a plastic bag, which he raised in explanation. But he knew he owed his old friend more.

They climbed into the front of the car, neither of them saying anything. For a few seconds they sat in silence in the darkness before Jean-Baptiste started up the engine, turned on the lights and accelerated away. The '*voiture en plastique*' was just as Marchant remembered it. The suspension was shot and the seats were threadbare. And there was no room for his long legs, which he had to turn to one side. None of this worried Jean-Baptiste as he drove down la route de la Plage towards the Atlantic, hunched over the wheel as if he was driving a Dodgem.

Marchant had to hold onto the roof bar on the first right-hand corner, which brought them parallel with the sea. After a few hundred yards, the road, now rue Rozé, turned back inland, but Jean-Baptiste drove straight on, taking a sandy track that ran along the top of the beach.

Marchant began to relax, breathing in the sea breeze. The fog of the Channel seemed a distant memory. The stars were as bright as scattered diamonds in the clear night sky.

'Was the harbourmaster happy?' he asked.

'No, but I've sorted it.'

'Thank you.' When Marchant had rung Jean-Baptiste, as he was passing the Needles, he had explained that he was in a tight spot with the Americans and needed some assistance. His most immediate problem was that he didn't have a passport, which might have caused difficulties when he arrived at Portbail. (Lakshmi had swum out to the boat with two passports and her phone, sealed in a plastic bag. The passports had survived, but the phone had died.)

Jean-Baptiste was well placed to help, and hadn't asked any questions. The Americans weren't his favourite allies in the war on terror. After a brief spell with the Commandos Marine, the French Navy's special forces, he had joined the Direction Générale de la Sécurité Extérieure (DGSE), France's MI6 counterpart. They had met when Jean-Baptiste was a liaison officer in London, hitting it off after they discovered a shared ambivalence towards authority and a taste for Bruichladdich whisky. Jean-Baptiste was also indebted to him after he had botched an operation to burgle the London offices of China Eastern Airlines. Marchant had assisted with the subsequent cover-up.

'We won't stay for long,' Marchant said as they continued along the edge of the sand. 'I just need somewhere to work out what I'm going to do.'

Jean-Baptiste shrugged. 'You can stay as long as you want. We're here for the summer.'

'How's Clémence?' Marchant had flown back from Morocco at the end of the previous year for their wedding outside Versailles. He had never been to such a stylish event, although the evening was a bit of a blur. Clémence had a younger sister.

'Working too hard. It's the first time she's taken a holiday this year. Travel, travel, travel.'

And now she would be asked to take care of Lakshmi, Marchant thought.

'I guess you heard about Salim Dhar's arrest,' he said.

'I may be on holiday in the sand dunes, but I'm not an ostrich, Dan. Of course I heard. But that's old news now. Did the radio on your boat not work?'

'You mean the oil refinery attack.'

'And the ones in Cornwall.'

'No?' Marchant could feel his stomach tightening.

'Britain is no longer linked to America by fibre-optic cable. The special bond has been broken. Explosions have been reported at various sites on your west coast. All of them are where these cables reach land.'

Dhar had always been precise in his targeting. Now, it seemed, his followers had struck at the heart of Britain's relationship with America, severing its umbilical cord. He felt another sharp pang of patriotism. His country was under attack, and it was within his power to protect it. *Only my freedom will bring you peace.*

162

'I thought that's why you left Britain,' Jean-Baptiste joked. 'You're better off here in France.'

Marchant returned his friend's smile. They were happy to be in each other's company. For a moment, Marchant forgot about Lakshmi lying in the back. Then she groaned and he turned to check on her, making sure her head wasn't knocking against anything as they bumped along the dusty track.

'She's asleep again,' he said, but Jean-Baptiste's mind seemed to be on other things.

'Was it really you in the Russian jet with Dhar?' he asked.

Marchant didn't say anything. News of the attack had gone around the world, but he had hoped that his own role in it was known only to Britain and America's intelligence agencies. But Jean-Baptiste had always been well-connected.

'I won't ask what you were doing,' he continued. 'I will just assume that it is why you are now on the run in France without a passport.'

Marchant paused before he spoke. 'I was trying to turn him.'

Jean-Baptiste seemed to think about this for a moment. Usually they avoided speaking about their work, unless they had to, but Marchant had just broken the rule. It was the least he could do in the circumstances. There was a limit to how much he could take without giving something in return. Jean-Baptiste wouldn't buy a cover story.

'Ambitious,' he said.

'And I got burnt. The only person who knew about the operation was Marcus Fielding, who I doubt will be Chief of MI6 for much longer.'

'I heard that too.'

'It's official?'

'Not yet.'

'Christ. I'm in a bigger mess than I thought.'

'So they caught Dhar, and now they want to catch you, thinking that you were working with him when in fact you were trying to turn him.'

'That's about it.'

'Why has Fielding left?'

'The Americans must have forced him out. It was hard for him to explain what one of his officers was doing with Salim Dhar in a Russian jet.'

'That is a tricky one,' Jean-Baptiste said, laughing.

Marchant was grateful that Jean-Baptiste wouldn't ask any more questions, even though his own explanation was inadequate. That was the nature of their friendship. But he was surprised that Jean-Baptiste's smile fell away so quickly.

'Are you sure nobody followed you across the Channel?' he asked, glancing in the rear-view mirror. Marchant knew better than to look around. They had left the beach and were now driving inland on a main road.

'I'm sure.'

'There's a car that's been behind us since Barneville-Carteret. If it follows us at the next turning, we've got company. The road only leads to our house, and we're not expecting guests.'

Marchant tried to think who might have tracked him across the Channel. Denton and Spiro were the people who most wanted to find him, and they both had assets that could be mobilised in France. He was confident that no one had seen him board the boat at Gosport. There was a possibility that the NSA or GCHQ had listened in to his phone call to Jean-Baptiste, but they would have to have been monitoring Jean-Baptiste's number, which was unlikely. The French were very protective of their agents, particularly against the prying eyes and ears of America.

'Hold on,' Jean-Baptiste said as he stepped on the accelerator. The fiberglass frame of the Mehari shook as he took the speed up to 110kph. He kept the needle there along the long straight road, braking slightly as it curved to the right. After the bend, he braked sharply and turned off to the left through two stone posts and down what Marchant remembered was the final approach to his family château. But instead of proceeding along the tree-lined avenue, Jean-Baptiste parked up, jumped out and swung a high wooden gate shut. The car behind would have not seen them turning off.

'Let's see who it was,' Jean-Baptiste said, looking through a crack in the gate. They both stood there like naughty kids, listening as the vehicle approached. It was a black people-carrier. The windows were dark but partially lowered in the front. As it passed, Marchant caught a glimpse of the driver, who was looking straight ahead.

'Friend of yours?'

Marchant closed his eyes. 'No.' He couldn't be certain, but the figure at the wheel looked like an SVR officer called Valentin. If the Russians knew he was in France, he had a problem.

52

Harriet Armstrong looked around the COBRA table and wished Marcus Fielding was there. She had not always seen eye to eye with him, but his erudite presence was comforting in times of emergency. She didn't want to dwell on where he was. It made no sense for Fielding to have gone to Russia. All she knew was that he hadn't fled as a traitor. It wasn't possible, not Fielding. She put the thought out of her mind as she turned to the assembled politicians, military chiefs and intelligence officers. There was only one other woman in the room, the Home Secretary, but they had yet to bond. Perhaps the crisis now engulfing Britain would bring them closer.

'According to the latest intel, terrorist strikes have been confirmed at the following targets,' she began. 'Satellite teleport comms hubs at Goonhilly, Cornwall; Madley in Herefordshire; and Martlesham in Ipswich. They have also taken out submarine cable termination stations at Skewjack and Bude, disabling the FA-1, Apollo, TAT-14 and AC-2 fibre-optic cables, as well as the Tyco transatlantic cable that comes ashore at Highbridge in Somerset. And the US Murco terminal at Milford Haven has been destroyed. Casualties have – thankfully – been minimal, but I hardly need point out the strategic nature of these targets. They are all central to our relationship with America.'

'And we're absolutely certain that this is a response to the capture of Salim Dhar?' the Prime Minister asked.

'I would say they're more a response to his being handed over to the US.' Fielding would have said the same if he had been here, Armstrong thought. She owed it to him. Like him, she had long argued that Britain's support for America, most notably during the Gulf War, was a significant factor in the rise of homegrown terrorism.

'Either way, these are not impulsive attacks,' the PM continued, ignoring her jibe. 'They must have been months in the planning.'

'Without a doubt,' Armstrong replied. 'And they all bear the hallmarks of Dhar. It's as if his arrest was a trigger for his followers to carry out a series of pre-planned attacks.'

The director of GCHQ took up her point. 'Dhar certainly has a considerable following in the UK. We can see that from the online chatroom activity. And they know what he likes: surgical strikes against US military and political targets. What we can't be sure about is whether Dhar authorised them.'

'Right now, I just need to know if this is the beginning,' the PM said. 'The markets are in turmoil, the recession's deepening. The British public doesn't have the stomach for a summer of terror.'

'We're assuming this is phase one,' Armstrong said.

'Are the Americans sharing intel?' the PM asked. His face had the look of a man who already knew the answer.

'Not with us,' Armstrong said. 'They're following "their own lines of inquiry".'

The PM turned towards the director of GCHQ.

'Cooperation is not a word I'd use to describe the present situation,' he said. 'The NSA isn't pooling anything.'

'We've increased security at all critical national infrastructure targets,' Armstrong said, hoping to lift the mood.

'What about Daniel Marchant?' the PM asked, turning to Ian Denton. 'Is there any news on him?'

'None, I'm afraid.' Denton was in quiet mode, Armstrong thought. The restrained tones of newly acquired power.

'Washington might start talking to us again if we could hand him over too,' the Foreign Secretary said.

'I'm aware of that,' Denton said. 'And we're doing all we can to find him. Jim Spiro is at least still on speaking terms, and I'm working closely with him to locate Marchant.'

Of course he was, Armstrong thought. Denton owed his promotion to Spiro. She was not surprised by his sudden change of attitude towards Washington. She had always thought of him as a chameleon. Now he found himself the sole beneficiary of a rapidly deteriorating relationship with America, much to the chagrin of everyone else. The Foreign Secretary and the PM had both had their arms twisted over the promotion of Denton. At least they had stood up to the bullying sufficiently to insist he was made only acting Chief.

'I thought Fort Monckton was a secure site,' the PM said tersely. He was not good at disguising his feelings, Armstrong thought. MI6 had already caused him enough trouble, what with Fielding's apparent defection and Marchant on the run. But Denton, America's anointed one, had suddenly become one of the most powerful people in the room.

'It is,' Denton said. 'But it was designed to stop people getting in, not escaping.'

'Can we rule him out?'

'In what sense?'

'Can we be certain that Daniel Marchant played no part in these bombings? I mean, given he was in the SU-25 with Dhar.'

Denton hesitated for a moment, knowing that all eyes were on him. He's enjoying this, Armstrong thought.

'I'm afraid you'll have to ask Fielding that. But as he's in Russia, we can only guess.' He paused again. Fielding's apparent defection was next on COBRA's crisis agenda, but it seemed that Denton wished to bury him now. 'If you want my honest answer, I think Marchant's involved in some way with these attacks. And if Marchant is involved, we must assume Fielding is too.'

53

Marcus Fielding wasn't initially aware that Denton had placed him in Moscow, but he knew his deputy would make the most of his disappearance. As it happened, Denton wasn't far wrong. Fielding had left the country, but he wasn't in Russia. He was in Warsaw, sitting in the office of Brigadier Borowski, head of Agencja Wywiadu, Poland's foreign intelligence agency. Both men were drinking whisky.

After leaving Legoland for what he believed was the last time, Fielding had taken a taxi to Victoria Station, where he kept a passport, money and a suitcase with two changes of clothes in a left-luggage locker. To return to his flat in Dolphin Square would have been too risky. He knew his number would be up the moment Denton opened the safe and saw the handwritten report by Stephen Marchant. Denton would go straight to the Americans, who would take the letter as evidence of what they had always suspected: MI6 was a hotbed of traitors. Stephen Marchant would be found guilty posthumously and Fielding branded a traitor by association.

So he had embarked on an emergency cover that he had never dreamed would be necessary. Placing his plastic box of office possessions in the station locker, he had taken the suitcase down to the men's cloakrooms beside Platform 1, where he changed into different clothes: affluent New England slacks, open-necked shirt. His spare passport was American, drawn up for him by Langley in happier times, in the name of a tourist from Boston who was visiting Europe in his early retirement. The cover story had been compiled a while ago, and Fielding reread the two-sheet legend before emerging from the cloakrooms as Ted Soderling.

After doubling back a couple of times on his way out of the station, he was satisfied that no one was following him. He bought a ticket for the Gatwick Express, then purchased a cheap pay-as-you-go phone with cash, using the transaction to polish up his New England accent. Although the circumstances were depressing, it felt good to be in the field again, and he had boarded his train with a copy of the *International Herald Tribune* under one arm and a spring in his step.

'We are still very sorry about what happened,' Borowski said, splashing more whisky into their glasses. It was unlike Fielding to drink, but these were unusual times. 'All of us.'

'Of course.' Fielding knew the air would have to be cleared before he could start asking favours. His oldest friend and colleague, Hugo Prentice, had been killed in London on the orders of one of Brigadier Borowski's agents, Monika, because it was believed that Prentice was a Russian asset. A ring of Polish AW officers had been blown, including Monika's brother. All of them were shot dead by the FSB, Russia's domestic intelligence agency, having apparently been tipped off by Prentice.

'Monika was acting alone,' Borowski continued. 'She was very close to her brother. It clouded her judgement.'

'I just want to assure myself that it really was Prentice,' Fielding said. 'He was a good friend. That's why I'm here.'

'Officially?' Borowski asked, trying to be delicate. It didn't suit him. He was a big walrus of a man, who reminded Fielding of Lech Wałęsa, the former Polish president.

'I don't know how much you've heard, but officially I'm on sick leave. My deputy, Ian Denton, is currently acting Chief.'

'And he's just issued a warrant for your arrest,' Borowski said, indicating a sheet of paper on his desk. 'Which I'm ignoring, of course.'

'Thank you.' Denton was more of a bastard than he thought. Now he must prove that he was a traitor too. 'I need to talk to Monika.'

'She's not well.'

Fielding had allowed Monika to return to Poland, despite the ongoing police investigation into Prentice's death. He was aware that she had hired a Turkish gang in north London to kill Prentice, but she had covered her tracks well. Nobody would ever be allowed to link Prentice's death with a Polish intelligence officer, something for which Borowski was particularly grateful.

'Can we go over the evidence one more time?' Fielding asked. 'What made Monika so sure it was Prentice?'

'Me, unfortunately. I had no idea she would react in the regrettable way she did. Her instructions were to prepare a case. I would then have brought the evidence to you.'

'So what convinced you?'

Borowski lit a cigarette, tilted his head back and exhaled, the smoke rising to the low ceiling, where it spread out as if in search of something – the truth perhaps.

'Nine months ago, we lost an asset in Moscow. He was an illegal, had been living there for ten years. One of our best. He was shot – the police blamed local gangs and an argument over money. Then we lost two more in quick succession. Both were illegals and part of the same ring. In Russia, we have always operated better without embassy cover. One was in Moscow, the other in Sochi.

'The coincidence was too much. We must have had a mole

in AW. When we lost the last two in the ring, we feared for our entire illegals programme. We worked all our Russian assets, pumping them for anything they had. One of them, a junior officer with the FSB, came back with a name. He said the FSB was being fed the identities of our illegals in Russia by an MI6 agent based at the British Embassy here in Warsaw.'

'Hugo Prentice.'

'Correct. I passed this on to Monika, to help her build the case. Bravely, she'd begun sleeping with Prentice, hoping to find out more. When they were in London together I sent her a message, telling her that a second FSB asset had come forward with Prentice's name. I wanted her to know she was on the right track. Her cover was not an easy one for a young woman, pretending to love a man who might be responsible for her brother's death.'

'But how would Prentice have known the identities of your illegals?'

'He had been stationed here for two years. MI6 and AW pool a lot of intel, as you know.'

'But not the names of each other's illegals.'

'No. Not officially. Hugo was – how do you say – unorthodox, old school. Played by Moscow rules.' Brigadier Borowski smiled, as if remembering better days. 'I would not have put it past him to find these things out. Unfortunately, Monika took the second FSB confirmation the wrong way and, well, you know the rest.'

Prentice had been shot dead in cold blood outside a restaurant near Piccadilly. Fielding thought back to the funeral, at Coombe in West Berkshire. A pitiless sun had shone down on black suits in idyllic countryside. It had been a difficult day.

'If I told you I didn't think Prentice was a Russian asset, would you be surprised?' Fielding asked.

'I would have been, until a few days ago.'

Fielding sat up, ignoring the smoke, which had started to circulate down towards him.

'What changed your mind?'

'The FSB agent who first gave us Prentice's name? It appears he's a plant. A *podstava*. We had our doubts about him. Now we know for sure that the information he gives us is being controlled by Moscow Centre.'

'So the Russians wanted to frame Prentice?'

'It would seem so. Please don't ask me why.'

Fielding already knew why. To protect the identity of Ian Denton, the real Russian mole in MI6.

54

Marchant had been to Jean-Baptiste's family château a few times, but he had forgotten how grand it was. Jean-Baptiste's mother, Florianne, had bought it twenty years earlier as a summer retreat. She spent most of the year in Versailles, but liked to have a place for her children and grandchildren to gather in the holidays. It had been a wreck when she took it on, but over the years she had gradually restored the main house and the rambling outbuildings that formed a loose courtyard.

Florianne had greeted Jean-Baptiste and Marchant when they had arrived a few minutes earlier. He couldn't remember ever seeing a more attractive seventy-year-old. Although she had a cigarette hanging loosely from her mouth, she hadn't aged the way most smokers do. Her skin was fresh, her face open, reflecting the youth that she liked to surround herself with. She wore white linen trousers and spoke English with a French accent so sexy that Marchant had to stop himself from laughing.

He could hear her now, talking outside with Jean-Baptiste about Lakshmi, while he took in the building in which they were to stay. It had only been half converted, and the main room was still clearly a barn. Old wooden troughs from which cattle had once fed ran along one wall, and a huge oak beam supported the roof. Beyond that was a bedroom, where Lakshmi was sleeping, a small bathroom and a tatty sitting room with old leather sofas and a Mac desktop computer. Marchant guessed it was normally used as a playroom. There were four grand-children in residence, playing down at the swimming pool, but Jean-Baptiste had explained that their parents (his sister and brother-in-law) were in Paris.

'She's still sleeping,' Marchant said as he came out to join Jean-Baptiste and Florianne.

'Clémence is on her way back from the shops now,' Jean-Baptiste said. 'She won't be long.'

'Do you want a swim while we wait?' Florianne offered, a barking Pomeranian at her feet. After their initial exchange in English, she had reverted to French. 'The boys are down there.' Her eyes were kind, but hinted at sadness too.

'I'll stay with Lakshmi,' Marchant said.

'I can sit with her, it's not a problem.'

'It's OK. Thank you.'

There was a pause in the conversation as Florianne took a drag on her cigarette. Marchant glanced around at the surrounding countryside. Apart from the farm opposite, there were no other houses in the immediate area, just flat fields dotted with white Normandy cattle.

'Here she is now,' Jean-Baptiste said as a car appeared at the far end of the track. The Pomeranian began to bark.

Ten minutes later, Marchant was sitting with Clémence beside the bed in the barn, talking to Lakshmi. She was in a bad way, drifting in and out of sleep.

'Was she on any medication for her injury?' Clémence asked, taking Lakshmi's pulse on her good wrist. Clémence was as Marchant remembered: fragile and intense, beautiful with her short hair, tired around the eyes. She didn't joke like Jean-Baptiste, and often Marchant felt guilty in her company for not taking life seriously enough. At times it seemed she was carrying all the world's troubles – poverty, famine, disease – on her slim shoulders.

'I think so. Painkillers.'

'The heart rate is high and her pupils are presenting symptoms of withdrawal. I would not expect this with ordinary pain relief. Does she have any history of drug abuse?'

'Lakshmi?' he asked, as a wave of adrenaline surged through him. It was one of those moments when he realised how little he knew about her. He suddenly felt vulnerable, exposed. What else didn't he know? Marchant had come across one or two agents in MI6 and the CIA with drug habits, but Lakshmi was too conscientious, too industrious.

'What is the English expression, Dan?' Clémence asked.

'Cold turkey?'

'This is her condition. She is having chills, muscle cramps, shivers. You need to run a hot bath for her, and then talk. Through the night if necessary. I don't want to prescribe anything until I know more.'

'She got cold, she had to swim out to the boat when we left England,' Marchant said. 'Maybe she has hypothermia?'

But he knew it wasn't that. Her sweating legs at the Fort, the sudden mood swings, her euphoria on the phone; all along, he had told himself it was something else – her injured wrist, the cold sea – but he knew now it wasn't. He had kept secrets from her – the name of the traitor in MI6, the reason he hadn't killed Dhar – and she had withheld one from him.

55

Spiro always liked the final approach to Bagram air base. The Hindu Kush made for a spectacular backdrop that quickened the pulse, although he knew its rugged grandeur hid an ugly truth. Afghanistan had little to commend it as a country. Just ask the Soviets, who had built the original air base here after they had invaded the country in 1979. But he had always felt more on-message here than in Iraq when it came to fighting the war on terror.

Salim Dhar had been taken to Tor Jail, an interrogation facility on the air base that was set apart from the newly built main prison. If it hadn't been for the Red Cross, Tor would have remained as anonymous as the CIA's various black sites around the world, but its existence was now widely known. In Pashto, Tor translated as 'black', and 'the black jail' was run by the Joint Special Operations Command. (It was not to be confused with 'the dark prison', or 'Salt Pit', a former brick factory outside Kabul where detainees had once been held before being transferred to Guantánamo.)

Spiro knew the JSOC people well, and everyone had agreed that Tor was the best place to send Dhar, at least for the time being. The number of inmates at Bagram, known by its liberal detractors as Guantánamo's evil twin, had tripled since the new president's arrival to around two thousand. Guantánamo hadn't taken any new prisoners since 2008, and the President had issued an executive order to close it within a year of his coming to office. Just like he had ordered the closure of the CIA's black sites and an end to the Agency's enhanced interrogation techniques.

Almost two years on, what had changed? Diddly squat. Guantánamo remained open, ditto some of the Agency's more clandestine sites, and a revised Army Field Manual had become the new gold standard for interrogation. The manual was meant to draw a line under waterboarding, but Spiro could still do almost what he liked with Dhar, thanks to its ten-page 'Appendix M'. Much of it was based on the same blueprint drawn up by SERE instructors at Guantánamo in 2002 – that lawless period after 9/11 when he and others in the CIA had been given a blank cheque from the bank of pain, as his old boss used to say.

Spiro glanced out of the window across the Shomali plain as his Gulfstream V taxi-ed off the long, 11,000-foot runway. Running south through the valley was the Panjshir river, taking its snowmelt towards Kabul forty miles away. It was here that the Taleban had fought with Ahmad Massoud's Northern Alliance. Before that, it had been a battleground between the Afghan *muja-hideen* and the Soviets. Abandoned tanks still littered the hillsides, and there were skull-and-crossbones signs everywhere warning of landmines. How long would it be before Bagram was aban-doned? Ten years? Twenty?

He flicked through a well-thumbed copy of the manual. To keep the bleeding hearts in Washington happy, a military psycholo-gist and a lawyer were meant to be present when he interrogated Dhar. He would see about that. Walling, face-slapping and stress positions were all still allowed under the new manual, provided they caused 'shock' rather than 'pain'. It was an interesting distinc-tion. The same was true of a technique called 'separation'.

Described in detail in Appendix M, it belied its innocuous-sounding name and could only be used on unlawful enemy combatants – those who weren't protected by the Geneva Convention, in other words.

Solitary confinement, sensory deprivation and overload, the induction of fear and hopelessness, sleep deprivation, temperature manipulation and an approach called 'pride-and-ego down' – these were all part of separation. If everyone was born with a gift, this last one was Spiro's. Taken to its limits, pride-and-ego down involved the ritual humiliation of a prisoner, beginning with calling their mothers and sisters whores and ending up forcing them to perform dog tricks on a leash while wearing female lingerie. Why was he so good at it? Spiro didn't want to go there, he just knew how to make others feel suicidal.

Dhar was in separation now. He had been ever since he had arrived from the UK twenty-four hours earlier, confined in a small cell. Ideally he would be kept there until he died of old age, but Spiro was too curious. He had wanted to meet Dhar ever since he had nearly ruined his day in Delhi fifteen months earlier, when he had got too close to assassinating the US President. That's not to say he would have minded if Dhar had been killed when he had been captured, but the Brits had been too careful with their triggers.

Just as Spiro was walking down the steps from his plane, taking in the heat of the Afghan afternoon, his phone rang. An unknown number. For a moment he thought it might be his wife. She still hadn't made contact, and he had been unable to get in touch with any of her friends. A part of him feared where she might have gone, but he didn't want to dwell on it.

'Who's this?' he asked.

'It's Lakshmi.'

56

Lakshmi had waited until Daniel and Clémence had left the room before she sat up. Her lower legs were clammy with sweat, and her stomach was cramping. She knew what was going on. She had been here before. It would get worse for a few more days before the pain would slowly recede.

She thought she was about to throw up as she sat on the edge of the bed, listening. Outside she could hear Jean-Baptiste, Clémence and Daniel chatting together on the gravel. It was a risk making a call now, but she wouldn't have a better opportunity. She needed to tell Spiro where she was. Sea water had killed her own phone, but Clémence's was in front of her now, left behind on the wicker chair. She had forgotten it, and would be back as soon as she realised.

It was a sturdy old Nokia handset, and Lakshmi hoped it could make overseas calls. As she had drifted in and out of sleep, she had heard enough to establish that Clémence often worked abroad as a doctor. Holding the phone in her shaking hand, she dialled Spiro's mobile, an American number that she knew by heart, and looked up at the high window. She could still hear talking, but only Daniel and Jean-Baptiste's voices. Where was Clémence? Had she remembered her phone?

The number didn't connect, so she tried again, worried that

Clémence would return at any moment. She rose to her feet, steadying herself as she climbed onto the chair, and looked out of the window, taking care not to be seen. She felt dizzy, and thought she would fall. Jean-Baptiste and Daniel were standing ten feet away, their backs to her, talking in low voices. In the distance she could see Clémence walking across a lawn to a swimming pool. Unable to get a connection, she climbed off the chair, stood to one side of the window and tried to hear what Daniel was saying.

'Fifty years on, the Americans still think MI6 is a Moscow outpost,' she heard him protest. Then the wind changed direction, or he lowered his voice, because she missed the next few words, only hearing the end. '. . . Stephen Marchant, then they thought it was Marcus Fielding. And they've always had their doubts about me.'

'Who hasn't?' Jean-Baptiste said, laughing.

'The problem is, the Americans are right. There is a Russian asset in MI6, but it's not me, it wasn't my father and it's not Marcus Fielding.'

'Do you know who it is?'

Daniel seemed to hesitate, or perhaps she just couldn't hear him any more. A part of her was jealous of Jean-Baptiste. Daniel had never quite been able to confide in her who the traitor was, as they had stood on the moonlit shore in front of Fort Monckton. '. . . Denton,' Daniel was saying quietly. 'He's ousted Fielding, and the Americans are backing him. He gave them Dhar on a plate.'

Lakshmi felt a wave of disappointment. Daniel had got the wrong man. It couldn't possibly be Denton. He was Spiro's appointment, a little creepy, but his trusty lieutenant. She tried to keep listening, but the voices came and went on the wind.

'You were right, they took Dhar to Bagram,' she heard Jean-Baptiste say. What he said next made her think she was relapsing.

'He won't be much use to you there.' What did he mean by that? 'Not unless you want to learn first-hand about America's enhanced interrogation techniques. But I guess MI6 knows about them already.'

'Very funny. As if the DGSE has never tortured anyone.'

'I didn't say that. Sometimes we do crazy things, but I'm not sure we'd ever try to turn the world's most-wanted terrorist.'

Lakshmi couldn't be sure she had heard Jean-Baptiste correctly. She didn't trust her own mental state, and the wind was distorting his words, but there was something about what he had said that made sense. Daniel hadn't held back from killing Dhar in Russia because they were half-brothers. It was because he was trying to recruit him.

She dialled the number again, her fingers fumbling. This time the line connected.

'Where are you?' Spiro asked.

'In France.'

'With Marchant?'

She paused, trying to order her thoughts.

'You sound compromised,' Spiro continued.

'I haven't got long.' The talking outside had stopped.

'What's he up to?'

'He thinks Ian Denton is a Russian asset.'

'Denton?' She could hear the derision in his voice. 'Has he been drinking? Talking to Fielding?'

'I don't think so.'

'Can you give me your exact location?'

'Northern France. We came by boat.' She tried to listen again for Daniel and Jean-Baptiste's voices, but heard nothing. 'I've got to go.'

'We can trace this call if you stay on the line.'

'I can't.'

183

'Stay with him, find out what he's planning to do.'

'There's something else. I'm not sure, but –'

'What?'

She thought again about what she had heard. Maybe she had just imagined it. There was no time to explain. Daniel and Jean-Baptiste had been silent for too long.

'I have to go.'

She hung up, and deleted the call history. It wasn't enough to fully cover her tracks, but it would be sufficient if nobody was looking. After putting the phone back on the chair, she climbed into bed. She should have told Spiro that Daniel had tried to turn Dhar, but perhaps she didn't believe it herself. A part of her wanted it to be true. However shocking the implications, it made her own betrayal of Daniel easier to bear, more justified. She was no longer doing it solely in response to blackmail.

If Daniel was helping Dhar with his *jihad*, she had no qualms about betraying him. Dhar had dedicated his life to destroying the country she called home. America had adopted her as one of its own, and she had promised to give something back. Wasn't that why she had signed up to be a doctor? Why she had joined the Agency? Both men needed to be stopped.

She closed her eyes and fell into a troubled sleep, unaware of the figure standing in the doorway.

57

'Are we ready?' Spiro asked, striding into a small, well-lit room in Tor Jail. The brick walls were painted white and the floor was grey concrete. It was easy to clean, and disguised any bodily fluids that might have been missed. The room had no ceiling, just a metal grille. The jail was housed inside a vast hangar built by the Soviets as a workshop, and its span roof arced high above all the cells. It reminded Spiro of an old railway station, except that it echoed to the sound of pain rather than steam, and smelt strongly of excrement.

'Yes, sir,' an overweight Military Police guard replied, handing Spiro a clipboard. He noticed that the words 'Fuck Islam' had been tattooed across the knuckles of the guard's hands. There was no military psychologist or lawyer present. Spiro had brought the interview forward without telling them. 'The Hadgie's had forty-eight hours of isolation, sleep-depped too.'

'Music?'

'2pac – "All Eyez on Me".'

'Now that's just plain evil, forcing someone to listen to that. What's wrong with Marilyn Manson?'

The guard flinched for a moment before realising that Spiro was smiling. 'He's been shackle-standing for' – the man checked his watch with professional pride – 'three hours and twenty. Diaper last checked three hours ago.'

'And?'

'Soiled.'

'Get it changed. I don't have to smell it to know Salim Dhar stinks of shit. Has he said anything yet?'

'Not a word.' The guard paused. 'There's something else.'

'What is it?'

'He's not like the other BOBs.'

Spiro had missed the crude lingo of the jail ghetto. BOB stood for 'Bad Odour Boys'.

'We gave him the usual welcome when he arrived, shaved off his beard, worked him over, strictly in accordance with our "shock of capture" routine.'

Vicious dogs, screaming guards and strikes to Dhar's body, Spiro thought. He knew the drill well. Make the first few hours of capture as terrifying and disorientating as possible, because that's when a detainee is most likely to drop his defences. It didn't take much. A well-aimed blow to the common peroneal nerve, just above the knee, could incapacitate the whole leg. Done repeatedly, it could necessitate amputation. Most people preferred to talk.

'And?' Spiro asked.

'Heartbeat stayed around 60bpm. BP was 110/70. That's weirdly low for someone in his situation. And he wasn't showing any of the other usual stress indicators. I ain't seen self-control like it. Whatever you say about him, the hadgie's disciplined. Mind and body.'

Spiro thought about this for a moment. He knew Dhar was going to be tough to break. It was why he wanted to do the job himself. He liked a challenge. He also owed it to Lieutenant Randall Oaks, a close friend and one of the six Marines who had been

killed by the drone strike in North Waziristan. Spiro had personally ordered the attack, thinking the target was Dhar.

'Is his mother here yet?'

'Sir, there's a problem with Dhar's mother.'

Salim Dhar's mother had been renditioned to the UK from
South India a few weeks earlier. Her presence in Bagram was
crucial to the interrogation progress. She was Dhar's weak point.

'What sort of problem?'

'We don't know where she is. Nobody does.'

Spiro had feared as much. He had put a call in to Denton
earlier about the mother, and knew from his tone of voice that
he was stalling. Fielding had insisted on taking custody of her.
Unfortunately, Fielding was now on the run, last believed to be
in Russia.

Two minutes later, Spiro was on his phone, holding for Ian
Denton.

'Ian, it's Jim. We need Dhar's mother.'

'That won't be so easy,' Denton said.

'Are you telling me Fielding's the only one who knows where
she is? She's at an MI6 safe house in the UK, right? That must
kinda narrow things down?'

'We're working on it. How's Dhar? We'd like to ask him a few
questions.'

'I'm not sure you'd want any of your officers out here at the
moment. And d'you know what? I'm not sure I want them here
either.'

Spiro didn't have to spell it out for Denton. They both knew
what he was talking about. Nine months earlier, the Court of
Appeal in the UK had ordered a communiqué between the CIA
and MI5 to be made public. Spiro and others had kicked up a
huge fuss, threatening to stop sharing intelligence with America's
oldest ally. The unredacted document revealed that a detainee,

Binyam Mohamed, had suffered significant mental stress during a CIA-led interrogation in Karachi. Knowing how he had been treated, MI5 still sent out an officer to interview Mohamed, contravening its own guidelines on torture.

'Perhaps we could just forward some questions,' Denton said. 'We're in crisis here, in need of leads. The attacks appear to be by Dhar's supporters. He must know who they are.'

'By all means send over your questions, Ian. But find the mother too, will you?'

Sometimes Spiro wondered about his decision to promote Denton. Didn't the guy realise what was going on? The CIA was running the show in the UK now. It would find the bombers who had targeted US interests, with or without help from the muppets in MI5 and MI6. What did Denton think Spiro was going to ask Dhar? How did he find life in the frickin' Cotswolds?

'One other thing,' Spiro said. 'Marchant's in northern France. He's with Lakshmi Meena.'

'What's he doing there?'

'That's what I'm trying to find out.' Something stopped him telling Denton about Marchant's belief that Denton was a Russian mole.

'Will she bring him in?' Denton asked.

'Not yet. I want to know what he's up to.'

After Spiro had hung up, he turned to the guard.

'I need a local. Medium height, brown skin. And female.'

58

Marchant had only caught Lakshmi's last few words on the phone, but he had heard enough to know that she had become a problem. She was still working for the CIA. Her imminent firing, the possibility of prosecution – he realised now that these were lies. And her drug habit, which she had managed to conceal from him, suddenly seemed irrelevant. She was hiding something far worse. He should have known, should have trusted his instincts.

Careful not to wake her, he took Clémence's phone and checked the call history. It had been cleared. Then he clipped open the back, removed the battery and slid out the SIM card. Clémence would have to use Jean-Baptiste's phone from now on. There was a chance the call had already been traced, but he was confident that Lakshmi had not spoken for long enough.

He sat down on the edge of the bed and looked at Lakshmi. Her face was pale and a few strands of hair were stuck to the side of her forehead; she had been sweating. He tucked them back, thinking of Leila, whose damp hair he had cradled after she had been shot in Delhi.

Her eyes opened, and she lay looking up at him. He shouldn't have brought her with him, especially with limpid eyes like those. Already he could feel his resolve weakening. Perhaps he should give her another chance, let her explain herself. But he knew he couldn't.

'I owe you an apology,' she said quietly, her hand resting on his. He wanted to remove it, but he forced himself to keep it there. 'I should have told you.'

'You should, yes.'

'It's not good to keep things from one another.'

'No.' Marchant closed his eyes. If she confessed, perhaps he could find a way to forgive her. She might have been coerced into betraying him, like Leila.

'I didn't choose this, Dan. It wasn't a deliberate act on my part.'

'I know.' Was she about to come clean? They looked at each other for a long time before she finally spoke, her voice shaking with a mixture of emotion and withdrawal.

'I was in agony in the restaurant. The medic gave me an injection. It took away the pain, but it brought something else back.'

Marchant listened with a heavy heart as she went on to tell him about her student drug habit, how it had been a misguided act of rebellion against her parents, and how she was determined to be clear of it again under Clémence's care.

'I'll tell Clémence everything, give her my full medical background, but I wanted you to know first.'

'That's good of you.' Marchant stood up and walked over to the window. Then he turned to face her. 'Who were you calling on the phone just now?'

Her face remained unchanged, but he knew his question had cut through her discomfort, triggering alarms deep beneath the surface. His own brain was working fast too, calculating how best to play her. He wouldn't force the phone issue, just watch how she reacted. He needed to see her betrayal for himself.

'I had a dealer in Gosport,' she began, lost in thought, buying time. 'He wasn't local. He came down from London when I called him. They'll travel a long way when they know you're desperate. I told him I'd pay anything. That time when I went to the guardhouse for you? After I'd chatted with them for a while, I went for a walk, along the fence by the golf course. There was no way I could get out of the Fort, so I scored through the perimeter wire.'

He had to hand it to her. She was good, even in detox. For a moment he believed her. Perhaps she really had arranged for a dealer to come down to Fort Monckton.

'So why were you ringing him from France?'

'He rang me.'

'On Clémence's phone?' He tried to conceal his disbelief.

She paused. 'I texted him first. On her phone. Asked him to call me back on the same number. I was desperate.'

'And what did you say when he rang?'

This time she paused for longer. Marchant wondered if the game was finally up, but she kept going. 'He asked me where I was, and —'

'You told him?' Marchant's voice was raised.

'I said I was in northern France. I'm sorry. You think he might not have been a dealer?'

He didn't know what he thought. He tried to recall what he had overheard her saying to Spiro on the phone. 'Northern France. We came by boat. I've got to go.' Again, he almost found himself being taken in by her story.

'Did you honestly think he'd come to France?'

'I was going to ask him if he knew of any dealers here. They all know each other.'

'But you didn't?'

'I hung up. Have you any idea how crazy you become, Dan? Right now, all I'm thinking about is how I want to steal your phone and ring him again. Tell him I'll pay for a speedboat to get the gear here quicker.'

She managed a thin smile, but he couldn't bring himself to reciprocate. He was too angry – with her, himself. He would let her cover story remain unchallenged for now. Like all good ones, it drew heavily on her own life, giving it an air of credibility. He would use her loyalty to the CIA to throw Spiro off the scent, feed him false information, providing she hadn't told him too much already.

'I'll get Clémence,' he said. 'Maybe she'll give you methadone to make things easier.'

'You do believe me, Dan?' she said, a sudden desperation in her voice.

'Believe what?'

'That I didn't want to go back there. To the past.'

'Is there anything else you're hiding from me?' It was his final throw of the dice, her last chance.

She hesitated before she spoke. Somewhere in the distance Florianne's dog began to bark. It was always barking. 'No more secrets.'

'I'll call Clémence.'

59

Dhar was ready for Spiro. It felt as if he had been preparing for this moment all his life. He had always known that one day they would meet, ever since he had learnt that it was Spiro who had waterboarded Daniel Marchant. It was Spiro, too, who had nearly cornered him in Delhi and who had almost thwarted his most recent attack on Fairford and GCHQ. His reputation at the CIA was well known among *jihadis*. He had been at the forefront of the infidels' so called 'war on terror' for almost ten years, relishing the freedom that had been given to the Agency in the aftermath of 9/11.

Young *jihadis* like Dhar had studied what had happened to their elder brothers at Camp X-Ray. They had familiarised themselves with the interrogation techniques of Survival, Evasion, Resist and Escape, knew their way around the Army Field Manual, even its notorious Appendix M. Copying the SERE instructors who had waterboarded fellow Americans to prepare them for capture, *jihadi* leaders had tortured their colleagues at training camps in Afghanistan and Pakistan, preparing them for Guantánamo and Bagram.

It wasn't only the body that had to be prepared, it was also the mind. And it was here that Dhar felt strongest. For as long as he could remember, he had been able to remove himself from his immediate environment, shutting off the outside world by focusing on an inner one. He credited his Hindu mother, who had taught him Patanjali's doctrine of *Samyama* meditation – *dhāraṇa* (concentrating), *dhyāna* (contemplating) and *samādhi* (loss of self). They had both needed to shield themselves from the man who thought he was Dhar's father.

Later, he had learnt the Islamic mental state of *al-khatir*, purifying the mind with a heightened sense of oneness. At a training camp in Kashmir, a psychologist had explained the science to him, how meditation dramatically reduces activity in the primary somatosensory cortex, the part of the brain where pain stimuli were assessed for their intensity and location.

When the guards at Bagram had first started to beat him, he had risen out of his bruised body and watched the scene from above, detaching himself from the pain. Now one of the guards was back in the room, standing too close to his face. Dhar recognised him by his stale tobacco breath. The guard started to pull at the masking tape that had been used earlier to strap a pair of headphones to his head. The tape pulled at his shaved skin, but he shut down the nerve endings, as if he was turning off a tap. It was nothing compared to what he had felt earlier. The music had stopped a few minutes ago. It had been too loud to ignore, but Dhar had parked the unholy sound in a remote corner of his head and built a wall around it, layer upon layer of bricks until it was no more than a distant thudding.

After the headphones had been removed, the guard untied the blindfold, but there was no light. The space he was in was so dark that he kept blinking to check that his eyes were functioning. The guard flicked on a torch and flashed it at his eyes. Dhar turned away. He was standing naked except for an oversized diaper, his hands shackled to a metal roof grille above him. The guard removed the diaper – rubber gloves again, like the ones they had

194

worn earlier for the body cavity search – and then he felt a jet of cold water as he was hosed down.

The guard left him on his own in the darkness, and for a few minutes there was silence. He steadied himself, swaying from the ceiling. The shackles around his ankles were biting into his flesh. He focused on his breathing, trying to ignore the pain in his chest where he had been beaten. Then he heard a voice in the next-door room. He knew at once that it was Spiro's.

'Bring her in here,' the voice said.

Dhar flinched at the reference to a woman. He knew his own weaknesses. They had been identified during his interrogation training. A closeness to his mother, and a chronic fear of insects. The brothers had laughed at the latter, but it was an entirely rational phobia. As a child in Delhi he had nearly died when a giant hornet had stung him. He had suffered an acute anaphylactic shock, and only the quick thinking of his mother had saved him. She had rushed him to a doctor's surgery in Chanakyapuri, where he had been treated with adrenaline. The CIA was unlikely to know about the incident, but they would exploit the fear if they did. More certain was their knowledge of his mother. She had been renditioned from India by Spiro, and was now in British custody. At least, that was what Marchant had told him. Had he been lying?

He heard the sound of a scuffle, and then someone being slapped. There was no reason to believe that Spiro had brought his mother to Bagram. He told himself not to listen. It was an old trick. Ever since the Spanish Inquisition, interrogators had learnt that torture by proxy was often the most effective way to get someone to talk. Pulling out the nails of a prisoner in an adjacent cell could have more of an effect than removing the victim's. Then he heard Spiro speak again.

'Your son Salim is in the next room. Are you going to let him hear you suffer?'

There was no reply. Dhar closed his eyes, calming his thoughts, letting the bad ones go.

'Why are you not answering our questions?' Spiro asked, louder now.

Another slap, followed by a muffled moan. Female, but it could have been anyone's. Despite himself, Dhar began to imagine that it was his mother next door, and saw her small body strapped to a chair. He let the image slip away as quickly as it had appeared, but it reared up again, more vivid this time, his mother's face distorted and bruised.

'How well does Salim know bin Laden?' Spiro asked. 'He must have spoken of him, boasted about it.'

It was a ludicrous question. Dhar had never met the Sheikh. Everyone knew they had their differences, even if they were more about means than ends. Spiro was just fishing. But the questions continued. Did she know he had been seen with Ayman al-Zawahiri? How long had they been colluding? When did your son first meet Anwar al-Awlaki? Each time, there was silence, as there would be if the same questions had been directed at Dhar.

He shared al Q'aeda's goal of removing America from the Arab Holy Lands and restoring the Caliphate, but he preferred military and political targets. Civilian casualties were problematic, particularly if they were Muslim, like the sixty guests killed at a wedding in Jordan in 2005. Such attacks alienated Muslim brothers.

Spiro was no longer talking.

'Has she been like this all day?' he eventually asked someone. His tone was more abrupt than before. The room fell quiet. Had Spiro left? Somewhere in the distance a cell door closed, the metallic click echoing around the vast hangar. Despite himself, Dhar could feel his heart rate rising. He didn't like the silence. It wasn't Spiro's style. Then he heard a scuffling sound, followed by the protests of a guard.

'Sir!'

'I haven't got time for this,' Spiro said as the sharp crack of a gunshot reverberated around the prison. The voices of other detainees called out like frightened animals in a forest. Then Dhar's cell door was open, and bright light streamed in. He turned his head away, but not before he saw a limp female figure being dragged away by her ankles.

Spiro stepped into the doorway.

'Your mother wouldn't talk,' he said as he closed the steel door behind him.

60

'I shouldn't have brought Lakshmi,' Marchant said, holding onto the side of the Mehari's door as Jean-Baptiste drove around a tight corner. They were heading down a farm track into the woods to the north of the château, in search of *sanglier*, wild boar, while Clémence helped Florianne prepare dinner. Lakshmi was sleeping again.

'Was it your Russian friend in the car?' Jean-Baptiste asked.

'I'm not sure. I can't think how they'd know I'm in France.'

Marchant had begun to convince himself that it wasn't Valentin in the black people-carrier. The Russian had been a thorn in his side ever since their paths had crossed in Sardinia. There had once been a chance to kill him – on a crowded Underground platform in London – but he had held back from pushing him onto the tracks.

'You must have upset them, talking Dhar out of his attack.'

'I'm not about to be awarded the Order of Lenin.'

They drove on in silence for a while, Marchant more conscious than ever that he had brought danger into his good friends' lives.

'Lakshmi can stay here. Clémence will keep her sedated,' Jean-Baptiste eventually said.

'Is she OK about her phone?'

'I am. It's better nobody rings her. She's meant to be on holiday, after all.'

After he had removed the SIM card, Marchant had asked Jean-Baptiste to post the handset to a poste restante near their flat in Paris. Jean-Baptiste had driven to Caen, where he had reinserted the card, turned on the phone, switched it to silent and sent it in a small padded package. They were both confident the number would not be traced – it was an SFR pay-as-you-go SIM, and Lakshmi hadn't spoken for long – but they didn't want to take any risks.

'You know, you're lucky to have found Clémence.'

'Come on, Dan, she's the lucky one,' Jean-Baptiste said, smiling. Sometimes Marchant wondered if Jean-Baptiste ever had days when he was depressed. He doubted it. The only time he had seen him sad was after they had been to a match at Twickenham, where England had beaten France. He had briefly played club rugby for Toulon, before signing up with the Commandos Marine.

'I wish I'd been as fortunate.'

Jean-Baptiste hadn't seen Lakshmi at her best, and he had only met Leila once. He would never criticise someone else's girlfriend, but Marchant could tell that he hadn't warmed to either of them.

'The trick is to choose someone from outside our work,' Jean-Baptiste said. 'Spies can never trust each other completely.'

'I thought I'd learnt my lesson. But Lakshmi, she ignored orders and helped me. She saw the bigger picture. Spiro must have black-mailed her.'

'So what now? If we take care of Lakshmi, what will you do?'

'That's what I wanted to ask you about.'

'Sounds ominous,' Jean-Baptiste said, pulling up at the side of the track. 'Sometimes we see wild boar over there, coming out of the wood. It's where the farmer feeds them, but he's not here today.'

'I need to prove that Denton's working for the Russians. It's the only way I can go back to Britain. And I owe it to Marcus Fielding.'

'Why did he go to Moscow?'

They were out of the car now, looking across a field towards the woodland.

'I don't believe he did. If he wanted to visit Russia without being seen, he would have been more careful. He may be getting on, but he's still good in the field.'

'You think Denton made up the story?'

'If everyone thinks Fielding's the Russian mole, Denton won't come under suspicion.'

'Maybe he'll take fewer precautions, drop his guard. Now would be a good time to watch him.'

Jean-Baptiste was a surveillance specialist, whether it was in the Normandy countryside or on a Paris street. He had soft feet and sharp eyes.

'I'll be arrested if I return to London. The Americans want to hang me along with Dhar.'

There was a pause while Jean-Baptiste scanned the forest edge with his binoculars. Marchant guessed he knew what was coming.

'There, to the left of the gate. Can you see them? Young ones, three of them. And two adults.'

Jean-Baptiste passed the binoculars to Marchant. He took them and looked at the family of wild boar, trying not to think of Obelix. Why had they bothered to bring a rifle with them? Jean-Baptiste could probably kill one of them with his bare hands.

'Will you go to London for me?' Marchant asked, still peering through the binoculars. He didn't want to see Jean-Baptiste's expression. 'Take a look at Denton?'

'I'm on holiday. Hunting wild boar, not Russian moles.'

'I know. And I wouldn't ask unless it was important. If the

200

Russians have an asset at the top of MI6, there are implications for France, too.'

'See, there's another male, on his own, to the right,' Jean-Baptiste said, reaching behind him for the rifle. 'It's better we take this one. He's a loner.'

Marchant tracked right and picked up the solitary boar, who was trundling down a track that ran parallel to theirs, about three hundred yards away, on the far side of a field. It hadn't spotted them or the other boar.

'Remind me again of the proof against Denton?' Jean-Baptiste said, the gun now at his shoulder.

'There isn't any. Not yet. That's what I need you to find.'

'And if I agree to go?'

'I'll stay here and look after Clémence and Lakshmi. It's not safe after the call Lakshmi made, but northern France is a big place. I'll take my chances. If you find something, I'll pass it on to MI5. Harriet Armstrong can't be happy that Denton's replaced Fielding.'

'I'll go,' Jean-Baptiste said, as the still country air echoed to the sound of his rifle. The boar fell on its side.

61

Dhar struggled to regain his composure as he hung from the ceiling like a carcass in a butcher's cold room. Spiro was in front of him, smiling. The infidel was just as he had imagined: thick-set, shaved head, a face worn down by years of inflicting pain. Dhar looked him in the eye and then turned away, processing what he had seen. Spiro would have milked it more if he had really shot his mother. He was bluffing, just as they had said he would. Fake executions were a common ruse. The CIA had done something similar with Abd al-Nashiri, mastermind of the USS *Cole* attack in 2000. The 'dead' body had been a prison guard acting the part.

'It's been a long time,' Spiro said. Without warning he spun and punched Dhar in the face. The shock was worse than the pain. Dhar braced himself for a second hit as Spiro rubbed his fist, but it never came. 'That was for Lieutenant Randall Oakes. Good friend of mine.'

Dhar spat blood and licked his bruised lips. He knew who Oakes was. He had been one of the six infidel Marines kidnapped by brothers in Afghanistan. A recording of Dhar's voice had been played into a mobile phone in the hut where the Marines were being held, attracting the attention of the NSA and then a drone armed with Hellfire missiles. Dhar had been far away at the time, hiding in Morocco's Atlas Mountains.

For the next few minutes Spiro talked of Dhar's father, Stephen Marchant, and his half-brother, Daniel, and how he had long suspected them both of treachery. He told him how the rot had started way back when with Philby, Burgess and Maclean, that America should never have trusted Britain again. Even Dhar was surprised by the tirade, his hostility towards the UK.

'I've always had my suspicions about the British House of Marchant,' Spiro continued, walking around the tiny room. 'You know, it was no surprise when it turned out that Salim Dhar was the bastard son of the Chief of MI6. Not to me, it wasn't. No goddamn surprise at all.'

Without realising it, Spiro was filling Dhar with strength at the time he most needed it. He could listen all day to stories of his father's so-called treachery. It gave him courage. He liked to hear how Daniel Marchant had got under Spiro's skin, too. It made him feel better about the deal they had struck. He was working with America's enemies.

'We're in no rush here, by the way,' Spiro continued. 'No rush at all.' He was standing in front of Dhar now, too close. A tiny drop of spittle had formed on his thin lower lip. For the first time he seemed to be mildly frustrated by his prisoner's continuing silence. Dhar smelt his sweat mixed with stale cologne, noted the glistening beads gathering at his pockmarked temples. If he struck quickly with his forehead, he might crack Spiro's nose, but he knew it would be a futile gesture. He had something else in his armory, something that would stop the American in his tracks.

'We can do it the hard way,' Spiro said, walking away from Dhar. 'Or you can talk and we can make this easier for everyone.'

'I'll talk,' Dhar said. Spiro paused and turned around.

'Good,' he said, failing to conceal his surprise. 'So the devil's got a tongue after all. And what exactly would you like to talk about?'

'Your wife.'

62

Clémence was not happy about Jean-Baptiste's sudden departure for London. He hadn't said he was going on Marchant's behalf, just that the office had called and it was urgent.

'Maybe it's better you stay single,' she said, standing at the foot of Lakshmi's bed with Marchant. They had moved Lakshmi into the main house, to a room closer to Clémence's. The wooden shutters were closed, but didn't quite meet in the middle, allowing sunlight to pour into the room. A jug of water stood on the bedside table, casting eerie, translucent reflections on the old stone walls.

'I'll try,' Marchant said. Lakshmi was asleep, her breathing steady.

'It's not the first time Jean-Baptiste has left me on holiday. And I know it won't be the last. But that doesn't make it any easier. We get very little time together.'

Clémence was like a ball of frustration tonight, Marchant thought, her small frame wound tight with stress.

'I guess it goes with the job,' Marchant said, feeling guilty. It was typical of Jean-Baptiste not to have blamed him for his trip to London. 'Thank you for looking after her.'

'She's tough,' Clémence said, tidying the bedspread unnecessarily. 'I like her. In another life, maybe we could have been friends.

She was making good progress. Sweating it out. Sedation will only delay her recovery.'

A moment later, Marchant's phone was ringing. It was the handset he kept for incoming calls, which meant it could only be Paul Myers. No one else had the number. He made his apologies, grateful for the excuse to leave the room, and walked out into the courtyard.

'You know you asked me to listen in to some Farsi, for old time's sake,' Myers began.

'Yes?' Marchant said.

'You're using it, aren't you?'

'What?'

'The voice-modulating hands-free. Your voice sounds different, a bit more than it should. Like –'

'Listen, what have you found?' Marchant told himself not to be so impatient with Myers, who was doing him a favour.

'Picked up some Revolutionary Guard chatter about Bagram and Dhar. They're definitely planning something, just like you thought.'

'What are they saying?' Marchant asked, his pulse picking up. He knew all about Iran's Islamic Revolutionary Guard Corps. Formed after the Revolution in 1979, the Corps was separate from the regular army, which had been tainted by loyalty to the deposed Shah. Among other things, it specialised in asymmetric warfare and thumbing its nose at the West. If anyone could free Dhar, it would be them.

'I need time to analyse it properly. A lot of it's indirect, coded phrases. But you were right about them wanting Dhar out of there.'

'Has anyone else heard this? The NSA?'

'You are joking? The NSA rely on us for this sort of thing. Wouldn't know a decent Farsi analyst if they saw one. Everyone thinks Mossad has the best Farsi desk, but we're –'

'What do you normally do with intel like this?' Marchant said, cutting him off, thinking fast.

'Pool it with the relevant Controllerates, run it past my line manager. Then she liaises with the Americans.'

'Don't share it with anyone, do you understand? No one.'

'I can't do that, Dan. You know that.'

Marchant was aware that there was only so much he could ask of Myers.

'Can you at least sit on it? Twenty-four hours?'

63

Spiro felt the blood drain from his face as if someone had pulled a plug. He turned away, wondering whether to hit Dhar again, but his strength had left him. He didn't like people talking about his wife, least of all Salim Dhar. Dammit, what did he know? What did anyone know?

To his colleagues at Langley, his thirty-year marriage to Linda must have seemed unusually strong. Perhaps it was because they had married when he was still in the Marines. As a military wife, Linda was used to putting on a brave face in public, never complaining.

Espionage was different. Most of the officers he knew at Langley were either divorced or separated. The long periods of travel, often at short notice, and an inability to offload at home after a hard day at the office put an intolerable strain on relationships.

But in fact Spiro's marriage was far from strong. Right now, he didn't even know if Linda was alive, let alone where she was.

The problems had started way back, when their disabled son had been born. Joseph had required a lot of looking after, which had taken its toll on their relationship. After years of dedicating herself to him while Spiro was away on tours, Linda had come to terms with her guilt and finally let others take over the burden of care. She was a changed woman, taking up photography, getting into shape at the gym. Spiro wished they had made the decision earlier. But then she fell in with a new crowd of people, younger than herself.

'This is my husband, Jim,' Linda had said one Saturday morning, after she had dragged him out for a coffee in Washington, DC, to meet a group of her photography friends. Busboys and Poets was at 14th and V, and it wasn't his kind of place, but she had insisted on it. Students and chinstrokers ate Oaxaca omelettes with pico de gallo as they read on their Nooks and Kindles. The walls were adorned with images of Gandhi and Martin Luther King. At the far end, the high-ceilinged restaurant merged into a non-profit bookstore. Not his kind of place at all.

'So what exactly do you do for the government?' the only other man in the group had asked after Spiro had initiated some awkward smalltalk about the previous night's Redskins game.

Spiro threw a glance at Linda. This hadn't been part of the deal. She knew he never talked about his job in public. And she knew not to talk about it to others.

'Come on, Jason, give the guy a break,' she said. 'It's the weekend.'

'It's just that in my world that usually means the Feds.'

Everyone seemed to stop talking at once, not just at their table but in the whole café. Spiro glanced across at Linda, who didn't quite seem sorry enough, and then turned back to Jason as he took a sip of his decaf coffee. He was holding the cup's handle delicately between thumb and index finger, his ringed pinkie sticking out. For a second he wondered if Linda was having an affair with him. He had long, fair hair and soft, almost cherubic features – more like a poet than a photographer.

'It's OK, no big deal,' Spiro said quietly. 'I work for the Agency.'

Jason sat back and folded his arms, looking at the others with smug satisfaction.

'What do you do? Run their black sites?'

'Not quite. I try to keep our country safe.'

'Right. By invading other countries. Remind me again about the intelligence that linked 9/11 with Saddam?'

'Jason, Jim's come along to see what we do,' Linda said, a hand on Spiro's arm. He withdrew it.

'Well, I'm not interested in showing him,' Jason said, finishing his coffee and standing up. 'And I don't think the rest of you should be either.'

The group watched in awkward silence as Jason walked out of the café.

'I'm sorry, Jim. He can get a bit passionate,' Linda said.

It was an unfortunate choice of words, but Spiro agreed to stay on. The remaining three women were easy on the eye, full of apologies and keen to tell him how pleased they were to have met his wife. He would look up Jason's file later. It turned out the women had recently set up Photography for Peace, a Washington-based project to capture 'whatever makes the world a more harmonious place'. They showed him some photos on an iPad, including a dove in flight and a peace sign formed by six hands, taken by Linda. She wasn't yet a member, at least that's what she told him on the drive home afterwards. She had wanted to clear it with him first.

A brief check revealed that Jason was a peace campaigner who had cut his teeth protesting against the 2003 invasion of Iraq. Since then he had been a staunch critic of Israel, opposed the war in Afghanistan and campaigned for a 'new and progressive non-militaristic US foreign policy'. He was currently on an FBI watchlist, although not under surveillance.

Spiro and Linda had a row when he told her about Jason's file. She was angry that he had checked up on him, and walked out of the house when he told her not to see him or her other friends again.

'He's just a frickin' photographer,' she had shouted. 'You're jealous, that's what this is really all about. Jealous that someone might just be interested in me for a change.'

'What do you know about my wife?' Spiro asked, glancing at the cell door as he turned to face Dhar again. His voice was quieter now. At this point in the interrogation the psychological advantage should have been all his, but Dhar had turned the tables. The mother stunt appeared to have left him unmoved, and he knew about his wife. Spiro had no idea how, but he would find out.

'We all carry secrets,' Dhar said. 'I was Stephen Marchant's.'

'Mine are strictly professional,' Spiro lied. He needed to flush out more, establish what Dhar knew.

'I know where she is.'

'Of course you do.' Spiro tried to play down his interest, but he realised how desperate he was to find out.

'It could have been worse. She could have been a *jihadi* like me.' A smile broke across Dhar's bloodied lips. 'But she chose to be a peace campaigner. At least nobody knows. None of your colleagues.'

Spiro didn't hesitate to hit him again. He punched him hard in the face, and followed up with a knee to the groin, thinking of Jason in the café. Then he hit him in the solar plexus.

'You're lying!' Spiro shouted, losing control of his immediate environment, breaking the first rule of interrogation.

Breathing heavily, Dhar spoke again.

'My Palestinian brothers are grateful for her support. It takes a brave American to stand up to Israeli soldiers in villages like Bil'in. Ramallah is not for the faint-hearted.'

Spiro knew he was telling the truth. She had gone to the West Bank with her peacenik friends. Professionally, it would be humiliating if it ever became known at Langley. Damaging, too. He had yet to tell the vetters about his wife's new social circle.

'You might never see daylight again,' Spiro said, walking towards the door.

'One thing I don't understand,' Dhar whispered, raising his head in defiance. 'Does this man Jason know she's married?'

64

Marchant stood up and stretched. The night was warm, and moths were crashing against the light outside the stable block. Jean-Baptiste was talking on the computer, the idle chat of a tedious stakeout. It was 9 p.m. in London, and he was in a hired car across the street from Ian Denton's flat on Battersea Bridge Road.

The previous night he had followed Denton's Range Rover home from Legoland, but the driver had taken several counter-surveillance measures, which worried Jean-Baptiste. Either they were routine or he had been spotted. He liked to think it was the former.

'He's working late,' Jean-Baptiste said. 'Last night it was 8.30.'

'He's the Chief.'

'I thought the point of being boss was that you got other people to do all the work.'

'That's true, but the buck stops with you when things go wrong, and Britain's currently under attack, in case you hadn't noticed. I'm amazed he's not sleeping under his desk.'

'He gets in early. This morning it was 5 a.m. How's Clémence tonight? Still mad at me?'

'You could have told her why you're really in London.'

'I will when I need to.'

Marchant looked across at the château, where a light was on

in an upstairs window. Clémence had taken Lakshmi under her wing, looking after her day and night. The phone call to Spiro three days earlier still worried him. Marchant's natural instinct was to move on, keep running, but he couldn't leave Clémence on her own. Lakshmi was his prisoner.

He knew, too, that it was safer to liaise with Jean-Baptiste in London if he remained at the château. The VOIP software on Jean-Baptiste's computer made it easy to talk to him over the internet, and harder for anyone else to listen in. As an extra precaution, Marchant had spoofed the IP address using a proxy server and downloaded free software for Tor, an anonymous routing network.

Tor was widely used by political activists in countries – Iran or China, for example – where they needed to disguise their location. MI6 had its own 'onion routing' network for field officers (available as a secure app or a download) that used a similarly layered approach to security.

'Here comes Denton,' Jean Baptiste said.

Marchant tried to imagine the scene: Denton sitting in the back of the Chief's official Range Rover, talking on the phone, enjoying his new power, Fielding's seat still warm.

'Special Branch driver gets out, opens rear door for Denton,' Jean-Baptiste continued. 'He glances up and down street – old school – says good night to the driver, goes inside. Front door closes. I'm not sure what I'm going to find out here, Dan.'

Marchant wondered too, but if Denton was going to do anything interesting, it would be after his Special Branch officer had left for the night. Earlier he had called Paul Myers on his pay-as-you-go number and asked him to hack into Denton's bank account, find out where he shopped, look for any unusual payments. Myers had been reluctant at first – he was already

214

feeling uneasy about delaying the Revolutionary Guard intercept – but Marchant knew it would appeal to his curiosity.

'His personal data will be well protected,' Myers had said, savouring the challenge already. 'Very well protected. The *News of the World*'s been after it for months. And Armstrong's. And the Prime Minister's.'

'Did they get anywhere?'

'Only with the PM's bank account. That's because they didn't understand –'

'It's OK, I'll take your word for it.' Marchant didn't have time to listen to one of Myers's technical explanations. They tended to be long and incomprehensible. 'Can you do it?'

'I can try.'

Two hours later, a triumphant Myers was on the phone again. In the past year, Denton had shopped almost exclusively online for his clothes, except for the House of Fraser in Hull, formerly Hammonds, where he had picked up two suits in person.

'There's just one thing that strikes me as odd,' Myers said. 'He buys his food at Waitrose.'

'What's strange about that? Just because he's from Hull, you think he should be shopping at Booths?'

'Listen, pal, I'm from the Midlands, and I shop at Waitrose. We're all middle-class now. It's not that. He could have the stuff delivered. Waitrose Home or Avocado if he's in London.'

'Ocado. Bit posh for Denton.'

'He buys his food at the Clapham Junction branch, St John's Road, every Tuesday and Friday evening. Pays with his partnership card. If I was Chief of MI6, I think I'd have it delivered, don't you?'

Myers had a point. And it was a Friday evening now. Perhaps Denton's solitary shopping trips were a thing of the past, the habit of a deputy, but it was worth a try, which was why he wanted Jean-Baptiste to stay on the case tonight.

'Be patient,' Marchant told him. 'Denton gets hungry on a Friday.'

'So you said. I'm also hungry, but I think I'll wait until I'm back in France to eat again. He's out. Closes front door. Checks up and down the street. Heading my way. Far side. Walking quickly.'

'He wants his dinner. He'll go down Latchmere Road, then turn right to Waitrose.' Marchant had called up Google Street View on the computer screen. 'Follow him. I think this might be it.'

65

Spiro poured himself a large bourbon and sat down on the edge of the bed in his living quarters in Bagram. They were on the far side of the base, away from the runway, but he could still hear the sound of aircraft. The base was always busy, giant C-5 and C-17 cargo planes landing day and night, F-15 and F-16 jets screaming down the runway. After vowing never to eat there again, he had just had another lousy meal at DFAC, the base's dining facility. He used to find it funny, but he hadn't felt comfortable tonight seeing the Muslim LECS (locally employed civilians) serving up bacon and pork dishes. It would only breed hatred for America, fill the world with more Salim Dhars.

He stood up and went over to the small window, from where he could see the Hindu Kush to the north and the Salang Pass. Beyond the perimeter wire, the grassy plains were dotted with solitary locust trees. A gathering ball of dust was rolling in towards the base, where it would coat everyone and everything in another layer of sand. It drove some servicemen crazy, particularly those who were billeted in the rows of canvas tents down by the hospital. Spiro had more of a problem with the permanent smell of aviation fuel that seemed to hang over the base like an accusing miasma.

Spiro had driven up to the Salang Pass once, where a treacherous road cut through the snow-tipped mountains at ten thousand feet. It was after a particularly gruelling interrogation. The detainee, a local taxi driver, had died in custody, five days after being captured. It had become clear later that he was innocent. Mistakes happen in war.

At least he knew Dhar was guilty. But he had got under Spiro's skin in a way he had never thought possible. In all the interrogations he had carried out in the frenzied aftermath of 9/11, at Guantánamo's Camp X-Ray and other detention facilities around the world, no one had had such an effect on him. He had been prepared for Dhar to spit at him, insult his religion and his parents, pour scorn on Western decadence and American imperialism – but it was the calculated nature of his attack that had taken Spiro by surprise. Each had known the other's weakness: Dhar's mother and Spiro's wife. Unfortunately, his had proved the greater.

Spiro had consulted earlier with a colleague in Joint Special Operations Command, and it had been decided to leave Dhar in separation for now. JSOC hadn't asked why Spiro would not be proceeding with his interrogation, and he hadn't volunteered an explanation. Instead, he had sarcastically reminded the duty officer that after thirty days, permission would be needed to extend Dhar's isolation to ninety days. Both parties knew it would be a formality.

He picked up his phone from the bedside table and tried to ring his wife's mobile again. It went straight to voicemail, but he didn't leave a message. He had left too many already. Things had not been great between them recently, but he would make amends, try to understand her changing needs. He might even work up an interest in cameras, if that's what it took. Glamour photography didn't sound so bad. It was only now she was gone that he realised how much he missed her. He needed to talk to someone, a friend who had been married for thirty years, but there was no one. Everyone he knew had messed up on the domestic front.

All he could do was focus on practicalities. If she was in Ramallah, his options were limited. He needed to get her away from there without anyone at Langley knowing who she was or what she had been doing. His relationship with Mossad, Israel's foreign intelligence service, had always been complicated, just like the Agency's. Otherwise he would ask them to bring her in.

His preferred option was to return to London. The UK was still reeling from the series of terrorist attacks on its infrastructure, and Washington was keen for him to be at the heart of the US response. His man, Ian Denton, was where he wanted him, running MI6, although the British PM had yet to make his appointment permanent. It was an annoying hitch, but only temporary. Denton owed his promotion to Spiro, and he would be happy to help. He had already told him his wife was missing. MI6 had a number of field officers in the West Bank who could spirit her back to London without too many questions being asked. He tried not to think of it as renditioning his own wife.

A few minutes later, he was on the phone to Denton in London.

'Has the smoke cleared yet?' he asked.

'We're surviving.'

'I can hear traffic. Bad moment?'

'I'm doing my weekly shop.'

'Christ, Ian, Chiefs don't buy their own groceries.'

'Northern ones do. Besides, I like the walk.'

'I'm coming back to London overnight. Are you free for a coffee first thing tomorrow? I need a favour.'

'I'll buy some blueberry muffins.'

66

'Looks like he's celebrating,' Jean-Baptiste said. 'He's heading straight for the fine wines. Bordeaux. I like this guy. For a moment I thought he was buying fruit juice from California.'

Marchant smiled at his old friend's prejudices as he listened to him on the computer. 'Burgundy would have been better.'

'I thought you British were obsessed with Bordeaux.'

'Not all of us.' It was Marchant's father who had introduced him to Burgundies, the *grands crus* of Musigny and Montrachet that still lay in the cellar at Tarlton. He was glad he hadn't moved on to any of them with Dhar.

'Now he's at the bakery. Muffins. Blueberry, I think. The all-American boy.'

It used to be a sausage sandwich from the canteen, Marchant thought. How people change. 'What's he doing now?'

'Looking for the barcode. Scans them.'

Earlier, Jean-Baptiste had described how Denton had gone up to a bank of 'Quick Check' handheld scanners when he had arrived at Waitrose, and Marchant had explained the joys of shopping with a barcode self-scanner, which wasn't yet widespread in France.

'Keep talking,' Marchant said. He wanted to know Denton's every move, however mundane or insignificant it might seem to Jean-Baptiste.

'White bread, sliced. Scans it. What's wrong with a baguette from the local *boulangerie*?'

'Doesn't keep.'

'I hate supermarkets. Now he's looking at – mustards? I don't recognise this. A small white pot? Taking one of them from the back of the shelf.'

'What is it?'

'Black writing on the lid. "Something Relish"?'

'Gentleman's Relish.'

'If you say so.'

'Anchovy paste. Patum Peperium. Very English. You put it on toast.' It was one of those foods, like Marmite, that was hard to explain to a Frenchman.

'He's scanning it – trying to. Looks at his scanner, then around the shop. Another look at the screen. Reading something. He didn't do that with anything else. Puts the pot in his trolley, picks up another and scans that one. Twice. Maybe the first one didn't work.'

It was then that Marchant began to wonder if they were onto something.

'Listen to me carefully, Jean-Baptiste. I think the scanner might be significant.'

'It's a weird-looking thing, isn't it? Like a Geiger counter. Maybe he's searching for weapons of mass destruction. An MI6 obsession, no?'

'Very funny.'

After more banter, Jean-Baptiste became serious again.

'Wait. He did something strange with his hands there. *Legerdemain*. While he was looking at a small packet.'

The internet voice connection began to buffer, distorting Jean-Baptiste's words.

'Say that again,' Marchant said.

'He picked something up – maybe blinis, I'm not sure. I think he stuck something on the packet, then put it back on the shelf. A sticker?'

'Are you certain?'

'No.'

Marchant shifted in the wicker chair, checking instinctively that the door behind him was closed.

'That's not normal.'

'Even for a supermarket?'

'You don't go around putting stickers on food. Not unless you work there.'

After picking up a treacle tart, Denton headed for the checkout, tracked at a distance by Jean-Baptiste, still talking on his hands-free mobile phone to Marchant.

'He scans a barcode on the till . . . hands back the scanner.'

'Normal.'

'Now he pays. With a card.'

'What's happened to the scanner?'

'The girl's put it in a basket, with lots of others.'

'Do you know which one he used?'

'I think so, yes.'

'Keep an eye on it.'

'What about Denton? He's leaving.'

'Let him go.'

Ten minutes later, Jean-Baptiste was loitering by the books and magazines, reading about Carla Bruni in a copy of *Hello!*, when an announcement was made that the store was closing. He rang Marchant.

'They're shutting,' he said.

'The scanners?'

'Still in the basket.'

'Can you see them from the street?'

Jean-Baptiste glanced over at the front of the store. The angle was not great, but it was possible. 'I think so.'

'Leave the store and hang around, see if they put the scanners back after they close.'

Jean-Baptiste didn't have to wait long before the stackers began restocking the shelves. They were young and from a range of ethnic backgrounds, some chatting, others yawning. It reminded him of a holiday job he had once taken with Carrefour. It had put him off supermarkets for life. After a few minutes, a woman picked up the basket of scanners and took them back to a wall panel near the entrance, where she placed each one in a slot. He watched carefully, and made a note of where Denton's ended up: top row, far left. Then he rang Marchant and told him.

'What time does the store open?' Marchant asked.

Jean-Baptiste glanced at the front door, where the opening hours were printed on the window.

'8 a.m.'

'You need to be there.'

67

Denton knew it had been a risk going out to the supermarket, but he had enjoyed the *frisson*. It was a foretaste of what lay ahead. There had been no sign of the DGSE agent who had followed him in his car the day before, but it was good to put others on alert. The French had always spied on the British in London, but it wasn't usually so obvious. It was something he would have to get used to as Chief.

After pouring himself a glass of Fleur de Boüard, he thought of what he was about to do. It wasn't without risk, but tonight was a celebration, a chance to mark his promotion. Besides, the damage had already been done. This time he was sure he was alone. His house had been swept for bugs the day before, partly in response to the French tail, but also as a routine precaution for an incoming Chief.

He had planned to eat first, but he realised he could wait no longer. Hunger would sharpen his senses. He closed the curtains in the sitting room, checked that the reinforced front door was double locked, and walked into the kitchen. The freezer was well stocked with bags of ice cubes, and he took out a packet, weighing it in his hand. How far was he prepared to push it? He fetched a bowl from under the sink and a pair of scissors from a drawer.

Upstairs in his bedroom, various thoughts flooded through

him as he closed the curtains and began to undress. They always did at this point. The lingering guilt, his attempts to expurgate himself through rational argument. It was a subconscious response to his role in the war on terror, nothing more. Disturbing, but beyond his control. The blame lay with others.

The visit to Morocco eight years earlier that had triggered it had been deniable, a small group of MI6 officers shown a level of human degradation that should never have been allowed. He hadn't volunteered to go, he had been sent. It took a while for the scenes to resurface, for him to acknowledge a dark desire to re-enact what he had witnessed. After the first time, he swore he would seek help, but it was futile. He couldn't stop himself. His only mistake was thinking he had been alone.

He went over to the bedside table and pulled out a pair of his ex-wife's old tights. Then he cut off a corner of the bag with the scissors and poured a dozen ice cubes into them, shaking the cubes down to the toe. After glancing at the clock on his radio alarm, he slid a few more ice cubes into the tights. Moving quickly now, he went back to the bedside table and took a solid metal ring from the drawer. It was part of a dog choker chain he had bought from a local pet shop. Attached to it was a smaller ring with a key and a long length of nylon string.

He slid the tights through the bigger ring until it was resting on top of the ice, then tied them high up on the curtain rail, so the ice-filled leg was hanging down. He placed the bowl on the floor beneath it to catch the drips. Finally, he relayed the string over to the ceiling light, and tied it to the lampshade. He had measured everything up before, but he glanced once more at the hanging ice, and followed the string back to the light above the bed. When the ice melted, the tights would slide through the ring and the keys would swing down on the string to where he was lying.

Five minutes later he was on his front, legs bent double and hog-tied at the knees and ankles so his heels were clamped against the back of his thighs. He had already inserted a nickel-plated ring into his mouth, locking open his jaws in a way that gave him a look of permanent shock (it was safer than a ball gag). All he had to do now was clamp his wrists into the handcuffs. He knew it was a risk binding his arms behind his back – it would make the key harder to pick up when it swung down onto the bed – but tonight was different. Fifteen ice cubes would keep him busy for at least four hours, longer than he had ever gone before.

He clicked the handcuffs shut, closed his eyes and imagined he was back at the al-Tamara interrogation centre outside Rabat, bound and gagged and pleading for his life.

68

After an early breakfast of a croissant and coffee with Florianne, who was less welcoming than the day before, Marchant looked in on Lakshmi. She was awake, and smiled faintly when she saw him. It was clear she was still heavily sedated. Marchant knew the French liked their pharmaceuticals, and he would have trusted Clémence with his life, but it was still upsetting to see Lakshmi so drugged up. He reminded himself of the phone call, her act of betrayal. But it was hard to imbue the limp figure lying before him with treachery.

'How are you feeling?' he asked.

'OK. A little sleepy,' she said, her voice slurred.

'We're going to stay here for a few days, then head back to Britain.' He wanted to see how she reacted, establish if her mind was still sharp. Returning to the UK was the last thing someone in his situation would do.

'That's nice,' she said.

Back in the barn, Marchant sat down in front of the computer, trying not to think about Lakshmi. If her body was free of drugs, they could talk properly, and he could find out what Spiro had done to buy her loyalty. Maybe then there would be a way back for her, for both of them. But he couldn't take the risk of letting her recover.

He checked his watch. In a few minutes he would ring Jean-Baptiste in London, where he would be waiting for the -supermarket to open. Marchant had been up half the night, researching barcodes. He was convinced that Denton had used the handheld scanner to read information on the pot of Gentleman's Relish, before placing his own code on a packet of blinis.

Technology had come a long way since the days of a few lines and numbers denoting a product's name and price. It was now possible for anyone to convert text into a barcode (and vice versa) and print it out, using free software and an ordinary printer. New two-dimensional QR (quick response) matrix barcodes could contain large amounts of data, including digital photos, which were easy to read with a mobile phone app. Supermarkets weren't far behind, introducing increasingly sophisticated handheld readers with multimedia colour screens. As a way of uploading and downloading information, it was more subtle than a transmitter concealed in a plastic rock, the method used by hapless MI6 colleagues in Moscow.

'You sound hungover,' Marchant said when he had connected to Jean-Baptiste.

'I tell myself every time not to drink your warm beer.'

'Someone's going to come in early and use Denton's scanner.'

'But you can't choose which one you're given. It's randomly selected.'

'You or I can't choose, but maybe Denton can.' Marchant glanced at his watch: 9 a.m. in France, 8 a.m. in Britain. 'Is the shop opening?'

'Yes, on time. Unlike your buses.'

'Any sign of anyone?'

'There's a man I've been watching for a few minutes. He was in the queue outside the doors. Medium build, suit, close-cropped hair. Ordinary looking, except his eyes. Definitely made in Moscow.'

'What's he doing now?'

'Walking towards the scanners with his trolley – and past them. Picks up some flowers. White lilies.'

'Damn. Anyone else around?'

'Wait, he's coming back, taking out his wallet. He's at the rack of scanners. A tall woman, dyed blonde hair, is in front of him. She puts her card in the machine and – yes – a scanner lights up. Second row down, fourth from the right. She takes it, our man steps forward. This could be a good game, guessing which scanner. If I ever have kids, I'll bring them here instead of the park. Hours of fun.'

'Just tell me what he's doing.'

'He's about to swipe his card. Which scanner is your money on?'

'Top row, far left.'

'*Et voilà*.'

Marchant's palms began to sweat. He tried to think through the best course of action if Denton was using the scanners to communicate with his Russian handler. The barcode might reveal instructions for where and when to meet, whether a meeting was on or had been cancelled. Or it might contain more complex information that could be read later by a scanning app.

It would be hard to prove anything without alerting Moscow. The weakness of the system was the overnight delay between the barcode being placed on a product just before closing time and it being read the next morning as soon as the store opened. If Jean-Baptiste could get access to the barcode during the night, he might be able to read and replace it without raising the alarm. But Denton wasn't due to go shopping again until next Tuesday, and Marchant couldn't afford to wait that long.

For the next few minutes he listened as Jean-Baptiste relayed the Russian's shopping habits: cold meats, sourdough bread, pickled gherkins, Stolichnaya vodka.

'No blinis?'

'He's walked straight past them.'

'He'll be back. What's he doing now?'

'Talking on his phone. Wait, he's heading round to the smoked salmon again – and to the blinis. I can move in from behind and get in quite close here.'

'Be careful.'

'He's picked up a packet, thirty-six cocktail blinis, from the back of the shelf. It's the same packet Denton handled last night. Now he's scanning it.'

For a few seconds, Jean-Baptiste said nothing. Marchant thought the line might have dropped. He told himself to relax. Jean-Baptiste had said he was standing close to the Russian. He was just being careful, couldn't talk. Then he spoke, his voice breathless, as if he was running.

'I'm blown. I've got to get out of here.'

'What happened?'

'I could see the screen of his scanner when he read the barcode.'

'And?'

'It was a photo.'

'Of what?'

'Me.'

69

Dhar sat cross-legged on the floor of his cell, staring at the two hatches in the steel door. One was at ankle height, the other waist height. At the top of the door was an observation aperture covered with a sliding steel plate and a grille. For twenty-three hours a day he was on his own like this. It didn't bother him, not yet anyway. By his reckoning, he had been in Bagram for three days.

Every eight hours the middle hatch opened and a tray of food was passed through. Once a day, both hatches slid open and he was asked to stand close to the door, his hands together in front of him. A silent guard then shackled his wrists and ankles, let him out of the cell and led him to a caged area measuring five feet by fifty feet. Known as 'the dog kennel', it was where Dhar was allowed to exercise for one hour. There was no natural light anywhere.

Dhar was indifferent about his exercise break. He was content in his cell, his mental strength and *Samyama* routines more than enough to allow him to deal with the solitude and the crude attempts to confuse his body clock. The single lightbulb had been left on for the first twenty-four hours, then he was in darkness for what felt like a further twenty-four. He presumed mealtimes were also being altered, but he listened to the rhythm of his body, forcing regular patterns of behaviour onto the empty days.

It was something he had learnt at the training camps, where he had survived longer than most in solitary confinement. While others had talked about their brains atrophying, the desperate need to talk to others and then to themselves, Dhar had encountered no such problems. To cope with the boredom and disorientation, he would choose a particular day from his past and live in it, second by second, hour by hour.

The day when he had met his real father, Stephen Marchant, was a favourite. It was the first and only time they had seen each other, in a black site in South India. His world had shattered and come together in those few moments when Marchant had told him that he was his son.

Today he would have no reason to live in the past. But he didn't know that when the middle hatch slid open. He rose from the cell floor to take the plastic tray. The food usually smelt worse than it tasted, and noxious vapours were rising off the small serving of *dhal*. Dhar didn't bother to acknowledge the American guards who brought him the food, but this time the tray bearer caught his eye through the observation aperture. He was an Afghani.

After taking the tray, Dhar held eye contact with the man, whose striking green eyes looked frightened behind the thick safety glasses worn by all the guards to protect them from anything thrown or sprayed at them by inmates. Small and wiry, the Afghani was one of many LECs who worked at Bagram. He nodded at the tray, the rubber seal of his glasses pressed against his glistening eyebrows. The *chapatti* was usually served flat. This time it was folded into a neat square, like a napkin. Dhar glanced at it and then looked back at the Afghani, who slid the middle panel shut and walked away.

There was only one place in the cell where Dhar could not be observed, and he sat there now with his back to the wall. The tray was in front of him on the floor. He leant forward, and was about to pick up the *chapatti* when he thought again about the Afghani. He sat back. The man had been trying to signal something to him. Was Iran about to keep its promise?

He recalled the last meeting with Ali Mousavi, his old ally in Iran, who had made contact while he had been training in Russia for the attack on Fairford and GCHQ.

'We have a job for you that would suit both our purposes,' Mousavi had said. He went on to give enough details for him to agree in principle. Dhar was losing what little enthusiasm he had for the Russians – there had been another clampdown on Muslims in Dagestan. The proposed Iranian operation was in the Strait of Hormuz and the target was American.

'First, though, I have a difficult mission in Britain,' Dhar had replied. 'I may need your assistance if I fall into the hands of the infidel.'

'Once your work is done there, we will help you all we can, wherever you are.'

Dhar was certain that Mousavi's offer had been genuine, and that Iran wanted to use his global popularity to win wider support for their own *jihad* against America.

He studied the tray of food, wondering what, if anything, was inside the folded *chapatti*. For a moment he thought it might be a key. He cursed the thought – it would take more than a key to get out of Bagram. Perhaps he had imagined the look of honesty in the Afghani's eyes, and was about to fall into a trap. Spiro would prefer him dead, particularly after their chat about his wife. But he had always trusted his instinct, and now it told him to trust the Afghani.

He leant forward and picked up the *chapatti*. There was definitely something inside it, bulging beneath the top fold. His hands were shaking. Or was it the *chapatti*? It seemed to be vibrating.

Slowly, he undid the thin bread, peeling back the layers with his index finger and thumb. Then he saw it: a two-inch-long Asian giant hornet. Before he could remove his hand, the confused insect twitched its carapaced abdomen in an aggressive arc and stung Dhar's finger.

The pain was instant, like a burning nail being driven up through his hand and along his arm towards his heart, but it was the memory that scared Dhar more. He was back in Delhi again, a seven-year-old child playing in a British expat's garden, his throat and tongue swelling as he struggled to breathe. '*Amma!*' he screamed. '*Amma!*' His mother had waved to him a few minutes earlier from a top window of the house, where she was babysitting.

He started to wheeze; his airway felt blocked. He didn't know if any words came as he cried out again, looking for his mother in the grille of the prison door. A heavy paralysis crept up his arm, the skin of which was already turning a deep red. White lumps bubbled up over the back of his hand and his knuckles. But it was his face that frightened him the most. He could feel it swelling up like a balloon, as if someone had attached a bicycle pump to his finger and was inflating his head through his arm.

Why had he trusted the Afghani, he thought, as he began to lose consciousness. This was Spiro's work, revenge for having taunted him about his wife. It wouldn't be the first time. The CIA had somehow discovered his phobia, just as they had known about Abu Zubaydah's fear of insects when they had interrogated him at Guantánamo.

'*Amma!*' he tried to shout again, writhing on the floor of his cell. He didn't care if Spiro saw him crying like a baby. He wanted his mother. The last memory he had was of the Afghani's pellucid eyes peering in at him. They still looked honest.

70

Marchant threw some of Jean-Baptiste's clothes into a bag and looked around the room, checking he hadn't left any evidence of his stay at the château. Clémence was in the main house with Lakshmi. He hadn't told either of them that he was going. It wouldn't be too long before Jean-Baptiste would be back. After his face had shown up on the Russian's scanner, he had left the supermarket as quickly as he could, driving straight to Heathrow, from where he had emailed Marchant some photos of Denton and the Russian. There was no point in him staying on in London if his cover had been blown.

'You must leave too,' he had said. 'At once. If they know about me, they know about you.'

He had told Marchant where he kept a sheaf of spare passports. All of them were French except one, which was British.

'Get yourself to Orly. I'll be at passport control to make sure you get on a plane. Where do you want to go?'

'Essaouira would be good.'

Marchant took the keys for the Citroën Mehari and headed over to the barn where it was kept, thinking about Morocco. His last few minutes with Dhar in Tarlton had been surreal, raising glasses of vodka and whisky to their shared *jihad* moments before British special forces had stormed the house. Marchant had asked how Dhar would contact him, if – once – he had managed to escape from Bagram. 'A camel herder in Essaouira,' Dhar had said, grinning, sounding like someone out of the Arabian Nights. Last time, it had been a storyteller in Marrakech. He trusted his followers in Morocco.

Jean-Baptiste was on the phone again as Marchant slung his bag into the back of the Mehari.

'I've booked you a ticket to Essaouira. Direct flight from Orly, plenty of holiday cover. I know the sector well. Have you got money?'

'I'm good,' Marchant replied, but he didn't feel great as he sat behind the wheel, his hand hesitating before he inserted the key into the ignition. It went against his instincts to leave Lakshmi with Clémence. Despite everything, he was still in two minds about her. While she remained heavily sedated, she was vulnerable. He didn't like that. But she was also working for Spiro, and knew Marchant's location. She had already demonstrated that she was prepared to betray him. He got out of the car and walked back to the main house, weighing up his options.

It was quiet as he entered the door to the kitchen. Too quiet. Florianne was usually at the long farmhouse table drinking coffee, or sitting outside beside the small lake at the back of the château. There was no sign of the Pomeranian, either. Marchant tensed. The incident with Jean-Baptiste at the supermarket had shaken him out of the complacency that had set in over recent days.

'Clémence?' he called, walking up the stairs. For a moment he considered returning to the car for the gun, which was in his bag. He had planned to hand it over to Jean-Baptiste once he was safely at the airport.

There was no answer.

'Clémence?' he called again, making his way quietly down the landing to the room where Lakshmi was sleeping.

He stopped to listen. Silence. Then he heard a muffled sound, and entered the room quickly. Clémence was sitting on the chair beside the bed with her hands tied behind her back. Her feet were tied too, and there was a gag in her mouth.

Lakshmi's bed was empty.

71

Lt. Col. (Dr) Patch McQuaid, emergency medicine flight commander at Bagram's Craig Joint Theater Hospital, was prepping the four-bed trauma bay for the imminent arrival of a Medevac helo when a patient from the internment facility was wheeled in through the door on a gurney. McQuaid had already been alerted by a doctor at the jail's small medical facility that a high-value detainee was coming over. He was suffering from severe anaphylaxis and his condition was critical, beyond their limited resources.

It wasn't the first time some jerk from JSOC had overstepped the mark during an interrogation, he thought, and it wouldn't be the last. He was through with putting prisoners back together after they had been broken apart by torture. It wasn't why he had joined the USAF, or why he had been deployed from Lackland Air Force Base in Texas.

The Craig Joint Theater Hospital prided itself on acting as the main hub for all forward surgical stations in Afghanistan, looking after US servicemen and locals, including the enemy. Only last week an injured Taleban fighter had been brought into the trauma bay, thrashing around and spitting at staff. It turned out the Marine who had shot him was on the next gurney in. The fighter eventually calmed down after an Afghani nurse, on a mentorship programme at the hospital, explained that he wasn't going to be killed.

The detainee lying in front of him now wasn't thrashing about, but he was clearly a threat to someone, given the level of security that accompanied his arrival. Half a dozen Military Police guards stood at the door of the trauma bay, M4 carbines at the ready. McQuaid recognised Jim Spiro, a spook whose path he had crossed before, waiting beyond them.

'Sir, he's not responding to IM adrenaline,' a young medical technician said, glancing up at the Military Police guards. 'And he's important.'

'Every patient is,' McQuaid said, looking down at the swollen body. 'Every patient is.'

'Some kind of crazy giant wasp was found in his cell. He was in the separation wing.'

'Just flew in through the open window, I guess,' McQuaid said, adjusting his stars-and-stripes scrub cap. 'We need oxygen and IV epinephrine, chlorphenamine and hydrocortisone. Titrate slowly and keep an eye on the monitor.'

'Sir.'

'What happened?' McQuaid called across the room to Spiro as he stabilised the patient, establishing his airway. His blood pressure was low, his heart racing. Urticaria wheals covered more than 90 per cent of his body. McQuaid had seen far worse in the previous six months, blast injuries that would wake him at night in his retirement, but the red, bloated figure was still shocking. He doubted if his own mother would recognise him. His face was without features, blown up like a basketball, eye sockets reduced to tiny slits, his nose hardly breaking the surface of the puffy flesh. Only his lips stood out, grossly swollen like a pair of baby bananas.

'Another fucked-up question-and-answer session?' McQuaid continued, still addressing Spiro as he glanced at the ECG monitor.

'Dangerous insect dropped into confined space with detainee? Oh shit, he's not talking, he's dying. Jesus, when are you people going to learn?'

Spiro appeared not to have heard his outburst. Either that or he was ignoring him. A lot of people did. McQuaid glanced up at the large American flag hanging on the wall. It was good that he was flying back to Texas in a week. He was beginning to lose it. Too many stressful shifts. A few weeks earlier, one of his radiologists had discovered a bullet lodged in the scalp of an Afghani. It turned out to be an unexploded incendiary round. Everyone except key personnel had to be evacuated from the hospital while a surgeon removed the UXO from the poor guy's head, assisted by the bomb-disposal team. Today had all the hallmarks of another hectic watch. Reports were coming in of an attack on a US patrol just outside Bagram. Two dead, four traumas on their way.

A member of the Afghan National Army (ANA) had been bitten by a snake and reacted badly. He was about to arrive too, no doubt with his entire family in tow. When locals were brought in, the place resembled one of the Pashtun villages beyond the perimeter fence. As if that wasn't enough, the base had been put on full alert after a rocket attack the previous day. It wasn't an unusual event.

Bagram had been attacked half a dozen times during McQuaid's latest tour, and he had grown used to the sight of the fifteen-foot-high blast walls everywhere, including a line of them between the hospital entrance and the helipad. The only consolation was that the Taleban's rockets and mortars were about as accurate as Ryan Rowland-Smith's pitching. Why the Houston Astros wanted to sign him next season was anyone's guess.

The first US traumas began to come through the door as McQuaid was administering epinephrine intravenously to the detainee. There were six in total, not four, and their injuries were some of the worst he had seen. McQuaid and his team remained calm, as they always did, but a chilling scream of pain and the sudden influx of people into an already crowded trauma bay began to nudge the atmosphere towards chaos. The simultaneous arrival of two ANAs with their snakebitten colleague and extended family didn't help. He was almost as swollen as the detainee.

'We should have taken him to Kabul!' one of the ANAs shouted. He was hysterical, accusing staff of ignoring his friend, who was lying on a collapsible gurney.

It was just as McQuaid began to explain how his hospital treated everyone as equals that the first explosion rocked the hospital. The blast, a white flash of heat, knocked him to the ground. Later he could only recall snatches of what followed, fleeting cameos of carnage. Amid the panic and the shouts of 'Incoming!' he remembered the lights going out and seeing the ANAs move purposefully through the smoke and debris towards the detainee. It only later struck him as odd that they had somehow managed to avoid the worst of the blast.

At the same time, he spotted Spiro lying on the floor next to the armed MPs, at least two of whom appeared to be dead. His sense of the order in which things happened was poor, but he was almost certain that there was a second explosion – he remembered another blinding flash – before he saw the ANAs and locals gathered around the high-value detainee's bedside. Had they lifted him up? Slumped in the corner, his ears ringing and dust in his mouth and eyes, McQuaid couldn't be sure. All he could remember was the ANAs walking out of the trauma bay, accompanied by the locals and a bloated figure on a gurney.

72

'I hate what he does, his work. Sometimes he goes for weeks, never calls. Then he's back in my life as if nothing happened. And now this. Who the hell was she? What was she doing in my mother-in-law's house? How dare she?'

Marchant knew that all he could do was roll with the punches. Clémence had every right to be upset. After spending three days looking after Lakshmi, she had been tied up and gagged. He did his best to keep out of the way as Clémence paced around the room, running a hand through her short hair. She could be very frightening for someone so small.

'I'm sorry,' he offered. 'I should never have brought her. As I said to Jean-Baptiste. It was a big mistake. Selfish.'

'You're all the same. British spy, French *espion*, what does it matter? You lie in your job and you lie at home to your lovers and your friends. I don't want anything more to do with this. After she tied me up, she looked at me with pity. Pity! As if to say, "You poor bitch, married to a spy." And she's right.'

'Clémence, Jean-Baptiste will be back in a few hours.'

'Is that what he said to you? He hasn't rung me since he left for London. Didn't dare, because he knew what I would say. And I can't ring him, because I don't even have my own phone any more.'

'It was my fault he went. I asked him to go.'

'But he knew this was meant to be a special holiday. The one time in the year when we can be together, be ourselves. First my phone is taken away from me, then my husband, and now I'm tied up by someone I've spent the last three days looking after. I even thought we could be friends.'

'I must go,' Marchant said. 'Find out where she's gone.'

Clémence said nothing for a while. She just stood in the middle of the room, smirking, nodding her head in anger.

'Go. Why not? You didn't protect me when you were here. Do you have a cigarette?'

'I don't smoke.'

'Nor do I. But I need one.'

'I had no idea she was –'

'You're right, you had no idea. Do you know what Jean-Baptiste asked me to do? Keep her as close to death as I could. That's not an easy thing for a doctor to do. We are trained to make people healthy. Actually, I don't blame her for running away. She was a strong woman, making a good recovery from an addiction she had beaten once and was determined to beat again. Why should she lie there, taking morphine when her body could be free of drugs? And why should I give it to her?'

From the moment he had found Clémence bound and gagged, Marchant had wondered how a sedated Lakshmi had managed to overpower her. Now he began to understand.

'Had you been giving her the right dose?' he asked.

'What is "right"? How would you know the correct dose? You're not a doctor. I gave her what I thought was right in the circumstances. She had suffered a minor relapse after two years of clean living. It was not right to sedate her so strongly.'

'Did you give her anything?'

Clémence paused, and sat down on the edge of the bed. Tears

243

were beginning to well. When she wasn't speaking – or shouting – she suddenly seemed vulnerable, a tiny figure in a dangerous world. Marchant was about to walk over and comfort her when she looked up at him, struggling to maintain her defiance.

'To begin with, yes. But then she was making such good progress. How could I stop someone from getting well? I didn't spend seven years at medical school so I could stop someone from recovering.'

So Lakshmi had played them all, faking her sedation. It was a pact between her and Clémence, the doctor who could do no harm. He should have known.

'Did she say where she was going?'

'I didn't ask. I heard her screaming, apparently in pain. I came running, and she was hiding behind the door. I had no chance.'

'Did she say anything to you at all?' Marchant asked, looking out of the window onto the courtyard below.

'Only that she was sorry and didn't want to harm me. She even checked that the gag in my mouth was not uncomfortable.'

'She's a spy too, you know that?'

Clémence smirked again, lost in thought.

'Then she's not like other spies I know.'

'She works for the CIA, who want me dead. Her job was to report back on me.'

'I thought you were lovers.'

'We were.'

'I'd better check on my mother-in-law. I heard a car drive off.'

'Florianne's?'

'I think so. It's a Golf, GTI. Her pride and joy. Lakshmi must have taken the keys from the kitchen.'

Two minutes later, Marchant and Clémence were untying Florianne, who had also been bound and gagged in her bedroom.

She was a strong, dignified woman and her pride was still intact, even as she sat at her dressing-room table, her feet and hands tied with silk scarves to the chair, another scarf in her mouth.

There was no sign of the dog.

73

'We've got orders not to let anybody in or out,' the young guard said as an HH-60 helicopter arced low over the main entrance to Bagram Air Base. Moments earlier he had watched it take off from the helipad beside the hospital, rising through the smoke that had engulfed the building. It was the second attack on the base in a week, but this one looked serious. The hospital had never been targeted before.

'Our friend is dying,' the ANA soldier pleaded, nodding towards the back of their Humvee. 'You saw when we brought him in.'

'I'm sorry,' the guard said, glancing across at the hospital, hoping the chaos of the situation was enough of an explanation. But he knew he was weakening. He couldn't forget the bloated body the ANAs had shown him fifteen minutes earlier, the concern of the relatives who had accompanied him. He had nearly retched when he had seen the puffed-up skin. Bitten by a snake, apparently.

'The hospital has been badly hit,' the ANA continued. 'We were lucky not to be killed.'

'Will he make it to Kabul in the Hummer?' the guard asked. He had heard on the radio that they were transferring patients and injured staff by helicopter to various forward operating bases. The worst were being flown out to Landstuhl hospital in Germany.

'If we go now,' the Afghani said. 'Many people are injured here. We will only add to their burden. It is better we go elsewhere.'

The guard glanced again at the back of the Humvee.

'Please check,' the Afghani said. 'I don't want to get you into trouble. We just want to save our friend.'

The guard walked around the vehicle and knocked once on the rear door. It was a new Humvee, one of many that the Afghan National Army had bought from the Americans. What he couldn't see was that the identification markings on the roof had not been changed yet. They still signified that it was a US military vehicle. The rear door swung open. Three locals stared back at him, heads covered with scarves, fear in their eyes. On the floor the bloated patient lay on a collapsed gurney. He wore uniform and his face was even more swollen than before, like a Kharbouza melon. The guard closed the door and vomited into the sand by the roadside.

'OK, you can go through,' he said. 'And take care on the way. Someone's got it in for us today.'

The driver smiled nervously and drove off. But when he reached the main road, he didn't turn south towards Kabul, he headed north. Shortly after Charikar, he turned left onto Asian Highway 77 and prepared to drive west through the night towards Herat, where they would switch vehicles for a smaller 4x4, change into civilian clothes and speed seventy-five miles with their patient to the Iranian border.

74

Marchant spotted the dog as he was crossing the courtyard in the Mehari. He pulled up at the gates, climbed out of the vehicle and walked across the lawn. At first he had thought it was a T-shirt belonging to one of the boys, who had left earlier in the day, but clothing would have sunk. The dog was floating head down, in the middle of the deep end.

Marchant had left Clémence with Florianne. He hadn't been able to look either of them in the eye as he had said goodbye, saying that Jean-Baptiste would be with them soon. Why should they believe him? He had failed to shield them from a dangerous woman he had brought into their home.

Glancing up at the house, he found a net that was used for cleaning the pool and slipped it under the dog. He lifted it up, hoping the net wouldn't break with the weight, and swung the animal onto the grass. It was obviously dead, but he still checked the soggy fur for signs of life. He didn't want Florianne to know that her beloved Pomeranian had drowned, silenced by the same woman who had tied her up in her own house.

Carrying it by the legs, Marchant took the wet carcass over to some bushes, and tossed it deep into the undergrowth. He didn't have the time – or the inclination – to bury it, he told himself, as he walked back to the car. It was just a dog. Then he saw a spade and a garden fork propped up against the raised vegetable beds. Damn, he thought. Damn the bloody Pomeranian, damn Lakshmi. Where had she gone? To the nearest village with a public phone, he guessed. She would ring Spiro, who would tell her to keep following him. So why had she left, and in such a hurry? What did she want to tell him?

There was no sign of anyone at the windows of the house as he jogged over to the spade, but he was careful to remain out of sight, cutting behind a row of poplar trees. After digging a shallow grave, he retrieved the dog and placed it in the cool earth beneath the bushes. He wasn't going to make a cross out of sticks, he really wasn't.

It was as he accelerated down the drive that Paul Myers rang him.

'I've got some news,' he said. It was hard to tell if Myers was excited or terrified. 'He's out.'

'Dhar?'

'Escaped an hour ago. We're in meltdown here. Americans suddenly wanting to share all our Farsi intel again.'

'Was it the Iranians?'

'We don't know, but I'm fucked if it was, Dan. Well and truly screwed. I shouldn't have sat on that intercept.'

Marchant hadn't heard Myers like this before. He had to calm him down, reassure him. At the back of his mind, though, he knew it had been asking too much of his friend to withhold the Revolutionary Guard intel for twenty-four hours.

'Where are you calling from?'

'My flat.'

'I'm almost certain it's the Iranians who sprung him.'

'Jesus, Dan. What are you getting into? There's an alert out for you, too. And for Fielding.'

'You have to pool what you heard. Otherwise it will look as if

249

you're covering something up. Can you alter the timings? Make it look like a mistake?'

'I don't know. I was in real time, not data mining. It doesn't look good for me, Dan. In fact, it looks shit.'

'I realise that.' Marchant paused. 'I know it's hard, but it's important, otherwise I wouldn't have asked. It will be worth it, trust me.'

'Not if I'm bloody arrested, it won't. There was an internal warning last week about Iranian sympathisers.'

'You're not going to get arrested, Paul. I promise.'

But he wasn't so sure.

75

Spiro's ears were still ringing when he took the call from the Director of the CIA. Technically, Salim Dhar was Joint Special Operations Command's prisoner at the time he had escaped, but Spiro was overseeing his interrogation, and Washington had decided that the Agency would take the drop.

He didn't hear much of what the DCIA said as he stepped into a corridor outside the medical bay. He couldn't hear much of what anyone said. But he understood the general message. His career was over if Dhar wasn't recaptured within twenty-four hours. So far there had been a successful news blackout of his escape. The attack on the Craig Joint Theater Hospital was being widely reported in the US media, but no mention had been made of Dhar. It wouldn't be long, Spiro thought, before news seeped out and the CIA was the laughing stock of the world.

He had refused to be medevacced out of Bagram. The worst traumas were already on their way to Germany, but he had chosen to be patched up at the internment medical bay. It was over-stretched but doing what it could in the aftermath of the mortar attack. As Spiro walked back in to have his hands bandaged, he looked around for the doctor who had made the initial assessment of Dhar. There was no sign of him.

He had rung in a panic, telling Spiro that a high-value detainee was about to die unless he received expert medical attention at the hospital. 'I've never seen anaphylaxis like it,' he had said. 'I've injected him with adrenaline, but no response. The guy's body will blow unless he gets proper treatment.'

The temptation to let Dhar swell until he exploded had been considerable, but Washington was adamant that he should be kept alive to stand trial, once he had told the Agency everything he knew. So Spiro had authorised the fateful transfer. He had been knocked unconscious by the blast that had ripped the roof off the hospital, but as he explained to the young medic who was dressing his hands, he had seen a lot worse in Iraq.

'That's the first war, when things were done properly,' he said. And probably before you were born, he wanted to add, but resisted. He felt old enough already. Apart from his hearing, which would return eventually, he had minor cuts to his face and hands, and a shrapnel wound across his right calf. He knew he had been lucky to survive, but he also knew you made your own luck in war.

It was now more than an hour since Dhar had escaped. Spiro had feared the worst from the moment he had regained consciousness. The timing of the mortar attack on the hospital was too much of a coincidence. At first, it had looked as if Dhar had missed his chance to cut and run, and was still lying on a bed in the trauma bay. It was only as the dust settled that Spiro suspected he had been switched with another patient.

Suspicion turned to sickening reality when it emerged that an ANA had been admitted with anaphylaxis at the same time. Spiro had called through to the air base commander and asked for as many helicopters to get airborne as possible. By all accounts, the ANA vehicle was heading for Kabul, but he wanted checks on all roads out of Bagram.

He also wanted to know what his wife was doing. As he left

the medical bay, his hands bandaged like ski gloves, he checked to see if she had rung. There were no missed calls, but the phone was ringing in his clumsy hands. He hadn't heard it, couldn't hear it now. Alarmed, he lifted the handset to his ear and detected a distant ringing tone. The damage to his ears was worse than he thought. He accepted the international call and explained that whoever it was would have to speak up. It was Lakshmi Meena.

76

'She took your mother's car,' Marchant said on the phone as he drove fast in the Mehari towards Barneville-Carteret. 'And I'm in yours.'

'Look after it,' Jean-Baptiste replied. He was at Heathrow, shortly to board his flight to Paris. 'There's a GPS tracker on the Golf. I installed it last year, borrowed from the office. Give me a second – I can see where she is with an app on my phone.'

Marchant waited while Jean-Baptiste found the car's location. There was no guarantee that Lakshmi was still with it, but it was a start. He had tried to ring Jean-Baptiste as soon as he had untied his wife and mother, but had been unable to get through.

'She's driving my mother's precious car on heavy medication?' Jean-Baptiste asked. 'That's not good.'

'Jean-Baptiste, I don't think she's sedated. Clémence wasn't giving her the proper dose.'

'Why not?'

'She's a doctor. We should never have asked her. She believed Lakshmi was recovering well. She couldn't bring herself to make her ill again.'

There was a pause. Marchant imagined Jean-Baptiste was trying to process the implications.

'Did anyone see her take the car?' he asked.

'No. I was at the computer. And Clémence —' He broke off.

'What? There's something wrong.'

'They're both fine.'

'Tell me what happened.' Jean-Baptiste was angry now.

'I'm sorry. She tied them up.'

'What's going on, Dan?'

'I said they're fine.'

'It doesn't sound like it.'

'Fine and angry. Clémence tried to ring you on the landline, but couldn't get through. I tried too.'

'I'm keeping my phone turned off as much as I can.'

'Is it safe for you to talk now?'

'We're taxi-ing down the runway.'

'I'm sorry about Clémence and Florianne, really I am. If it's any consolation, Lakshmi took care not to hurt them.'

'Find the bitch. Clémence spent three days of her life looking after her – she won't be happy. That's why I try to keep our worlds separate, Dan, to stop things like this happening.'

'I know.'

Jean-Baptiste paused before speaking again. 'I've uploaded some photos to the email you gave me. They show Denton and his friend in the supermarket. I don't know who he is, but I'm sure he's Russian.'

'Thank you.' Jean-Baptiste hadn't actually sent the photos. It was too risky. To avoid detection, he had put them in the draft folder of an anonymous Hotmail account. 'It's my fault about Lakshmi. I should never have brought her here.'

'Just find her for me. She went north at first, but now she seems to be heading towards Caen on the N13.'

'Can you tell if she's stopped anywhere since leaving the château?'

'No stops. If you head straight for Carentan, you should catch up with her on the N13. But be careful, eh? With the Mehari. It's only plastic. And try not to damage my mother's Golf.'

77

'I wanted you to be the first to see them,' Brigadier Borowski said, walking around the small kitchen. They were in an AW safe house in Marki, a suburb in the north-east of Warsaw. Fielding was at the table, sifting through a sheaf of black-and-white photos, a half-empty bottle of whisky next to him. He was unshaven and still wearing the American clothes of his cover. Sleep had eluded him since he had been in Poland. His back was playing up, too. It always did at times of stress.

'How did you get these?' he asked.

'We go back a long way, Marcus, and at the moment I feel very indebted to you, but please don't ask me for the name of our best asset in Moscow.'

Fielding looked up at the Brigadier's broad smile. 'I'm sorry.'

'I felt I hadn't helped you enough with your questions about Hugo Prentice. To lose a close friend is never easy, but to know his death was a mistake is even harder. After we met, I called a meeting and we decided to utilise our asset at the heart of Moscow Centre. It's not something we do very often. Every Western intelligence service should have one, but we're among the few who actually do. As a rule we use him at times of national crisis only, to reduce the risks. But our mistake about Prentice makes this, in my opinion, an emergency.'

'I appreciate it.'

'I have put the images on a memory stick for you. Please use them carefully. It's important Denton has no means of contacting his handler once you confront him with the photos. Otherwise our asset could be blown.'

'Of course.'

Fielding ran through the likely order of events, how best to present the evidence in his hands. It might not be him who did the confronting. He was still shocked by the images before him. The sight of Denton naked was one thing, but it was the overpowering atmosphere of incarceration – the cell-like surroundings, the shackles – that most unsettled Fielding.

Ian Denton had been a colleague for twenty years, his deputy for the last year. Fielding knew he had separated from his wife, but he had never suspected him of anything like this. But then, what did anyone know of anyone else when the curtains closed? The Russians knew. They must have made it their priority to find out. Once they had photographed Denton in such compromising circumstances, the blackmail would have been easy. There may have been no wife to embarrass, but Denton would have agreed to anything to prevent the photos surfacing. They would have destroyed his career. Now Fielding had to make sure they did.

'I never thought the British were like this,' the Brigadier said, looking over Fielding's shoulder at one particularly shocking photo. Denton was holding a razor blade close to his bloodied and swollen penis. Fielding detected the faintest trace of smugness in his voice. He couldn't blame him. 'I thought this was what you did to the other side.'

'That was the Americans,' Fielding said. 'In places like Szymany, a black site in your country, I seem to remember.'

Szymany was where the Americans had taken Daniel Marchant. After flying him out on a rendition flight from Fairford, they had waterboarded him at Stare Kiejkuty, a former outpost of the SS's intelligence wing during the Second World War. It was Prentice who had rescued him.

'We all have our price.'

As Fielding made to leave, Brigadier Borowski's phone rang. He stood in the doorway, handset to his ear, and then said something in Polish that Fielding couldn't catch. He wasn't fluent, but he knew enough to get by.

'Some surprising news from Afghanistan,' Borowski said, clipping the phone shut as he turned to Fielding. 'Salim Dhar has just escaped from Bagram.'

78

Marchant could see the Golf up ahead. They had just passed Bayeux. He had rung Jean-Baptiste for an update on her position, and tried to reassure him again that his wife and mother were out of danger, but he wasn't happy. Marchant didn't blame him. He liked to think he had taken some of the sting out of Clémence's anger, but she would still give Jean-Baptiste hell when he returned. He imagined Florianne could be a handful too.

He overtook the car in front of him, cursing the Mehari for its lack of suspension. There were now only two cars between him and Lakshmi. He had to move quickly, knowing she would recognise the Mehari as soon as she saw it in her rear-view mirror. He waited for another straight stretch of road and then accelerated past the first and then the second car, dropping in tight behind the Golf. Lakshmi was clearly visible in the driver's seat. Why hadn't she stopped at the first opportunity and rung Spiro? Then he saw the reason. She was talking on a mobile phone. Either she had taken Florianne's from her room, or it had been left in the car.

Marchant tried to think through what Lakshmi might have discovered at the château. If she wasn't sedated, she could have overheard everything. He had talked indiscreetly with Jean-Baptiste, as old friends, even field officers, sometimes did, but it had been on the assumption that Lakshmi was unconscious. Whatever it was she had heard, Spiro now knew. He drove alongside the Golf and waited for Lakshmi to look up, keeping an eye on the road ahead.

She glanced across, and was startled to see Marchant. He had expected better of her, thought she would have seen him coming. Capitalising on her surprise, he turned the steering wheel sharply to the right, knocking the Golf sideways with a sickening crunch of plastic. The Mehari wasn't heavy enough to bump her off the road, so he veered away before knocking into the Golf again. Meena had got the message. She took the next slip road off the N13, but she didn't slow down and pull over.

After joining a smaller road, she accelerated away, leaving Marchant no choice but to try again. He spotted a gap in the oncoming traffic and pulled out, bringing the Mehari level with her. The road had begun a sharp curve to the left. Marchant was now in the wrong lane on a blind corner. He turned into the Golf for a third time, just as he saw a lorry coming around the corner towards him, lights on, horn blaring.

79

Despite the incessant noise in his ears, more like a guttural roar now than ringing, Spiro had caught most of Lakshmi's call from a car in France. Daniel Marchant had turned Salim Dhar. His initial reaction was to dismiss the idea out of hand. But as he left the detention centre at Bagram and headed towards the accommodation block, her faint words began to make more sense.

Marchant's presence in the cockpit of a Russian jet had always troubled Spiro. According to Fielding, Dhar had scaled back his attacks on Fairford and GCHQ thanks to Marchant's powers of persuasion. Spiro hadn't believed him at the time, but maybe Marchant really had struck an eleventh-hour damage-limitation deal. They had also been together at the house in the Cotswolds shortly before Dhar was captured. Had they been finalising terms?

Spiro watched as a Chinook helicopter took off nearby. It was unnerving not to hear the distinctive thudding of its twin blades that he knew so well. The roar in his ears provided a more general soundtrack, the amplified din of war as blood coursed through his auditory arteries. The most compelling reason for believing Lakshmi hung over him like the black smoke still drifting across the air base. He tried to ignore it at first, not wanting to contemplate the implications, but by the time he reached his room, he knew it was true. If Marchant was running Dhar, he was no good to him in Bagram – just as Meena had heard the Frenchman say. Which meant that Marchant was in some way involved with the jailbreak.

'Ian, it's Jim Spiro,' he said, talking too loudly into his mobile phone.

'Are you OK?' Denton asked. 'I heard you got caught in the blast.'

'Can we talk about Dhar?'

'Our station head in Kabul just rang with the news.'

'Lakshmi Meena's called in from France. She overheard Marchant talking to some shady French guy, possibly DGSE. She thinks Marchant's recruited Dhar as a British asset.'

'Not with my authority.'

'I kinda figured that. If it's true, he was acting on his own, or more likely on Fielding's orders. Either way, you need to look into the possibility that someone other than Fielding and Marchant might have helped Dhar escape. Fielding's in Russia, Marchant's in France. They couldn't have done this on their own.'

'Someone in MI6?'

'Or Five. Or GCHQ. The goddamn SAS, for all I know. We're looking for anyone who was sympathetic to Marchant and Fielding.'

'That's quite an allegation.'

'Is it? How about a former Chief of MI6 once passed US intel to Moscow. I'd call that quite an allegation.'

'Britain's no friend of Dhar.'

'Neither was Russia, but they helped him. If you don't start asking around, we will.'

80

Marchant braked hard and dropped in behind Lakshmi again as the lorry thundered past. He didn't want to think how close he had been to being shunted back down the road by a ten-tonne juggernaut. He didn't want to think of the damage that had already been done to the Mehari either, or to Florianne's Golf. This time Lakshmi slowed down and pulled into a lay-by. Marchant followed her, reaching for the gun in the bag on the passenger seat. Once both cars were stationary, he slipped the gun down the back of his jeans and walked over to the Golf.

Lakshmi sat impassively, waiting for him. It was as if they were strangers in an American movie, he the traffic cop, she waiting for her ticket. It was hard to think that only a few days earlier, they had shared a bed at the Fort. Life had seemed full of promise then.

'You could have got us both killed,' she said, staring ahead, hands still on the steering wheel.

'You left in a hurry. I figured you might not want to stop.'

'I didn't see you in my mirror.'

'Careless – for someone so good in the field.'

'Don't try to flatter me.'

'Are you getting out?'

'Is that a question?'

Marchant didn't answer. Reluctantly, Lakshmi stepped out of the Golf. She must have calculated that he was armed. It was windy, and she ran a hand through her hair as she looked across the open French countryside. In another life, Marchant would have shared the view with her, but he wasn't in the mood for sightseeing.

'Did Dhar give you the gun?' she asked.

So she had heard him talking to Jean-Baptiste about Dhar.

'I need to know what you've told Spiro.'

'Will you let me tell you why first?'

'I'm guessing blackmail.'

'You make it sound so matter-of-fact. It wasn't something I agreed to lightly. Spiro threatened to destroy my father, his business, everything he's worked for, unless I complied.'

'When did he do that? At the Fort?'

'After you decided not to tell me that Denton was a traitor.'

So she knew about Denton too.

'I thought we really had something,' she continued. 'I was ready to leave the Agency to give us a chance. But Spiro gave me no option. I owe everything to my parents.'

'Including your smack habit? Or were you faking that, too?'

'That was the real deal, Dan,' she said, turning to face him. 'It will be for the rest of my life.'

Marchant paused, holding eye contact. For someone who had just come off hard drugs, she didn't look so bad. Beautiful, in fact. The original heroin chic. 'I really need to know what you've told Spiro,' he repeated.

'Spiro laughed when I told him you thought Denton was a Russian asset.'

Marchant looked down at the ground. It was a delicate situation. He had to establish what she had told Spiro without telling her anything she didn't already know.

'What else did you tell him?'

'Is there anything else?'

'You tell me.'

'Dan, I don't know what game you're playing, but Salim Dhar just got out of Bagram.'

'That was careless too. Did Spiro tell you that?'

'Two minutes ago.'

'How was he?'

'Deaf. He very nearly lost his life in a mortar attack.'

'Now that would have been a shame.'

Marchant had been trying to imagine what had happened in Bagram ever since Myers had told him the news. A mortar attack sounded like the Taleban, who had increasingly close links with Tehran.

'For some reason, Dhar was being treated at the air base hospital. They should have let him die, don't you think? Or did you have other plans for him?'

'I don't know what you're talking about,' Marchant lied. He had to hear her say it.

'He might be your half-brother, Dan, but Dhar's spent his entire adult life trying to destroy my country. He very nearly killed our President.'

Marchant hadn't heard her talk about America in such proprietary terms before.

'And now his followers are trying to destroy my country,' he replied. 'Have you listened to the news recently? Britain is on its knees.'

'So why?'

'Why what?'

'Why are you running him, Dan?'

She had finally said it, what he feared the most. 'Is that what you think, what you told Spiro?'

She didn't answer. An articulated lorry drove past, followed by a line of cars. When they had gone, she turned again to Marchant, speaking quietly this time.

'Just what sort of a deal have you cut with him?'

Now it was Marchant's turn to remain silent. He glanced down the road. A solitary vehicle was approaching.

'I remember you once telling me there were other ways to win the war on terror,' he said. 'It wasn't all about Guantánamo, enhanced interrogation techniques, drone attacks, Jim Spiro. He can't kill them all, you used to say.'

'I still believe that. But there are lines that can't be crossed.'

'And you think I've crossed one?'

'I don't know, Dan. It doesn't seem to surprise you that Dhar's at liberty again. Or even concern you. That really scares me. The thought that you might have helped in some way with his escape.'

Had she told Spiro that, too? The solitary car was getting closer now. For the first time, Marchant began to worry. It was a black people-carrier.

'What exactly did you tell him?' he asked, a hint of urgency in his voice. Time appeared to be running out.

'I overheard Jean-Baptiste say that Dhar wouldn't be much use to you in Bagram. I didn't want to believe it. I tried to convince myself that I'd misheard, but when Spiro said Dhar had just escaped, it made sense. I hope to God you know what you're doing.'

What happened next took place behind bulletproof Perspex, at least that was how Marchant saw it – as if he was watching events through a safety screen. The people-carrier was driving fast, but it slowed as it passed them, almost to walking pace. Marchant saw the gun at the rear passenger window before he had time to draw his own.

'Get down!' he shouted to Lakshmi, but his words came after

the gun had fired. He knew it was aimed at him, but he felt nothing, protected by the Perspex. They both fell to the ground, Lakshmi more awkwardly, on a patch of muddy grass beside the Mehari. Even if they had managed to duck in time, the car's fibreglass shell would have offered little protection against the bullets, one of which had hit Lakshmi in the stomach.

She made no sound as she lay on the grass, bewildered, a hand on her bleeding abdomen. Marchant shouted – a mix of anger and guilt – and stood up, firing off three rounds at the people-carrier, which was now driving away at speed. The rear window exploded into myriad shards, but the car sped on.

81

Denton put the phone down and walked over to the window of his office, trying not to break into a sweat. What was Marchant doing with someone from DGSE? It was too much of a coincidence. Two days earlier, he had been alerted to a tail. Someone from the French intelligence agency had been following him around. MI5 had dismissed it as routine, a welcoming party for a new Chief of MI6, but now it began to look like something more.

He told himself he was worrying unnecessarily and went back to his desk, thinking over what Spiro had said about Dhar's escape. He had enough on his plate without the CIA making wild accusations about British complicity. The events in Bagram had already kicked off an ugly row in Whitehall.

He thought again about Marchant, what he might be doing in France. If anyone could turn Salim Dhar, it was his half-brother. A rapport of some sort clearly existed between them. And then there was Fielding, who had never quite been straight with him about Dhar and Marchant, always holding something back. But nullifying a terrorist was one thing, turning him into an asset quite another.

What advantage did he – or Fielding – think it could possibly bring MI6? Dhar had focused his *jihad* on America, but his followers weren't averse to tearing Britain apart, as recent events had proved. And what about his escape? How could Marchant, on the run in France, possibly have helped?

Early reports suggested that the Taleban had played a central role in the jailbreak, possibly with assistance from Iran. Denton knew the handful of MI6 officers who worked the back channels with the Taleban, and none of them had ever been close to Marchant. The Increment was another possibility, but it was highly unlikely that a rogue element had been drawn into helping with a jailbreak in Afghanistan.

Then it came to him. At the COBRA meeting he had just left, the PM had rounded on the Director of GCHQ, asking why his analysts had not picked up any Taleban or Iranian chatter before the attack. Marchant had friends in Cheltenham, people like Paul Myers, the analyst who had revealed the truth about the drone attack on the six US Marines in North Waziristan. He worked the Farsi beat, and had been one of Leila's many admirers. If anyone had heard the Iranians say something, it would have been him.

Denton picked up the phone and rang Spiro back.

'Can I borrow your interrogation facility at Fairford?'

82

Lakshmi was drifting in and out of consciousness in the passenger seat as Marchant drove fast towards Caen. He had left Jean-Baptiste's damaged Mehari in the lay-by and taken Florianne's Golf. There was no doubt in his mind that he had been the intended target of the shooting, or that Valentin's finger had been on the trigger. The Russians must have followed him from the boat, and would have been on the lookout for a Mehari.

'Try to stay awake, Lakshmi, keep talking to me,' he said. He hoped the hospital in Caen would be easy to find.

'Please don't let them give me painkillers.' Lakshmi was holding a dirty towel to her bleeding stomach. Marchant had found it in the boot, and feared it was for the dog. 'I can't go there again.'

'I won't.' A relapse, or a *rechute*, as Clémence had called it, was the least of Marchant's worries. Lakshmi was losing blood, and needed urgent treatment. He banged his hands on the steering wheel in frustration as the car in front of him stopped at traffic lights. There was a chance to jump them, but they were now in a city and he didn't want to draw attention.

He would get Lakshmi admitted to hospital as an emergency, give Jean-Baptiste an update, and then fly out to Morocco. Lakshmi was no longer a threat, but the Russians were onto him. It would have been too risky to call for an ambulance and wait by the roadside. Instead, he had phoned Jean-Baptiste and told him about the shooting. After showing more concern for the Mehari than for Lakshmi, Jean-Baptiste had given him directions to the University Hospital on avenue de la Côte de Nacre in Caen.

'Seriously, I'll look after her, don't worry,' the Frenchman had said. 'I've spoken to Clémence, and she has forgiven her. Sadly, she hasn't forgiven me.'

'Has Dhar really agreed to work for you, or is it wishful thinking?' Lakshmi asked, her voice slow but clear. Marchant glanced across at her. She was slumped into the corner of her seat like a drunk. Her usually open face was distorted in pain. For a fleeting moment, he wondered if she was faking her injury, just as she had faked her sedation.

'He's agreed.'

As soon as the words left his lips, he realised she was going to die. He could confide in her at last, tell her the truth. It took death for them to be honest with each other.

'What will you get out of it?' she asked, more breathless this time. Marchant picked up a bottle of water from his door, checked the traffic lights and held it to her lips. She drank a little; the rest poured down her face onto her shirt. The lights changed, and he accelerated away.

'We share the same father. He was British. Dhar never felt comfortable waging his jihad against the land of his father. He's promised to shield Britain from future terrorist attacks. We could do with that right now.'

'What will you give him in return?'

Marchant looked across at her again. Her voice was barely a whisper now. They weren't going to reach the hospital in time.

'I've already given it. His freedom.'

He had never spelt out his deal with Dhar before. He hadn't told Jean-Baptiste the details, and there had been no opportunity to talk it through with Fielding. The way he had just explained it, the pact sounded Faustian, like the one his father had made with Primakov.

'It's blackmail,' she whispered. Marchant thought he saw a smile trying to break through her pain.

'It's not,' he said.

'We've both been blackmailed.'

'I thought you were betraying me for nobler reasons.'

'I was.'

Marchant drove on in silence. When he looked back at Lakshmi, her eyes were closed, her hand less tight on her stomach.

'Keep the towel pressed firmly,' he said too harshly, reaching across and pushing it against her bloody hand. She opened her eyes and looked at him.

'Britain will be safe, but –' she faltered, whispering. 'Will Dhar still be at war with America?'

Marchant drove on, not wanting to look at her, following the signs for URGENCES through an endless lattice of small roads and low hedges that ringed the university hospital. It had begun to rain hard, and the wipers were struggling to clear the water from the windscreen.

'Yes,' he said. 'Dhar will still be at war with America.' He knew Lakshmi was gone. After a while he turned to check. The hand holding the wet towel had fallen across her lap, her head had rolled forward. Tears pricked his eyes.

'But Britain will be safe,' he continued, staring ahead, his hands too tight on the steering wheel. 'Isn't that what matters? What this is all about? Why I signed up to Six? Why you joined the Agency? We talk about making the world a safer place, but in the end we just want to protect our own back yards.'

But as he pulled up outside the hospital, he knew he was lying. He sat there for a moment, still looking ahead, hoping to hear her breathing above the sound of the rain and the wipers. He didn't want to turn off the engine, fearing the silence.

'I was close to my father too,' he said quietly. 'I would have done anything for him. I hoped you'd come round to what I'm trying to do with Dhar. But I never told you, did I? Never trusted you.'

He cut the engine and looked across at Lakshmi. She had lost too much blood. Leaning over, he touched her eyes, closing them like delicate clamshells, and moved to kiss her goodbye on the lips. He hesitated. It was from moments like this that he had guarded himself. He kissed her on the forehead. They had both tried to trust each other, but it wasn't to be.

An image of her at the temple in Madurai came to him, barefoot except for ankle chains, her forehead dabbed with crimson *tilak*. He preferred to think of her like that. She had looked strong then, at home in Mother India, proud to be American. At times he had let her in, but not completely, not the way he had done with Leila. And now he knew why.

He promised to tell her father that she had loved him.

83

'Are you free to talk?'

Paul Myers took the call at his bedsit in Montpelier, Cheltenham, where he had been confined since the attack on GCHQ that had nearly killed him. He wasn't ready to return to the office; not yet.

'Who is this?' he asked, sitting up at his desk. A bank of computer screens flickered in front of him. The voice had been crudely distorted. The effect wasn't as subtle as his own modulator, the one he had given Marchant. Instinctively, he wanted to know more, not about the caller but the technology. He guessed it was Eastern European.

'Can you talk?' the voice asked again. Myers thought about routing the unknown caller through his laptop, trying to reverse the modulation, but it would take too long. He had also worked out who it was: Marcus Fielding. There was something about the upper cadences, a faintly nasal quality that hadn't been knocked out by the software.

The former Chief of MI6 was on the run, just like Daniel Marchant, who had caused him enough grief already. Try as he might, it was proving hard for Myers to cover his tracks over the Revolutionary Guard intercept. The last thing he needed was Marcus Fielding making his life even more complicated.

'It's a secure line,' Myers said.

'I need to make contact with Marchant.'

Fielding wasn't bothering with any niceties, like introducing himself or apologising for potentially losing Myers his job.

'I've got a number.'

'That would be helpful.'

A call from Fielding had always made his palms sweat, and this one was no exception, even though he was no longer Chief. Myers went over to his bedside table, where he kept a notebook for middle-of-the-night ideas. At the back he had written down Marchant's number, using a simple shift-key code. But just as he was reading it out to Fielding, his doorbell rang. The postman had already called, and he wasn't expecting visitors. He never was.

'I've got to go,' he said after reading out the number, but Fielding had already hung up.

Myers looked down onto the street. Two men were standing in front of the door that led to his flat and the three others in the building. He thought he recognised one of them from work, but he couldn't be sure. Moving quickly, he logged into GCHQ from his desktop computer and checked for a final time that his CX report on the Farsi intercept was not showing in the Gulf Controllerate files. He had deleted it from his own account, but a trace could still be found in the auxiliary data silos if someone was looking for it. The information was gathered from keystroke logging, a security measure that everyone at GCHQ was subject to, particularly those, like Myers, who had authorised computer terminals at home. Every keystroke, every action on a keyboard was tracked and later automatically analysed for unusual patterns of behaviour, such as deleting files.

After signing out, he pressed the intercom button by the front door and asked who it was.

'GCHQ security,' a voice replied. 'Routine homeworker check.'

Routine my fat arse, Myers thought, as he considered his

options. He wasn't like Marchant, who would escape out of the window or grab a pizza box off the floor and bluff his way past the men, pretending he had delivered a Margarita instead of an American Hot. That wasn't his style. He was too much of a coward. Instead, he looked around the room in the vain hope that there might be somewhere to hide, a place where he could curl up in the darkness, eat a large chocolate bar and pretend none of this was happening. They wouldn't be interested in the copies of *Fly RC*, a magazine for remote-control plane enthusiasts, scattered on the bed, or the *Persian Pussy* porn mags stacked under it. They would be looking for evidence to link him with the jailbreak. Why did he agree to sit on the information for twenty-four hours, as Marchant had asked?

Preparing himself for the worst, he buzzed the men in. Suddenly remembering the notepad by the bed, he walked over and ripped out the back page, which had Marchant's coded number on it. He scrunched it up and popped into his mouth as the two men reached the top of the stairs.

84

Marchant held Lakshmi in his arms, standing in the swing doorway marked URGENCES. It was the second time in a week that he had carried her limp body. The first had been on the boat at Portbail, where he had handed her over to Jean-Baptiste. This time she was heavier, a dead weight.

The staff rolled a stretcher in and laid her down on it. They worked with quiet professionalism, and were more optimistic than he was as they took her away to the Emergency Room. He knew it was too late, but they would do all they could to try to revive her. He explained to the duty nurse that his friend had been shot in the stomach, and she told him he would have to stay in the waiting area until the police arrived.

That was all he could do for Lakshmi. The moment the nurse turned her back, he was out the doors and walking back through the rain to the Golf. It didn't feel right to leave her behind, but he had already said his goodbyes. He sat at the wheel for a moment, breathing deeply, watching the condensation form on the inside of the windscreen.

He felt less strongly about her death, now the seat beside him was empty. The only trace of her was a bloodstain on the uphol-stery. She had chosen her country above what might have existed between them. He had chosen his. And yet, they had both acted with a knowingness of each other's position, a mutual respect, an acknowledgement that this was the only way it could be.

The intelligence services had long been a magnet for patriots, but he had never seen himself as one, not overtly, like his father. The same was true for her. Circumstances had drawn it out of them. Perhaps it had something to do with being abroad, seeing your country from afar, in a wider context. The reports of Britain in flames had gone to his core, reminding him why he had joined MI6, why he was now spending so much time trying to turn Dhar. And her patriotism had been stirred by the thought of Dhar being free to attack America once again.

His phone buzzed twice before he was aware of it ringing. The only person who had this number was Paul Myers, but it wasn't him, unless he was calling from a different phone. He thought of not answering, but decided to take the call on the hands-free given to him by Myers.

'We don't have long,' a distorted voice said. Marchant wondered if his modulator was playing up, and adjusted the headphones.

'Who is this?'

'The Vicar.'

85

Myers didn't know where he was, but it was within an hour's radius of his flat by car. He had focused on the geography of his journey, the time spent blindfolded, as he tried to work out what was happening to him. The two men who had come to his flat had explained that they wanted to take him for a routine security check, but he feared the worst when they showed him into the back of a car with darkened windows. For a brief, unrealistic moment he had thought about running, but he was overweight and unfit. And he was still hurting from the bomb blast of a week earlier.

No one had been rough with him. Not yet. There had been no intimidation or threats of violence, but he was still more scared than he could ever remember being. At school the bullies had always masked their initial approach with a veneer of kindness, luring the fat boy into dark corners with smiles and false sympathy. It was the not knowing that unnerved him. No one had said a word since he had got into the car. His questions went unanswered, his pleadings ignored. Then they gagged him.

All he knew was that he was now sitting on a plastic chair in what felt like an aircraft hangar. He couldn't be sure, because he was still blindfolded, but the acoustics suggested a high roof. He had also heard the sound of an aircraft taking off close by. At one point he had caught an American accent. Perhaps he had been drugged and was in Afghanistan, Bagram. They did that on TV, took people to the scenes of crimes to jog their memories. Was he about to be shown the blast hole in the perimeter wall through which Dhar had escaped? Forced to confront the consequences of his actions?

He told himself to stay calm. They weren't going to hurt him. His hands and arms were tied, but he was sure he hadn't left the country. He was still in Britain, where they didn't do torture. He just wished someone would remove the blindfold. If they started to play rough, he had already decided that he would tell them everything: the Revolutionary Guard intercept, Marchant's interest in Dhar's escape, the voice modulator he had given him. There was nothing in it for him any more. He had helped Marchant enough over the past few years, and their friendship had proved more trouble than it was worth.

'It's Paul, isn't it?'

Myers jumped. He had assumed he was alone. The voice sounded close to him. It was also familiar. He was good on regional accents, global as well as local, even better at people's attempts to conceal them.

He tried to reply, but a noise came out instead, as if the gag was still in his mouth, although it had been removed a few minutes earlier. Instinctively, he moved his jaws and licked his lips.

'I hope you're not uncomfortable,' the voice went on. He knew who it was now. Ian Denton, the new Chief of MI6, born and bred in Hull – on the eastern side of the city, if he had to be more specific about the accent. 'The blindfold is nothing sinister, just a security precaution. Someone will untie you in a moment.'

'Why am I here?' Myers asked.

'You won't be for very long if you answer a few routine questions.'

When did 'routine' become such a dreaded word? Myers wondered. Routine questions, routine tests. Used by police or doctors, it presumed guilt rather than innocence, sickness rather than health.

'About what? Why have I been brought here?'

'Daniel Marchant – you know him, don't you? Good mates.'

Myers paused. It was time to cut Marchant free, save himself. 'Not any more,' would be the sensible answer. Denton clearly knew they had once been allies. 'Not any more,' he repeated to himself.

'Are you friends with him?' Denton asked again.

'Yes.'

Myers swallowed and saw himself at a distance, from across the hangar, or wherever he was.

'Do you know where he is now?' Myers wanted to scream, 'Tell him everything!' – but the fat boy couldn't hear him.

'Fort Monckton?' he offered. 'I haven't heard from him for a while.'

'So you didn't tell him about the Revolutionary Guard intercept you made the other day? Didn't tell anyone, in fact.'

'I don't know what you're talking about.' If Myers ever made it back to his flat, he would do something about the keystroke-logging software. Denton must have accessed data security at GCHQ, followed the trail back to his terminal.

'The intercept that, if it had been pooled with the appropriate directorates and properly analysed, would have given warning of an Iranian-backed assault by the Taleban on Bagram Air Base?'

Myers kept silent, trying to work out why he was being loyal to Marchant. Up until now, he had never had any issues with Denton, but if a choice had to be made between him and Marchant, he would side with his old friend every time. That much he knew. And hadn't Marchant said it would all be worth it? He had always shared Marchant's distrust of America, and they had once – improbably – loved the same woman, Leila, which should have made them enemies but had brought them closer. If his reluctance to betray Marchant constituted bravery, the motive was overrated. He wanted to throw up.

'Perhaps I'm being unfair,' Denton continued. 'You did pool it, just a day later than you should have done. When it was too late.'

'I haven't been so well recently. I was caught up in the –'

'I know what happened. The bomb dropped on GCHQ nearly killed you. As I recall, your mate Daniel Marchant was in the cockpit. Who needs enemies?'

'I didn't realise the significance of the intercept,' Myers said. 'Not at first. I was working in real time. A lot of the CX is analysed later. When I heard about the jailbreak, I went back over the intercept and pooled it, thinking it might be helpful.'

'Come on, Paul. You're one of the best Farsi analysts Cheltenham's ever had, and you didn't realise the significance of heightened Revolutionary Guard activity on the Iran–Afghanistan border?'

'Not in real time, no. The exchange was heavily coded.'

'The truth is, you deliberately withheld it. At the request of Marchant.'

'The desk is very overstretched. Sometimes we all miss things. It's human nature. We've got more Farsi speakers than the Americans, but we're still short-staffed. Everyone is, even Mossad.'

'I'm going to ask you this one last time, Paul. Then it's out of my hands. Did you tell Daniel Marchant about the Revolutionary Guard intercept? And did he ask you to delay pooling it?'

Myers paused before he spoke, his voice more defiant than he expected. 'No.'

'Untie him,' Denton said, as if he was a director suddenly calling 'Cut' on a scene. All around him, Myers heard activity, people moving, papers being shuffled. He exhaled loudly, letting out an involuntary whistle of relief, but then Denton spoke again. 'Then strip him naked.'

86

It was twenty-four hours since Salim Dhar had reacted to the hornet sting in Bagram detention facility. His face was still swollen, but his breathing was easier, and it felt as if his body was slowly reclaiming its original shape. He had been seen by two doctors since arriving in Iran. The small medical room he was in now was clean and comfortable, and the only evidence that he wasn't a regular patient was the silhouette of two armed guards standing outside the door.

The doctor who had just visited him refused to answer any of Dhar's questions, unless they concerned his medical condition. He had appeared frightened, and shook his head silently when Dhar asked him their exact location. All he would confirm was that they were somewhere in Iran. There was something about the windowless room, though, that made Dhar feel sick. It was almost as if it was swaying. He put it down to his heavy medication.

Dhar couldn't remember how he had been extracted from Bagram, or anything about the journey to this place. His last memory was of being stung in his cell, and looking up to see the green eyes of the local Afghani who had brought him his near-fatal meal. It seemed he had been right to trust him, although it had been a dangerous decision to induce an anaphylactic shock. Both doctors had confirmed that the sting had been intentional.

The Iranians had clearly done their homework. Dhar had only once spoken of his fear of insects, at a training camp in Kashmir, dating it back to a hornet sting that had nearly killed him as a child in Delhi. The information must somehow have found its way to Ali Mousavi and the Revolutionary Guard.

Dhar felt around on the bed for the TV remote and clicked on the screen in the corner of the room. He had tried to watch it earlier, but had felt too tired. After flicking through some local channels, he found a news programme. It was carrying a report on Britain, where the authorities were still investigating a series of terrorist attacks on critical national infrastructure. He tried to concentrate, but found it difficult. His medication made him drowsy. Drifting in and out of sleep, he managed to establish in his mind which UK cells might be responsible.

Later, the programme switched to Afghanistan, and an attack on the hospital at Bagram Air Base. There was no mention of his escape. It wouldn't suit either the Americans or the Iranians to make his disappearance public.

'How are you feeling? I've brought you a small gift.'

Dhar looked up to see Ali Mousavi enter the room, accompanied by an armed guard, who hung back at the door. Mousavi beckoned to the man and he came forward awkwardly, holding a large plastic bowl of apricots. He placed it on Dhar's bedside table, watched by a beaming Mousavi.

Dhar didn't say anything. He wasn't sure he could speak. Instead he raised one arm in acknowledgement, bending it at the elbow.

'The doctors tell me you will be better within the week,' Mousavi continued, gesturing for the other man to leave. Dhar hadn't seen Mousavi in uniform before. He usually wore sharp, Western-looking suits, and he spoke impeccable English with a hint of an

American accent. Despite these shortcomings, Dhar liked him. They had worked well together in the past, perhaps because Mousavi wasn't a typical military man. To look at, he had the appearance of a well-groomed newsreader, tall, with a trim moustache and soft skin. Dhar had always remembered his hands, which were smooth like a woman's: thin, effete fingers, perfectly manicured nails.

Mousavi's background was in academia. He had studied abroad before beginning a second career in VEVAK, Iran's internal security agency, and then the Revolutionary Guard. A period of study in America had committed him to removing the Great Satan's stranglehold on the world. And he was intelligent enough to know how to do it. Nobody knew more about the theories of asymmetric warfare than Mousavi. Iran didn't possess the firepower of its adversaries, but there were other ways to defeat an enemy.

'Our men did well,' Mousavi said. 'The Zionists are too embarrassed to tell the world you have escaped.'

Dhar tried to smile, but the effort hurt, creasing his heavily creamed face. The room began to sway again, and he wanted to ask Mousavi where he was. But when he tried to speak, no words came, just a pain at the back of his throat.

'I was planning to come tomorrow, when the doctors tell me you will be feeling stronger, but I had to see you with my own eyes.' Mousavi paused. Dhar could see that he was embarrassed, not used to his sentences tailing off into silence. His manner was more suited to coffee-house badinage. Dhar lifted his arm again, to give him encouragement.

'I also have something else I must share with you. It seems we have an ally on the inside, at the heart of British intelligence. According to one of our assets in the UK, somebody at GCHQ managed to listen in to a conversation when we were planning the attack on Bagram. The analyst heard important operational details, but chose to tell no one until afterwards. It may have been an oversight, but it seems the delay was deliberate. The analyst has been arrested. There is a chance that the mission to rescue you might have failed before it had started if this man had reported what he heard.'

Dhar closed his eyes, feeling his blood pulse through his swollen eyelids. The room was no longer swaying. He hadn't thought about Marchant since his arrival in Iran. The delay at GCHQ had all his hallmarks, getting someone else to do the dirty work.

'Do you know who this person might be?' Mousavi asked in a voice that suggested he knew already. Dhar would have sat up if he could. Instead, he tried to clear his thoughts, chase away the fog of medication. How much did the Iranians know about Marchant? They would be aware that the Englishman was his half-brother, and that he had been in the cockpit with him over Fairford. But they couldn't know about the deal they had struck at Tarlton.

As far as the Iranians were concerned, Marchant was on the run, suspected of treachery and sympathetic to Dhar and his anti-American views. Dhar would keep it that way. There was no need to tell Mousavi about the finer details of their pact, that Dhar had agreed to shield Britain as best he could from the global *jihad*.

Dhar rocked his head from side to side. In time they would talk about Marchant, but not now.

'Whoever this person is,' Mousavi said, 'we owe him a great debt of gratitude.'

Dhar managed a smile, ignoring the pain in his lips. He would thank Marchant, in his own way and in accordance with their private arrangement. When he was stronger, he would send messages to Britain, halt the attacks. It was the least he could do in return for his freedom.

87

Marchant watched the fishermen on the sea wall in Essaouira as they gutted their catch. In the blue sky above, seagulls circled, swooping in to catch entrails as they were tossed into the air. The scene was equally chaotic below. Wooden handcarts laden with glistening fish – red snapper, sea bass, flounder and cartons of sardines arranged in neat lattice patterns – were being wheeled into the fish market to be auctioned off. Some would make it to the row of cafés around the corner, where tourists could choose fish from elaborate displays and eat them with chips on draughty benches.

Marchant had walked past them earlier, escorted by a pushy waiter. 'You want Jew fish?' he had said. Apparently, salmon had been popular with Essaouira's once-thriving Jewish population, before it had migrated to Israel in the early 1950s. 'Maybe fish and chips? Better than Harry Ramsden's.'

It had been windy ever since he had arrived in the coastal town, sand blowing in from the Sahara. In the distance, Atlantic waves were bursting into bloom against the high city walls of the medina, while across the bay, kite-surfers soared into the sky. They seemed to defy gravity as they hung in mid-air, thirty feet above the waves. Marchant had learnt how to do it back in Britain, at Watergate Bay, on a weekend break from Fort

Monckton. If circumstances had been different, he would have given it a go.

Today, though, he had other things on his mind as he left the fish market and headed back up the narrow lanes towards his *riad* in the heart of the medina. Marchant liked this part of town, the rich mix of Arab and French cultures. It reminded him of happier days in Marrakech. The buildings were four storeys high, and the alleyways sometimes too narrow for the handcarts. Occasionally they would break out into sunlit squares, where old men sat on plastic chairs drinking coffee. At other times they took him further and further into the old part of town, a labyrinthine world where Berber workers ate lamb chops off smoky coals and Muslim women emerged from ancient *hamams*, faces glowing.

'*Schoof, schoof,*' someone urged as he passed a shop selling Djembe drums from Mali. 'Look, look.'

Marchant declined, moving through the crowds, always vigilant. To his left, a carpet-seller from the Sahara limped up and down outside his shopfront, a cigarette wobbling in his mouth. Occasionally he singled out a wealthy-looking tourist and asked him to venture inside to see his shop. 'I am from Zagora. Only the best-quality rugs.' Up on the right, a man was selling individual swigs of milk from a jug.

Marchant had considered staying in his *riad* but he wanted to know if the Russians had tracked him to Morocco. He was confident they hadn't. After leaving the hospital in Caen, he had driven fast to Orly airport, where Jean-Baptiste was waiting for him. He had given him the keys for the Golf and the Mehari, apologising for the damage to both, and explained that he feared Lakshmi was dead.

'I'm sorry,' Jean-Baptiste had said. 'I know what she did to Clémence and my mother, but I'm still sorry.'

'She'd switched sides and was working for Spiro,' Marchant had replied. 'She needed to be stopped.'

'Would you have shot her if the Russians hadn't?'

Marchant didn't know the answer. He looked at him for a moment and then turned away.

'There's a gun in the bag,' he said, handing a holdall to Jean-Baptiste.

The Frenchman took it, glancing around him. They were standing near the crowded check-in desk for his Royal Air Maroc flight to Essaouira. 'Have you used it?'

Marchant nodded. 'Dhar's fingerprints are on it too.'

Jean-Baptiste raised his eyebrows. Marchant would have understood if he had handed it back. The gun of the world's most wanted terrorist was as incriminating as evidence could get.

'Check-in and passport control are expecting you. Keep to the far left desks. When you get to Essaouira, you're on your own.'

Marchant felt on his own now as he followed the narrow lane back to Lunetoile, a discreet *riad* on rue Sidi Mohamed ben Abdullah. Watched by several cats, he let himself in with the key the Zimbabwean landlady had given him and walked up three flights of wooden stairs that looked down onto a tiled central area. His room was on the top floor. He had asked to see it before paying a deposit. It was chic and clean, with a view of the sea, but what sold it to him was that it would be possible to leave in an emergency via the surrounding rooftops.

His plan was a simple one. Everything had seemed simpler after he had taken the phone call outside the hospital in Caen. Fielding, his voice distorted by a less sophisticated modulator than the one Myers had given Marchant, had been calling from Poland. Between them, they now had enough evidence to remove Denton from office. It just had to be revealed at the right time and to the right people. Marchant was still shocked by what Fielding had managed to uncover, but not entirely surprised. There had always been something suppressed about Denton; he just hadn't thought it was anything quite as extreme as this.

Before going down to the fish market, Marchant had stopped off at an internet café, sat at an inconspicuous terminal and logged into a Hotmail account, where he found five photos attached to an email in the draft folder. Mischievously, Fielding had entitled the email: 'Man is born free . . .' Marchant wasn't bothered what pain Denton chose to inflict on himself. More troubling was the thought of him savouring the pain he might have inflicted on others. The allegations about MI6 complicity in torture suddenly took on a different hue, particularly as Denton was overseeing the internal investigation.

Marchant walked out onto the terrace of his rooftop room and looked around at the medina's other world, the one high above the bustling streets and squares below. On the roof opposite, a woman was hanging washing, occasionally stopping to look out to sea. To his right, a cat prowled along the edge of a building, seemingly unaware of the hundred-foot drop to the street below. And in the distance, in a medley of competitive roof extensions, two tourists were sunning themselves in a precariously perched conservatory.

Fielding had given Marchant the personal mobile number of Harriet Armstrong, Director General of MI5, and he dialled it now on one of several pay-as-you-go phones he had bought in the medina. It was a private number, and he hoped no one was listening in. Armstrong's relationship with Fielding had not always been warm, particularly when she had briefly flirted with the Americans, but they had become close allies in recent months.

She had also shown a strange loyalty to him when they were in India, and had never had much time for Denton. What Marchant was about to tell her now would lift her spirits.

'It's your favourite runaway. Can you talk?' he asked into the hands-free as Armstrong picked up.

'Who is this?'

'It's about Denton.'

'Wait a moment,' Armstrong replied. Marchant could hear her say something, perhaps to her PA, then a door closed. He hoped she was clearing her office. 'OK, I'm the only one listening. I won't ask where you are or what you're doing. Or why your voice sounds different.'

Marchant couldn't blame her for being terse. The terrorist attacks would have put her under enormous pressure, made worse by Dhar being free again.

'I've been in touch with Fielding. We've both been working on information that there's a Russian mole high up inside MI6.'

'You sound just like the Americans.'

'It wasn't Hugo Prentice, and you know it's not Fielding.'

'Surprise me.'

'Ian Denton. And we've got the evidence to prove it.'

Marchant didn't have long, but he was happy to let Armstrong remain silent for a few seconds while she digested the news. It was a lot to take on board.

'What sort of evidence?' she asked quietly. Her bullish, head-mistressy manner had disappeared.

'Seems like Denton's into B&D. The Russians caught him trussed up in chains a few years ago, took photos, threatened to go public unless he agreed to work for them.'

'No wonder his wife left him.'

'Fielding's got the photos.'

'How?'

'You can ask him when he gets his job back. I've also got pictures of Denton meeting a Russian contact in London.'

'London?' Armstrong paused. He wondered if she was pouring herself a drink.

'When?'

'Last week.'

'Christ. When D4 was meant to be babysitting him. At his request – he thought he was being followed. But they didn't see any Russians, just an irritating Frenchman from DGSE.'

Jean-Baptiste, Marchant assumed. His friend wasn't so good at covert surveillance after all.

'I've run some checks on the Russian Denton met,' Marchant continued. 'I don't know who he is, but he's not working under diplomatic cover.'

'Another bloody illegal. Are you sure he's Russian?'

Marchant thought about the evidence. One man seen buying blinis in Waitrose – it wasn't exactly belts and braces. Jean-Baptiste's evidence was no better. *Ordinary looking, except his eyes. Definitely made in Moscow.* For a moment, Marchant wondered if he had made a terrible error, but then he reminded himself about Primakov's letter.

. . . Moscow Centre has an MI6 asset who helped the SVR expose and eliminate a network of agents in Poland. His codename was Argo, a nostalgic name in the SVR, as it was once used for Ernest Hemingway.

For a while, everyone had thought the mole was Hugo Prentice, a mistake that had led to Prentice's tragic death. But Primakov had known otherwise. The real Argo was Ian Denton.

Marchant's confidence was returning. Denton's obsession with barcodes was not normal behaviour. It was clandestine, and had evaded Armstrong's watchers in D4, whose job it was to counter Russian operations in Britain. And why would the

Russians have compromising photos of Denton if it wasn't to blackmail him?

'I'm sure he's Russian,' Marchant said. 'He was using super-market barcode scanners to exchange data. Maybe you'll recognise him when I send the pictures over.'

'And when are you planning to do that?'

'When's the next COBRA meeting?'

88

'It really doesn't have to be like this,' Denton said, taking his jacket off as he walked around Myers. He had toyed with various possibilities, but decided that strappado, or reverse hanging, would yield the quickest results with the overweight analyst from GCHQ.

First, he had stood him on a chair and bound both hands behind his back. Myers seemed to be in shock, and hadn't protested. Then Denton had tied his wrists to a rope attached to the hangar roof and asked him again about the intercept. When he refused to answer, Denton kicked away the chair. Myers's arms had dislocated instantly under the considerable weight of his body – popping like snapped carrots – and he was now swaying naked in front of him.

'All I need to know is what you told Marchant about the intercept, and what he said to you. Tell me that and we'll take you to a good hospital, where they can click your shoulders back into their sockets and send you home.'

'I don't know what you're talking about,' Myers repeated.

Denton was impressed by the loyalty Marchant inspired in his friends. He had never subjected himself to strappado, but he knew the pain was excruciating. Yet Myers had not once deviated from his story. He had screamed and cried, and relieved himself twice, but showed no signs of telling Denton what he wanted to hear.

Perhaps he was rushing him. In the past, in Morocco and Pakistan, he had taken longer, but he didn't have the luxury of time today. He needed to be back in London, prepare for tomorrow's COBRA meeting, do his weekly shop in Waitrose.

'Please take me down,' Myers said quietly. 'I didn't know how important the intercept was at the time. The exchanges were coded. I went back and deciphered them when I heard about Dhar's escape. It was a mistake.'

'Quite a big one. I don't want you to feel bad, but the world was a much safer place with Dhar behind bars. You can make amends by telling me what you told Marchant.'

Denton walked slowly around the drafty hangar, waiting for a reply he knew would never come. They had the place to themselves after Spiro had given him the keys for the afternoon. The hangar was in a remote corner of RAF Fairford, and Denton knew this wasn't the first time an interrogation had taken place here. Pairs of steel rings had been fixed in a row along the far wall at shoulder height. Below each pair the ground was stained. The sliding door at the other end of the hangar was bolted and chained. It looked as if it hadn't been opened for years.

'Do you believe in circumcision, Paul?' Denton asked from across the hangar. The scene had more appeal from a distance. There was a greater sense of incongruity, a sharper contrast between Myers's flabby white body and the industrial setting.

It became even more interesting as Myers started to breathe harder, blowing in and out as if he was impersonating a steam engine.

'It's just that it's hard to tell,' Denton continued, walking back towards Myers. 'Everything's gone a bit small down there.' An opposite reaction to his own.

'I've got nothing else to say to you!' Myers shouted, raising his head, squinting at where he thought Denton was standing.

Normally he wore glasses, thick ones, but Denton had removed them. His blind defiance was impressive. Denton had read little in Myers's files about bravery in the field. Quite the opposite. His line manager had expressly recommended that he should never venture outside GCHQ.

'Muslims do; people like Salim Dhar.' Denton was standing directly in front of him now. He pulled a small knife from his pocket and flicked open the blade, holding it inches from his face. 'I don't think we'll need anything bigger, do you?'

89

Spiro had mixed feelings about being back in London as he waited outside the office of the US Ambassador. His influence over Britain's intelligence services relied on support from Washington, and he wasn't sure how much longer he could count on that. Dhar's escape from Bagram hadn't exactly played well in Langley. Short of shooting the President, Spiro couldn't imagine anything more damaging to his career. It made his worries about an AWOL wife pale into insignificance. She still wasn't answering his calls, and Denton hadn't seemed keen to help when he had rung him from the airport.

'We're not an offshoot of Relate,' Denton had said, after Spiro had raised the possibility of MI6 lifting his wife from Ramallah.

The fact that he had now been kept waiting for almost twenty minutes to see the Ambassador only added to his growing sense of insecurity. In the past, Turner Munroe would come to see him in his CIA offices at the other end of the embassy building. Spiro knew it wasn't just his own power that was waning, it was the Agency's.

'Sorry to keep you waiting, Jim,' Munroe lied a few minutes later, closing the door behind them. 'Just taking a call from Fort Meade.' Of course you were, Spiro thought. The NSA now had more people working in London than the CIA. 'Are you OK?' he continued, glancing at Spiro.

'Never felt better,' he said, taking a seat. A bead of sweat gathered at his temple as he unnecessarily smoothed the bandages on his hands. Spiro always felt unhealthy in Munroe's presence. There wasn't an ounce of fat on the Ambassador's tanned body as he sat down behind a large desk. Spiro looked away, glancing at the spacious surrounds. If the size of a man's office was a reflection of his ambition, he thought, Munroe was aiming for the White House. What did he do in here? Use it as a running track?

'We're contingency planning for Dhar's escape leaking to the media,' Munroe said. 'Diplomatically, we're going to feel the heat.'

'Right now I don't give a dime about diplomacy.'

Munroe didn't respond. He took his time, always a sign that he was keeping something back. Spiro hated it when someone else held all the cards.

'The Ambassador in Paris called this morning. An American woman was shot in Normandy, brought into a hospital in Caen. I think she's one of yours. Lakshmi Meena?'

'Badly injured?' Spiro asked, struggling to keep his voice neutral.

'Dead on arrival. I'm sorry.'

Spiro gazed out of the window, where the grey streets of London offered little comfort. A light drizzle was falling on office workers hurrying to overpriced sandwich bars. Daniel Marchant had always got under his skin. It was why he had once ordered him to be waterboarded. He was slowly taking Spiro down. First, it was Dhar's escape, now it seemed he had shot one of his agents.

'She was on an operation in France,' Spiro said. 'Staying close to Daniel Marchant.'

'I thought he was on the run, whereabouts unknown.'

'He was. Like I said, Lakshmi was on an operation. Covert. That's what we do. Risk our lives in the field rather than staring at a bunch of computer screens all day long in Maryland.'

Munroe ignored the jibe at the NSA. 'Was it successful?'

'She did her job, like all my officers do.' Spiro wasn't going to tell him that Marchant might have helped Dhar to escape. Munroe would pass on the intel to the NSA, and the matter would be taken out of his hands. This was his mess, and he would sort it.

'Then at least she didn't die in vain. Do you know who might have killed her?'

'That's fairly obvious, isn't it?'

Munroe stood up and set off on a walk around his office. For the first time, Spiro noticed he was wearing running shoes, brand new ones. Perhaps he was breaking them in.

'You've never liked Daniel Marchant, have you?' the Ambassador said.

'And you've always stuck up for him. Ever since he tried to kill you at the London Marathon.'

'He didn't try to kill me, Jim. He saved my goddamn life. If it wasn't for his courage, I would have been blown into a thousand pieces on Tower Bridge. And it looks as if he tried to save Lakshmi Meena too. Paris sent over some CCTV photos. Lifted from hospital security.'

Munroe went back to his desk and handed Spiro a black-and-white photo. It was of Marchant with Meena in his arms, entering the hospital.

'I'm not sure he would have brought her in if he had shot her,' Munroe said.

'Do we know where he went afterwards?'

'Unfortunately, CCTV outside the hospital wasn't working.'

'There's a surprise. What do you expect from the French?'

'Someone else came to ask about Miss Meena an hour later.'

Munroe passed over another photo. It was of a well-built man talking to a duty nurse.

'Who is he?' Spiro asked.

'DGSE, apparently. According to Harriet Armstrong, her officers followed the same man around London earlier this week. He was tailing Ian Denton.'

'Denton?'

'New intelligence chiefs always attract a bit of attention, even from so-called friendly nations.'

'France isn't friendly. And the DGSE are fucktards. Before Meena died, she rang me. Said Marchant was lying low with a DGSE officer.'

'Could it have been this man?' Munroe asked, nodding at the photo in Spiro's hand.

Spiro didn't answer. If it was, what the hell was he doing in London following Denton?

'Can I give you some advice, Jim? We haven't always seen eye to eye, but I don't like watching anyone go down, particularly a fellow American. Don't get too close to Denton.'

'Is there something I should know?'

But before Munroe could answer, Spiro's mobile phone rang. It was his wife.

90

Salim Dhar was feeling stronger by the hour. A combination of heavy steroids and antihistamines had reduced the swelling on his body to a faint rash. His face still felt bloated, but every time he checked in the mirror of his medical room he was surprised to see that his cheeks were no more than a little puffy. His only concern was the moments of dizziness, when he felt unsteady on his feet.

Ali Mousavi was talking on his phone outside in the corridor. For someone normally so calm and measured, he was unusually agitated. Iran had been goading the West all year with its nuclear programme, he had explained, and now Israel and America were on the point of losing patience. Earlier in the day, a second US Carrier Strike Group had entered the Strait of Hormuz, off the coast of Iran, a development that seemed to have lit a fire in Mousavi's eyes.

'I am so sorry, Salim,' he said now, as he stepped back inside the hospital room. '*Inshallah*, the day is drawing closer when we will give America more than a punch in the mouth.'

'We?'

'You. With more than a little help from the Islamic Revolutionary Guard Corps. I must show you something.'

Mousavi inserted a DVD into the player below the TV screen.

He then came over and stood next to Dhar's bed, operating the DVD with a remote. Moments later, they were watching a flotilla of fast-attack inshore craft surge across a stretch of the Strait of Hormuz. The commentary was in Farsi, but there were English subtitles. From what Dhar could tell, the footage was from a recent Revolutionary Guard exercise entitled 'Great Prophet Muhammed Six War Games'. A stream of missiles and rockets streaked across the sky, fired from launchers mounted on the boats. When the drama was over, smoke pouring from a forlorn target vessel in the distance, Mousavi turned to Dhar.

'Impressive, no? The exercise was in April. You might have seen clips on the news, or maybe YouTube. We put them up there to scare the West.'

Mousavi smiled. Dhar thought back to their meeting when he had come to see him in Russia about a possible operation. He hadn't gone into details, but had hinted at a waterborne attack on America.

'Our navy is strong, but no match for that of the United States. The only chance to strike at the enemy is with these asymmetric swarm attacks. However many weapons systems their ships may have, what can they do if fifty – maybe a hundred – small boats speed towards them, firing missiles and torpedoes as they go. Their helicopters will take out most of them, but not all. And it only requires one, just one, to get through.'

'Is this what you have brought me here for?' Dhar asked.

'Let's talk later. It's important you rest.'

Dhar didn't like Mousavi's evasiveness. In the past, he had always controlled his own operations, down to the smallest detail. He had never been answerable to others. The Russians had let him plan the attack on Fairford, happy to provide the hardware and then stand back. The same had been true in Delhi. Iran had sourced the sniper rifle and done little else. It was how he operated. But things were different this time, a sense of impotence hanging over him. Dhar knew he was indebted to Iran for his freedom, but he preferred to be in control of his own fate.

'Where am I?' he asked.

'Is the swaying not a clue?'

Mousavi pretended he was about to fall over, then steadied himself like an unfunny clown.

'I thought that was my medication. Are we on a boat?'

'Not quite. An oil platform. The Revolutionary Guard has naval bases on islands such as Abu Musa, Larak and Qeshm, as well as at the Abadan oil terminal. But our most secure one is right here, in the middle of the Persian Gulf. Nobody knows about it. The Americans think we are drilling for oil.'

Dhar was relieved to know that the cause of his unsteadiness lay outside his body. The last time he had been at sea was after he had ejected from the SU-25 and been picked up by the Russian trawler. That seemed a long time ago now.

'It is earlier than we planned, but the Americans have forced our hand,' Mousavi said. 'There is a chance for personal greatness in the coming week, an opportunity to alter the geopolitical landscape in the manner of 9/11. These propaganda videos are all very well, but the boats are old Swedish Boghammars from the 1980s, or poor imitations from North Korea and China. They look good on YouTube, but then they sink. They are rubbish, cheap children's toys. Half of them are on the seabed since this film was made. We need new boats.'

Like a businessman making a PowerPoint presentation, Mousavi clicked on the remote again. Another expanse of water appeared on the screen. It wasn't the Strait of Hormuz this time, and there was nothing military about the commentary, which was in English. A sleek, ice-blue powerboat was travelling fast around the southern coast of Britain, the white cliffs of Dover visible in the background.

'It's called the *Bradstone Challenger*,' Mousavi said. 'A fifty-one-foot long Bladerunner. Top speed is 72 knots – that's more than 80mph. It circumnavigated the UK in twenty-seven hours and ten minutes, averaging 53 knots, including fuel breaks. A record that still stands. This boat doesn't go over waves, she cuts through them.'

'And you want one?' Dhar asked. The side of him that had thrilled to the fighter jet enjoyed watching the boat as it powered up the English Channel. He had always enjoyed speed, ever since his gaming days at the training camps in Kashmir, where young *jihadis* had whiled away their downtime on counterfeit Xboxes run off car batteries.

'One? I would like fifty. Sadly, this is a sports model, and only two were ever made, by a British company, with help from a US defence contractor. But one is up for sale, and if we buy it we will reverse-engineer fifty copies. As you can see, it remains stable in rough water, even at high speeds. It doesn't bounce up and down like our current boats, making it a perfect firing platform.'

'Why can't you buy it?'

'We're trying, but there's a hitch. The US Commerce Department's Office of Export Enforcement' – he almost spat out the words – 'has discovered our intentions and is attempting to block the sale. The boat is currently in Karachi. We thought the deal had been concluded in Durban, but delivery has been held up. It is on board an Iranian vessel under a Hong Kong flag. When it docked at Karachi, the Pakistanis said there was something wrong with the paperwork – the Americans had obviously put pressure on them.'

Mousavi paused, watching the Bladerunner scythe through the waves. Then he turned to Dhar. 'We need someone on the ground in Karachi who can sort it, a Westerner. Someone who can convince Pakistan that the end user is a godless playboy in the Gulf, and not the Revolutionary Guard.'

'Our British friend?'

Mousavi nodded. Both sides were still treading carefully around the subject of Daniel Marchant, unsure how much to reveal. Earlier, Dhar had confirmed that Marchant must have been the one who was instrumental in delaying the GCHQ intercept, explaining that he had long been waging his own secret war against America.

'But are you sure you can trust him?' Dhar asked. It was still a big leap for the Iranians to make. Until recently, Marchant had worked for the foreign intelligence service of the Old Fox, Iran's historic enemy.

'You do.'

'He's my half-brother.'

'Without his help, we might not have got you out of Bagram.'

'But he's British.'

'And not welcome at home. I gather he's wanted by MI6 as well as the CIA. And not for the first time.'

'Just like his father – my father – Marchant's quarrel is with America. He still loves his own country.'

'We have many quarrels with the British, but today our fight is with the US. Will he help us?'

'If he thinks he's doing it for me – and acting against America.'

'Then we must bring him to you.'

91

Marchant slipped the internet-café owner five hundred dhirams and sat down in front of the computer. He had looked at four cafés before choosing this one. It was in a quiet street off rue Sidi Mohamed ben Abdullah, where he was staying, and had a small booth at the back for private use. The owner was also happy to close for twenty minutes. It was just before 9 a.m., and trade was always slow in the morning.

Marchant didn't want to dwell on what the booth was used for. Watching hardcore porn downloads, he guessed, or explicit live webcams. All he knew was that it suited his purposes. The computer had a working camera mounted above it, and the background behind him – a pale blue wall – was anonymous.

According to Armstrong, COBRA would be reconvening in five minutes. It had been sitting on and off ever since the terrorist strikes began a week ago. Marchant had been the subject of a few COBRA meetings in his time, but he had never attended one, virtually or in person. He tried to picture the scene around the table. It was unfortunate that the VOIP video connection would only be one-way. He would like to see Denton's face.

Marchant knew it had been a risk taking Harriet Armstrong into his confidence, but it was a calculated one, based on her dislike of Denton. It would also allow her to bank some of the credit for identifying Denton as a Russian mole, which MI5 had so far failed to do. Marchant hoped she would return the favour. Already she had arranged for extra Special Branch officers to be on standby in the building, and she had agreed to oversee the patching through of Marchant to COBRA's video-conferencing bridge.

All he had to do now was download Tor, the anonymous routing network, and choose a suitable proxy server to mask the internet café's IP address. To keep Myers happy, he would use a botnet too.

After Tor had downloaded, Marchant checked the lock on the door – he had insisted on a key – and dialled up a VOIP address for COBRA that Armstrong had given him. COBRA used its own secure video-conferencing network, but it could receive VOIP calls from the outside world. As he waited for a connection, he ran through the precautions he had taken, hoping they would be enough to conceal his location. All COBRA's incoming internet traffic was submitted to Deep Packet Inspection, technology that was being increasingly used by the NSA and GCHQ for online surveillance, filtering and intercepts. Iran and China were big users of DPI too.

He glanced at his watch. It was 9 a.m. The line began to ring.

92

Ian Denton had left Myers's body out of shape but intact. He needed more time, something he didn't have. Circumcision had failed to break him. On the drive back up from Fairford to London the previous night, he had begun to doubt whether Myers had talked to Marchant and whether, between the two of them, they had helped in any way with Dhar's escape. It was a wild allegation for Spiro to have made, but Denton was happy to pursue anything that might further discredit Marchant. Spiro's talk of him staying with a DGSE agent in France had been unnerving, particularly if it was the same agent who had followed him around London.

He would wait to see what others had to say at the morning COBRA meeting that was convening now. Dhar was top of the agenda, and security was tight. More Special Branch officers than usual had been present downstairs, checking bags at the entrance to the Cabinet Office building. There had been another attack this morning, on a small technology firm in Edinburgh that made hydraulic parts for America's nuclear submarines. Nobody had been killed, but the premises had been destroyed by fire. The attack had badly damaged morale. It was the first for a few days, and the British public had begun to believe the wave of terror was over.

Just as proceedings were about to get under way, Spiro walked into the low-ceilinged room and sat down beside Denton. Denton thought he looked a mess, unshaven, his sunken eyes heavy with exhaustion. It wasn't normal for the Americans to attend COBRA meetings, but Spiro's presence was a sign of the times. Despite Dhar's escape, the US's influence in Whitehall remained as pervasive as ever.

Denton acknowledged Spiro, wondering how long he would remain in London. Earlier, he had told him about the lack of progress with Myers. Spiro had sounded weary, almost resigned. He was a shadow of the man who had ordered his Marines to surround Legoland. If he went, Denton must take care not to be dragged down with him. He wouldn't go quietly, and Denton suspected he had come here today to point the finger at Britain for Dhar's escape.

'Welcome, everyone,' the PM began. 'We're pleased to have Jim Spiro with us – and particularly pleased that he's alive and well after the horrific events in Bagram. Jim will update us on Salim Dhar's current status, then we'll focus on the new and specific threats to Britain and how we're combatting them.'

But moments after Spiro began to talk – 'To cut to the chase, we believe Salim Dhar is currently hiding in Iran' – the distinct, insistent sound of an internet call was heard in the room. Spiro fell silent as others stopped shuffling papers to listen.

93

Harriet Armstrong looked at her watch as the PM welcomed everyone. Marchant was due to ring in two minutes' time, at 9 a.m. She glanced up at the screen at the end of the room, top right of a grid of eight. It was here that Marchant would appear if he called. Before the meeting had started, she had spoken to the member of staff who looked after COBRA's communications, explaining that she was expecting an important call from an officer in the field. The young woman had agreed to patch it through on the speakers and up on screen four.

The PM had eyes only for Armstrong as he talked. Responsibility for Britain's safety seemed to rest on her shoulders alone. She didn't think her job could get any worse, but the bomb in Edinburgh had proved her wrong. It was a miracle that nobody had been killed. She felt an acute sense of personal failure – she always did whenever a terrorist managed to get through. The PM had remained civil when she had briefed him, but it was clear that he felt she was failing too.

The phone call from Marchant yesterday had only added to her problems. She didn't know whether to trust him, but mention of Fielding had offered some reassurance. She missed the former Chief's measured authority, his lapidary asides, particularly at COBRA meetings like this one. After listening to Marchant's allegations about Denton, she had invoked the Regulation of Interceptions Act to retrieve archive CCTV footage from the Clapham Junction branch of Waitrose. Sure enough, the acting Chief of MI6 was there, just before closing time, shopping for one.

It was a faintly tragic scene, one she could relate to. She had been buying single portions ever since her husband had left her. But there was no evidence of any exchange of information using barcode scanners. No Russians, either. But Denton was too experienced to operate within the sightlines of security cameras. She would have to see what Marchant came up with.

The PM had turned to introduce Spiro, who had the haunted look of a prisoner of war, hands bandaged, a face that had not slept. Compared to him, the others around the table appeared strong and healthy, which Armstrong knew was not true. The airless room was like a morgue, staffed by the dead. She hoped to God the bombings would stop soon. Britain and those appointed to protect her couldn't take much more. But there were few leads, and no sign of respite.

As Spiro began to talk she heard the sound of an internet call. She nodded at the female member of staff, glanced at Denton and took a deep breath.

94

Spiro knew the voice as soon as he heard it, but it was still a shock when the image of Daniel Marchant flickered into life on one of the screens behind him. He turned his leather-backed chair around to take a proper look, realising he had lost his audience to a bigger act.

'Sorry to interrupt the war on terror, but there's something I need to share with you,' Marchant began. His voice was clear, but the image was buffering.

There was a flurry of activity to Spiro's left, where the Director of GCHQ was now on his feet. At the other end of the table, an adviser whispered urgently in the Prime Minister's ear.

'Who put this through?' the Director asked. 'Which address did he dial into? DPI will track it, work out where he's calling from.'

'I didn't quite catch that, but it's a waste of time if you're trying to establish my location with Deep Packet Inspection,' Marchant said. 'I'm using an anonymous network via a proxy server in Lichtenstein – oh yes, and I accessed it through a botnet.'

The Director hesitated for a moment before sitting down. Like Spiro, he knew there was no chance of getting any authorities in Lichtenstein to help track down the call. Marchant could be anywhere. And even if IT forensics did manage to trace the call back to a computer, which might take days, the botnet meant they would probably kick down the wrong door and arrest a spotty teenager in Poland playing World of Warcraft.

'It's been painful viewing to see my country under attack and not be able to do anything about it,' Marchant continued. His image had now stabilised on the screen and was synced with his voice, which was being relayed through speakers on either side of the bank of screens. 'But I think the attacks will stop now that Salim Dhar's out of jail.'

Now that you've sprung him, Spiro thought. He considered standing up, telling everyone what Lakshmi had overheard, that Marchant was a fraud, but it wasn't clear if the microphones on the table were working. Not that anyone would be listening. The room was mesmerised by the sight of Marchant on the screen. He looked like a backpacker who had crashed a dinner party. His straw-blond hair was tousled, his collarless shirt unbuttoned too far.

'There are those, I know, who think I am in some way responsible for the attacks,' Marchant said. 'The Americans, for example.'

'Too damn right.' Spiro could contain himself no longer. To his surprise, Marchant appeared to have heard him.

'Things are worse than I thought if the CIA is running COBRA,' he said.

'Hand yourself in, Marchant,' Spiro heckled. 'Myers has told us everything.'

It was a lie, of course. Denton had failed to get a single frickin' word out of Myers down at Fairford. Marchant continued speaking, unfazed. Perhaps the audio link had dropped.

'But it's not just Jim Spiro who's trying to frame me,' he said. 'It's also Ian Denton, who I hope is present.'

Everyone turned to the acting Chief of MI6, who remained motionless in his seat next to Spiro. The temperature in the airless room was rising. There was no Whitehall protocol for this sort of thing. It had never happened before. Only Harriet Armstrong seemed relaxed, watching the screen with interest rather than alarm. Spiro wondered what she knew.

'We should patch this call through to Fort Meade,' he whispered to Denton, loud enough for the Director of GCHQ to hear. 'Their DPI would track it in seconds.'

Spiro knew this was another lie, but he said it to reassure himself. He didn't like the way Marchant had rounded on Denton. The Ambassador's words were still ringing in his ears, along with all the other noises in his ears: *Don't get too close to Denton.*

'As you all know, my old Chief, Marcus Fielding, had to leave the country in a bit of a hurry,' Marchant continued. 'He wasn't defecting – of course he bloody wasn't. He was forced out of office by a bitter deputy who saw an opportunity to discredit him – and me.'

Again, all faces swung round to Denton, as if they were watching a tennis match.

'I know my presence in the cockpit of the Russian SU-25 was unorthodox.'

Unorthodox? Spiro had heard enough. He stood up, gesturing at the screen.

'This man was party to an act of war against the United States. What are you guys doing just sitting here, letting him run circles around you? He's gone rogue. His half-brother is Salim Dhar, for Chrissake. He's as good as a terrorist himself. After shooting down a US Air Force plane, he bombed GCHQ. What more frickin' evidence do you need?'

'Jim, we just need to hear what Marchant's got to say,' the PM said. 'Unlike your country, ours is being subjected to a sustained terrorist assault, and so far we don't have too much to go on.'

'And you think this guy will help you? I'll give you a lead. He just sprung Salim Dhar from Bagram jail.'

There was silence for a moment. Marchant appeared to have heard Spiro's outburst, and had paused, looking down and to the side like a confused interviewee on a live TV programme. Spiro sat down. He hoped Denton might say something to back him up, but he had withdrawn into himself, lowered his lizard eyes, the way he used to do.

'As I was saying,' Marchant continued. 'I'm aware my recent actions have thrown up more questions than answers – about me and Marcus Fielding. One day I hope both of us can explain everything. In the meantime, there's something you should all know about Ian Denton. His rise to become Chief of MI6 – acting Chief – was not driven by personal ambition, it was the result of blackmail.'

A low murmur travelled around the room like a Mexican wave. Spiro gripped his upper arms, as if he was cold. The noise in his ears grew louder. He didn't want to dwell on what Marchant was about to say next, but he knew it would be bad. The whole day was shaping up to be a disaster. His wife was in London, and wanted to meet for a chat. He was relieved she was no longer in the West Bank, but he hadn't liked her tone of voice – he didn't know the exact word for it, but it was the opposite of conciliatory.

'For the last fifty years,' Marchant continued, 'Moscow Centre has dreamed of having an asset at the top of MI6. Kim Philby almost made it, and they nearly got there with Ian Denton, thanks to the support he received from Washington.'

Where was Marchant going with this? Spiro glanced at Denton, who was staring into the middle distance, teeth gritted, his jaw pulsing. His own stomach had tightened. The Ambassador had been trying to warn him. *Don't get too close.* Denton had been his appointment.

'Fortunately, the Prime Minister and the Foreign Secretary had the good sense not to fully endorse Denton's appointment,

317

sparing MI6's blushes,' Marchant continued. '"Acting Chief" won't look so embarrassing when they come to write the history books. If someone could access the following website – www.dirtylittlesecret.org.uk – there are some photos I'd like to share.'

Without warning, Denton stood up, gathering his papers as if to leave. 'I haven't got time to listen to these baseless lies,' he said.

'Actually, would you mind holding on, Ian?' Armstrong said, glancing across at the PM. 'Allegations of this sort, however unfounded, are my department. And.I'd like to clear this up now.'

Denton turned to the PM, who was looking at Armstrong.

'Harriet's right,' the PM said. 'We need to sort this.'

Denton sat down again, his limbs almost seeming to give way beneath him. Spiro noticed Armstrong nod at a female member of COBRA staff. A moment later, the screen next to Marchant displayed a government website. Everyone waited, listening to the sound of a tapping keyboard as the URL address Marchant had given was typed in.

Another murmur, this time louder, mixed with a single female gasp. Spiro traced it to the typist, who had a hand clasped to her mouth. He preferred to look at her than at the image on the screen. It showed a naked Ian Denton bound in chains, clearly in physical pain but sexually aroused nevertheless. Not a pretty site at the best of times, but even more troubling in the cavernous surrounds of COBRA.

Spiro couldn't bring himself to look at Denton sitting next to him. No one could. People glanced at the shocking image several times, as if to check, and then anywhere except at the man himself. Awkward wasn't the word for the car-crash atmosphere, Spiro thought: a head-on collision between the English reserve that usually prevailed in this room and the obscenity now depicted on the screen. For the first time he could remember, the sound of Daniel Marchant's voice came as a relief.

'This photo – I will spare you the others – was taken three years ago by the SVR, who used it to blackmail Denton. At the time, he was disillusioned with his career at Six – always being overlooked for the top jobs, never quite being given the nod, a bit of an outsider. So why not accept Moscow's offer? The extra money was handy, and of course the consequences would have been fatal to his career if the photos ever surfaced. And if anyone believes these images are fabricated, Denton communicated with his Russian contact in the Clapham Junction branch of Waitrose last Friday night. I've posted photos of that on the website too.'

'Could we see them, please?' It was the PM, clearing his throat as he leant forward to talk into his table mike.

'There's a link at the bottom of the screen.'

A moment later, Denton was clearly identifiable in a grainy photo, but there was no one else in the frame.

'He's leaving a message disguised as a simple retail barcode,' Marchant said. 'If you click on the next link . . .' He paused. '. . . You'll see his Russian contact at exactly the same place – the blini counter – reading the message with his barcode scanner.'

'His real name is Dimitri Khrenkov,' Armstrong said. 'A Russian illegal living in the UK under the name of Duncan Spence.'

Since when did she get in on the act, Spiro wondered. The PM was surprised by Armstrong's comment too.

'Did you know about this?' the PM asked, as Armstrong dialled a number on her mobile.

'Marchant contacted me before this meeting,' she replied. 'D4 managed to trace Khrenkov.'

'What are you planning to do with these images?' the PM asked, looking up at Marchant.

'If Denton isn't removed from his job with immediate effect and Marcus Fielding reinstated as Chief, the website will go live.

Search engines won't have any trouble finding it – I've keyworded the images with "Torture" and "MI6".'

'Counter-intelligence,' the PM said, turning to Armstrong. 'It's your call.'

Everyone looked up as the door to COBRA opened. Two uniformed Special Branch officers stood there, waiting for instructions.

'Arrest him,' Armstrong said, snapping her phone shut.

95

Salim Dhar made his way out of the medical room and along the corridor, following behind Ali Mousavi and two armed guards. The legs of the oil platform were resting on the seabed, but the superstructure was still prone to swaying. Mousavi refused to confirm their exact location, but it was somewhere in the Strait of Hormuz. The main shipping lanes were clearly visible in the distance, three oil tankers crossing the horizon.

Two minutes later, after making their way down a metal staircase and through a warren of deserted corridors, Mousavi stood at the entrance to a steel, wheel-locked door. Dhar calculated that they were on the lowest level of the platform's living quarters, the sea not far below them. Ushered in by Mousavi, he stepped through the door and found himself in a small indoor boatyard. Tools were scattered everywhere, as if they had just been put down, but there was nobody about. Dhar had already noted that, apart from Mousavi, only two medical staff and the two guards had seen his face. He guessed that Mousavi had ordered the boatyard and the living quarters to be evacuated before his arrival.

In front of him, taking centre stage, was an unpainted vessel. It shared the contours of the *Bradstone Challenger*, the powerboat Mousavi had shown him in the TV news footage, but it had none of its glamour or finish. The boat was hanging from a small derrick, and below it big bay doors were set in the floor.

'I thought the Bradstone was still in Karachi,' Dhar said.

'The real one is. We have mocked this one up, based on technical specifications we managed to acquire from a Bladerunner dealership in Dubai. The boats they sell are not as high-spec as the *Bradstone*. Our people are reverse-engineering what they can, but we won't be able to make proper progress until we have the real thing. Still, it gives you an idea of the size and shape. And inside, the controls are identical, so you can get a feel for them. Take a look, why not?'

Dhar walked over to the hull, climbed up a short ladder propped against it, and slid into the cockpit. There were two big bucket seats at the front, one for the helmsman and one for the navigator. Behind them a long wooden bench ran down one side of the boat to the shell of a galley area. A wooden seat curved around the stern. None of the interior had been finished or upholstered apart from the two seats in the cockpit.

'This is where their loose women sat,' Mousavi said, gesturing at the cabin. He was on the top rung of the ladder, looking into the cockpit. 'When they weren't lying about naked on the deck.'

Mousavi smiled, but Dhar didn't want to think of the craft as a place of pleasure for the decadent infidel. As he sat behind the wheel, studying the bank of six monitor screens in front of him, he preferred to concentrate on the boat's military possibilities, the damage it was capable of causing. In recent days, Mousavi had talked more about the operation that lay ahead. It was not without risk, but the target was so iconic, the global ramifications so immense, that Dhar had struggled to sleep at night, his mind filled with the images that would soon be circulating around the world.

'Does it actually work?' he asked.

'Of course. But it's not as fast as the real thing. It doesn't have the thousand-horsepower Caterpillar engines. Or the Arneson surface drives. Later we will lower it into the water for you to practise. It's easy to operate. You'll enjoy it.'

'What about the torpedoes?' Dhar asked, thinking back to the first time he had sat behind the controls of the SU-25 jet. He had felt daunted then as the Bird, his Russian instructor, had talked him through the flightdeck. This was much simpler.

'That's why our engineers have built this one. To work out how and where to install them inside the hull. The plan is to fit the real thing with "hoot" supercavitation torpedoes – our own version of the Russian "shkval" system – as soon as it arrives. During recent tests, they travelled at 200 knots, twice the speed of normal torpedoes and too fast for any American ship.'

Dhar was impressed, but he wondered if he would ever be on the side that wasn't reverse-engineering others' technology. Mousavi had talked to him earlier about supercavitation. It was a way of creating a bubble of gas around an object as it moved through water, reducing friction and allowing it to travel at much faster speeds.

'I need to send a message to my people in Morocco,' Dhar said, still sitting behind the controls.

'Every time you contact the outside world it is dangerous – for all of us.'

'How do you expect me to ask Daniel Marchant about helping in Karachi?'

'I was not thinking of asking him.'

'He might not come quietly. It's better he knows I'm involved.'

Dhar couldn't explain the real reason he wanted to send a message to Marchant. It wasn't to reassure him about Karachi, but to honour their private arrangement. Thanks to Marchant he now had his freedom, but Britain was still burning. And that troubled him more perhaps than it should. There were over-zealous brothers in London who needed to be stopped.

'Let me first send word to him,' Dhar said. 'Then your people can liaise with mine and bring him here.'

'Send word? How will you do this? No one is allowed to leave until the next shift of oil workers arrive – that is why we brought you here. To the outside world, to the Americans, this must appear like a functioning oil platform.'

'I don't need anyone to leave. Just give me an internet connection.'

96

Marchant stepped out of the internet café and glanced up and down the street. Nobody was around. He thanked the owner, who turned the sign on the door back to 'Open', and set off towards his *riad*. The call to COBRA had gone well. Denton had been arrested, and the PM, after a private discussion with the Foreign Secretary, had agreed to Fielding's return. The only surprise was Spiro's presence. Luckily, no one had been in a mood to listen to his accusations about Marchant and his role in the Bagram jail-break. Spiro's influence in Whitehall was clearly waning.

There was still a risk, though, that the Americans could make trouble for him. They hadn't forgotten his role in the downing of an F-22, and they would try to blame him for Lakshmi's death. At no point in his video conference with COBRA had Marchant discussed his own return or a possible amnesty. For the time being he wanted to remain abroad, unaccountable. There was work to do. Dhar was out there somewhere and had promised to protect Britain. Marchant just hoped his half-brother had detected his hand in the jailbreak. That had always been the deal: Dhar's freedom in return for Britain's safety.

As he reached rue Sidi Mohamed ben Abdullah, Marchant heard a noise behind him. He turned to see a group of fifteen, maybe twenty, street children surge around a corner and run towards him as a pack. They were laughing and playing, one of them scuffing a deflated football along. Marchant tried to move to one side to let them pass, but they were already around him, streaming past on either side. The children were all smiles and there was no menace, but none of them acknowledged him, which struck Marchant as odd.

Then something touched his hand. Was he being naïve? Had they fleeced him like a swarm of locusts? He felt for his money, and a scrap of paper, screwed up in a tight ball, fell to the ground. It must have been pressed into his palm. He looked up to see the last of the children disappearing around the corner. The child turned back, catching his eye, and was gone.

Marchant didn't unfold the paper at once. After doubling back on himself, he walked past the internet café and turned into a small side street before cutting back to rue Sidi Mohamed ben Abdullah. Somebody had known he was at the café, which meant he had been careless. He was certain no one had followed him, but they might be watching now.

He put the paper in his pocket, unfolded it with his fingers and then brought it out, glancing at it briefly. One word was written on it: 'Abdul'. He balled the paper and threw it down an open drain.

Dhar had told him at Tarlton that he would make contact through the camel herders of Essaouira. The most obvious place was on the main beach, at the far end of which he had seen herders standing around in the wind and surf with their camels, waiting for tourists. He hadn't been over there yet, but he set off now, assuming that Abdul was in some way connected to Dhar.

Essaouira felt different as he left through the south-eastern gate of the medina and headed towards the beach. He was no longer a visitor, he was a target, the focus of someone's surveillance. No one was who they seemed any more. Women on the promenade wall were selling henna designs for hands and feet. One of them glanced up at him as he passed. A row of laminated cards showing different patterns was laid out on the pavement in front of the women. Some were complex, like matrix barcodes. Relax, he told himself. The women were just trying to earn a living.

The beach was shrouded in a heavy sea mist but it was still busy, a riot of football matches. This was no casual Sunday knock-about, Marchant thought. Proper pitches had been marked out in the sand. Players, mostly young men in their teens and twenties, were wearing formal strips, the refs dressed in black and brandishing whistles.

Marchant walked down to the water's edge, kicking a ball back to a player as he went. Two runners jogged past, listening to iPods. A few people were swimming. Stray dogs roamed the foreshore, searching for food. Up ahead, a man appeared out of the mist and headed across the sand towards him, hood up, his arms dripping with watches. Marchant was firmly in his sights.

'Rolex?' he asked. Marchant smiled but said nothing, walking on. 'Breitling?' His time in Marrakech had taught him not to be drawn into dialogue. 'Sunglasses?' he heard behind him.

The kite-surfers were further down the beach, on the far side of the bay, away from the swimmers. Nobody was on the water yet. The mist was slowly lifting, the sun breaking through in patches like dim torchlight. In front of him, a group of French beginners was being given a lesson by an instructor. Their kites and strings were laid out like giant jellyfish.

An ephemeral layer of sand rippled across the beach towards Marchant as he walked on towards the camels. Some stood in the mist, others were lying down, the occasional grunt carried in the wind. One pair necked like lovers – anything to attract the tourists. Competition for business was fierce, the modern world undermining the camels' ancient draw. Beyond them, a column of quad bikes snaked through the sand dunes, ridden by a family of tourists. In the far distance, Marchant could make out a rider on a solitary Arab horse, galloping through the shallow surf.

One of the herders broke away from a group and approached him, pulling on a reluctant camel.

'Five hundred dhirams, half an hour,' he said. His heart wasn't in it, Marchant thought. Had he given up on tourists, or was he Dhar's man?

'Not now. Maybe later,' Marchant said.

'OK, my friend. If you want camel ride, my name is Saif. Here's my card.'

Marchant took it and walked on towards a row of beach cafés and water-sports shops, where rival flags billowed in the wind like tribal standards. At the first café, a man in a tattered blue overcoat moved between orange sun loungers, a bulging plastic bag in his hand.

'*Cacahuete! Cacahuete!*' he shrieked, bursting into a toothless, gummy song. '*Bom-be-bom-be-bom-be-bom-be-bom. Cacahuete! Cacahuete!*' He was selling roasted peanuts and almonds.

A group of chic French students in bikinis called him over to their sun lounger, where they were crowded around smooth-chested teenage boys in swim shorts. Music played on a mobile phone while they smoked. Empty beer bottles were stacked on the table. Marchant thought the almond seller was about to be given a hard time, but he was greeted like an old friend.

'Camel ride?' a voice said beside him. The man had approached with the stealth of a professional.

'How much?' Marchant asked.

He knew at once that this was Dhar's man. There was something about him: a fierceness in the eyes.

'Four hundred and fifty dhirams, half an hour. No haggle.'

'I haven't come all this way not to haggle,' Marchant said,

detecting the beginnings of a smile on the man's weatherbeaten face.

'Nobody haggles with Abdul,' he said. 'Would you like to walk with me?'

Two minutes later, they were far enough away from the beach cafés to talk. Abdul was showing off his camels, giving Marchant an assessment of each one: '. . . dull eyes . . . shiny hair . . . nervous . . . firm ears . . . broad cheeks . . . strong straight legs.' For a moment, Marchant thought he had been mistaken for a camel buyer.

Then Abdul's tone changed as he fastened a strap on a saddle. 'I have an address for you,' he said. 'In London.' He barked a command and the camel collapsed to its knees, as if it was deflating.

Marchant tried to concentrate on the camel, to look as if he was sizing it up for a ride, but Abdul's words threw him. He had been expecting coded instructions of some sort, a way to meet up with Dhar or at least make contact with him. Dhar would never return to Britain, even if he had been on the vodka again. So why had he been given an address in London?

'If you care for your country, you must pass it on,' Abdul continued, the camel now fully seated on the sand. 'Time is running out.'

97

'I'm not naïve, Jim,' Linda said. 'But somehow it was easier when you were in the Marines, fighting a war.'

'We're at war now, just on a different battlefield, with different weapons and a different enemy.'

Spiro and his wife were walking beside the Thames, past the Globe Theatre. When they had met outside the South Bank Centre, she had let him kiss her on the cheek, but pulled away when he tried to hug her. She was looking tired after her flight from Beirut, and had done her hair in a different way, but otherwise Spiro thought she seemed OK.

'Jason's taught me to see the world differently,' she said.

Spiro had told himself not to react when Jason's name cropped up, as he knew it would. But try as he might, he bristled at the thought of her spending time with the doughnut puncher he'd met in Busboys and Poets.

'Oh come on, Linda, don't bring him into this.'

'Excuse me? You and I don't have a future if we can't talk about Jason.'

'Is that so? Is he the reason you went away?'

They stopped to look at each other. Spiro had always thought it odd when couples argued in public seemingly unself-consciously, but right now he didn't give a damn what the people passing by thought.

'Jason's gay, OK?' Linda said, her voice quieter. 'I thought that was fairly obvious.'

Spiro had suspected as much, but the idea of Jason teaching his wife 'to see the world differently' still made him mad. He knew his jealousy made no sense, but that was how it was. He was tired, and was already feeling humiliated by Denton's demise.

'I'm sorry,' he said, as they walked on. 'It's been a bad day.'

'And you can't talk about it.'

'How long have we been married? Thirty years? Not a bad run. What I don't get is, why now?'

'Why not?'

'Where did you go, Linda?' He needed to ask, in case Dhar had been lying. 'Why didn't you answer my calls?'

'You wouldn't have believed me if I told you. I can't believe it myself. I've been a military wife all my adult life, staying at home, looking after Joseph, waiting for you to walk through the door, not knowing where you've been, when you'll be away again.'

'And I appreciate it, you know I do. I should have done more, encouraged you to do your own thing. Photography, whatever.'

'The timing was never right. You know that.' He guessed she wouldn't want to talk about Joseph. The decision to send their disabled son away into full-time care still sat uncomfortably with both of them.

'I wanted to do something for myself. Not as your wife, but as me. Photography for Peace has given me some self-respect. When Jason asked if I wanted to go with the group to Ramallah, I saw an opportunity.'

So Dhar hadn't been lying. It would have been so much easier if he had. His supporters must have been with them on the West

Bank. Had the Israelis watched them mix with her and Jason and their group? His CIA career would be over if Mossad started circulating photos of his wife with Salim Dhar's *jihadi* friends. He told himself to calm down. They could discuss the damage to his career later. Today was about her. Everything had always been about him – that was the problem.

'An opportunity for what?' he asked, trying to be conciliatory.

'To see conflict for myself, first-hand. To try to understand why we fight each other. Why you were sent off to war in Iraq. What drives you and the Agency now.'

They walked on in silence for a while. Then she spoke. 'You don't seem too surprised. I thought you'd be mad at me for going to a place like Ramallah.'

'I'm an intelligence officer.' He was tempted to reveal that he already knew where she had been, but decided against it. 'We're trained to conceal our emotions.'

He swallowed hard, and felt his eyes moistening as they walked on. All he wanted was for them to be back in Virginia, ordering double pan-fried noodles and spicy chicken from P.F. Chang's at Tysons Corner as they watched old episodes of *The Sopranos*. Their marriage hadn't been perfect, but it had worked, and he would do all he could to make it better now.

'I know what you're thinking,' she said, linking an arm in his. It was the first sign of affection she had shown. 'That I fell blindly in love with the Palestinian cause, and hated the young Israeli soldiers who trained their sights on us when we threw stones at them.'

'Well, didn't you?'

'It wasn't as simple as that. I came away thinking peace will never be achieved if both sides continue as they are. It's not a new idea, it's never going to win me the Nobel Peace Prize, but nothing will improve unless one side or the other has the courage to change its own behaviour.'

'I'm not sure that's going to happen any day soon, honey.'

'Perhaps not. And I'm in no position to change things. All I can do is exhibit a few photographs at Busboys and Poets. But you are. You can make a difference.'

'Me? How?'

'In your war on terror. By stopping the torture. Treating your enemies as prisoners of war rather than as enemy combatants with no rights.'

Spiro detected Jason's words in what she said. He could hear the watercooler chat in the office already: 'Heard about Jim's wife? Some butt pirate's turned her into a beatnik.'

'One, these are not nice people we're dealing with here,' he said, resentful that he was having to justify his job to his own wife. 'Two –' he dropped his voice, glancing around them – 'we don't do torture. And three, I don't even want to begin listing all the atrocities we've prevented as a result of information gathered from enhanced interrogations.'

'I know all that, Jim. Don't treat me like a fool. I'm not asking you to put in for a transfer to payroll, I just want you to try to change your behaviour at a personal level, that's all. These things can only start with the individual. There must be times, even at the Agency, when it's down to you, your call alone, whether to treat someone as a fellow human being or as a goddamn farm animal.'

An image of Salim Dhar hanging from the ceiling in Bagram flashed through his mind. Could he have done things another way? Would it have made a lick of difference? He doubted it.

'And if I do? If I try?'

'Perhaps you and I can make a go of things. Give ourselves another chance.'

98

Harriet Armstrong sat in the Range Rover, looking out across the Thames, waiting. She was in East Greenwich, in the shadow of an old coal-fired power station. It reminded her of earlier days, when she had been a young officer with MI5. Her life then had seemed like one long wait, a never-ending series of stake-outs, cold coffee and male colleagues with marriage problems.

Twenty minutes earlier, a team of armed police officers from CO19 had broken down the front door of an old dockworker's cottage in a parallel street. Four men had been arrested. Bomb-making equipment on an industrial scale had been found in the house and a metal scrapyard that backed onto the garden, along with plans for more devastating attacks, one of which had been imminent.

She had moved fast after taking the call from Daniel Marchant. He had not gone into detail, and she hadn't asked him to. All she knew was that MI5 finally had a lead.

'You need to get people down there now,' Marchant had said.

'Thank you.' She never liked anyone telling her how to do her job, but she had hoped her gratitude sounded genuine. 'I'm picking Fielding up from the airport later,' she had added, knowing he would be pleased.

A text came through on her phone. The crime scene had been

secured. She tapped on the glass that separated her from the driver and the Range Rover sped off. A small crowd had gathered at the far end of the street, mostly residents who had been evacuated from their homes while the terraced cottage and the scrapyard had been searched for explosives. A police officer on the front door stood aside as Armstrong walked into the house.

Forensics teams in blue overalls and facemasks were busy at work. She knew her presence was unhelpful, but she needed to see for herself where so much of the pain of the past few weeks had been conceived. She also wanted to know how Marchant knew, what linked him to the terrorist cell. At the COBRA meeting he had said the attacks would stop now that Salim Dhar was free. Did he mean that Dhar himself would stop them? If so, how did Marchant know? Was he in touch with Dhar?

She couldn't believe that he had helped Dhar to escape, as Spiro had alleged – but who really knew? They were half-brothers, after all. Marchant had always been Marcus Fielding's private project, someone he was not prepared to share with anyone else. It had driven Denton to distraction. She hoped Fielding might be more open with her on his return.

The cottage was a simple two-up, two-down, with a kitchen and bathroom recently added at the back of the ground floor. It was tidier than she had expected, except for the second bedroom. Two mattresses lay on the floor, on either side of an architect's design board which was on a slant facing the sash window. The blind was down, and the solitary bulb hanging from the ceiling wasn't working – CO19 had cut the electricity before the raid – but there was enough light to see what was on the board. Rough, hand-drawn sketches of Sellafield nuclear power station and the National Grid substation in Sheffield, along with professional surveillance photos of both sites. But it wasn't these that caught her eye. It was a photo of a young Salim Dhar, posing with an

AK47 at a training camp, stuck on the wall like a picture of a saint.

She stared at him for a moment, and was about to leave the room when another piece of paper caught her eye. Someone had written down an address in Victoria. Next to it was tomorrow's date.

99

Marchant was drinking coffee at one of the cafés at the back of the beach, near where the camels mustered. Trance music played over the speakers as tourists lounged around in the wind and sun, but he couldn't relax. The sea mist had cleared to reveal Île de Mogador on the horizon. There had once been a prison on the island. Now all he could see was the tower of a mosque, its white brickwork picked out in the sunlight.

Abdul was down on the beach, away to his left, chatting to other camel herders. Business was slow today. Nobody wanted to ride out to the fort ruins of Bordj el Berod, which had supposedly inspired Jimi Hendrix to write a song. Perhaps the tourists were wising up, Marchant thought. Hendrix had not visited Morocco until two years after 'Castles Made of Sand' was released.

He took another sip of coffee. Two trawlers were returning to port. Seagulls swarmed behind their sterns like clouds of smoke. An inflatable rescue boat headed slowly across the bay. A lot had happened since Dhar had been picked up by the Russian trawler in the Bristol Channel. Marchant wondered where he was now, whether Abdul knew the sender of the message he had given, let alone what it meant. He doubted it.

Dhar would have communicated using his own human version of anonymous routing. Each link of the chain would only have

337

been aware of the messenger either side of him. Somewhere along the line, at the start perhaps, Dhar might have used technology, left a message in a draft email folder, just as Fielding had done. But Dhar was a firm believer in using the spoken word rather than modern comms, which were no longer safe from the prying eyes and ears of GCHQ and the NSA.

A few minutes earlier, Marchant had rung Armstrong on another new pay-as-you-go phone, standing at the water's edge where no one could overhear him. After the call, he had dismantled the unit and slipped its parts into his pocket before binning them. Armstrong had sounded happy. If, as Marchant thought, the address in London was that of a terrorist cell, it meant that Dhar was playing ball. He would catch the news tonight, see if there was any talk of police raids in Britain.

Marchant watched as a kite-surfer walked down towards the water, carrying his gear like a parachute. Ahead of him people were starting to rip across the waves, soaring into the air as the wind rose. Would he still be able to do it, Marchant wondered, as a waiter wrestled with a parasol in front of him. He had deliberately chosen a sun lounger at the back of the café. There was no one behind him and he had clear sightlines, allowing him to clock everyone who entered or left. He could keep an eye on Abdul too, see who he talked to.

Abdul had asked him to return in half an hour, once he had passed on the message. He hadn't elaborated, just said that there was something else he needed to discuss. The plan had sounded messy, putting Marchant on edge. He waved for a waiter, settled up and made his way over to Abdul, satisfied that he was alone.

'It is better you ride,' Abdul said, gesturing at his camel, which was kneeling down.

'Where are we going?' Marchant asked. 'To meet Jimi Hendrix?'

'Don't mock us. We all have to earn a living. It is safer to talk if people think you are a dumb tourist who has paid too much to ride a lazy camel.'

'People? Who's watching?' Marchant asked, mounting the animal. Abdul was making him increasingly nervous.

'There are new faces on the beach today, people I haven't seen before.'

'What sort of people?' Marchant must have been losing his touch. He had seen nothing suspicious from the café.

'Maybe Russians.'

Ten minutes later, Marchant was riding down the beach, scouring the horizon for threats. He had thought about cutting his losses and heading back to the medina, but he needed to know what else Abdul had to say.

'You had another message for me,' he said, glancing around. Someone had started up a quad bike in the dunes, at the end of the row of cafés.

'You must travel to Bandar-Abbas,' Abdul replied.

Marchant closed his eyes as they rode on in silence. It made sense. Dhar was hiding with the people who had sprung him from Bagram. Travelling to Bandar-Abbas on the Iranian coast would be risky, but he needed to see Dhar again, thank him for the address in London and reassure him of his own role in the jail-break. If Dhar was to be an effective MI6 asset, it was important that he was run properly. Marchant didn't just want the details of one cell in London, he wanted a constant flow of intel from the heart of the global *jihad*. That was the deal.

'How do I get there?' he asked. But before Abdul could reply, Marchant heard the sound of a horse galloping up behind them.

He spun round. A man riding bareback on an Arabian piebald mare drew up alongside them, pulling on the reins. His face was half covered by a red scarf, which he lowered to talk to Abdul.

His accent was different from that of the Berbers of Marrakech, but Marchant caught enough to know there was something wrong.

'It is not safe for you to be here,' Abdul said, turning to Marchant. 'You must take my friend's horse.'

'Who is it? Where are they?' Marchant asked, scanning the beach. The scene looked innocent enough in the July sunshine. The wind was up, and a fine spray hung over the sea where the waves were breaking. Half a dozen bright kites zig-zagged through the sky, dragging their surfers across the choppy water.

Then he saw them, two quad bikes rising into the air as they came over the crest of a distant sand dune.

'Russians,' Abdul said. 'Please, there is no time.'

The rider had already dismounted and was holding the mare beside the camel. Marchant slipped down from the saddle and jumped across onto its bare back, feeling the horse's warmth. His father had been a keen rider, taking him and his twin brother through dried-up riverbeds in Rajasthan when they were young. Later he had taught Marchant how to play polo, which they had watched in Delhi. The horse bucked, unhappy with its new rider, but the man still had hold of the bridle and brought it under control with a curse. Marchant had never ridden bareback before.

'Go,' Abdul said. 'We will try to delay them.'

Without hesitating, Marchant dug in his heels and galloped down the beach, away from the cafés and towards the ruins of Bordj el Berod. He was barely in control of the horse, which was strong and wild, but a survival instinct had taken over. He glanced behind him. The quad bikes were approaching Abdul. The other man was on foot, waving frantically for the quad bikes to stop. They didn't have a hope. The Russians weren't giving up. Marchant was pretty sure they blamed him for Dhar's failure to complete the mission at Fairford.

340

He cut down to the water's edge, where the sand was soft – too soft for the quad bikes, he hoped. This end of the bay was deserted. Anything could happen down here, Marchant thought, and no one would know. He needed to get back to the cover of crowds, where it would be harder for the Russians to shoot him. They had missed him once, killing Lakshmi. They wouldn't miss again.

Riding back up the beach, he took the horse in a long, sweeping arc. To his left, he could see a man lying motionless on the sand, and Abdul slumped on his camel. The quad bikes were heading straight towards him. Either he could head up into the dunes, where the going would be tough for both horse and bike, or he could drop down to the sea again and ride back to Essaouira. But to do that he would have to pass in front of the quad bikes, and he didn't know if he had enough time.

He galloped across the beach on a diagonal path towards the sea. His horse seemed to sense the urgency, and found more speed, or perhaps they were on harder sand. The quad-bike riders saw where he was going and tried to cut him off, but he reached the water with a lead of two hundred yards. It was now a straight race back to the headland and around to the cafés. He could feel the horse beginning to tire in the wet sand, but his pursuers were staying higher up the beach. They were still behind him, but were closing fast. One of them had drawn a handgun.

A shot rang out as Marchant rounded the headland. He was running out of options. Fifty yards in front of him, an instructor was teaching a group of teenagers how to kite-surf. He guessed it was an introductory lesson, because none of the students were standing on their boards, which were lined up in the shallow water beyond them, bobbing about like toy boats in the splashy surf. The instructor was holding the bar of a kite, but it wasn't attached to his chest harness. Instead, he passed the bar to each teenager in turn, allowing them to feel the force of the wind.

Marchant glanced to his right. The quad bikes were now level with him. They were risking the softer sand and had come further down the beach towards the water without losing speed. Turning his horse into the shallow water, Marchant headed straight for the group of teenagers, hoping they would get out of the way. The horse seemed to enjoy being in the sea and accelerated again, panting hard, kicking up spray.

Marchant knew he only had one shot at what he was about to do. He shifted his weight to the left. A terrified cry went up from the teenagers as it became clear that the crazy tourist on the horse wasn't just buzzing their lesson with a ride-by – he was galloping straight through the middle of them. They split in all directions, but the instructor seemed to freeze, holding onto his kite.

As Marchant rode past, he leant down, grabbed the kite bar from him and leapt free of his horse. The wind was strong enough for him to be carried a few yards, like the surfers who were jumping waves in the distance. He landed beside one of the boards, and it took only a second to slot his feet into its grips. Without looking behind him, he bent his legs, braced his arms against the pull of the wind and pointed the board out to sea.

Just as he began to pick up speed, a gust of wind blew down the beach, ripping him off balance. The kite dropped down low, almost touching the waves, and dragged him through the shallow water, first on his front, then on his back, arms above his head. Water sluiced through his mouth, up both nostrils, down his throat. He struggled not to think of being waterboarded, tried not to panic.

Normally he would have released the bar, but he knew he had to hold on if he was to stand any chance of escaping. Gagging on the salt water, he managed to lever himself upright. A plume of water seemed to explode beside him as another gunshot rang out, then another. He trimmed the angle of the kite, adjusted his feet on the board, and set off again, this time skimming across the waves like a flying fish.

100

'Welcome home, sir,' the immigration officer at Heathrow said. Fielding nodded, took his US passport and walked on. He was still travelling in the name of Ted Soderling, his American tourist cover, which meant his real ID must have been flashed to every desk in immigration. Americans might be all over Whitehall, but they didn't call Britain home, not yet. Armstrong had been thorough.

Earlier in the day, Brigadier Borowski had rung through to Fielding's safe house to tell him the international warrant for his arrest had been lifted. Borowski had done some research of his own too, calling in a favour at the British High Commission in Warsaw. Ian Denton had 'fallen ill', and many of the decisions he had made as acting Chief, including the order to arrest Fielding, had been rescinded.

Fielding took it all to mean only one thing. Daniel Marchant had managed to show the SVR photos of Denton to Harriet Armstrong, along with his own evidence from London. He had thought about calling her himself, but old habits died hard. A small part of him still suspected a trap, so he had asked Borowski to speak with Armstrong to confirm that the coast was clear for his return.

Fielding didn't have any luggage, so he was soon standing outside Arrivals. Armstrong had told Borowski that she would meet Fielding in person, which seemed unnecessary, but they had much to catch up on. A few moments later, a black Range Rover swept up in front of him and a rear door opened. A second car drew up behind with a Special Branch security detail.

'There was really no need,' Fielding said as he climbed in beside Armstrong.

'I'm sorry we're in my car,' she said. 'Yours is still being swept and checked.'

Armstrong wasn't overtly warm in her greeting. She never was, hiding behind a veneer of primness that Fielding had long dismissed as affected. But he sensed, as he looked across at her, that she was pleased to see him. The corners of her pinched mouth twitched with a suppressed smile as they sat in silence, waiting to join the M4. Perhaps she was just feeling pleased with herself. She had every right to be. Britain would sleep more easily tonight. A major terrorist cell had been arrested in Greenwich – he had watched a report about it on the plane.

'I'm sorry about the photos,' he said. 'There was really no other way.'

'I've seen worse.'

Fielding wondered where. MI5 was under investigation for collaborating in torture during the aftermath of 9/11, as was MI6. Before he left London he had made the mistake of putting Denton in charge of the search for the rogue MI6 officer. There was less urgency now. When he was back in the office, he would cross-check the files with Denton's movements. Or maybe he would ask Anne Norman to do that. She had never liked Denton, and the process might prove cathartic.

'Were you surprised?' he asked.

'Hindsight's a wonderful thing. When Marchant called about Denton, a part of me was disappointed. You know, that there was no higher motive.'

'People don't betray for ideology any more.'

'Perhaps not, but blackmail? It's so . . . tawdry. We're all tarnished by it. It reminds us how cheaply our profession can be bought.'

'I blame myself. Not for Ian's sexual preferences, of course, but for his bitterness. I didn't manage him well. I should have spotted the dissatisfaction, the depth of it. He was always an outsider, that's why I brought him on. To shake things up a bit. He didn't burn those agents in Poland because of love for Russia. It was out of hatred for us – Prentice, me, the old guard. The club. Philby once said that in order to betray, one must first belong. Ian never belonged.'

'But would he have betrayed us if the Russians hadn't black-mailed him?'

Fielding didn't know. He had asked himself the same question many times in recent days. 'Moscow Centre saw someone who was hesitating on the ledge, an aggrieved deputy who needed to be pushed before he jumped. All I know is that there are still good people out there, fighting for what's right. And Daniel Marchant's one of them.'

'So you always say. You're going to have to be honest with me, Marcus. Let me know what's going on between him and Dhar.'

'How do you mean?' But he knew exactly what she meant.

'He's always been your private project.'

'I knew his father well. I promised I'd look after Daniel.'

'Where is he now?'

'I don't know.'

'But you spoke with him while you were away.'

'Once. To give him the photos.'

'He rang me yesterday.'

'Then you've talked to him more recently than I have.'

'He gave me the address in Greenwich where four men were arrested. The place was a hub, a nerve centre for coordinating a

346

network of smaller cells around the country. We've since picked people up in Truro, Bristol, Edinburgh, Sheffield and Cumbria. And we've found enough bomb-making material to blow up half of Britain.'

Fielding was good at not reacting, but even he struggled to remain unmoved at this.

'Sounds like it was a good lead,' he said.

'Good? We stopped an imminent attack on Sellafield. Twelve hours later and we would have been looking at a nuclear disaster.'

'I don't know why you sound surprised. As I've always said, Marchant's one of the best.'

'How did he know, Marcus? How did he know something that's eluded us for weeks?'

'How do any of us know? By doing what we do: lying, manipulating, deceiving.'

'They were also planning another attack, more personal.'

'On what?'

'I went down myself to the house in Greenwich, took a look around. There was a scrap of paper with a private address on it. House number, street, directions from the nearest Underground station.'

Fielding looked up. 'Whose?'

'Mine.'

'Marchant will be pleased.'

'I owe him my bloody life, Marcus.'

'Like I said, he's good.'

'Try telling that to Spiro.'

'I gather he was at yesterday's COBRA.' Fielding had heard of Spiro's presence at the meeting, thanks to another favour called in by Borowski. Friendly intelligence agencies across Europe were monitoring events in London, anxious to see how much America would bully its oldest ally.

'At one point he made an allegation about Marchant. Everyone else was too interested in Denton to notice, but his words stayed with me.'

'What did he say?'

'That Marchant helped Salim Dhar escape from Bagram.'

'And how did Spiro think he might have done that?'

'He didn't elaborate. But there was something else he said. "Myers has told us everything."'

'Paul Myers? GCHQ Myers?'

'I assume so. He's been working at home ever since the attack. I tried to ring him last night, no answer. Apparently he hasn't logged into the network for twenty-four hours, which is unlike him. He normally sleeps with his keyboard.'

Fielding had always had a soft spot for Myers, ever since he had humiliated Spiro at a Joint Intelligence Committee meeting. He didn't like the thought of Spiro spending time on his own with him. Enquiries would be made.

Neither of them spoke for a while. Armstrong checked through some paperwork. Fielding stared out of the window at the passing scenery. The M4 as it approached London always struck Fielding as a depressing introduction to Britain, with its billboards and boarded-up office blocks. The only sight that cheered him was the onion dome of the Russian Orthodox Church in Gunnersbury, a vivid splash of cobalt blue in grey suburbia.

He knew he would finally have to take Armstrong into his confidence about Dhar and Marchant. Her support would be crucial in the coming days, and there wouldn't be a better time to get her onside. The terrorists responsible for making MI5's life a misery had just been arrested. Peace was returning to Britain. And a plot to kill Armstrong had been thwarted. If ever she had reason to be grateful to Dhar, it was now.

'What I'm about to tell you must never go beyond you and

me,' he said, turning from the window to face her. 'The Prime Minister can't know, nor the Foreign Secretary, nor the Home Secretary. No one. It's better for all concerned if they remain ring-fenced.'

'From what?'

'Daniel Marchant is running Salim Dhar as a British asset. Dhar's war is with America, not with us. And we've just received our first dividend.'

101

Marchant was more than five hundred yards offshore when he allowed himself to slow down, bearing away from the wind. A crowd had gathered around the quad bikes on the beach. He guessed the camel herders were remonstrating with the riders, accusing them of killing two of their friends. It would be an ugly scene. The Russians were quite prepared to shoot themselves out of trouble.

Marchant's arms were tiring. He had been on a long tack without a harness, with only his adrenaline to keep him going. Kite-surfers rarely ventured out so far. He looked around for others nearby, but they had moved further around the bay, scared off by the shooting. If he kept going, he told himself, he could reach the Île de Mogador and safety. It was his only plan, although the inflatable rescue boat he had seen earlier was now heading in his direction.

The last thing he wanted was to be picked up and taken back to shore, even if the Russians had gone. Someone would have called the police, and he would be asked to be a witness, which meant questions, ID and an unwelcome appearance on the grid. He was travelling on the French passport Jean-Baptiste had given him, which he had wrapped loosely in a plastic bag, but he feared it would be ruined.

The rescue boat was approaching fast. Marchant turned his board away, hoping to make it clear that he didn't need assistance, but the boat tracked him.

'Are you injured?' a voice called out in French.

'*Non, ça va bien,*' Marchant called back.

'Where are you heading?'

Anywhere but the beach, he thought.

'Île de Mogador,' he offered, unable to think of a better answer. There were two people in the boat: one at the wheel, and the one talking to him, leaning over the side. They were young and dressed in T-shirts and long shorts, like the men who ran the kite-surf shops beyond the cafés. One had a pair of sunglasses in his short, curly hair.

'We thought you were going to Bandar-Abbas.'

Marchant felt his whole body relax, as if he had just crossed the line after a marathon. He let his kite spill its wind and fall towards the sea. The boat was alongside him as he sunk, exhausted, into the water.

'Are you friends of Abdul?' he asked in French.

'He was meant to take you down to Diabat.'

'Abdul was shot.'

Neither man said anything. Instead, they pulled in the kite and its tendril strings. Marchant was certain they were here to help him, sent by Dhar. Diabat was further down the beach, beyond the ruined fort. He grabbed the side of the boat and hauled himself in.

'The other man was shot too,' he said. 'The one with the horse.'

'We know Abdul by name, we spoke on the phone, but –'

'You've never met him.'

Both men nodded. Marchant reassured himself that they were here to help him. The only way they could know about Bandar-Abbas was if they were linked in some way with Dhar. It was

351

anonymous routing again. For safety, nobody knew anyone else in the chain.

The boat accelerated, turning left and away from Île de Mogador, which was still a long way off. He realised now that he would never have made it.

'Where are we going?' he asked, shivering in the wind.

'Diabat. New people will drive you out to Mogador airport. You will be given a ticket to Paris, where you will take a flight to Dubai. From there, you will fly on to Bandar-Abbas.'

102

Ali Mousavi was in his business-presentation mode again, talking Dhar through a series of slides and videos in a small room on the ground floor of the oil platform, near the indoor boatyard. Two soldiers kept guard outside. Dhar was happy to sit back and listen, eating white-fleshed apricots and drinking from a plastic bottle of Damavand mineral water. The after-effects of his anaphylactic shock had finally worn off, and he was beginning to feel himself again. His injured leg was still sore, and life on an oil platform induced occasional bouts of claustrophobia, but otherwise he was focused and ready for what lay ahead.

Mousavi's presentation was helping his recovery. Dhar was impressed with the scale of Iran's ambition and the country's understanding of its own military limits.

'Carrier Strike Group 10 deployed from Norfolk, Virginia, for a six-month tour of duty on 21 May,' Mousavi said as an aerial photograph came up on the screen. It showed a group of American warships at sea, spread out in formation. 'CSG 10 currently consists of four destroyers, three frigates and the flagship, the aircraft carrier USS *Harry S. Truman*, which comes with its own embarked air force, Air Wing Three, also known as Battle Axe.'

'And what does "Battle Axe" include?' Dhar asked, spitting out the American moniker.

'Eighty aircraft – Seahawk helicopters, early-warning Hawkeyes, electronic attack Prowlers, Hornets and Super Hornets.'

Dhar, his shoulder muscles involuntarily flexing at the last words, wished he hadn't asked. He knew they were fighter jets, but he couldn't stop an image flashing through his mind of the insect that had stung him in Bagram.

'Are you all right?' Mousavi asked.

'Carry on,' Dhar said, annoyed at his own weakness. He took another apricot.

'The Strike Group passed through the Suez Canal and entered the Persian Gulf earlier this week as part of a major build-up in the Fifth Fleet's area of operations. A German frigate has also joined them, and we think the Israelis have moved submarines into the Strait. Our threats to block and mine the Strait have drawn the enemy in, as expected. We've seen it all before, but this time the Zionists are looking for contact. And so are we.'

Mousavi paused, waiting for an image of an aircraft carrier to appear on the screen.

'Our target is the *Truman* – call sign CVN75, America's eighth Nimitz-class supercarrier, nickname "Lone Wolf". Later this week it will pass through the Strait, close to where we will be holding our biggest ever naval exercise.' Mousavi paused. 'There are more than six thousand personnel on board the *Truman*, and the commanding officer's a Jew. The ship keeps a Torah on the hangar deck.'

An image of a naval officer appeared on screen. They both remained silent.

'Is this a suicide mission?' Dhar asked. The more he had heard about the operation, the more he suspected it would require the ultimate sacrifice. Mousavi turned to look at him, pausing before he spoke.

'Not for you, of course. But there will be many martyrs. We

aim to have more than a hundred fast-attack boats at sea, including our new Seraj and Zolfaqar craft, and our Bavar 2 stealth flying boats. Most will be manned, but some won't.'

Mousavi switched the image to a photo of a heavily armed powerboat. The caption read YA MAHDI – SONAR-EVADING, and it was travelling at speed. There was no crew on board, making it look like a ghost ship, Dhar thought.

'The Americans will use the excuse of transit passage through the Strait's shipping lanes to conduct a naval exercise in what they claim are international waters,' Mousavi continued. 'They do this often.'

'Can people in Iran see the American ships from the shore?'

Mousavi nodded. 'Of course. It's like the British seeing hostile warships from the white cliffs of Dover. It can be very provocative, but also to our advantage. When the Americans pass through later this week, we will carry out our own naval exercise. A wave of unmanned Ya Mahdis will approach the convoy. The Americans will expect them to turn back, assuming they are part of our naval exercise, but they won't. When the Americans open fire – it is essential the first shots are theirs – we cry foul and retaliate in overwhelming numbers.'

More photos, aerial images of a row of twenty speedboats in a line, surging forward, followed by another line, and another. The Iranian flag billowed from the stern of each boat, and anti-ship missile launchers were mounted above the cockpits. They were crewed by men wearing bandanas. Dhar thought they looked like pirates. Mousavi began to pace around the room, gesturing like an impassioned academic as he spoke.

'At the heart of a swarm attack lies confusion. It is essential that the enemy is overwhelmed in his mind by the sight of so many boats coming towards him. He must enter a state of true sublimity – the anarchic spectacle before him appalls and fascinates in equal measure. At first, he will see only one or two boats, but then three, five, ten, twenty. We call this the 'sorites paradox', or the 'paradox of the heap'. One boat does not make a swarm. Maybe ten don't. Who knows? It is like grains of sand. When do they become a heap? After thirty grains? Thirty-five? It is impossible to tell. With a flotilla of fast-moving boats, there is an elusive tipping point when it becomes a swarm.'

'Why do you need me?' Dhar asked, unsure whether Mousavi's esoteric take on asymmetric warfare was reassuring or naïve.

'Because Salim Dhar has become a talisman for the global fight against Zionism. Some choose to stay hidden; you have always fought on the front line. I cannot deny that morale is low in Iran. Salim Dhar is the West's public enemy number one, a *jihadi* with a record of spectacular strikes against America. Your presence will help us achieve an even bigger victory against the Great Satan. It will unite our nation, justify our need for a nuclear deterrent and send a message to *jihadis* everywhere, triggering a pan-Islamic war against the Western world order.'

Fine words, but Dhar knew there was a degree of realpolitik too. His involvement would take some of the diplomatic heat off Iran in the aftermath of what was effectively a declaration of war against America. If it failed to ignite a wider conflict, Tehran would distance itself from the attack, accusing him of being a rogue asset who had hijacked a routine naval exercise. But he could live with that.

'Picture the scene,' Mousavi said. 'The USS *Truman*, flagship of the US Navy, 100,000 tonnes, $4.5 billion, listing in the Persian Gulf, smoke billowing from the bridge as it sinks beneath the waves. The images will travel around the world like 9/11, only this time there will be no moral ambiguity, no civilian casualties.'

'And I will be on board the *Bradstone Challenger*.'

'Our very own "lone wolf" that will land the fatal blow. Providing, of course, that your friend delivers it from Karachi.'

'He will.'

'You will be well protected. Initially, Seahawks and UAVs will be your greatest threat, but they will be more concerned with targeting boats in front of yours. As the swarm gathers, the Phalanx Close-In Weapons System will become an issue. Every US warship has Phalanx. It is a fully automated, radar-guided Gatling gun that fires 4,500 rounds of armour-piercing tungsten per minute. Too many. By the time you arrive, they will be out of rounds and the *Truman* will be within range of your own weapon systems.'

Mousavi cued up a short video. It showed a torpedo streaking towards a destroyer and hitting it amidships. The force of the explosion seemed to lift the boat out of the water as it buckled in two and burst into a ball of flames.

'There's something else you should know about the torpedoes our engineers have developed for *Bradstone Challenger*,' Mousavi continued. 'The single greatest threat to a ship of *Truman*'s size is fire. That's what sunk HMS *Sheffield* in the Falklands War. She went down in deep water six days after being hit by an Exocet missile. And it was fire that disabled most of the US aircraft carriers in the Second World War.

'Your boat will have two torpedoes, each equipped with a small thermobaric charge. If the *Truman* is pierced below decks, the ensuing fireball will be catastrophic. And it only takes one torpedo to get through. In the Battle of Midway, the Japanese carrier *Akagi* was sunk by a single bomb striking the upper hangar deck. It exploded amidst the planes, which were armed and fuelled for take-off.'

Dhar was impressed. But no matter how Mousavi chose to cast the operation in the classroom, he knew the reality. It was a martyrdom mission. The knowledge wasn't unsettling, because the prize was so great. A supercarrier was the embodiment of all he despised about America. According to Mousavi, 'Give 'em Hell', the USS *Truman*'s motto, was written everywhere around the ship to remind the crew of their duty. The *Truman* was iconic, the ultimate symbol of America's global arrogance, patrolling the world's seas as if it owned them. It was also vulnerable, more so than ever, an outdated form of warfare more useful for its strategic value than its tactical effectiveness. And like the *Bismarck*, it was an irresistible target.

Until recently, Dhar had felt he could achieve more in life than he could in death. But he had been lucky to survive the attack in Britain, even luckier to escape from Bagram. Time was running out, but there was still much to be done: America still occupied the Arab lands.

Mousavi was right. The stage was set to humiliate America in an attack that would reverberate far beyond the narrow confines of the Strait. Without him, it would be merely an act of aggression in a long-running local dispute. America would retaliate, destroying Iran's navy and possibly its nuclear facilities, oil prices would rise slightly and the world would move on. With him, the attack would serve as a rallying cry, a call to arms in Palestine and Pakistan, Yemen and the Caucasus. Islam had reached a pivotal moment in its history, an opportunity to wipe out arrogant materialist powers. It would be the greatest victory since the Prophet Muhammad, despite his army facing over-whelming odds, triumphed at the battles of Kheybar and Badr.

They shall fight in the way of Allah and shall slay and be slain.

103

Spiro spun the numbers on the combination lock and pulled at the chain on the old hangar doors. He tried not to dwell on what he might find inside. Few people visited this corner of RAF Fairford – access was restricted to senior CIA and JSOP personnel – but he still looked around the deserted airfield before stepping inside. The hangar was dark except for a shaft of cold blue light filtering in through a vent high up on one wall.

It wasn't the prospect of finding a tortured body that troubled Spiro. He had seen enough of those in his time. It was the thought that whatever had happened in the hangar over the past forty-eight hours might one day percolate back to Linda. There would be ways to cover it up, of course. There always were. Paul Myers wouldn't be the first GCHQ employee to be found dead in unexplained circumstances. But he knew he would be an accessory to the crime, even if he hadn't been there in person. It was he who had given Ian Denton the use of the facility.

So why had he come? Marcus Fielding had called him earlier. To be fair to the Brit, he could have rubbed his face in it, but Fielding had chosen to remain civil.

'Now's not the time for recriminations,' he had said. 'We both believed in Denton. I made him my deputy, you made him Chief.'

'Acting. Do you still believe in Daniel Marchant?' Spiro had asked.

'He's just exposed Ian Denton as a traitor.'

'In between busting Dhar from Bagram.'

'You know there's no evidence for that, Jim.'

'At least we were right about the existence of a Russian mole in MI6. Give us credit for that.'

'You just thought it was me. But let's move on. I have a small favour to ask.'

'Make it quick. The DCIA's called me back to Langley.'

'Denton interviewed a British intelligence officer down at RAF Fairford. Paul Myers, a Farsi analyst at GCHQ. You may have met him once.'

'Don't recall the guy, but I heard as much.' Spiro wasn't going to give Fielding any easy wins. Of course he remembered Myers. He was the fatass who humiliated him over the tape recording of Dhar's voice. Nor was he going to tell Fielding that he himself had facilitated Myers's interrogation.

'For some reason, Myers hasn't been at work. He's not answering calls, seems to have vanished. Tempting though it would be to surround Fairford with British troops, I thought I'd give you the opportunity to find out what's happened to him first.'

'I'll ask around.'

There had been no need. Spiro knew exactly where Myers was. He just wasn't sure if he was still alive. Denton had said he needed more time with him. Then he was arrested at the COBRA meeting and Myers had been forgotten. Paying him a visit now was the least Spiro could do, given he was passing through Fairford on his way back to Langley.

The metal door banged behind him, reverberating through the hangar. Spiro flicked on a row of switches, and the hangar lit up quarter by quarter. The last switch bathed Myers in a

360

pool of harsh white light. His naked body was hanging from a rope tied to his wrists, and there was something awkward about his shoulders and arms. Spiro could see what had happened. Denton had hanged him in reverse – some people called it a Palestinian hanging. He thought of Linda, tried to imagine her on the West Bank, waving placards, naïvely hoping for a more peaceful world.

He walked over to the body, a handkerchief to his nose. He couldn't see Myers's face, as his head had rolled forward, but he glanced at his injured groin. Dry blood was smeared around his stomach and thighs. Spiro thought he was inured to such scenes – he had seen far worse in Guantánamo and Bagram – but this time he felt repulsed.

Perhaps it was the excrement on the concrete floor. It was the one smell he couldn't abide, the only thing that had made his stomach turn when he was in India. Usually he got his subordinates to clean up a detainee before he set to work on them. And it was why he always insisted on diapers.

Spiro glanced again at the concrete floor and realised that Myers's feet were just touching it, enough to take the weight off his arms. Before he had left, Denton must have lowered him, which meant there was a chance he was still alive. Spiro moved forward, watching where he trod, and put a hand to Myers's neck. It was warm.

For the next five minutes he worked quickly. After cutting Myers down, he washed his face with water and sat him against the hangar wall. He was still unconscious, but there were signs that he was coming round – the odd grunt, his lips beginning to move. Both his shoulders were dislocated, and Denton had been busy with a knife below the waistline. Myers, though, had refused to talk. Perhaps he hadn't known of Dhar's imminent escape from Bagram. Perhaps Marchant was blameless.

'You're OK, buddy,' Spiro said when Myers eventually opened his swollen eyes. 'We're going to get you patched up at the medical unit here, then send you home.'

He hoped Linda would forgive him.

104

'We cannot be complacent, but it does seem that the cell arrested in Greenwich yesterday was responsible for coordinating the recent spate of attacks, and had others planned.'

The Prime Minister was in an uncharacteristically good mood, Fielding thought, as he listened to him address COBRA. It was a top-table meeting today, heads of houses rather than prefects. Only one seat was empty: Spiro's. He had attended the last COBRA meeting, despite it being for UK personnel only, but after Denton's departure and Fielding's return, his days in London were at an end.

'We all owe a great debt of gratitude to Harriet and her team,' the PM continued. 'They have worked around the clock to track down the perpetrators.'

The quiet noise of Whitehall approval spread through the room. Earlier that afternoon, the UK threat level had been lowered from 'severe' to 'critical'. Armstrong glanced across at Fielding. No one present would have read anything into the look, but he saw gratitude in her tired eyes. He would let her enjoy her moment, even though they both knew it wasn't deserved.

'I also want to take this opportunity to welcome back Marcus Fielding. As you know, he was' – the briefest of pauses – 'taken ill a few weeks ago, and then, regrettably, a warrant was erroneously issued for his arrest. I'm pleased to report that Marcus is no longer ill, and no longer wanted by Interpol.'

The PM tried to make light of the last remark, but no one was laughing.

'As for our colleague Ian Denton, he is now on extended sick leave. Stress is a debilitating illness, too often ignored in today's pressurised workplace.'

Fielding couldn't believe the government was trying to brazen out the Denton affair, hiding behind the farcical cover of sick leave, but that was the agreed line. Everyone around the table knew the truth, but the PM was having none of it, at least for the time being. According to Armstrong, the Americans were as keen as the British for Denton's treachery to be covered up for as long as possible, given he was their appointment.

Those who had witnessed Denton's unmasking at the earlier COBRA meeting had been reminded of their responsibilities under the Official Secrets Act. The PM must have known it was a temporary measure, Fielding thought. Sooner or later the government would be forced to come clean, admit that MI6 had been penetrated at the highest levels by Moscow.

'Which only leaves us with the problem of Daniel Marchant,' the PM continued. 'As you are aware, the Americans are keen for him to be questioned about his role in the attack on one of their military jets at Fairford. The British government would like to talk to him about the bombing of GCHQ, too. It seems he fled these shores and was last seen in France. But I'll let Marcus fill us in.'

Fielding had run his strategy past Armstrong before the meeting. He glanced in her direction now, just before he looked up at the table of faces. He hadn't planned to be entirely honest, but those assembled in the room were due an explanation of sorts.

'It's no secret that the Americans have long wanted to remove Daniel Marchant from the field,' he began. 'They suspected his father of treachery, and believed he himself was a renegade and a liability. His presence in the cockpit with Salim Dhar certainly seemed to confirm their case against him. There are others, too, who feel strongly that Marchant should be removed.' A glance across at the Director of GCHQ. 'After downing an American F-22, Dhar went on to attack Cheltenham, causing structural damage to GCHQ and killing one member of staff. Marchant, of course, was still on board, making him effectively party to an act of war against his own country.

'I realise this deserves a more thorough explanation than I've given in the past, but you'll understand if I still can't go into operational details. What I can tell you is this: Marchant is as committed as we all are to finding Dhar and bringing him to justice, despite their family tie.' Was there a quiet intake of breath? 'As I have said before, his options in the cockpit were severely limited. He did, however, succeed in talking Dhar out of far worse attacks on Fairford and GCHQ, a point that Washington continues to overlook. He also played a central role in drawing attention to Ian Denton's . . . illness.'

Fielding glanced across at the PM, as if to emphasise the folly of his attempted cover-up, but the PM's head was down.

'Marchant's current whereabouts are classified, but I can tell you that he is doing all he can to locate Dhar. And as his half-brother, he may well succeed where others fail. To this end, I have asked MI6 station heads around the world to offer him assistance. Unfortunately, the Americans remain committed to detaining him, which makes his search for Dhar even harder. I'm confident, however, that he'll succeed. We've handed Dhar over once already, and we shall endeavour to do so again.'

'Thank you, Marcus,' the PM said, trying to sound breezy.

'Rebuilding our relationship with Washington remains a priority, and nothing would help us more than recapturing Salim Dhar. If it takes a maverick and a liability, someone who has brought MI6 and his country into disrepute, so be it.'

It was clear to Fielding that the PM didn't approve of MI6's continued support for Marchant, a view he suspected was shared by everyone in the room except Armstrong. They would rather the Americans took him away to be waterboarded again. Anything to appease Washington.

Fielding sat back, wondering if he had said enough. All he needed now was time while he worked out how Marchant was going to run Dhar. So far the product – a single address in Greenwich – had been copper-bottomed, but he needed more. Dhar was a high-risk asset. He could change his mind or be killed at any time. Speed was of the essence, but there was still no contact from Marchant. It would only be so long before the CIA caught up with him.

105

The last time Marchant had passed through Dubai airport, he had been on his way back from India. A few hours earlier, he had cradled the dead Leila in his arms, the back of her head removed by a sniper shot from Salim Dhar. The bullet had been intended for the US President, who was visiting the Lotus Temple in Delhi at the time, but Leila had stepped in the way – intentionally or by mistake, he still wasn't sure. His own head had been a mess too, confused by his love for a woman who had betrayed him.

His thoughts were clearer now as he walked across the smooth marble floor of the airport's main atrium, past the yellow Lamborghini Gallardo that was being raffled, and under the fake palm trees that reached up to the glass roof. He was on the way to see Dhar in Bandar-Abbas, where the Iranians were looking after him.

They were looking after Marchant too. A lanky, unsmiling agent had met him in Paris and flown with him to Dubai, steering him through a channel where passports were not examined. He had been given a new one for each sector, well-crafted forgeries that he hoped one day to show the cobblers in Legoland. In five minutes he would be boarding a fifty-minute flight across the Persian Gulf to Bandar-Abbas.

His only concern was how to let London know what he was

doing. There had been no opportunity in Morocco to call or to buy a phone. Dhar's men had driven him straight from Diabat to Essaouira airport. One of them had then flown with him to Paris, where he was handed over to the Iranians, who had made it clear that he wasn't to contact anyone.

He understood their suspicion – Iran only had Dhar's word that he could be trusted – but it was still a problem. Fielding would be back as Chief, and expecting him to be in touch. At least he would know by now that their deniable operation to run Dhar as an agent was up and running again, and yielding results. Marchant had caught a news bulletin on the plane about four arrests in Greenwich.

He tried to slow down as they passed the duty-free counters selling mobile phones, but his minder dropped his pace too. He was good at his job, Marchant thought. Nobody watching would suspect that he was effectively the Iranian's prisoner. He would try a blunter approach.

'I need to buy a new phone,' he said, stopping in front of one of the counters. 'Mine was destroyed in Morocco. Salt water ruins the circuits, you know.'

'You can buy one in Bandar,' the Iranian said, walking on. If he was irritated by his charge's request, he didn't show it.

'They're cheaper in duty-free,' Marchant replied. He felt like a teenager pestering his parents. The Iranian came back to where Marchant was standing. The man behind the phone counter began to think he had a customer.

'We currently have a promotion on all BlackBerry products,' he said hopefully, looking first at Marchant and then at his minder.

Marchant was considering whether to continue the charade when his eye caught someone looking at phones at the next-door counter. He recognised him at once as Felix Duffy, a fellow recruit on his IONEC course at Fort Monckton. The last Marchant had heard, Duffy was rising fast up the Gulf Controllerate. Was it chance – it was a standing joke that there were more intelligence officers at Dubai airport than passengers – or had Fielding sent him?

'OK,' Marchant said. 'I'll wait till we reach Bandar-Abbas.' The Iranian was not going to let him buy a phone. Marchant's main priority now was getting a message to Duffy. 'But I do need a slash.'

Two minutes later, he was washing his hands in a bright and airy cloakroom, watched by a young Malayali who was employed to keep the place clean. (Marchant reckoned there were almost as many South Indian workers at Dubai airport as there were spies.) His Iranian minder had stayed by the entrance after first checking the cloakroom, but Duffy was too experienced to enter while Marchant was still inside. It would only have aroused suspicion.

Marchant looked around him. If Duffy had been sent by Fielding, he would expect a message, word from Marchant on what he was doing, why he was going to Bandar-Abbas. The walls of the cubicle had been too clean to leave graffiti. The South Indian smiled as he passed him a paper towel. Then Marchant noticed a plastic-framed panel on the wall behind him. A list of columns informed customers when the cloakroom had last been cleaned: time, name of cleaner, supervisor's signature.

'Pen?' Marchant asked, spotting one in the attendant's top pocket.

The man wobbled his head from side to side as he retrieved a felt-tip. Marchant pulled out his passport and found a ten-dollar bill left over from Morocco. After swapping the bill for the pen, he glanced around the empty cloakroom, smiled at the cleaner and signed in the supervisor's column.

SINBAD, he wrote, copying the staccato uppercase of the previous signature.

The Iranian was waiting for Marchant when he came back out onto the concourse. As Marchant suspected, he told him to wait while he went to check the cloakroom. A few seconds later he returned, and informed him they were late for their flight to Bandar-Abbas.

106

'What makes you so certain there's a second cell?' Fielding asked as he poured Armstrong a large glass of Talisker in his office. It was late in the day, the western sky smudged red by the setting summer sun. She had declined his offer of Moroccan tea.

'Forensics have found something on a hard drive retrieved from the house in Greenwich,' Armstrong said. 'Another wave of attacks is planned. It seems there's a completely different network of cells out there, with different targets. This time they're not interested in infrastructure, they want civilian casualties – as many as possible.'

'And there was nothing more specific?'

Armstrong looked a wreck, Fielding thought. If you chose to dress formally, as she did, the cracks were more obvious when things went wrong.

'The two networks were operating in isolation from each other. The Americans aren't pooling anything. They're doing their own thing and shoring up security on all US assets in the UK. We've asked about making Dhar's escape from Bagram public – the attacks might stop if his supporters knew he was free – but Washington won't hear of it.' Fielding knew where the conversation was leading. 'Has Marchant been in contact again?' she asked, as if it wasn't a non sequitur.

'As it happens, he's just shown up on the grid in Dubai,' Fielding said, pushing his chair back and stretching his long legs out to one side of his desk. 'One of our assets in Paris immigration recognised him boarding a flight to Dubai. We alerted our UAE station and made contact.'

'And?'

'And what? Marchant wasn't able to communicate freely, but I hope to have more for you soon.'

Fielding thought again about the message from Dubai. Marchant had managed to make contact, leaving a single word for Felix Duffy, who had passed it on, unclear of its significance. But Fielding knew exactly what it meant.

'Is that it?'

'I'm sorry, Harriet. You know as well as I do how difficult these things can be. Dhar is no ordinary source. He can't be bounced into providing product. My biggest concern is keeping the CIA off Marchant's back. If they discover he's in Dubai, they'll lift him, and Dhar's usefulness to you and me will be at an end. He would never communicate with anyone else.'

'Of course. It's just that I'm not sure the country could cope with another wave of attacks.'

What you mean, Fielding thought, is that *you* couldn't cope. He had never seen her looking so worn out. Ironically, he himself was feeling ready for the fight that lay ahead, fresh from his time off in Poland.

'Right now,' Armstrong continued, 'Dhar remains our only lead. And quite frankly, I don't care what he's got planned for the Americans, as long as he gives us another address.'

Ten minutes later, Fielding was alone in his office, standing at the buttressed bay window. The Service's centenary cartoon by Matt was back on the wall, its fairy spook still making him smile, the London Eye turned in the distance, and Anne Norman was

372

keeping ministers at bay with her usual robust charm. He could hear her now on the phone, deflecting another call from Whitehall. When he had arrived back from Warsaw, she had given him ten minutes to get his feet under his desk, but then the floodgates had opened: a tirade of complaints about the acting Chief.

Ian Denton's worst offence, it seemed, had been to ask for two Yorkshire teabags in his mug. 'It looked like mud, and must have tasted far worse,' she had fumed. Never mind Denton's dubious sexual proclivities or his apparent allegiance to Moscow, Fielding thought. Ann was a simple snob at heart, shamelessly allergic to northerners.

Now Denton was out of the way, all should have been well with the world, but Fielding knew it wasn't. London had never felt more unsafe. Down to his left, a police roadblock on Vauxhall Bridge checked traffic, while helicopters circled above. At Armstrong's request, the UK threat level had returned that afternoon from 'severe' to 'critical', meaning a terrorist attack was once again imminent. All police leave had been cancelled and the army had been put on standby.

He thought again about Armstrong. Dhar's intel had saved many lives, including her own, but it didn't make the operation to run him any easier. The risks couldn't be greater for everyone, including himself. He trusted Marchant's judgement, but what exactly were the terms he had struck with his half-brother? They must have come to some sort of agreement when they met at Tarlton. Dhar seemed committed to halting the terrorist attacks on Britain, even if they had been launched in his name after he was captured. But had Marchant agreed to help with Dhar's escape in return?

Denton had believed as much, accusing Marchant's friend Paul Myers of sitting on a GCHQ intercept that might have prevented the jailbreak. Myers had denied everything, in an act of loyalty that had cost him his foreskin and very nearly his life. A few minutes earlier, Spiro had called to tell him that Myers was in the medical unit at RAF Fairford.

'I've done all I can for the guy, Marcus,' he had said. 'He's not in a good way, but he'll survive.'

'What happened to him?' Fielding had asked.

'Seems like Denton prefers Roundheads to Cavaliers.'

It had been an unusually cultured quip for Spiro. His career would be over this time. For years Washington had been looking for a Russian spy in MI6. Finally, it had found one, but it had been Spiro's man. He was having wife trouble too, if the rumours were to be believed. But then, most people in intelligence ended up single.

Anne Norman's voice came through on the comms console.

'I've got the station chief in Dubai on line two. Says it's urgent.'

'Put her through.' Fielding walked back over to his desk. Esther Bannerman was good, one of a bright new generation of women fast-tracking their way through the Service, possibly to the top.

'We've just watched Marchant board a flight to Bandar-Abbas,' she began.

It was as Fielding thought. 'No more communication?' he asked.

'Nothing. He's being babysat all the way by the Iranians.'

'And the CIA?'

'We kept them looking the other way. I don't think they saw him. The Russians were in town too, but this is Dubai. It might have been a coincidence.'

'I doubt it. You sound anxious.' Fielding knew she had once carried a torch for Marchant.

'I don't know what Dan's planning to do in Bandar, but we've just heard that the Revolutionary Guard is about to embark on another naval exercise, bigger than Prophet 6 in April. And the second Carrier Strike Group is currently in transit in the Strait. We've warned all our assets.'

'You mean he's entering a potential war zone.'

'I suppose I do, yes. This time the stand-off is more than sabre-rattling.'

'All the more reason to have people on the ground.'

Fielding hung up and walked around his office, hoping to shake out the tension in his lower back. He was certain now that the Iranians had helped to spring Dhar from Bagram – with or without Marchant's help – and were shielding him in the naval port of Bandar-Abbas. The first and last letters of SINBAD, the word Marchant had written in Dubai airport, were 'SD', Salim Dhar's initials, leaving 'INBA' – in Bandar-Abbas.

Dhar and the Iranians had worked together once before, narrowly failing to assassinate the US President in Delhi. The military build-up in the Gulf was nothing new, but Dhar's presence in the region changed things. So did Marchant's. Had he been summoned by Dhar, or was it his own decision to visit, hoping for more information about imminent attacks on Britain?

Fielding's fear was that the Iranians planned to use Dhar in another act of proxy terrorism. If Marchant was drawn into it too, Fielding would have to cut him free. He wouldn't be able to defend him – or protect himself – if an MI6 officer was complicit in a second attack on America. The downing of a US F-22 had destroyed what was left of the special relationship. There would be no more product from Dhar, but sometimes the price for good intelligence could be too high.

107

Marchant held his arms up while two armed guards frisked him. He had already been searched when he boarded an oil-platform supply vessel in Bandar-Abbas, posing as an international worker about to begin his shift. And he had been checked again after arriving on the platform. It was nothing personal, he told himself. All the oil workers he had arrived with – Ukrainians, Indians, Iranians – had been subjected to the same high level of security.

His geographical knowledge of the Strait of Hormuz was patchy, but he reckoned he was near the shipping lanes to the south-west of Bandar-Abbas, and north of the Tunb islands that were disputed between Iran and the United Arab Emirates. He had seen them from his cabin porthole on the journey over in the supply ship. They sat in the middle of the lanes, and were a permanent source of anxiety for the West. The Revolutionary Guard was known to use them as bases for naval exercises, making them a threat to the oil – 33 per cent of the world's seaborne supplies – that passed through the Strait each day.

After the guards were satisfied, one of them nodded, and opened the door for Marchant. The room appeared to be in a medical wing, and he wondered if he would find Dhar ill in bed. But it wasn't Dhar who was waiting for him. It was an Iranian military officer. Had he walked into a trap?

'Welcome,' the officer said, extending a hand. 'My name is Ali Mousavi. I hope your journey was not too tiring.'

Marchant nodded, detecting a faint American accent.

'Take a seat, please, relax,' Mousavi said, gesturing at a chair. Some mineral water and a plate of dates had been laid out on a small table. Marchant sat down, glancing around the small, windowless room – the bed, the TV in the corner – checking that he hadn't missed Dhar. The meeting could go either way, despite Mousavi's apparent hospitality.

'Your brother will be here shortly,' Mousavi continued. 'He speaks very highly of you.'

Marchant remembered now where he had heard the name before. It was an Ali Mousavi who had recruited Leila.

'I just wanted to thank you in person,' Mousavi said.

'For what?' Marchant's mind was racing as he thought back to Leila's treachery, her death in Delhi. He needed to focus, stick to the part he must play. Dhar would have told them of his anti-American credentials, his run-ins with the CIA. It was the only reason the Iranians would trust him.

'Somebody in your country omitted to pass on intelligence that might have stopped Salim Dhar from escaping.'

'It was the least I could do,' Marchant said, not missing a beat. He was relieved that Myers's omission had been noticed. It meant Dhar would know he had helped with his escape, which was the basis of their deal.

'Did you work for GCHQ?'

'No, but an old friend does. He's a Farsi analyst. I called in a favour, told him to sit on anything relating to Dhar.'

'It's a mystery how someone in GCHQ heard our conversation, but your brother is free, and he clearly has you to thank.'

Mousavi wasn't taking any chances. Marchant didn't blame him. He wanted to be certain that the Englishman in front of him could be trusted. Relations between Britain and Iran had never been worse. But trust him for what? They wouldn't have let him visit Dhar unless it suited their own agenda.

'Can I ask you something?' Mousavi said. 'It's a little left-field.'

'Go ahead,' Marchant replied, trying not to be distracted by the Americanism.

'Did you really think you were drowning when the CIA waterboarded you?'

'It's a trick of the mind,' he said, fixing Mousavi with a stare. He was determined not to be unsettled by the question. 'Your body isn't really about to drown, your brain just thinks it is.'

'Salim said you resisted longer than most.'

'I wasn't going to give the Americans the satisfaction of breaking me.'

'Quite.'

Had Marchant passed the test, or should he do more, compare notes on what it was like to be an enemy of America? What else had Dhar told Mousavi?

'I also understand that you still love your country,' Mousavi continued, smiling. 'The Old Fox.'

Marchant felt his mouth go dry.

'To love a country is one thing, living there is quite another.'

'An international warrant exists for your arrest, issued by the British. It wasn't so easy bringing you here.'

'And it will be difficult for me ever to return.'

'That's hardly surprising. Your attack on the F-22 was spectacular, the stuff of American movies, *Top Gun*. It suddenly made all things seem possible. If they ever forgave you, would you work for MI6 again?'

'My spying days are over.'

'But I thought it ran in the family. Your father was a famous spymaster, Chief of MI6.'

Again, Marchant wondered how much Dhar had told him, where the conversation was going.

'It served his purposes. The CIA accused him of being a traitor.'

'And was he?'

Marchant paused before answering. 'He betrayed America, yes.'

'While remaining loyal to Britain. At the end of the day, espionage has more to do with expediency than ideology, don't you find? Please don't rule out working for MI6 again.'

Christ, Mousavi was sounding him out for recruitment, Marchant thought, just as he had once done with Leila. He could picture her stretching in the morning sunshine before the London Marathon, pushing her hair out of her eyes, one hand on his shoulder.

'I won't.'

'It may serve our purposes, too.'

108

Adam Southover, navigation officer on the crowded bridge of the USS *Winston S. Churchill*, remained calm when he saw the Iranian speedboats in the distance on the port bow. He was British, and serving on the guided-missile destroyer as part of the US Navy's personnel exchange programme. For the past two hours he had been officer of the deck, in charge of the ship's navigational safety as it passed through the Strait of Hormuz.

'This is a United States warship,' the radio officer said. The Americans had been trying repeatedly to make radio contact on VHF Channel 16, but with no success. 'I am engaged in transit passage in accordance with international law.'

The ship's siren emitted five short blasts. Southover checked their position again, and looked up at the speedboats. The destroyer's radar plot had been tracking them for a while, picking up small contacts at five miles out, but they had stayed north of the inbound shipping lane. Now they had cut across it and turned to close, weaving in and out of each other's wake as they approached the *Churchill*.

'There are five of them, sir,' the petty officer of the watch said, looking through binoculars. 'Single outboard engines.'

'Armed?' Southover asked.

'Unconfirmed, sir.'

Southover thought through his options as he asked over the intercom for the captain to come to the bridge. The boats were still more than three miles away, but they were closing fast. Two years earlier, five Iranian patrol boats had buzzed three US Navy warships in the Strait, not far from where they were now. The Pentagon had released video footage suggesting that one of the warships, the USS *Hopper*, had been close to opening fire after a voice was heard on the radio saying: 'I am coming at you. You will explode.' But the reality was less dramatic. The threatening voice was probably the work of 'Filipino Monkey', one of many anonymous pranksters (bored fishermen) who liked to heckle shipping on Channel 16 in the Gulf.

This time there was silence on the radio. Southover didn't believe the Iranian boats were hostile, but he could take no chances. There was always the possibility that they might be the first wave of a swarm attack.

'Continue bridge-to-bridge flashing lights,' he ordered, taking a deep breath. 'And sound GQ.'

It was an order usually given by the commanding officer, but time was running out. A repeated klaxon alarm pierced the air as an announcement was made over the ship's speakers. 'General Quarters, General Quarters. Condition One throughout the ship. All hands, man your battle stations.'

He watched as the Phalanx Gatling gun swivelled urgently on its mount, lowering its barrels towards the incoming boats. Other weapons were brought to battle-ready, too, including single and double .50-calibre machine guns and the 5-inch lightweight gun on the foredeck. Swarm attacks were notoriously difficult to defend against, not least because multiple targets consumed so much ammunition. If the Pentagon got its way, all US warships would soon be equipped with rapid-firing lasers designed to burn through a boat's hull with

100-kilowatt rays. No ammunition required, just a power supply from the ship's generator.

A minute later, the *Churchill*'s commanding officer appeared on the bridge.

'I have the con,' he said.

There was no time for the usual more formal handover – not that the captain was one to stand on ceremony. Southover liked him. He was a cultured man, twenty years out of Annapolis, and they got on well. When they weren't discussing books, they would banter about the common language that divided their two countries: 'lieutenant' vs 'leftenant', 'soccer' vs 'football', 'aluminum' vs 'aluminium'. Only once had their linguistic differences nearly threatened an incident, when Southover had said 'making a sternboard' instead of 'coming astern'. This time, though, the captain's manner was businesslike, his face taut as he listened to the radio officer repeat his warning.

'Incoming small craft, you are approaching a United States warship operating in international waters. Your identity is not known, your intentions are unclear. You are sailing into danger and may be subject to defensive measures. Request you establish communications now or alter your course immediately to remain clear.'

Silence. A burst of Filipino Monkey might have relieved the tension, Southover thought. Or a Horse's Neck, with brandy, not bourbon. The one thing he missed on board the *Churchill* was alcohol. On a Royal Navy ship, an incident would be dissected over a drink or three in the wardroom next time they were alongside, and they would have risen the following day with splitting headaches and eyes like gundogs' bollocks. US Navy ships were dry.

He looked across at the speedboats again, dancing across the waves, seemingly without a care in the world. Each one must have cost $10,000 tops, versus $1.8 billion of US hardware. On paper there was no contest, but they were at sea, in one of the most volatile stretches of water in the world.

'Incoming unidentified small craft, you are sailing into danger and may be subject to defensive measures,' the radio officer repeated. 'Request you establish communications now or alter your course immediately to remain clear.'

The crew had rehearsed endlessly for such scenarios, most recently in a 'swarmex' exercise off Canada's Pacific coast involving remote-controlled fast-attack craft, but a ball still tightened in Southover's stomach. The *Churchill* was the lead ship in a convoy passing through the Strait. Behind her was the USS *Normandy*, another guided-missile cruiser, and behind her, the aircraft carrier USS *Harry S. Truman*, flagship of Carrier Strike Group 10.

'Prepare to fire warning shots, 250 yards in front of target,' the captain said. The information was relayed to the single .50-calibre machine gun on the port side. 'Let's give them one more roll of the dice.'

Moments later, there was a buzz of interference on the ship radio, and then an Iranian voice spoke clearly.

'American Warship 81, this is Iranian Navy patrol boat on Channel 16, come in, over.'

The captain raised his eyebrows.

'This is American Warship 81, over,' the radio officer said.

'American Warship 81, this is Iranian Navy patrol boat. Request shift to Channel 11, over.'

'This is American Warship 81 shifting to Channel 11, out.'

There was a pause before the Iranian spoke again. 'Request present speed and course, over.'

The captain shook his head. 'Wrap it up.'

'This is American Warship 81,' the officer said. 'I'm operating in international waters, out.'

The whole bridge listened as the radio crackled, but there was no more contact.

'They've turned around, sir, heading north,' Southover said.

'Question is,' the captain said, 'was that the main dish, or just an *amuse bouche*?'

109

'Thank you for my freedom,' Dhar said, embracing Marchant. 'We can talk freely here,' he added, whispering in his ear.

Dhar was pleased to see his half-brother. Although he was used to living in isolation, life on an oil platform in the Persian Gulf was not for him. It was not so much the swaying as the sense of being physically apart from the rest of the world, as if he was on his own small island. In his case, it was exaggerated by the need to keep him apart from the other workers on the rig. His only company had been Ali Mousavi, whose Americanisms were starting to grate. He was bored, too, with the windowless room, which was too closely associated in his mind with his recovery from anaphylaxis.

'You asked me to help in your escape from Bagram,' Marchant said, sitting down in the chair again. Dhar walked across the room and sat cross-legged on the end of his bed, resting his chin on his hands.

'And in return I promised to do what I could to protect Britain' – a glance at the closed door – 'a family arrangement that there is no need to share with our hosts.'

'The address in Greenwich was very helpful,' Marchant said. 'A cell was arrested, and the attacks have stopped – at least for now.' Dhar sensed that his visitor's gratitude was qualified.

'But?' he asked. Marchant looked up at him. 'You don't think I've kept to my side of the deal.'

'The attacks were extensive, and you have a big following in Britain,' Marchant replied. 'I'd be surprised if there was only one cell. And I doubt that they know you're no longer a prisoner in Bagram.'

'I did not authorise these attacks. Britain is not a priority of mine, despite its many failings. But they were carried out in my name after I was arrested by the British. That's why I gave you the address in Greenwich. I wished for the assault on my father's country to stop.'

'And will it?'

'*Inshallah*. But you're right, many brothers will still be angry at my capture. And there's a second cell in London. Unlike me, it does not choose to discriminate between civilian and military targets. Nor does it see any difference between America's foreign policy and Britain's.'

'I need the address, Salim.'

'And you will have it. I presumed that's why you came. But first I need your help with another operation against the infidel.'

Dhar saw the faintest twitch under Marchant's left eye. Would he object, protest that the terms of their agreement had been breached? America was already trying to arrest Marchant for his apparent role in the downing of the F-22. Participating in another strike against the US would make him almost as wanted as he was.

'What do you have in mind?' Marchant asked, a smile beginning to form. 'I enjoyed our last airborne outing. '

Dhar remembered why he liked Marchant – his coolness under pressure, a trait they shared. It was no surprise, of course, that they had so much in common.

For the next ten minutes he told Marchant about Mousavi's

386

need for high-speed boats, his belief in asymmetric swarm attacks when faced with a more powerful enemy. They talked, too, about his escape from Bagram, the giant hornet cocooned in a warm chapatti, his desire to work for the Iranians again. And they agreed that Russia would not be happy with either of them after the aborted attack on the Georgian generals at Fairford. Finally, they discussed the mocked-up Bladerunner in the oil platform's boat-yard, the real *Bradstone Challenger* in Karachi and how every fleet, even a swarm, needed a flagship, a queen bee.

'If you can secure the boat's release and bring her here, I will give you another address. But you don't have long. The second cell will not have taken kindly to the arrest of their brothers in Greenwich. I do not trust these people. They have been talking for some time of attacks that will result in the death of hundreds, maybe thousands.'

'A nuclear hellstorm.'

He noted that Marchant had remembered his words. 'I do not wish to blackmail you, but it is important you deliver the boat.'

110

At 5 a.m., Harriet Armstrong gave up trying to sleep. She had been driven back from her office at Thames House at midnight, and had hoped for a few hours' rest before returning at 6 a.m., but it wasn't to be. She had tried Shabad Kriya, a form of bedtime meditation she had learnt after her trip to India, two hot toddies and the latest le Carré, but none of them had helped. Her mind refused to slow down, too troubled by the prospect of a second wave of attacks.

She had never shared the Prime Minister's relief following the arrests in Greenwich. The bombings had stopped, but the prospect of other cells remained very real. The coalition, however, had an electorate to consider, and made as much political gain out of the arrests as it could. She couldn't blame them. They hadn't experienced the sickening feeling she had felt on 21 July 2005, when it had suddenly seemed that the 7 July bombings were part of a bigger pattern.

It was against protocol, but after taking a shower she decided to walk into work rather than be driven. Her Special Branch protection officers would appreciate the break. They had been feeling the pressure in recent days, too. Her apartment was near Victoria Station, around the corner from where Daniel Marchant kept a ground-floor flat. Special Branch insisted that she take a different route home each day from Thames House, but she often seemed to drive down his street.

She decided to go that way now, for no other reason than that Marchant was on her mind and had been all night. Wherever he was, he held the key to a peaceful Britain. Fielding was right. There was only so much pressure Marchant could put on Dhar to reveal more intel, but she hoped he appreciated the gravity of the situation.

There was no sign of life in Marchant's flat as she walked past in the grey dawn. Wooden-panelled shutters kept out the light, and the lavender in the windowbox was wilting. Checking the street in both directions, she rang the doorbell. If someone had asked her why, she wouldn't have been able to give a rational answer. Perhaps he was hiding in London, under everyone's noses, but she knew he wasn't.

Chiding herself, she walked on, wondering if she should drop in on medical services when she arrived at the office. Her brain felt slippery, ideas and images sliding in and out as if at will. Nothing stuck. Her body was out of kilter too, as if it was over-flowing with adrenaline. At the slightest provocation, her scalp tingled: the slam of a door, a car backfiring. All night she had lain in bed, her muscles tensing. Whenever she did drift off, she would wake with a start after a few seconds, her heart racing, blood pounding in her ears.

She tried to breathe deeply as she cut down onto the Embankment at Vauxhall Bridge Road. Across the water, a few lights were on in Legoland, but the Chief's ramparted office was dark. She was grateful that Fielding had told her the truth about Marchant and Dhar. One day she would repay his loyalty.

It was just as she passed the Morpeth Arms that she noticed a figure down by the river, on the north side in the shadow of the bridge. She had glanced back to see if anyone was behind her, and a sudden movement below had caught her eye. The tide was out, and it was still barely light, making it hard to see the figure against the mud, but she was certain that someone was there. She leant over the wall to get a better look, but the muddy foreshore was deserted.

She walked on, admitting to herself for the first time that she was failing to deal with the crisis before her. It happened more often than people acknowledged in her line of work, where success was invisible and failure all too apparent. She tried to focus on patterns, in the hope of anticipating the terrorists' next targets.

The first wave of bombs had hit critical national infrastructure with American links. So far, civilian casualties had been mercifully few. The explosion at the Murco oil refinery had killed four workers, as well as the bombers, and there had been one death at the Skewjack cable terminal in Cornwall – an office receptionist who had re-entered the evacuated building. It was a miracle that no one else had been killed, but the extent of the bombings, the geographical spread, had created a heavy fear among the public. It would not easily lift if there were more bombs, particularly if they targeted people rather than infrastructure.

Her phone began to ring. It was Fielding.

'I didn't know you walked to work.'

'I couldn't sleep,' she said, glancing across the river at Legoland. Being watched wasn't a pleasant feeling. 'Your lights were off, otherwise I would have waved.'

'I think better in the dark. I was going to ring you at a more respectable hour.'

'Have you heard from Marchant again?'

She tried to conceal her desperation, but it was no good. She sounded pathetic.

'No, but he's on the move. I've just had word that he's flying to Karachi. He's got a minder with him, but if he reaches Pakistan, he may get a chance to make contact.'

'Ring me if he calls in. Please.'

'You'll be the first to know. And Harriet?' She didn't say anything. 'Don't overdo things.'

But she knew she already had. She was shot through to the core, seeing threats where none existed, missing others. She took a deep breath and walked on.

111

Marchant waited in the humid foyer of an office overlooking the port of Karachi, flicking through a copy of *Containerisation International*. Outside it was dark and overcast, another monsoon downpour imminent. His Iranian minder was still with him, and still not smiling. He had accompanied Marchant on the supply vessel from the oil platform back to Bandar-Abbas and on the flight to Karachi, via Dubai, sticking to him like gum on a shoe. Once again, there had been no opportunity to make a call to Fielding, but this time the frustration had been greater, given what he had to share with London.

It had been a massive gamble to assist with Dhar's escape from Bagram, but the stakes were far higher for Marchant now. He was helping the Revolutionary Guard to acquire a high-performance powerboat that could alter the balance of power in the Gulf. This went well beyond the terms of his original deal with Dhar, but he had no choice. If he didn't deliver the boat, Dhar wouldn't give him the address of a second cell that was planning to kill hundreds, possibly thousands, of innocent people. And protecting Britain from terrorist attacks was why he and Fielding had agreed to run Dhar in the first place.

He had no choice, he told himself again, as he stood up and walked around the foyer. There was a damp, musty smell that

reminded him of Delhi in the monsoon. He had smelt it somewhere else, too – on the curtains of the hotel in Madurai where
he had stayed with Lakshmi. He thought of her again, beside him
as he had driven to the hospital in Caen. *It's blackmail*, she had
said of his deal with Dhar. *We've both been blackmailed.*

He tried to focus on what lay ahead. The Americans would do
all they could to stop him. As far as he could establish, they had
already tried hard to prevent the *Bradstone Challenger* from
reaching Bandar-Abbas, using sanctions drawn up to prevent Iran
from obtaining military-use technology.

When it had first arrived in Durban from Antwerp, the powerboat was on a merchant vessel called the *Iran Mufateh*, which was
registered to the Islamic Republic of Iran Shipping Lines. Both
were on a US watchlist. The *Iran Mufateh* subsequently changed
its name to the *Diplomat*, and then to the *Amplify*, re-registering
to a front shipping company called Starry Shine and flying under
a Hong Kong flag. By the time the US Department of Commerce's
Office of Export Enforcement realised what had happened, it had
already left for Bandar-Abbas.

The US considered intercepting it at sea, but feared a diplomatic
incident. Instead, it turned to Pakistan for help. The PNS *Zulfiquar*,
a Pakistan Navy frigate, intercepted the *Amplify* and escorted it
into Karachi, where the *Bradstone Challenger* was removed from
the hold for inspection. Relations between Washington and
Islamabad had since deteriorated, following a drone strike that
had killed civilians inside the Pakistan border, and the boat was
languishing in a dry dock.

Marchant's brief was to ensure *Bradstone Challenger* completed
its journey. To that end he was playing the role of 'Jez Giddings',
a wealthy Western playboy who wanted his toy back. He had been
dressed in a sharp suit by Ali Mousavi and given a Rolex Yacht-
Master (fake) and a British passport (also fake), along with an

impressively thorough cover story, which he had memorised on the flight. If the Pakistanis could be persuaded that the end user was a private individual based in the Gulf, and not the Revolutionary Guard, they might release the boat. To help them in their decision, Marchant's minder was carrying a briefcase packed with $100 bills.

A buzzer disturbed the heavy afternoon atmosphere. Marchant glanced up at two small lightbulbs on the wall of the port office foyer. One was green, the other red. The green one was lit. From nowhere, a sleepy *peon* in a faded khaki uniform appeared and showed them both into the main office.

'I'm sorry to have kept you waiting,' a beaming official said, shaking their hands. He was short, but exuded power, or at least wealth. Marchant noticed the Cartier watch and a well-fed stomach bulging beneath his Ralph Lauren shirt. His office was less affluent. A calendar on the wall displayed a photo of a high-stacked container ship, and a large ceiling fan stirred the air. The walls were painted a municipal cream colour.

'How are you finding our weather?' the official asked, as he settled down behind his desk.

Remembering the subcontinent's preoccupation with the monsoon, Marchant had checked the reports in the *Dawn* newspaper on the flight from Dubai.

'Eighty-five per cent humidity today,' he offered.

'Too much,' the official said, holding one hand up and twisting his fingers as if he were changing a large lightbulb. His forehead glistened with a patina of sweat. 'This evening will be better, when the south-west wind comes in off the sea. A little drizzle, but very pleasant. Tomorrow will be a total wash-up.'

'Thank you for agreeing to meet us,' Marchant said, keen to move things on.

'Not a problem, not a problem.' An awkward pause. 'My difficulty is that the Americans have sent me this,' he said, picking up a fax from his desk and brandishing it in the air. 'A "stop order" preventing the export of your beloved *Bradstone Challenger*, isn't it.'

'On what grounds?' Marchant asked. He had agreed with his minder beforehand that he would do all the talking.

'Shall I read the damn thing to you? "The *Bradstone Challenger* is powered with two US-origin Caterpillar C18 engines and two Arneson surface drives, items subject to the regulations and classified under Export Control Classification Number 8A992.g." We love bureaucracy in Pakistan – a legacy of your fine country – but even I find this ridiculous. Poppycock. Apparently your boat contains "greater than a 10 per cent *de minimis* of US-origin items".'

'Isn't the real problem the end user? For some reason they think it's Iran, and not me.'

'My friend, all our lives would be much easier if you can provide evidence that you are a wealthy private individual, and not on the US Treasury's list of Specially Designated Nationals.'

It was the verbal cue that Marchant had been waiting for. Fearing it might have been missed, the official glanced at the case resting against the minder's legs. Up until now, he had studiously avoided looking at it.

'That shouldn't be a problem,' Marchant said.

He nodded at the minder, who picked up the case, walked over to the official and placed it on his desk. The man opened and then closed it, putting it on the floor by his chair. It was all done in reverential silence.

'I think we can lose this,' he said, smiling, as he screwed up the fax and dropped it into the steel-mesh bin beside him. 'These things get mislaid all the time. As our American friends enjoy reminding us, our country's communications are positively Third World. I will need your passport, though. To make a copy. Forms will need to be filled.'

Of course they would, Marchant thought. Duplicated and

rubber-stamped, too. He stood up and handed over his fake passport. Then he shook the official's hand, eager to wrap things up in case anyone changed their mind. The beaming official pressed a buzzer on his desk. For the first time, Marchant saw a smile on his minder's face.

'We will have the boat put back on board MV *Amplify* at once,' the official said.

Without speaking, he handed Marchant's passport to the *peon*, who had entered the room in response to the buzzer.

'I was hoping to deliver it myself,' Marchant said, watching as the *peon* left the room again.

'To Bandar? Why not? It's less than seven hundred nautical miles. That would take no time in such a boat as this.'

'There's one other thing,' Marchant said, glancing at the phone on the desk. 'Can I make a quick call? My mobile, the battery –'

'Of course, of course,' the official said, resting a hand on his shoulder. 'My office is yours.'

'Thanks. Actually, it's a private call – girlfriend trouble.'

Marchant pulled his best three-in-a-bed smirk, then glanced at the minder, checking how he would react. He wouldn't want to upset the deal, but he also had strict instructions to keep his charge incommunicado. There was a pause while the official turned to the minder and then back to Marchant.

'Be my guest. Come, let us leave this playboy of the Western world to his women troubles. Your passport will be returned on the way out.'

The minder hesitated, but the official was already ushering him out of the door like a guest who had outstayed his welcome. Marchant waited until the door had closed before he dialled Fielding's direct line in London.

112

Fielding took the call moments after he had spoken to Armstrong. He had been surprised to see her from his office window, walking along the north side of the Thames.

'I haven't got long,' Marchant said.

'Are you on a secure line?' Fielding asked. His comms console had identified the number as a business line in Karachi, Pakistan.

'There's no choice. I'll have an address later today – for a second cell. They're targeting civilians.'

'And what do we give in return for this information?' Fielding asked.

There was a pause, and for a moment Fielding thought the line had dropped. 'A boat. Quite a fast one. If I don't deliver it, there's no address.'

It was worse than Fielding had feared. The Iranians had been on a shopping trip in recent months, trying to buy up high-performance powerboats from around the world for use in swarm attacks. Their most recent attempt had been thwarted by the Americans in Karachi, where Marchant was calling from.

'Our cousins might not be pleased.'

'It's your call. If you want that address, you're going to have to keep them off my back during transit. I'll do all I can to disable the boat once I've got the information.'

Fielding was about to ask for a stronger guarantee when the line went dead.

113

'At least we were right about there being a mole in MI6,' Spiro said, watching the Director of the CIA pace around his airy office in Langley. Spiro was sitting on a bisque sofa in the window. It was a good sign. The last time he was in trouble, he had been shown to the hard-backed chair opposite the DCIA's desk. Today was a sofa meeting. It was also 'with coffee', another good omen. The coffee had yet to arrive, but at least it had been ordered. No one was ever dismissed with coffee.

'We just backed the wrong guy,' the DCIA said. 'Jesus, what is it with the Brits? The sooner we're out of there, the better.'

'I shouldn't have supported Denton,' Spiro said. He had already decided that contrition was his best option, even if it didn't come naturally.

'I'm more concerned about finding Salim Dhar.'

'So am I.' On his way up to the DCIA's office, Spiro had walked past the new operations room dedicated to Dhar's recapture – a sprawling web of maps, computer terminals and flow charts on the second floor.

'You still have a big role to play here, Jim,' the DCIA said. 'I know Dhar was lost on your watch, but you found him once, and you more than anyone know how to find him again.'

Spiro looked up, sensing he was about to discover why he hadn't lost his job.

'I'm giving you one last chance,' the DCIA continued. 'I can't protect you any more if you screw up again.'

'How can I help?'

'I read your report about Daniel Marchant's role in Dhar's escape from Bagram, how you think Dhar's been turned by the British. I'm beginning to believe it. We think Dhar's in Iran, but we can't be certain. We do know where Marchant is. He showed up on the grid in Karachi a couple of hours ago, flew in from Dubai.

'If you're right, Fielding's behind all this, using Marchant to run Dhar. Not that it's helped Britain so far. You know this guy better than most. Find out where he's going, and if we need to cut him some slack, so be it. Dhar is the priority here, and Marchant may be the only one who can lead us to him.'

Much to Spiro's surprise, the DCIA walked him down to the operations room, where he was introduced to the hand-picked staff charged with finding Dhar. There was no need. Spiro knew them all, too well.

'Jim will be heading up the hunt now,' the DCIA told everyone. 'I'm sure you'll give him all the help he needs.'

Spiro wasn't so sure, but this was a welcome show of support, a public message to rival colleagues. He hadn't been brought back to Langley to be dismissed, as he knew everyone had hoped – he was here to kick Salim Dhar's butt.

Just as Spiro was feeling better about life, the DCIA turned on his way to the door.

'Jim, I nearly forgot to ask. How's the wife? I heard she'd been away.'

The entire operations room fell silent. How much did the DCIA know? Had he brought him down here to humiliate him in front of Langley's finest? To tell them all that Linda Spiro had been throwing stones at Israelis in Ramallah?

'She's back, thanks,' Spiro said.

'Glad to hear it.'

114

The wheel of the *Bradstone Challenger* was made of black leather and steel, and was smaller than Marchant had expected, the size of a dinner plate. For some reason he had imagined a large wooden helm. His Iranian minder was behind him, lounging on a padded leather banquette at the stern. It was curved and looked like a Jacuzzi. Marchant had been at the wheel for ten minutes, following a brief lesson on the various navigation screens in front of him.

'Are you in the navy?' he called out above the roar of the Caterpillar engines. Earlier, the Iranian had manouevred the vessel out of the busy docks at Karachi with knowing ease.

There was no answer. Marchant glanced around. The minder had fallen asleep, his head resting on a round cocktail table. The cabin was dark except for the navigation screens and a line of blue floor-lighting under a shallow step. The décor was gunmetal grey, broken up by coral-red cushions on a leather sofa that ran down one side of the cabin. The whole scene reminded Marchant of the back of a limousine, or a sleazy room at a nightclub. Jez Giddings, his cover, would have loved it.

He checked the oil and fuel gauge dials. They were above a large compass on the instrument panel. In different circumstances he would have relaxed, enjoyed the sensation of carving through the Arabian Sea on a clear night at 35 knots, but now wasn't the time. The Americans might be tracking them. He hadn't told his minder why he had wanted to take the wheel. He wasn't sure himself. But a part of him sensed that in the coming hours he might need to know how to operate a Bladerunner.

He glanced at his fake Rolex Yacht-Master. It was past midnight. They had left Karachi at 8 p.m., after the port official had personally overseen the boat being lowered into the water. The plan was to hug the Pakistan coastline throughout the night, travelling at 35 knots. Any faster and they might attract unwanted attention. The port official had spoken with the Lieutenant Commander (Marine Wing) of Pakistan Coast Guards, who had agreed to turn a blind eye to their transit, but several American warships were on exercise up ahead in the Gulf of Oman.

'I thought about joining the navy once,' Marchant said, as much to himself as to his sleeping minder. He suddenly felt very alone on the dark water. The boat was cutting through the waves, but there was still an incessant thud on the bottom of the hull. 'Always loved boats.'

They expected to reach Iranian waters just after 3 a.m., when they would be met by a Revolutionary Guard patrol boat that would escort them into the port of Chabahar for refuelling. From there it was a seven-hour journey to Bandar-Abbas, travelling at 40 knots. By then he might even have had a conversation with his minder. There was nothing like sharing a boat to get to know someone. The Iranian had made no mention of the phone call from the office in Karachi. Marchant was convinced that he had smelt alcohol on his breath. The port official must have plied him with a quick whisky, something with which to toast his suitcase of dollars.

'My father used to keep a yacht down at Dittisham,' Marchant continued. 'A Westerly 22. Took it across the Channel once, lost the rudder.'

Did he keep on talking because a part of him sensed that his minder was not asleep? If that was the case, he should have sensed that the man had quietly risen to his feet and was standing behind him, a length of plastic tubing in his hand. Afterwards Marchant blamed the hypnotic motion of the boat for his carelessness. All he could do now was try to prevent himself from being strangled.

'Who did you call from the port office?' his minder shouted as Marchant gasped for air. Already he was feeling light-headed, his resistance fading. He attempted to get his fingers between his throat and the tubing, but it was too tight. The boat was beginning to veer to starboard, towards the shore. 'Tell me who you called!' the Iranian shouted again.

Marchant tried to think, but he was losing consciousness. Should he stick with the girlfriend line? Hope to persuade him that he really did have women problems? The man would know he was lying.

'OK,' he managed to say, his legs kicking beneath him like a demented tap dancer. Only the truth was going to save him. 'I'll tell you.'

'Who?' The tubing tightened.

'London.' He felt the minder's grip slacken a notch, enough to stop him from passing out. 'I was calling my boss, the Chief of Britain's Secret Intelligence Service. I'm still working for MI6.'

Marchant knew he only had a split second to strike, the synaptic moment in which his assailant's brain processed the significance of what he had just been told, calculating the implications for the mission, for his own career. In one movement, Marchant clasped his hands together into a single fist and swung them upwards as hard as he could, above his head, as if he was chopping wood. They connected with the soft tissue of his minder's mouth, flattening his lips and splintering his front teeth.

Marchant leapt out of his chair, pinning the Iranian's arms by his side. He swung his head into a steel luggage rack by the cabin door, and then again, harder this time, grabbing his hair with one hand as he smacked his head into the rack. The body fell limp.

Breathing hard, Marchant grabbed the wheel, turning the boat back out to sea, and reduced speed to 10 knots. Then he dragged the Iranian up onto the deck, where he removed his phone and wallet. He couldn't say they had ever bonded, but he hesitated as he heaved the body up onto the gunwale. The man was still unconscious, and wouldn't survive in the water. After glancing around at the dark, empty sea, Marchant slipped the body over the side. He knew too much. Then he rang Fielding on the Iranian's phone, tossing it into the night after he had finished.

115

'All well at Langley?' Fielding asked, looking through a sheaf of surveillance photos on his desk.

'The sun's shining,' Spiro replied. 'But I don't suppose you're calling about the weather.'

'You never know with the British. Thanks for looking in on Paul Myers. He's making a good recovery.'

'Listen, Marcus, I'm kinda busy right now. Trying to find Salim Dhar. You know how it is.'

'Congratulations on the job, by the way.' Fielding had heard that Spiro, far from being sacked, was heading up a new unit tasked with finding Dhar. The Agency never ceased to amaze him. 'I had the DCIA on the phone earlier,' he continued.

'Uh-huh.' Fielding had his attention now.

'He was asking about your wife. Whether I'd heard the rumours she'd been in the West Bank.'

Spiro didn't say anything.

'No actual evidence, of course, just canteen talk.'

'Thirty-year marriages provoke a lot of jealousy around here,' Spiro said.

'I'm sure. I told him I knew nothing about it. Which isn't strictly true. The West Bank's long been a personal interest of mine, a former beat. One of my old contacts in Ramallah emailed some images this morning.' Fielding looked more closely at a photo of Linda Spiro, camera around her neck, a rock in one hand. '"Photography for Peace", I think they're called.'

There was a pause. 'What do you intend doing with these images?' Spiro asked, his voice quieter now.

'Nothing. If Daniel Marchant reaches Bandar-Abbas.'

116

Fielding's timing was suspiciously immaculate, Spiro thought as he stepped back into the operations room.

'Sir, we have an unidentified vessel approaching Iranian waters,' a junior officer said. 'One mile off the Pakistani port of Gwadar, travelling at 35 knots.'

Spiro looked up at a video image of a powerboat. The footage was being relayed from the electro-optical camera of an RQ-170 Sentinel drone fifty thousand feet above the Gulf of Oman. Operated by the USAF in Nevada, the drone's main role in the region was flying over Iran in search of radioactive isotopes found in nuclear weapons facilities, but it had been repositioned to monitor Iran's recent naval exercises.

'What the hell's that?' Spiro asked.

'We're just working on it,' the junior officer said. An adjacent screen flickered as maritime recognition software scrolled with dizzying speed through a series of photographs – Iranian fast-attack gun boats, private launches, small military hovercraft. It stopped when it had found a match.

'It's called a Bladerunner 51, sir. There's a dealership in Dubai, and –'

'– and there's one impounded in Karachi,' Spiro said. 'At least, that's where it's meant to be. Jesus, whose frickin' side are the Pakistanis on?'

'Sir, this came through earlier,' another officer said, handing Spiro a report and a stack of photos. Spiro sifted through them. One was of Daniel Marchant entering a dock building in Karachi, taken with a long lens. Marchant looked more suave than Spiro remembered.

'Is this boat armed?' Spiro asked. 'Can we zoom in? Get a better still from the Sentinel's synthetic-aperture radar?'

Spiro watched as the video feed was replaced by a high-quality still image of the Bladerunner.

'According to the file, it wasn't armed when it originally left Durban.'

'I wouldn't put it past the Pakistanis to have added a bit of firepower,' Spiro said, walking over to take a better look at the image. 'Although it doesn't appear to have any obvious weapon systems.'

'It may have been fitted with torpedoes,' the junior officer said. 'That's what we told the Bureau of Industry and Security before they issued their stop order.'

The BIS could go to hell, Spiro thought, as he studied the silhouette of someone in the cockpit of the boat. Was it Marchant? If it was, he cut a solitary figure, but a part of Spiro envied him, out there in the field. What was his game? Was he going to meet Dhar? He thought again about Fielding, his threat about the photos.

'Sir, five minutes before the Bladerunner enters Iranian waters,' another officer said. 'If we're going to disable it, we need to act now.'

'Let it go,' Spiro said.

117

'Why do you want to see him?' Ali Mousavi asked.

'He brought us the boat, didn't he?' Dhar said. 'I wish to thank him – and to say goodbye.'

Dhar watched as Mousavi walked around the medical room. The Iranian had arrived on the oil platform a few minutes earlier. He had come from the military shipyard in Bandar-Abbas, where the Bladerunner was being checked over and fitted with its super-cavitation torpedoes.

'He killed one of my men. A loyal colleague. Why would a friend of ours do that?'

Dhar didn't know, but he presumed that Marchant had tried to make contact with London and had been caught. According to Mousavi, the minder had been sent with Marchant expressly to prevent any contact with the outside world. But when the boat had been met by Revolutionary Guards as it entered Iranian waters, the minder was missing.

'What does Marchant say?' Dhar asked.

'He claims they were attacked by pirates. There are many Somalis in these waters, but they do not have boats to match the Bladerunner's speed. No one does. Marchant is lying.'

'Where is he now?'

'Here, on the platform, where he will stay. It is best for everyone.'

Dhar walked up to Mousavi, closed his eyes as if in prayer and then opened them. 'Bring him to me.'

His tone was cold and threatening. It was meant to be. He was running out of time. Mousavi stared back at him. For the first time, Dhar saw fear in his eyes. It was as if he was weighing up the whole operation that lay ahead of them, the swarm attack, the Bladerunner, wondering if he had chosen the right person to lead it or was being drawn into something beyond his control. Dhar waited for him to look away.

'Of course,' Mousavi said. 'You are brothers. I cannot stand between you. But I must be present, I insist. We can no longer trust this man.'

A small flame of doubt began to flicker in Dhar's own mind. He hoped Mousavi hadn't noticed. 'Would he have delivered the boat to us if he was still working for the West?' he asked, hoping to extinguish the thought.

'Perhaps that is *why* he was able to deliver it,' Mousavi said. 'We were never expecting him to complete the journey. The Bladerunner is classified as "military use technology" by the Americans. It's on a US Treasury watchlist, the subject of international sanctions. How is it possible for such a boat to travel across the Gulf of Oman without being intercepted by the CIA or the US Navy?'

Another flicker. Dhar didn't have an answer. It was the British who wanted the address of the second cell in London, and the British who knew that Marchant had to deliver the boat in order to get it; but they wouldn't have the authority to allow the Bladerunner free passage. Only the Americans could do that. Was his half-brother playing them all?

Five minutes later, Marchant was shown into the room by two armed guards. He was handcuffed, his face bloodied and his clothes dishevelled, stumbling as he walked. Dhar guessed he had

411

been blindfolded as well as beaten up. He kept his head bowed as his eyes adjusted to the neon lighting. Mousavi nodded at the guards, who returned to their position outside the door. Dhar looked at his half-brother and then at Mousavi.

'Are you working for the Americans?' Dhar asked. He knew as soon as he had spoken the words that it was an unfounded charge. Of course Marchant wasn't. He had suffered more than most at America's hands, spent much of his adult life on the run from the CIA, culminating in him being renditioned and waterboarded. America didn't treat its own agents like that. Not yet. He wanted to be angry with Mousavi for suggesting the idea, but instead he turned his frustration towards Marchant.

'Answer me!' he shouted, kicking him hard in his downturned face.

Marchant looked up, his face full of disdain.

'Our hosts here think you are,' Dhar continued, already putting distance between himself and the accusation. He hoped Marchant would notice.

'What do you think?' Marchant said. His lips were swollen, his voice slurred.

'I think you were lucky to travel from Karachi to Bandar-Abbas without being intercepted by the Americans. Perhaps too lucky.'

Marchant paused before answering, wiping something – blood, spit – from his mouth with the backs of his shackled hands.

'A US warship tried to make contact on Channel 16 after we'd been jumped by the Somalis, but we ignored it. For the whole journey we stayed in Pakistani waters and then Iranian waters, never more than twelve miles offshore.'

Was this enough to satisfy the Iranians? Dhar glanced across at Mousavi, who seemed to have relaxed. He was happier too.

And feeling guilty for doubting his half-brother. It was time to give him the address in London.

'Like our father, your loyalty is to Britain and our common enemy is America,' Dhar said, walking around Marchant as if he was inspecting an animal at market. 'Thank you for bringing the boat. *Inshallah*, it will help us to strike a mighty blow against the infidel oppressor.' He paused, judging the moment. It was now or never. 'I wish I had been able to stay longer in your country. Perhaps gone to London. I've never been there.'

Marchant lifted his head, as if he understood the importance of what was about to be said. Dhar doubted whether Marchant would manage to find a way to communicate with London, but if they were both to die today, as seemed likely, he wanted to honour their deal. As it said in the Holy Qur'an: *Those who take a small price for the covenant of Allah and their own oaths – surely they shall have no portion in the hereafter, and Allah will not speak to them.*

'I read in a foreign magazine once about a place called Hoxton Square,' Dhar said, looking at Mousavi, who was checking messages on his phone, unaware of the direction the conversation was taking. 'There is a gallery there called White Cube. Many artists live in the area, in the surrounding houses, around the square. Their art is not to everyone's liking. Sometimes they push the boundaries too far, lose sight of their target audience. They need to be stopped.'

'I'll tell them,' Marchant said. He didn't thank him, but Dhar saw gratitude in his eyes. Regret, too, for they both knew it was probably too late.

'What are you talking about?' Mousavi asked, putting away his phone. He seemed preoccupied.

'Misguided artists who attack society,' Dhar said, smiling at Marchant.

413

'Come, now is not the time for banter, even between brothers. My colleagues in Bandar-Abbas have messaged to say the flagship is ready.'

'We are done. I have thanked my brother for bringing us the Bladerunner,' Dhar said, taking Marchant by the shoulders and kissing him on each cheek. 'And, for the record, I do not believe he is an American spy.'

'We shall see,' Mousavi replied.

'Good luck,' Marchant said as the two half-brothers stood facing each other. Somewhere deep inside him, the flame began to flicker again. Dhar wondered if he had misjudged his brother, missed something in his bruised cerulean eyes, which suddenly looked different, more distant? But before he could challenge him, Marchant was being ushered out of the room by Mousavi and down the stairs, where a boat was waiting to take him to the mainland.

118

'Marchant's reached Bandar-Abbas,' Fielding said, replacing his phone. Armstrong was standing in the window, unable to sit.

'We're out of time, Marcus, aren't we?' she said, her back still to him. She had invited herself over to Legoland, hoping, Fielding suspected, that it might somehow encourage Marchant to make contact quicker. Fielding hadn't objected. It had been a difficult few hours for everyone as pressure mounted from the government and the media to find the second cell of terrorists.

'He'll call,' he said, trying to sound confident. He wouldn't tell Armstrong that Marchant had arrived in Iran as a prisoner rather than a hero, bound and blindfolded and under armed guard. She wasn't listening anyway.

'Every policeman in the country is on the streets, my own officers haven't seen their families for weeks,' she said. 'We can't do much more, can't stop people living their lives, not in Britain. There are seventeen music festivals opening across the country this weekend. What should I have done? Shut them all down, told the organisers we've been unable to find the bombers but we think they might be about to blow up your main stage?'

'You've done everything you can, Harriet.'

Fielding rarely felt sorry for others, but he pitied Armstrong now. It was the loneliest hour for any intelligence chief, when all ideas were spent and the clock was ticking down. And it was worse for Armstrong. The buck stopped with the Director General of MI5 when the terror was home-grown.

'Have I?' she asked.

Before he could answer, an incoming call flashed up on his comms panel. It was an Iranian number.

119

Marchant took out the first guard with a blow to the back of the head, catching him by surprise after he had called him into the medical room. The second guard put up more resistance. It wasn't easy with his hands bound together, but Marchant used the metal cuffs to his advantage, wielding his wrists like a mace, just as he had done with the minder on the boat.

When both guards were finally lying still on the floor, he felt around in their pockets and found a metal key, a pair of electronic key cards and two mobile phones. The key fitted the handcuffs, and he released his wrists. Then he removed the guards' handguns and slipped them into the waistband of his trousers.

He had waited twenty minutes before attacking them, long enough for Mousavi and Dhar to have left the oil platform for the mainland. His head was throbbing, still in pain from the beating he had taken earlier on the naval patrol boat. At least he had had time to think as he had been shut away below decks, a chance to stand back from the deal he had entered into with Dhar.

His priority remained getting the London address to Fielding, but after that he would do everything in his power to stop Dhar. He couldn't stand by while an American supercarrier was attacked by a boat he had provided. He owed it to Lakshmi. She was right: he had been blackmailed. The operation to run Dhar was over.

Marchant didn't understand Lakshmi's loyalty to America, but he no longer shared Dhar's deep hatred of it either, regardless of what had been done to him in America's name. He hoped his father would understand.

He pulled out one of the mobile phones and dialled Fielding's direct line.

'It's dropped,' Fielding said. 'I'm sorry.'

Armstrong turned away, biting her lip.

Marchant cursed the phone. The signal strength was poor, and the call had not connected. He tried the other phone, but the signal was no better. He needed to ring again from somewhere else on the oil platform. After listening at the door, he locked it behind him with one of the electronic keys, and moved down the corridor towards the staircase. The only sound was a low-level hum that reverberated through the floors and walls of the platform. He assumed it came from the drilling rig. As far as he could tell, the platform was fully operational, despite its covert military role. During the Iran–Iraq war in the 1980s, oil platforms had been fitted with anti-aircraft guns, and there had been no secret about their strategic use.

He made his way down the staircase to the lower deck, where Dhar had spoken of a small indoor boatyard and a mock-up of the Bladerunner. There was still no phone signal. He pushed at an outside door and walked out onto a gantry where, incongruously, someone had planted flowers in a row of clay pots. The dash of colour – crimson red, blue – brightened up the industrial setting, gave him hope.

He checked the superstructure above and around him. No one was about. The entire living quarters seemed to be deserted. Then he looked out to sea, towards Bandar-Abbas. In the distance, a line of small fast-attack gunboats was heading out towards the Strait. Behind it was another line of boats, then another. The swarm was gathering.

He dialled Fielding's number, and this time it began to ring.

120

'Hoxton Square,' Fielding said aloud, for Armstrong's benefit. 'Can you be more specific?'

'That's all he told me,' Marchant said. 'It might be an artist's house, maybe a studio, but the cell's somewhere in the square.'

Armstrong was already on the phone, dispatching CO19 and her own officers to Hackney. They would have to close the entire square. It would take time to search every house, and there was a danger the terrorists would try to escape.

'You need to give the Americans a heads-up about something too,' Marchant said. 'A warning.'

'I didn't know you cared.'

'The Revolutionary Guard's navy is currently massing fast-attack boats in the Strait.'

'They've been doing that for days. It's part of an ongoing naval exercise.'

'Not today. This time it's for real.'

121

Marchant watched as wave after wave of boats surged out into the Strait, heading past Qeshm island in his direction. No wonder the oil platform was deserted. Everyone was at sea. He estimated there were about a hundred boats, maybe more. On the far horizon, towards Oman, he could make out the profiles of several warships, including the distinctive angled outline of the USS *Harry S. Truman*. Was that the target?

An array of the world's most sophisticated weapons stood between the swarm and the *Truman*, but it had never had to deal with more than a hundred hostile boats approaching at once. It would only need one to get through. Was Dhar in the Bladerunner?

Marchant went back inside. He needed to find the indoor boatyard that Dhar had mentioned, and try to get out into the Strait on the mocked-up Bladerunner. Dhar had apparently been on it with an instructor, so he knew it was seaworthy. He hoped it hadn't been requisitioned for the swarm attack.

He headed down the corridor, trying to calculate where the boatyard might be. As he turned a corner, he heard voices approaching and slipped into an open doorway, one of his guns drawn. Two men in bright orange overalls walked past, chatting in Hindi. He waited until they had gone, then continued along the narrow corridor to a door at the far end. He looked through a glass panel, but inside was just a staff canteen, deserted except for a solitary oil worker.

There was only one place left to try. Turning right, he followed another corridor, surprised by the size of the living quarters. It was like being on a big ship: a maze of endless narrow walkways, metal staircases and portholes. Up ahead there was a heavy door with a wheel-lock that suggested tighter security. He held one of the electronic keys he had removed from the guards' pockets against a panel on the wall, but nothing happened. He tried the other key, and this time there was a click. Turning the wheel, he swung the heavy door open. The place was deserted. It was just as Dhar had described: a small indoor working boatyard. In front of him was what he was looking for: a crude copy of the Bladerunner, suspended from a launch derrick like captured booty.

It took time to work out how to operate the big bay doors in the floor of the boatyard, but after twenty minutes he was at the wheel in the cockpit as the automatic derrick lowered the ersatz Bladerunner slowly towards the sea. There was no one to switch off the derrick, so his plan was to start up the engines once the boat was afloat and accelerate out of the two thick lifting straps.

As soon as he felt the water take the weight, he turned the ignition key. The engine failed to start. A moment later, he heard shouting above him. Armed guards were out on the gantry he had stood on earlier. More were peering down through the empty bay doors. He tried the key again, pulling out a gun from his trousers. This time the engine started, just as the guards above him began to shoot. He returned fire, roaring away from the oil rig into the Strait.

122

Dhar eased the throttle forward, taking the Bladerunner's speed up to 30 knots as he passed the main entrance to the naval base at Bandar-Abbas. It was a calm day, the sea flatter than it had been all week. The base was on a natural promontory to the south-west of the city, and was shaped like a trident. There was a central channel with two docks forking off it.

The last assault boats had left the base ten minutes earlier. At Mousavi's request, Dhar had stood on the eastern dock and watched them depart, acknowledging the cheering crews in their streaming bandanas. Dhar's brief appearance was high-risk, but the base was secure and his presence seemed to give the crews heart. The air had filled with cries of '*Allahu akbar!*', the mood defiant, incendiary, as Iranian flags were waved and American ones burnt. Every vessel in Bandar-Abbas seemed to be on the water, including an impromptu gathering of fishing boats that formed their own swarm, the men on board sounding horns and firing AK47s in the air.

The first boats to leave the base had been the unmanned Ya Mahdis. Even these had received a cheer, perhaps because no one expected to see the ghost boats again. Operated remotely, they formed the sacrificial front line of the swarm. Their purpose was to provoke the Americans into an engagement by not turning away from their warships. Once the first shots had been fired, their role was to keep drawing the fire of the Phalanx Gatling guns. Over-eager radars would lock on to the multiple contacts, expending all the Phalanx ammunition by the time Dhar finally arrived on the scene.

At least, that was the plan. Dhar wasn't convinced. In his mind he was ready to die, and he had prepared himself accordingly, asking Mousavi for a copy of the Holy Qur'an to take on board. After the last boat had left the base, he had turned to it in the incongruous surrounds of the Bladerunner's sleazy cockpit. Now, as he increased his speed to 50 knots and steered a course between the islands of Qeshm to starboard and Larak to port, he recalled verse 8:65 again:

O Prophet, rouse the believers to fight. If there are twenty among you, patient and persevering, they will vanquish two hundred; if there are a hundred then they will slaughter a thousand unbelievers, for the infidels are a people devoid of understanding.

Battle had already been joined on the horizon. He could see plumes of smoke, but it was impossible to tell if damage had been done to any American warships. He doubted it. The early phases would be a massacre. After the unmanned Ya Mahdis had come the Bavar 2 flying boats, looking like giant water boatmen as they had filed out of the naval base, with only their wings to stop them sinking. The fast-attack Seraj vessels had followed, 107mm rocket launchers bolted onto the tops of their cockpits, machine guns strapped to their decks. Then, finally, the more sophisticated Zolfaqar assault boats, named after the sword of Ali, the Prophet's son-in-law, in the belief that their missiles would bifurcate the infidel's ships.

All Dhar could hope for was that Mousavi's calculations were right, and that by the time the Bladerunner arrived on the scene the American warships' guns would have fallen silent. *Inshallah*, it would then be up to him. *Those who believe fight in the way of Allah, and those who disbelieve fight in the way of the Shaitan.*

According to Mousavi, his two torpedoes had an 80 per cent kill probability at a range of four miles. Dhar had wanted to be on his own in the Bladerunner, but the launch mechanism for the torpedoes was complicated, and there hadn't been enough time to train him. Mousavi had insisted he took an experienced operator, who was in the seat next to him. No one needed to know, Mousavi had said. The operator was a man of few words, which suited Dhar.

He wished the same could be said of Mousavi, who was gabbling away now on the encrypted ship-to-shore radio.

'Everything is going according to plan,' he said. 'Our boats began to fire their rocket launchers eight miles out from the *Truman*, not at the enemy ships, but a little in front of their own. The plumes of spray where the rockets are falling will partially block the enemy's line of sight, disrupting their anti-ship weapon systems until we are within firing range.'

'Has the enemy lost any ships?'

'We have shot down one of their Seahawks.'

A single infidel helicopter wasn't exactly a victory. Dhar didn't want to ask how many Iranian boats had been destroyed, but he soon found out.

The scene ahead, as he rounded Qeshm island, was one of devastation, smoke rising from numerous small boats, some of them sinking, others limping away. The sky was thick with helicopters, many more than Mousavi had predicted, the air rever-berating with gunfire. Anti-radar chaff shimmered above the sea like celebratory tinsel, mocking the scene below. Beyond it, a solitary rocket streaked away from one of the few Iranian boats still operational. It was clear that Mousavi was lying. Nothing was going to plan.

The engagement was taking place at a point in the Strait where the shipping lanes, each two miles wide, passed through the territorial waters of Iran. International ships traversed the Strait under maritime transit passage laws, which meant that the USS *Truman* was technically in Iranian waters. Dhar knew it would never be more vulnerable. That was why Mousavi had chosen the moment to unleash his swarm. But the Americans appeared to have been expecting it. Was it Marchant? Had he warned Washington?

Dhar accelerated to 70 knots. The Bladerunner was so much smoother than its poor relation on the oil platform. A moment later, it was strafed by deafening gunfire that ripped a hole in the roof. The damage appeared to be superficial, but Dhar now knew he was within range of the Phalanx Gatling guns, and that they hadn't run out of ammunition.

'Range to *Truman*?' he asked the operator.

'Seven thousand metres,' he said. Dhar glanced across at him, and spotted a small bottle in his hand.

'What's that?' he shouted.

The man's hands were shaking.

'Give it to me,' Dhar said, taking the miniature of whisky. He threw it out of the open cockpit roof. 'And prepare to fire the torpedoes.'

He took the Bladerunner up to 80 knots. Despite the wake from other boats, it maintained its stability in the water, a perfect firing platform.

'Six thousand five hundred metres and closing,' the operator said.

Perhaps Mousavi's plan had worked after all. The closer he could get to the target, the higher the chance of success. The boats in front of him seemed to move apart, clearing a way for their flagship. For the first time, Dhar allowed himself to look properly at his target, the vast bulk of the USS *Truman*, the 'Lone Wolf'. It dominated the horizon, unwieldy, aggressive, arrogant. 'Give 'em Hell' – wasn't that its crew's motto as it policed the world? *Inshallah*, he would send all six thousand of them to hell.

But just as he was about to give the order to fire, his eye was caught by a boat approaching fast on the starboard bow. Why hadn't he seen it before? Where had it come from? And why did it have no markings? A collision seemed unavoidable. It took him a split second to realise what it was, and who was at the helm.

123

Marchant knew now that Dhar's target was the USS *Harry S. Truman*. It was too big to resist, too iconic. And whether by fate or chance, his Bladerunner had not yet been shot out of the water. Perhaps it was its speed, or its lack of military markings. Either way, it was bearing down on the *Truman*, a crisp white wake spraying up at its stern like a fantail as it steered through the wrecks of burnt-out boats. By Marchant's crude calculations, it would reach the aircraft carrier in three minutes. Unless he could intercept it first. Marchant kept his hand firmly on the throttle, taking his own boat up to 60 knots as he steered a course towards Dhar.

Thirty seconds until impact.

Black smoke billowed out of his boat's struggling engines, making it look as if it had been hit by American fire. Maybe that was why he hadn't been hit either. Or had the Americans concluded that an unmarked boat heading away from their warships didn't pose an immediate threat? They would target it if they recognised the man at the wheel.

Twenty seconds until impact.

Unlike Dhar, Marchant was standing in the open air. His boat's canopy had fallen off soon after he had accelerated away from the oil platform. He was drenched – the boat shared none of the

Bladerunner's ability to cut through waves. But despite its inferior specifications, it was closing in on Dhar's boat. He was approaching at an angle, and he still seemed to have the element of surprise.

Ten seconds until impact.

As each second passed, Marchant wondered at Dhar's endgame, the scale of his ambition. The sound of gunfire from the US warships was less intense than earlier, and the Seahawks seemed to be holding back after one of their number had been shot down. What was Dhar doing? Marchant could see no obvious weapons on board, no crude rocket-launchers or machine guns. Had the Bladerunner been packed with explosives in Bandar-Abbas? Was it a martyrdom mission?

Time had run out for both men, two brothers united by a father, divided by loyalty, racing towards a shared fate. If Marchant had been asked what his own endgame was, he might not have answered, except to say that he was prepared to lose his life to stop Dhar taking the lives of six thousand others. It wasn't an act of heroism, just a simple case of maths.

Dhar had a clearer vision as he ordered the torpedo to be fired. '*Allahu akbar!*' he cried.

There was a moment before their boats collided when the two men looked across at each other. Dhar saw his father; Marchant his twin brother Sebbie, lying in the wreckage of a car crash in Delhi. A second later, both boats disintegrated, engulfed in a fireball that could be seen for miles around, but not before twenty-five feet of steel had exited an improvised firing tube and accelerated away at 200 knots towards its target, propelled by a liquid-fuel rocket.

124

Rajan Meena didn't hear the bell the first time it rang. He hadn't heard much since his daughter had died.

'There's someone at the door,' his wife said, coming into the living room. He looked up from the chair by the window, catching a glimpse of Lakshmi in her eyes. He wasn't cross at her for not wanting to answer the door. The last relatives from India had left the day before, and she couldn't face another expression of condolence, more flowers, however well meant. They had wanted to take Lakshmi's body back to Chettinad, but she had once told them that she wished to marry, have her children and be cremated in Virginia. 'I'm an all-American girl now,' she had smiled. It was after she had been accepted by the CIA, and they hadn't known if she was joking.

Rajan rose to his feet and walked over to the front door.

'Who is it?' he asked.

'My name's Daniel, Daniel Marchant. I knew your daughter.'

'I wanted you to have these,' Marchant said, handing Meena's mother a pair of silver ankle bracelets. Her husband had shown him in to the living room of their house, a modest residence near the main shopping mall in Reston.

'Did she give them to you as a present?' she asked.

'Yes.' It was a lie. He had removed them from her ankles before he had carried her into the hospital in Caen. In a weak moment after she had betrayed him.

'Then you should keep them.'

'I think it's better they're here, with her things.' Marchant glanced up at the mantelpiece, where a chorus of candles was burning around a photograph of Lakshmi and a statue of her eponymous goddess. He tried not to linger on either.

'As you like,' she said.

'I also wanted to tell you something.' He paused, gathering himself. Her mother had something of Lakshmi in her, the way she bit her lower lip. 'Lakshmi had to make some difficult decisions in her work.'

'We were very proud of her,' her father said.

'You were right to be. Other people might have struggled, deciding who to be loyal to, sometimes who to betray, but she was always guided by her parents, her love for you both. And her love for this country.'

Marchant let himself out and walked over to the waiting car, a black Chevy Suburban with darkened windows. When he returned to Britain he had another grieving parent to visit, but it would be a very different conversation with Salim Dhar's mother.

'How was it?' Fielding asked, sitting next to him on the back seat.

'Awkward. I've never found love or patriotism easy things to talk about, particularly when they involve America.'

'You'd better get used to it. The night's still young.'

'Are we heading straight to the White House?'

'A drink with the Defense Secretary first.'

'And we really have to go through with all this?'

'Turner Munroe's laid on a dinner in your honour. It's the

431

beginning of a beautiful new relationship between Britain and America. And Jim Spiro's proposing the toast.'

Two hours later, Marchant adjusted his bow tie as he watched Spiro rise to his feet in the East Room at the White House. He recognised some of the people around the table – Munroe, the DCIA, top US Navy brass and Harriet Armstrong, who had arrived late – but most of them were faceless, just as they should be.

It was a 'one plus' evening, which at least meant he wouldn't be grilled on operational details, even though all the guests had been heavily vetted. That would come later in the week, at Langley, where he had been invited by Spiro. Spiro's wife, Linda, intrigued Marchant. He hadn't even known he was married until they had been introduced at the bar.

Since Marchant didn't have a 'plus', vetted or otherwise, he had been put next to Fielding, who was similarly partnerless. Armstrong, also single, was beside the DCIA. As Marchant marvelled at the surprising longevity of Spiro's marriage, Armstrong caught his eye. They hadn't had time to talk properly about the second cell, but he knew how grateful she was. Five men had been arrested in a basement flat on Hoxton Square, minutes before they were about to leave for a lock-up in Spitalfields that was packed with explosives. A second network of smaller cells had been arrested around the country. Their targets remained classified, but he would find out from her later.

The sound of spoon against glass cut through Marchant's thoughts. Spiro waited for silence.

'We're gathered here tonight to give our thanks to a very special British colleague,' he began. Spiro didn't have to do this, Marchant thought. It would be killing him. Munroe must have insisted on it as part of the healing process. 'I think it's fair to say that Daniel Marchant and the CIA have not always got along.' Fielding let out a loud, solitary laugh. 'And in recent months, there hasn't been the normal warmth that characterises relations between London and Washington.' A few nervous eyes turned to Fielding, but this time he remained silent.

'But I'm not here to rake over the past. We're gathered tonight to salute Daniel, whose bravery in the Strait of Hormuz saved many thousands of American lives. The world's a safer place without Salim Dhar. I've always said that. His body might not have been found, but all he stood for has sunk to the bottom of the Gulf, where it belongs. His personal, bigoted *jihad*, aimed at ripping out the heart of America, should never be confused with other Islamic struggles around the world, in places like Ramallah, which deserve a fresh approach from all sides.'

Marchant noticed Spiro give the briefest of glances at his wife. 'And on that note, I'd like everyone to raise their glasses to Daniel Marchant, to the special relationship reborn, and to Iranian technology. They reckon the torpedo missed by a frickin' half-mile.'

Spiro sat down as laughter rang out all around him. A few people came over and slapped Marchant on the back, and for a moment it almost felt good to be in America. It was a lavish scene before him: Bohemian glass chandeliers, fine food, decent wine – Burgundy, of course – and the Lansdowne portrait of George Washington staring down at them. (Fielding had pointed out that it was in fact a copy. The original was at the Smithsonian Institution.) In a nice touch, there was even Bruichladdich on offer afterwards. But when a waiter tapped him on the shoulder and whispered to him that he had a phone call, which he could take in an adjoining room, the candles seemed to begin to burn rather than glow. Nobody knew he was here, except those who were in the room. Perhaps there had been a news leak, and a reporter was trying to interview him?

He couldn't tell anyone anything, of course. The story of how he jumped clear of his boat moments before it collided with Dhar's would never be known beyond the walls of Legoland and Langley. And no one would ever hear how the torpedo might have hit its target if it hadn't been knocked off course at its launch. Or how he had stayed under water for as long as he could, rising to the surface after the boats had exploded and being picked up by a US launch. His only injuries were from burning oil on his forearms. If the second torpedo had exploded, he would have been killed, but the thermobaric charge was faulty. Dhar hadn't appeared, dead or alive. A body would have been helpful, closed a chapter of Marchant's life. Instead there was only flotsam.

By the time he picked up the phone in a small, book-lined room, his palms were moist, his mouth dry. The caller ID was unknown, but the hiss on the line sounded international.

'Who is this?' he asked, but he already knew.

AUTHOR'S NOTE

In August 2005, the *Bradstone Challenger*, a British- and American-built high-performance powerboat, broke the record for circumnavigating Great Britain. Its time of twenty-seven hours and ten minutes still stands.

Five years later, the powerboat was bought by Iran's *Islamic Revolutionary Guard Corps* (IRGC). The DTI in London and the US Commerce Department's Bureau of Industry and Security had tried to block sale, fearing the *Bradstone Challenger*'s military potential.

At a press conference in August 2010, Rear Admiral Ali Fadavi of the IRGC Navy told AFP: 'It [the *Bradstone Challenger*] holds the world speed record. We got a copy [on which] we made some changes so it can launch missiles and torpedoes.'

Fadavi added that Iran would have reverse-engineered many *Bradstone Challenger*s within a year. 'We will be everywhere and nowhere to face the enemies.'

ACKNOWLEDGEMENTS

Big thanks to AFN, who helped with the naval scenes. To former 'Jungly' helicopter pilot Jerry Milsom. To Dr Andy Beale, who steered me through anaphylaxis. To Alex Goldsmith and Mike Wright for their French. To Giles and Karen Whittell for their support and American insights. To David Stevenson, for reading the manuscript. To Matt, who had to be ensnared in a honeytrap before revealing the secrets of his cartoon trade. To Mike Strefford, for sharing his knowledge of botnets and anonymous routing. To Sue Hunt for the Riad Lunetoile in Essaouira. To Mark Mangham for explaining mobile-phone technology. To C. Sujut Chandrakumar for his Indian wisdom. To Len Heath for his unswerving optimism and advice. To Will at Watergate Bay, where kitesurfing as an idea took off. To Toby at The Nare, who helped with the opening coastal rescue scene. To Jake Farman for his car knowledge. To Jess Walsh-Waring, for nearly getting the title. To Cécile, Etienne and their children for the real 'voiture en plastique', and to Marie Antoinette for the château in France. To Charlotte Doherty, Duncan Spence and Hope for Youth Northern Ireland. To Shirley Roff for her rock-solid support. And to Mrs Bumphrey for checking the latin.

Thanks, as ever, to Sylvie Rabineau at Rabineau Wachter Sanford & Harris in California. To Kevin McCormick at Langley Park, McG at Wonderland Sound and Vision and Jessie Ehrman at Warner Bros. To my peerless agent Claire Conrad, and Rebecca Folland, Tim Glister and Kirstie Gordon at Janklow & Nesbit. And to my inspirational publisher at Blue Door, Patrick Janson-Smith, who has been ably assisted by Laura Deacon, Robert Lacey and Andy Armitage at HarperCollins.

Two excellent blogs provided much insight into the Iran's Revolutionary Guard Navy, swarm attacks and asymmetric warfare: www.geopolicraticus.wordpress.com and www. informationdissemination.net

Thanks too to Guy Dinmore, Rome correspondent for the *Financial Times*, who broke the story about the Iranian purchase of the *Bradstone Challenger*. It was his investigative article in April 2010 that sowed the seed for this story. And to Gordon Carrera, whose book *Life and Death: The Art of Betrayal in the British Secret Service* has proved invaluable. I can't thank by name some of those who have helped in person with the intelligence content of this book, but MF, DM and HA, whom I've known since Delhi, have once again been invaluable. Thanks also to MC.

Most importantly, I must thank my family. My three brothers, Chris, Andrew and David, have always been supportive, as has Andrea Stock, my stepmother, whose title suggestions nearly made the cut. Stewart and Dinah McLennan, to whom this book is dedicated, have been there throughout, letting me stay at the Nook in Cornwall, where some of this book was written, and helping with the sailing scenes. My three children, Felix, Maya and Jago, have been a constant source of inspiration, helping to solve problems of plot, character and action – particularly action – over the breakfast table.

Above all, I want to thank Hilary, my wife and muse, for riding the ups and downs of the last four years with such patience, faith, love and good humour. The rollercoaster ride began with the publication of *Dead Spy Running*, took in a Hollywood film deal, and a husband's mid-life crisis that led to him changing career. Hilary held her nerve when others might have blinked. The ride is far from over, but I could never have got here without her.